COLLIDE

Also by L. R. Johnson

NEVER FOREVER

COLLIDE

L. R. Johnson

HAWAII Way Publishing

HAWAII WAY PUBLISHING
4118 West Harold Ct., Visalia, CA 93291
www.HAWAIIWAYPUBLISHING.com

HAWAII Way Author/Speakers Agency can send authors to your live event. For more information or to book an event contact HAWAII Way Publishing at:
HAWAIIWaypublishing@gmail.com, or 559-972-4168
Printed in the United States of America
First printed in 2016
ISBN 978-1-945384-01-1
Copyright © L. R. Johnson

Author may be contacted at lrjohnson.author@gmail.com
Author website www.lrjohnsonauthor.com

For Dad – Thank you for encouraging me.

You never doubted.

PREFACE

Memories Lost

The room was filled with several insidious beings, a scene Donovan was all too familiar with. This was a part of the work he detested the most. He didn't want to be here, but this man's corrupt desires forced his hand. Donovan's height reached a good foot above the man's stout build, making Donovan appear even more menacing. A heavy debate had transpired between the man and a friend who had tried to stop the transaction, causing heavy amounts of sweat beads to form around the stout man's receding hairline – despite the cool air.

Turning towards Donovan the man begged, "Please, you don't have to do this. I have a family and…"

"You should have thought about them before you decided to ruin their lives." Donovan's voice was dark, yet a tinge of regret coated his tongue.

The man's eyes pierced into a part of Donovan he hadn't felt for years. How could he justify what he was about to do? Just because he was trapped in this situation didn't mean he should damn someone else to this life – if it even is a life. What is wrong with wanting something so bad you are willing to sacrifice everything for it?

The man slowly turned towards his dark-haired friend who had tried to stop the exchange, gazing into his eyes sorrowfully. The two men were a yin and yang of each other. Where one was stout and fair with the beginnings of a receding hairline, the other was tall and thin with dark, thick hair and olive complexion. Though the two were opposite in appearance their friendship was intertwined like a thick rope.

The dark-haired man's eyes narrowed as he pleaded to his friend in a weak whisper, "If this needs to happen, let it happen to me. I have no family, nothing that will be destroyed by the outcome."

The dank air within the room hung thick and dark like a heavy blanket suffocating the room and making it hard to breathe. Donovan was familiar with what was transpiring. Gripping his fingers into a tight fist he fought back the urge to give in to his now natural instinct. Locking his sights onto the two men in front of him he silently watched their useless debate. There was only one way out of this situation and that was if Donovan would let him go, and that could never happen.

The stout man grabbed hold of his friend's shoulders, uttering firmly, "No, this is my fault and I take responsibility for it, but I need you to do me a favor. I need you to…"

Instantly the door opened, causing the two men to turn towards the intruder. "Father, what are you doing?"

A blithe voice rang in Donovan's ears as he turned abruptly towards the intruder. The girl's eyes locked onto his and for a brief moment he was reminded of who and what he used to be – a good man. Though his past was now just a grain of virgin sand in a murky moat, for a brief moment Donovan was able to see the grain and grab onto it.

Donovan watched her eyes transform from a bright, joyful appearance to one of fear and disgust. Her smile dropped, ripping out her heart on its way down. Donovan's eyes remained locked onto hers like two magnets colliding, mentally grabbing hold of her with fervor and strength – refusing to let go. Her eyes too were locked onto Donovan's, though hers told a very different story. One of betrayal, rage and despair, something he couldn't look upon anymore.

"Please leave, sweetheart. I need you to go – now," the stout man uttered to his daughter. His voice echoed loudly with guilty pain.

"No," she snapped back.

A growling voice instantly cut into the small, yet crowded room, making everyone freeze with fear. A man stepped out of a dark corner from the far side of the room. He seemed to materialize from the bleak shadows draped mysteriously from the corners of the room, like tattered curtains ready to reveal the main event. "You are pathetic, Donovan. Do I have to do everything myself?"

"Darius, please don't," Donovan uttered, trying to stop Darius, but it was too late.

Darius's black eyes deepened as he tore across the room. A swirling wind ripped through everyone as Donovan rushed over to the girl. His eyes locked onto her now silver-dollar-size blue eyes for the last time. He quickly lifted his hand, wrapped it firmly around her throat and gently squeezed. He watched as the light within her eyes slowly diminished, leaving the room a black plague where there once was light.

CHAPTER 1

∞

A Call to Something Dark

Slowly I walk through the mist-laden grounds of the small, yet beautiful Clayton California cemetery. The large marble headstones dot the vast area – an ominous reminder of how so many lives have been tragically altered by a loved one's death. Large cement angels sporadically mark the cemetery, guarding over family members' gravesites and the souls of those within their midst. Huge pine trees flank each side of the road that leads to the large entrance, giving mourners the appearance of entering a royal compound instead of a campus of death.

This has become my normal for the past year. A heavily weighted and unanswered walk towards my father's grave has consumed my every Saturday. His death is something that will haunt my vacant memory. No matter how hard I try to remember any details of his death – I can't. His death will remain a mystery to me and my life has become pathetic since his death – not like it was worth anything even before his death.

Standing dolefully in front of my father's headstone I stare in disbelief as streams of familiar briny tears etch their streaks into my face. Deep sorrow swells vigorously within my soul, expanding like an overinflated balloon getting ready to explode. Reaching towards my father's headstone I tenderly stroke the top rough edge, feeling the unfinished marble scrape at the epidermis layer of my fingertips like a rough file ripping away the coarse dead edges of my skin. Intense grief takes possession over me, causing me to fall to my knees. Burying my head into my hands, I expel the deep loneliness rushing through me.

My fragile mind drifts further into a dark cryptic corner where the veil seems to be lifting slightly. My weightless body is instantly cloaked by a thick, bleak shadow. It pours over me like melting black chocolate, merging into every crevasse and seeping into my essence. The penetrating haze fuses with my agony, causing my breathing to intensify. Mentally I attempt to pull the thick darkness away – but it is to no avail. The darkness seeps further into me. The dark gloom completely engulfs me with a heavy weight, dissolving into me and devouring my soul. Panic is my only guide now as the blackness takes over. A beguiling and captivating sensation suddenly rings in my mind and dances on my skin, tempting me to embrace it.

A low, haunting rumble in the far corner of my subconscious mind calls to me, "Lauren. Come." This voice is a rumbling roar, like a lion's deep guttural growl echoing with threads of sexuality sewn into it.

The deep familiar tone of his voice calls to me like a moth to a burning flame. The temptation is too strong. My mind begins to embrace the familiar, yet haunting request. "Here I am. Take me to your empty shelter." I relax as the darkness bleeds deeper into me.

A buttery smooth sensation unexpectedly surges through me, cutting a bright slit through the blackness. A loud, tangible voice erupts through the silence, "Lauren, stop!" The firm order jolts me out of my dreamlike state, summoning me to wake.

The thick gloom which had encased me shatters, allowing the sunlight to illuminate my soul once again. Closing my eyes even tighter in fear, I slowly slide my hands up into my thick dark hair, pushing the wild strands out of my face. Suddenly I feel something soft and velvety gently brushing up against my hand. Snapping my eyes open I discover a bouquet of large, vibrant red roses placed directly in front of my father's headstone. This emblem of remembrance has just appeared. They were not here when I arrived. The delicate petals stand erect with grace, yet fortitude in their purpose. Frantically I look all around, hoping no one has witnessed my pathetic display of grief and apparent breakdown. Perhaps it's the same person who seemed to shout at me to stop? Uneasiness spins within my stomach as I nervously gaze around an obviously vacant cemetery. It is so still in here that even the birds have vacated the premises. Fear still tap dances on the edge of my skin as the memory of my experience twirls within the silence all around me. Realizing my embarrassment and my disbelief of what has just happened, I decide to leave. Not wanting to be alone, I gather myself together and head over to Clayton's small but quaint Main Street.

The narrow tree-lined street consists of small postcard-looking buildings with unique shops within them. You can easily walk from one end of the street to the other in very little time. This area of town is always quieter than the stucco prison everyone my age gravitates to – the mall. It's amazing to me that any of the businesses here can even survive, but this is the kind of semi-secluded peace I am searching for right now.

The breeze showers over me as I walk down the sidewalk attempting to wash away the anxiety still rolling down my spine. As I wring my hands aggressively, an unnerving sensation of being watched prickles the back of my neck, causing the hairs to stand erect. After my already scary situation, this is not the type of feeling I need right now.

Pretending to adjust my ponytail I begin frantically looking all around for anyone staring in my direction. Shifting my eyes side to side I attempt to catch the perpetrator in the act. But to my chagrin, not a single person is even looking in my direction. The sidewalks on both sides of the street are nearly empty. I inhale a deep breath, making an attempt at slowing down my quick, shallow breaths. Beads of sweat form delicately on my temples. One drop gently glides down my jawline as I try to reassure myself that it's just my imagination.

As I hesitantly proceed down the nearly abandoned street, a deep yearning within the pit of my stomach pulls me towards a little yellow building that houses a small travel agency. I have never used this travel agency – or any other for that matter – but I believe my mother, on the other hand, keeps this company in business. Since my father's death my mother constantly goes on extravagant trips with her friends. She has never been an involved mother and since my dad's death she has emotionally detached herself from me. I have a mother, but I have never had a mom.

As I walk up to the little yellow building, I notice etched on the glass of the door is the name of the travel agency, "Martha's Travel Experts." I have heard the name Martha before from my mother. I am sure Martha is one of her travel friends with whom she goes on her extensive vacations. A thin layer of envious bile coats the breath within my mouth. Irritation scales my spine, causing me to stand erect as I stare bitterly at the travel agency. I have always desired to see the world, but never could afford it. My mother has enjoyed flaunting her trips in front of me but has never invited me on any of them. My mother knows how to get what she wants. Positioning her husband and friends where they can best serve her is a skill she has mastered.

Standing in front of the building I begin debating why I am here when a sudden familiar sensation rushes through me again. My muscles coil up like a spring getting ready to discharge. A deep, invading sensation rips through me. Someone isn't just staring at me, it feels as if they're tearing through my soul, making it hard to breathe. A shiver races up my spine, causing my shoulders to tremble in fear. Without hesitation I quickly rush into the travel agency, trying to escape my attacker. Wanting to create a physical barrier between me and whatever is doing this I vigorously slam the door, causing the glass on the door to vibrate violently. Turning sharply around I face the agent, giving her a sheepish and apologetic grin.

The salt and pepper haired woman, who at one point must have been comfortably sitting at her desk, now is erect in her chair. "Oh my! Are you all right sweetie?" Placing her hand slightly over her chest she grips her shirt protectively.

Smiling embarrassedly at the woman I affirm ruefully, "Sorry. I didn't mean to shut it that hard." I didn't want to tell her the real reason why I slammed the door and worry her for perhaps no reason at all.

"That's all right dear. Is there anything I can help you with?" She sighs as her muscles deflate, leaning back onto her comfortable office chair once again.

My almond-shaped eyes widen as my breath increases slightly, "No, sorry, I just thought I would come in and…" Suddenly my mind stops. People don't just walk into a travel agency just to look around. Most people have a good reason as to why they enter a travel agency, and I have absolutely no reason. Quickly my mind begins racing, trying to come up with a motive. Frantically I look all around the office, when out of the corner of my eye I see a shelf full of travel brochures. This is my saving grace. "…and grab some travel brochures to get a few ideas on a trip I am planning." Hopefully she believes me. I am such a horrible liar.

Walking over to the shelf I impulsively grab at the loose brochures, taking six different ones without even looking at the destination. It isn't like I will ever be going to any of these places anyway. As I frantically grab my last one I hear the agent suddenly laugh sharply behind me. "Those are some beautiful places that you have chosen, but I can tell by the variety of the locations you have no idea where you want to go."

My palpitating heart instantly hammers against my chest in fear that she has seen through my ridiculous story. I stand here frozen as my eyes soak in her tender, yet striking, features. The woman, whom I can only assume is Martha, is an attractive lady perhaps in her mid to late fifties. Soft lines painted across her face by life's unstoppable aging power delicately reveal themselves. Dark hair that is lightly dusted with the most beautiful shades of gray frames her oval face. Her straight hair hangs effortlessly, hitting her shoulders as it brushes her silk shirt like fringe on a lampshade. Wrapping my hands vigorously around the brochures, I begin wringing them into a tight roll. Hopefully these are free. After the torturous crumpling I am inflicting on the innocent brochures there is no way I will be able to put them back.

Stopping my destruction on the pamphlets, I gulp softly, asking in a shaky voice, "What do you mean?"

Walking gracefully towards me she utters respectfully, "Well, for starters look at what you have chosen." Gently she retrieves the brochures from my iron grip and flips through them one by one. "You have two on Paris, two more on Canada, one on Italy, and this one is on New Orleans. You are breaking the number one rule in planning a vacation, sweetie. You are thinking too broad. You need to narrow your choices down. Do you want to travel somewhere out of the country, or do you wish to stay within the United States?" Her petite frame looks even smaller standing next to me. I am not a large girl, but I am a hell of a lot taller than her.

I stare straight ahead as disbelief rushes through my dumbfounded mind, not quite sure how to answer her. I was absolutely expecting her to see right through me, but instead she actually believes me. To my dismay she is, in fact, trying to help me narrow down where I want to go. I didn't think this far in advance. I had only planned on grabbing some information, then leaving quickly.

Smiling hesitantly, she adds softly, "If you would like we can look at some places on the computer so we can narrow down your choices?"

"Thank you very much for your help, but I think I agree with you. I just need to honestly sit down and think about where I want to actually go first and foremost. Maybe when I have it figured out I can come back," I agree flatly, trying to hide the thick duplicity rippling heavily within my voice. I muster up the most believable smile I can, though I truly have no plan of ever coming back.

"Oh, if you wish," she mutters, slightly surprised by my response.

A thick tone of disappointment rolls vigorously from her voice. I am sure I was going to be her only break from her monotonous Saturday. I hate deceiving people – it's just not in my nature. She seems like a very nice person, but there is no way I am going anywhere other than Clayton anytime in the near future. My personal jet-setting ways are a lot like my life: stagnant, sad and no hope for change.

"Thank you very much," I state. Although it sounds pretentious, I truly mean it. She gave me a great escape from whatever seemed to frighten me – even if it was just from my own mental breakdown. My muscles have now successfully relaxed and my frightened mind has stopped its attack on me. Needing to end this web of lies I am weaving, I grip the pamphlets firmly in my tense hand, uttering insincerely, "I promise when I make my decision I will come right in and use you. Do you have a card?"

"Yes, hold on, I will get it." Walking over to her well organized desk she hastily grabs a business card from the top. "Here you go. My name is Martha Beckley. I am the owner here so call me any time."

This is definitely my mother's friend. There is no way I am going to give her my name now. I am pretty certain my mother does not speak too highly of me. Gripping her card tightly I add, "Thank you, Martha. I will." I quickly shove the card into my back pocket. "I am Laur…" Hesitating, I remember that this is my mother's friend and I have no desire for my mother to ever find out I was at a travel agency, least of all from one of her friends. "My name is Lori. I will call you when I have made my decision, thank you," I mutter quickly.

I make for the door, trying to get the heck out of this place before my streak of good luck ends. I can just see my mother walking through the door, thus exposing the deceitful predicament I innocently stumbled into.

Grabbing the doorknob, I immediately bolt through the door almost as fast as I had previously entered it. As I rush down the steps I hear Martha in the background mutter, "Now that is one strange girl."

She is absolutely right. I am a strange girl. I have no right trying to blend in with society. What am I thinking? Every time I change my routine I pay the price for it. I wish things would have turned out different for me, but they didn't. I just have to come to grips with the way my life is now.

CHAPTER TWO

Paradigm Shift

Strange or sinister events, as far as I can remember, have never occurred in my life. I am a dreamer, not a doer. I have always been a homebody type. I preferred staying home with my father over any excursions. In high school I would just go through the daily motions – completely content with my ordinary life. I read about bizarre and wonderful things happening to other people, but this past weekend's experience left me questioning what is real in my life. The only thing I discovered is I'm pathetic. Obviously my life is so pitiful my subconscious had to create something that wasn't real. I need to stop pretending I make a difference in this world. I have made a decision to not focus any longer on my stagnant life. I just need to continue going through my monotonous daily motions, fully accepting my dismal existence.

Deafening silence tumbles over me as I gaze out at my empty apartment. There is no one here but me. No dog or cat, no husband, no boyfriend, no friends for that fact. I am utterly and completely alone. I don't go anywhere, and even if I try it all blows up in my face. I have placed archaic landmines all around myself where no one can reach me, least of all touch my soul. What a dismal mess I have gotten myself into.

Despondently I stare at myself in the bathroom mirror, completely horrified at the ragged mess now standing before me. Deep heartache creeps into the corners of my blue eyes, causing tears to well up and seep out the corners. My fair, velvety skin is completely overtaken by red splotches now forming ranks around my eyes. These splotches spread out vigorously in an all-out attack over my entire face.

I've been sleepwalking and rambling through life with a pointless destination. Willingly I surrendered a part of me the night my dad died and I have been trying to recover myself ever since then, but I have no idea how. A sponge of despair presses over me, sucking up every last bit of self-esteem. Turning away from my horrible reflection I hastily walk into my bedroom, throwing myself forcefully onto my bed. Hopelessly I lay here staring up at the ceiling fan spinning around and around in useless circles. It doesn't matter how fast I make that ridiculous fan go, the stupid thing will never go anywhere. It is attached to my ceiling by one simple bar. But what if that bar was gone? Would the fan just simply fly away? What if I break free? Will I take flight or will my life spin completely out of control?

An oppressive weight pushes down on me, causing my figure to feel heavy. My mind slowly loses the unyielding battle against my exhausted body. Shadows melt into my vision and slowly devour everything around me with a thick murkiness. Gradually I sink deep into the mattress as the heavy weight of my mind drags me deeper into a hypnotic state.

Obscurity slowly breaks apart like glass shattering into millions of pieces. When the darkness clears I discover I am in a substantial room with a myriad of enormous windows flanked all around me. As I turn and gaze out the windows I can see the bright lights of what is apparently a large city flooding the dim room with colored lights.

Feeling the cold from the hard tile seep through me I suddenly realize I am sitting on the floor in the corner of the room. I try to get up, when all of a sudden I feel something keeping me down. Frantically I start searching all around for the reason as to why I am down here on the floor; when to my horror I notice the room is full of people staring and pointing at me like I am a bizarre attraction in a sideshow.

The scrutinizing onlookers are all dressed to the hilt. The men are all clothed in tuxedos while the women are wearing designer gowns. The loud, thumping music playing in the background sends pulsating vibrations to roll vigorously along the floor. It appears everyone is partying and having fun while taking their entertainment at my expense.

Unlike everyone else I only have on blue jeans with a plain white t-shirt – that's it. Tucking my bare feet vigorously underneath my legs, I begin contemplating what I am doing here dressed like this. I need to get out of here immediately. Quickly I jump up when immediately I'm snapped back down to the ground by something wrapped around me. Meticulously I look myself over for any sign of bruising caused by the jerking motion, when I notice I am chained to the corner of the room like I'm their entertainment for the night. Fighting back my fear I start yelling for help, hoping someone will care enough to drag me out of this hell. But everyone keeps on partying, walking by me like I'm not uttering anything at all.

Panic sets in, causing me to attempt to scream at the top of my lungs, but nothing is coming out of my mouth. The more I try to push the sound out of me, the more my vocal cords tighten up, restricting any sound to escape. Peering intently around the room I frantically try to find anyone who will be willing to help me.

As I gaze intently at the crowd I notice all their faces have an obscure haze placed over them, as if their identity has been intentionally fogged out. Swirls of muted color hover deliberately in front of all the gawking people. Though I cannot see their eyes I can feel their penetrating stares looking through me. No one appears to even care about my predicament. They all are having a great time, blissfully unaware of my pleas as I continually try yelling at the top of my lungs.

As I frantically examine myself I notice there is just one small chain enveloped securely around my waist. It is connected to the wall by just one small and feeble-looking eyehook. I should be able to break through this with very little effort.

Looking around, trying to make sure that no one is watching me, I wrap both my hands firmly around the end of the chain. Placing my feet securely against the wall for more leverage I begin pulling forcefully on the chain, but nothing will give. My strength feels like a mirage of hope – like I have absolutely no power in me at all. Weariness and fatigue consumes every part of my powerless body. I have no idea how I am going to break out of this binding prison. I yell again for someone to help, but it is another useless attempt. Frustration and anger wash over me as I begin thrashing violently around, trying to break free. A surrendering riptide consumes me as I give in to the despair, collapsing to the ground.

A deep uneasiness pushes through my belly, rippling out and up my spine and causing the hair on my arms to stand straight up. The disquiet from someone's intrusive eyes gazing forcefully upon me slithers deeper into me. A sensation of promising respite electrifies my mind. I look up, trying to see who this possible Good Samaritan is, only to discover that except for his intoxicating eyes, this man's face is intentionally blurred out.

He proceeds to walk slowly toward me with a smooth and graceful stride, captivating me with every step he takes. His stunning height towers over all the mindless partiers as he effortlessly proceeds to walk past everyone. His astonishing presence is heightened by his dark, slim-fitting suit accentuating his lean, yet muscular build. Gracefully he continues in my direction, ignoring all the gawking onlookers' attention gravitating toward him. His near black shimmering hair adds to his mysterious presence, allowing him to seamlessly pass through the crowd.

I can sense his gaze bypassing my temporal body, connecting straight to my soul, like he sees into my deepest, darkest desires. Though something deep within me is warning me to be terrified, for some strange reason I am not frightened at all by him.

His obscure face and eyes never waver from my scrutinizing gaze as he stands just inches away from me. Slowly he bends down, wrapping his large hands firmly around the chain binding me. The muscles within his hands quiver viciously, causing the veins in his hands to protrude slightly. Pulling forcefully on the stubborn chain he instantly pulls the eyehook out of the wall, releasing me from my imprisonment.

Panic immediately consumes me as I start spinning violently out of control. Swirls of color and rushing wind whip violently around me. Everyone in the substantial room begins running and yelling as complete chaos erupts. I no longer can make sense of what is whirling erratically around me anymore. I try to grab hold of anything to stop myself from this bizarre event I am being sucked into.

Suddenly, out of nowhere, I hear a very loud ringing noise as if it is coming from the furthest corner of my mind. It progressively grows louder until it no longer is ringing in the furthest part of my mind. Hastily I throw my hands out, attempting to reach for the faceless man, when immediately the ringing stops. The annoying sound is now replaced by my mother's shrieking tone, "Lauren, are you there?"

Hearing my mother's voice in the distance triggers my consciousness. Quickly I sit up out of bed, causing the blood to rush violently to my head and briefly dissolving my vision.

"Mom," I call out, gazing around my room.

"Lauren, if you are there and haven't left for work yet, pick up the phone," she demands fiercely.

Vigorously I rub my eyes, trying to bring back my clear vision. I look over at the clock as a sense of panic shoots violently through me. Blinking my eyes wildly I gaze again at the blurry clock. Horror floods over me as I discover it is seven forty-five in the morning. "Oh no, I slept in. I can't be late for work, William will kill me."

Numbing twinges race up me as I jump out of bed, hysterically looking all around my room. The good news is I am not chained to the corner of some strange building. It was just a bizarre dream. The bad news is that no matter what I do, I am going to be extremely late to work.

Grabbing my phone, I ask, "Mom, hold on. Let me turn off the machine." Rushing to my bathroom I vigorously throw cold water on my face. "Wake up, Lauren, it was just a dream, wake up."

Trying to fake a bubbly voice, I utter breathlessly, "Hey mom, I can't talk long, I'm running really late." Perhaps she won't hear the sleep still residing in my voice.

"Lauren, are you okay?"

"Yes. Why?"

"You sound groggy, like you just woke up." An acidic disapproval coats her voice, corroding her words.

Great, now I am going to hear it from my mom on how I not only have no life, but I am lazy. "Mom, is there a reason why you called me this morning? I really don't have time for your judgments," I snap.

"What, I can't just call to say hi to my daughter?" The thick sarcasm in her voice rolls through the phone, slamming into my ear. In all my life I don't think my mom has ever called just to say hi. There is always a reason for her calling me.

"Mom, like I said, I'm in a hurry, so why are you calling this morning?" I bite off each word forcefully.

"Well, now that you have finally asked about me… yes, there is a reason. I want to let you know I will be gone for about three weeks."

"Three weeks. Where are you going?" I utter in surprise.

"Well, the girls and I have been planning for the past few months a girls' getaway. We are going to be traveling through Europe for three weeks. I am so excited. I need a break."

"You need a break?" I sneer under my breath.

"What did you say, Lauren?"

"Another trip?" I quickly add, trying to hide my real statement. "Didn't you just get back from one two months ago?" I sigh.

"Yes. But you know me. I can't stand still for very long… besides, there is nothing for me here."

Ouch, I guess I fall into the nothing factor. How can I get out of this conversation? It's bad enough I know how pathetic my life is, but my mom has to remind me that I mean nothing to even her. Slapping my hand against my forehead in angst I plead inaudibly, "Someone, help me. I will do anything to get out of this dismal situation."

Suddenly my mother interrupts my pleading, "Lauren, I've got to go. Someone is at my door."

Surprise electrifies my mind at the perfect timing. "No problem, I've got to go, too," I state flatly.

"Ok, goodbye then."

Sighing softly, I utter, "Bye…Mom."

I wish I could thank whoever the person was at her door. They will never know how grateful I am for this life preserver they threw to me. A strange, uneasy feeling suddenly washes over me as my mind envisions the faceless man again. His dark, yet familiar presence haunts my mind, giving me the feeling something is about to change.

CHAPTER 3

A Slight Glimpse

Impatiently I sit in my car while stuck in bumper-to-bumper traffic. It is bad enough I was already running late for work, but now I'll be even later. Well, at least I already called William and told him I was going to be late. This is an absolute first for me. I have never been late to work before.

I have worked for William since I was seventeen. My dad got me the job right out of high school and after he died I just couldn't leave the company. My father and William were best friends for as long as I can remember. There is not a single memory I have that doesn't involve William in it. Since my father's death, William has taken on the role of my overprotective father. Despite the obvious fact that I am not a child any longer, I honestly have enjoyed him inheriting the role. He gives me the fatherly advice I sometimes miss and secretly still need.

Drumming my fingers against the steering wheel I begin impatiently gazing out at the endless sea of congested cars. Suddenly I notice an unbelievably unique car up ahead. My frame tingles with excitement at the possibility of seeing this amazing looking car. Living in the areas surrounding San Francisco I have gotten used to seeing extremely expensive cars. I have become numb to the everyday sight of a Rolls-Royce, Mercedes, and even an occasional Ferrari thrown into the vast sea of desirable cars. Hell, I even drive a BMW. But this is not your typical car. From its stunning and unique appearance, I can only assume this is a rare experience. I stare intently at the sleek back bumper of this miraculous vehicle for some identification or hint as to what kind of car this is. The only thing I can see is a large symbol of what appears to be a backwards capital E and a B merging together.

Most of the car is painted a breathtaking plum color, causing my mouth to water slightly as the sun shimmers off of it. But the back portion of the car is what catches my eye. A black color appears to mold perfectly around the car. It engulfs the back bumper as it wraps its way ominously around the sides. There are two silver, elongated air intakes running smoothly down the sides of the back window. The smooth, curved lines intricately flow over every detail, giving it very little air resistance. This car was made for extreme speed, not bumper-to-bumper traffic. This car would make even the wealthiest man turn green with unyielding envy.

As I slowly inch my way closer to this amazing car a nervous twinge surges violently through me. Suddenly, I am neck and neck with it. Nonchalantly I gaze toward the car, trying to take a peek at the inside, but to my dismay I see nothing but my own reflection. The windows are tinted a jet black color, causing it to reflect only the views of the outside world around it. There is no way anyone is ever going to be able to look through those dark windows. Turning dejectedly, I quickly glance back at the traffic lying in front of me, slightly disappointed I was robbed of my chance to see inside the miraculous vehicle.

All of a sudden I notice the car's window slowly rolling down, revealing the black coffee leather inside. A buttery smooth sensation creeps up my back, wrapping itself around my shoulders. A familiar black cloak covers me, causing my heart to beat out of control. Everything around me but the car dissipates, leaving me with only one desire…to see the driver. Slowly he comes into view. His black hair frames his chiseled jawline as it merges down into a smooth, strong neck. A familiar sensation mingles with the black cloak enveloping me. Peering in I try to see his obscure face when suddenly my heart begins pounding like I have been running for miles. The speed of my breathing intensifies until I start having a hard time catching my breath. Panic takes over me and I try to focus intently on breathing. The lack of oxygen causes my head to spin rapidly.

Out of nowhere comes a strange, yet recognizable sensation of someone staring at me, but the driver is not even looking in my direction. This feeling penetrates deep within my heart like someone is peering directly into my soul. The feeling is getting more intense, as if the intruder is prying into my deepest desires. Gripping at my chest firmly, I begin wondering if this is coming from the mysterious man. Looking back over at the car I discover the tinted window is back up, blocking my vision of him again.

Suddenly the intense sensation that had been flowing through me dissipates like a drain being pulled from a flooding tub. It's as if the perpetrator sensed that I could feel him reading my soul. Slowly my heart rate returns to normal as the pressure on my chest gradually subsides, slamming the door to my soul shut.

Instantly I gaze into my rearview mirror only to discover the mysterious car is now just a small, distant spot in the reflection. I don't even remember passing him. It only felt like a few seconds, but it must have been longer. I try to watch the car in my rear view mirror, but soon I reach my exit. As I take the exit my shoulders drop as I realize the astonishing car and passenger are gone, never to be seen again. The only thing left is the overwhelming feeling I had just been violated in the most sacred way – my soul. I try to get my thoughts back in order as I pull up to the office, but I can't get rid of the lingering feeling of the faceless black-haired man from my dream and now, perhaps, from my recent reality.

Running in to the office I try not to call attention to myself. I am now over an hour and a half late and I know I am in for some major trouble. Quietly I slide into my desk, trying to melt into the boring décor. My desk is basically just that, a desk set in the middle of a three-sided pegged board cubicle.

The office is laid out like a labyrinth of cubicles where the corkboard walls of the maze come only to about my neck in height. The twists and turns of the portable walls are laid out in a way as to utilize as many desks as possible in this small office space. Everyone is stuck in their own sections of the brilliantly laid out labyrinth in an attempt to lessen the distractions of employee conversations.

Quickly I pick up the phone, attempting to slither in unnoticed, when suddenly I feel a sharp, irritated tap on my shoulder.

"Excuse me, Lauren, can I please speak to you in my office?" the low, stern voice demands as irritation rolls viciously off his tongue.

Turning briskly toward the harsh voice I discover William anxiously towering over me with the most unpleasant expression on his face. A dark, annoyed countenance veils his usually soft face. Though he is mad, his handsome features show through his stern appearance. He has strong, masculine features feathered by just a few distinguishing age lines which gracefully encircle his stunning hazel eyes. His soft olive skin is set off by his dark, thick hair dotted with a few small sections of gray, giving him the ideal salt and peppered look. For his age he is absolutely handsome; no one would have any idea how old he actually is.

Slowly I follow him toward his corner office. As I weave throughout the maze of cubicles I can see the harsh glares from everyone. I am constantly avoided like the black plague. Though no one talks to me, they all have fun talking about me. Usually they talk about me being romantically involved with the boss, which makes me sick to my stomach. William is like a father to me. Just the utter thought of it sends chills racing vigorously over my body. I know I'm not the most popular person in the office, but this is ridiculous.

As I pass slowly by Stacie's desk, I overhear her whispering loud enough for me to hear, "She's so strange. It's about time she gets in trouble. Just because she knows the boss doesn't mean she should get away with things."

Narrowing my eyes I turn abruptly towards her, giving her my best dirty look – though I've never been good at giving them. It always looks more uncoordinated than anything else. But no matter how ridiculous it comes across I had to try. She glares sharply back at me, giving me a smug smirk. Snapping my head instantly forward I proceed to walk into William's office as he slowly closes the door behind me.

As soon as the door shuts I turn towards him, pleading apologetically, "William, I am so sorry. I called you this morning to tell you I was going to be late, but then I got stuck in the morning traffic. I had no way to tell you."

He just stands there in front of me, quietly shaking his head. Silently he walks over to his desk, slowly sitting in his chair. Placing his elbows forcefully on top of his desk, he cups his hands vigorously over his face. The already deep furrow between his eyes deepens even more as he peers through the openings in his fingers, focusing intently on his desk. I can feel the overwhelming anxiety flooding out of him like a geyser, filling the room with intense pressure. Keeping his eyes down, he lets out a loud, gruff exhale. "Lauren, have a seat," he sighs, pointing to one of the two leather chairs purposely placed in front of his desk.

Reluctantly I obey, gradually moving toward the ominous chair. A nauseous stabbing sensation stings my stomach as I languidly sit down, placing my quivering hands beneath my legs. My heart palpitates rapidly as I gaze down at my feet like a child who has just been caught stealing a cookie. It has been such a long time since I have been reprimanded by a father figure that this archaic feeling catches me off guard, like an unsuspecting lamb being caught in flood waters.

"Lauren, you know I think of you as a daughter." His voice quivers slightly.

"Yes," I mutter softly. My eyes remain affixed to the floor as the thick, palpable air encases me in his irritation.

A sharp exhale rushes from his mouth followed by a quick, thick sigh. His deep exhale is laced with a hidden relief tickled with an infuriating growl. The air within the room weakens slightly as I hear a low, unrelenting chuckle swirl within his throat; the kind that says I'm mad, but I'm more relieved you are safe. With that obvious reassuring sound, I look up ruefully at him.

Breaking the silence, he whispers, "When you called you said you would be a little late, not nearly two hours late. I was worried about you. I didn't want to be the one to call your mother and tell her you were missing." He gulped softly when he uttered the last word.

First of all, two hours does not constitute missing. Second, unless I was missing for days my mom would not worry. In fact, she would actually be rejoicing in the fact that she has finally gotten rid of me. I mean nothing to her other than her being able to say she is a mother.

Honestly I am glad he cares, but he will never have to worry about me. Since my dad died he feels like he owes him this and watches out for me, but I am almost twenty years old. I don't do anything that would cause him to worry. I don't party, I don't go anywhere, and I have no life.

Frustration instantly starts to bubble within me, burning my nerves. My hands begin quivering as my muscles tighten up. I can feel myself starting to lose control. Slowly I take a deep breath in through my nose, exhaling softly, trying to calm the wild beast within me. "I told you I hit the morning traffic and instead of taking thirty-five minutes to get here it took me over an hour. I had no way of letting you know I was going to be even later than I had already said," I huff, reminding him firmly of our earlier conversation.

"My point!" he yells as he throws both his hands up in the air then slams them back on the table forcefully. Reaching into the center drawer of his desk he grabs hold of something. "I am giving you this." Sliding his cupped hand across the desk he adds, "Let's just say you need it for the company."

A slight smile tickles the corners of his thin mouth as he opens his fingers, revealing a small black cell phone. "It's a cell phone," he exclaims like he is informing me of something I have never seen before.

"No shit, William," I snap disrespectfully. Okay, I know I don't own one, but that doesn't make me clueless. I think I know what a cell phone looks like. He is now being ridiculous. "You are giving me a cell phone? Why?" I roll my eyes in irritation over his overbearing and unwanted father-like reaction.

His eyes instantly widen like rubber bands snapping, causing his now dark hazel eyes to bulge slightly. "Watch your mouth, Lauren," he states briskly. Quickly his expression changes as he tries to soften the tension in the air. As he nods his head in pride a slight sheepish grin races across his lips. His eyes peer up at me, locking onto mine with a sincere expression in them.

"Before Max died…" he sighs heavily as he utters my dad's name, "I told him that if anything ever happened to him I would look after you and I am not about to go back on my word."

"You are being ridiculous. I was only two hours late and I told you this morning I was going to be late," I utter in response.

As I look at him I notice his interwoven fingers tightly clenched, causing them to turn a slight purple color. He gazes respectfully down at his hands while his thumbs spin in little fast circles around each other. There is a long, hollow pause as the quiet pierces forcefully through me, causing me to feel guilty for telling him that he is being ridiculous, even though technically he is. Swallowing my pride, I agree weakly, "William, I'm sorry. I'll take the phone. Thank you." I give him a quirky little smile.

"Lauren, I know I'm probably being overbearing, but please just humor me. I never had my own children and you are the closest thing I have to a daughter, so if I'm being unreasonable, I am sorry. You don't have to have the phone if you really don't want it," he states reluctantly.

His reverse psychology tactic is completely evident, but it doesn't matter. Instantly I stand, walk over to him and bend down, giving him a tight hug. He is overreacting, but his heart is in the right place.

"Thank you. I think I'll keep the phone – it may come in handy sometime. Is there more you want to talk to me about or can I go now? I am already two hours behind on my work," I state sarcastically as I give him a mischievous smile – this time he smiles back.

As I turn to walk out I feel his excitement permeate the room at his triumphant victory over me. Hastily I walk back to my desk, acutely aware that people are talking about me. I just want to get back to my little corner of this maze, sit down and do my work. Subconsciously though, I know this is an unrealistic dream, because as I walk by Stacie she looks up at me, giving me a sneering look of disdain and uttering slyly, "Weirdo."

"Oh, just ignore her," a gentle, low voice exclaims. "She's just jealous. She just wishes she could get away with being two hours late."

As I glance up my eyes slowly scan the tall lanky guy leaning up against his cubicle. His thin, yet muscular arms are folded tightly against his lean torso. A gentle smile spreads across his handsome, yet soft, boy-like face. His dark blue eyes sparkle with a genuine trust. Larry is that one guy that all the girls have an office crush on. It isn't necessarily because he is drop dead gorgeous, but more like the boy next door. His smile causes most girls to forget what they were talking about and just melt at his feet – not me, though. I will not add my air to inflate anyone's ego. He gets enough of that from all the girls here, especially from Stacie. I have no desire to have an infatuation over any guy, least of all Larry. Nothing personal, I am sure he is a nice guy, but he is definitely not my type.

Larry's smile widens as he artfully slides his hand through his thick California-blonde hair. His dark blue eyes narrow while his smile intensely tries making me forget about what Stacie has just said.

"Thanks, I guess," I mumble. I'm not sure if Larry's trying to be nice or if he just wants me to be his next conquest. I am the only – and I mean only – girl in the office who does not hang on every word he says or follow him around like a lost puppy dog. This uncommon situation before me makes me believe he is probably talking to me to make Stacie jealous or he is irritated because I don't throw myself all over him. It's not just him – I don't throw myself at anyone. And I definitely hate talking to people here…or anywhere. I go to work and home and that's about it.

"So did William let you off easy?" Larry whispers.

He starts following me toward my desk. Irritation climbs up my spine, rolling across my shoulders. Gripping my hands into tight fists I fight back the urge to tell him to mind his own business. Gazing towards Stacie's desk out of the corner of my eye, I notice she is now standing up, intently listening to what I am going to say. I'm not about to give them the satisfaction of knowing what really happened, contributing more fuel to their gossiping fire.

A devious plan rolls through my mind. I am going to make it look and sound good. Picturing someone in my mind that pulls out my anger – Stacie – I allow the rage to flow up my now stiff back, poisoning my mind. Forcefully I narrow my eyes, deepening the furrow between them. Clenching my soft jaw so as to make the corners quiver slightly and summoning up as much anger in my voice as I can, I abruptly turn towards them so they can see my face, uttering firmly, "No, for a moment I thought I was going to lose my job. He is the most ridiculous and unreasonable boss." I strongly emphasize the last part, putting an acidic edge to it. I hope he doesn't hear any of this or I am going to have to owe him a huge apology.

Judging by Larry and Stacie's bulging shocked eyes they honestly believe me. I have robbed her of the opportunity to spread the rumor I am sure she had mentally prepared. They were expecting me to say he let me off easy – the truth – but I can't tell them the truth, for both William's sake and mine. A bubbling surge of joy gnaws at the corner of my mouth as I look at Stacie's shocked face. Her wide black eyes mirror her wide mouth. The vast emptiness within her mouth reveals her perfect white teeth framed by her full red lips. She is stunning when her mouth and attitude don't get in the way.

As I start to turn to walk away I feel a tug on my arm. "Lauren, I am truly sorry you got in trouble. It's kind of a silly reason to get in trouble. It's not like we all haven't been late before."

I hear Stacie give a sharp exhale and utter viciously, "Bitch." If she's at all jealous because Larry is talking to me she has nothing to worry about. I never, nor will I ever, have any feelings for him. He is not my type. To tell you the truth I have no idea what my type is. I tend to like the dark, mysterious and unrealistic guys. I think I am just waiting for Mr. Take My Breath Away or Mr. Unrealistic. Let's just make the person so impossible he can never hurt me.

As I walk back to my cubicle I hear Larry saying, "Stacie, that was totally uncalled for." Though his voice is sharp towards her it is a useless attempt, like a knife trying to cut off honey. No matter how harsh he speaks he will never stop the flow of thick guile pouring out of her mouth.

Staring at the blank cork wall in front of me I try to wash the morning from me when I sense someone standing behind me. Turning brusquely in my seat I notice Larry standing behind me. "Are you all right, Lauren? She shouldn't have called you that," he sighs in disgust.

"It's okay, Larry. She doesn't bother me." That is a total lie, but I'm not going to give her the satisfaction of knowing that it really did bother me. At this point I just want to get started on my work, because I am terrified at what else can go wrong today.

Looking irritatingly up at Larry I notice his hands twisting around each other as he begins slightly chewing on his full bottom lip. "Hey, you know Lauren, a bunch of us are going out this Friday. We thought it would be fun to go to some dance clubs in the city." A slight exhale rushes out of him as he adds, "Do you dance?" His question is polite while his voice becomes breathy.

I remain motionless while my mind begins firing off the events of this screwed up day – and it's not even lunch yet. A churning sickness rises and hangs out at the base of my throat as I stare up at him in disbelief.

"Well, Lauren, do you dance?" he impatiently asks again.

His eyes gaze intently at me as if they are trying to lure the words out of my mouth. I know he wants some kind of response, but my mind has turned to a heap of useless flab. Placing both my hands up to my face I begin softly drumming the tops of my cheekbones, causing a gentle slapping sound. The sour tinge in my throat rushes up to my head, waking all my senses. Suddenly my imagination takes hold of my thoughts. I can tell him no, but then my life remains in this unyielding rut. And if I tell him yes, my life could possibly spin out of my control. Shaking my head slightly I force out my overactive imagination. I am complicating this situation. He just asked me a simple question. He didn't technically ask me to go. Blowing a heavy sigh out I give him an ambiguous answer, "To tell you the truth Larry, it has been a long time since I have danced, so I don't know if I can." The blood quickly rushes to my face, turning it a deep crimson color.

"Well, to tell you the truth I can't dance either, but I do have a lot of fun. So do you want to come with us?" he asks more aggressively this time, leaving little doubt of his intentions.

A forceful rush of air explodes frustratedly out of my mouth. He didn't just ask if I can dance this time. He point blank has laid out his intentions, forcing me to now have to give him a solid answer. Grabbing hold of my nerves I quickly answer, hoping to get this over with, "I guess I will." Instantly after the last word was uttered I recall him using the term "us" in his question. An immediate rush of regret tickles the base of my skull. I need to know who the "us" is going to be.

"Who else is going?" I groan.

"Well, me of course, plus Maria, two guys from processing, and…" a long, breathy pause slithers out of him, thickening the air between us. His hands begin nervously wringing and twisting vigorously around each other. Hesitation stutters out of him as he tries to say a name…a name I already know.

"And Stacie, right?" I sharply add.

He gives me a slight apologetic smile, "Is that going to be a problem?"

Dropping my head in disappointment I begin shaking it in disbelief. At this point it doesn't matter if she comes or not, I have already made up my mind this is going to be a big mistake. I don't dislike Stacie as much as she hates me. I can't wait to see her face though when Larry tells her I am going. "No, it won't be a problem," I reluctantly answer.

The pitch of his voice rises, matching his exuberant expression, "I'm glad you are going. You will have fun, I promise."

"I wouldn't promise something you have no control over," I state hesitantly.

A huge smile spreads vividly across his face. This is the first time I can actually see why the girls love his smile, it is contagious. I just hope I am not making a big mistake, giving him any misguided intentions.

"All right, then we'll see you Friday night at nine o'clock." Stuttering slightly, he adds, "If you want I can meet you at the office, and then you can ride with me to the club."

I don't want to give him the wrong idea. "That's okay, I think I'm just going to drive there myself. I have further to drive than the rest of you. That way when I am done I can just drive straight home instead of having you have to take me to my car." Hopefully that worked. I never realized before how quickly I can come up with lies. I'm not sure if it's a good thing or a bad thing, but in this case it's a very good thing.

As I turn around to finally get started on my work, I can feel Larry's enthusiasm as he walks away. I start thumbing through all my paperwork when suddenly in the background I can hear Stacie arguing with Larry. The razor edge tone in her voice cuts through the air with anger as she discovers Larry has invited me – and I said yes. Ignoring their heated discussion, I try to get back to work, but I can't help wonder how in just one day things have taken a drastic turn. How just last night I felt like I had missed the boat of life and I had been left floating on a buoy with no hope. I had completely given up on staying afloat in the water of life, but now it seems a second boat or a second chance has been given to me. I just need to let go of the buoy and climb aboard. Well, I wanted my life to be different – I guess I need to be careful what I wish for. Trepidation washes over me as I suddenly realize… I hope I am getting on the right boat.

CHAPTER 4

Let the Game Begin

Several times I almost back out of going, but deep down I know I have to do this. My heart starts pounding vigorously against my chest as I approach the looming exit. An entire gymnastics class seems to be doing somersaults within my stomach as the nervous energy builds within me. My slick, sweaty palms are having a hard time gripping the steering wheel. This is absurd – I'm not heading off to hell, I am just going dancing.

Reluctantly I gaze ahead at the haunting glow of the parking structure as my breathing begins to increase in speed. The quick, shallow breaths are intensifying and make me feel like I am going to hyperventilate. A cold sweat begins exuding off the nape of my neck, causing me to tremble with fear.

Slowly I pull into the parking structure when I instantly see Larry's gleaming, smiling face. Pulling my car next to his red Jeep I try to fake the best smile I can. Forcing the corners of my mouth up I give a facetious, yet slightly sinister-looking smile as my hands firmly grip onto the steering wheel. The steering wheel has immediately turned into my security blanket. As long as I am holding onto it and remain in the car, I can still leave. Once I let go it will be too late, I won't be able to change my mind.

My motionless eyes stare straight ahead as I attempt to rally all my internal strength. Suddenly there is a quiet tap at my window. Nervously I gaze over at Larry standing outside of my car door. His gentle face intertwines with his mesmerizing smile as it showers over me, washing away some of my fear. Apprehensively I roll down the window. I leave the engine running while I am still debating on whether I am staying or leaving.

"Lauren, I am glad you came. I hate to say it, but everyone was taking bets on whether you would show up or not. My bet was on you coming tonight, so it looks like I won," he admits with a slight laugh.

"You haven't won yet," I sharply reply.

Instantly a loud, boisterous laugh explodes from him like I had just told some ridiculous joke. But I'm not joking. I may have shown up, but that doesn't mean I am going to get out of this car. I haven't let go of my refuge – the steering wheel – yet. All it will take is me throwing the car into reverse and I will be out of here.

He must have been reading my expression because he quickly utters, "I've won, because you are not leaving." A threatening smile spreads across his face as his thick, blond eyebrows spring up teasingly. His eyes scan over my protective barrier as he adds, "By the way, nice car."

Jittery thoughts bounce in and out of my mind, making it hard to hear anything he is saying. Shaking my head rapidly I snap myself back into reality. "What did you just say?"

"I said, nice car," he repeats.

I don't see my car as nice. I just see it as a constant reminder of my father. This was his car before he passed away. When my dad died my mom didn't need a second car and couldn't stand seeing it sit in the driveway, junking it up. So she decided to sell it. I couldn't stand the thought of her selling it to some stranger. It oozed his smell and memories from every seam.

I asked her if I could have the car instead of her selling it. But of course, this is my mother, heaven forbid her do anything nice for me. She couldn't just give me the car. I had to buy it from her, paying the full asking price. I ended up having to use the money from my inheritance to pay for my own father's car. Her excuse for doing that was I will now have more of an appreciation for the car since I bought it – which was a bunch of bullshit. She just wanted the money.

I didn't care that I lost the money though. I am now able to have a part of my father with me. All I have to do is sit in his black

BMW, close my eyes... and smell. His musky scent permeates the tan leather, filling my mind with visions of his handsome, strong face. A faint aroma from his cologne still haunts every faded stitch on the driver's seat. Dark oil marks taint the leather where his hands had gripped at the seat and steering wheel. A simple cleaning could easily wipe these marks away, but these are the scars left on the car which now match the scars his death has left on my heart.

Turning towards Larry I utter reluctantly, "Thanks, it was my father's car."

Slowly Larry leans in towards my open window, when suddenly Maria walks up to the car. "Hey Lauren, you showed up," she mutters rudely, giving me a quick, sharp glance.

Instantly she turns her attention away from me, grabbing possessively onto Larry's arm. Glancing at him sharply, she urges, "Are you about ready to go in? We don't just want to sit here all night. Now that Lauren finally decided to show up we can go." She looks at me, giving me the same snotty smile Stacie gives me all the time.

Turning his attention back to me, Larry asks sincerely, "Hey Lauren, you can walk with Stacie and I, if you'd like?"

Quickly I glance over at Maria, noticing her wide eyes now match her equally wide mouth like she has just heard the most appalling suggestion. I want to explain to her that she has nothing to worry about – I'm not going to accept his offer – but I am having too much fun watching her petite frame squirm. The sides of her straight brown hair are pinned back, leaving a high beehive bump on the top of her hair. Two thin strands flow down each side of her heavily made-up face, leaving no natural features to shine through.

Instantly I want to laugh. Is he really that naïve, or is he just trying to be nice? There is no way Stacie will allow that. She would have an absolute meltdown if I walk next to him. Judging from Maria's wide eyes and appalled expression, there is no way in hell it's going to happen.

I realize I have completely misjudged Larry. Though I'm not physically attracted to him, he is a really nice guy. He is the kind of guy where his personality brightens your day and wins you over. I can tell he is just trying to do everything he can to make me feel comfortable, like I am welcome here. Yet I know ninety percent of the people here either don't want me to come along or don't know me enough to even bother to care.

"Thanks Larry, for offering, but it's probably best if I don't." Giving him a quick, reassuring wink I roll up the window and hesitantly turn off my car.

"Well, if you're not going to walk by me then you need to stay with the group. That way I know you haven't escaped to head back home." Though he seems slightly disappointed, he gives me a quick wink in return as a huge smile spreads across his face.

Standing up he turns towards everyone, shouting, "Is everyone ready?"

Everybody's heads nod in excitement but mine. Instantly I get the nervous, sick feeling again as my stomach begins tossing and turning once more. I'm not sure if I can go through with this. Can't we just stay here in the parking lot? I would feel so much better with that scenario, but I know that no one else would.

Slapping his hand softly on the hood of my car, he states firmly, "All right, let's go." Giving me one last smile, he walks over to the awaiting group.

As I get out of my car I gaze around at the dark, secluded parking lot, noticing all the rows of cars lined up perfectly in this open structure right in the heart of downtown. My stomach curdles with negative anticipation for what lies ahead of me. As I walk over to the group my vision is bombarded by the repulsive outfits Stacie and Maria have on. I feel like I have just walked into a porno audition room. They each have on a denim skirt – if that is even what it is. Their skirts are so short they barely even cover the bottom curves of their butts. Their shirts leave very little to anyone's imagination. Thin spaghetti straps meet up with silk and lace, giving it a lingerie appearance. Their clothes barely cover the necessary parts to prevent them from being arrested for public nudity. Scanning their exposed bodies I notice they are both covered with pronounced goosebumps over all their limbs. Even in

May, San Francisco's cold fog blankets the town, giving a piercing wet cold to the air and tonight is one of those nights.

Wrapping my arms tightly around myself I gaze down at my outfit. Though my slim-fitting jeans and lightweight shirt completely cover me, it reveals my slender hourglass figure, allowing men the use of their alluring imagination to their benefit. A sudden rising sense of empowerment I have never felt before crawls up my spine, causing me to unfold my arms and stand erect. A sense of satisfaction rolls across my shoulders as I discover for what feels like the first time that I don't need to wear so very little to feel beautiful.

The empowerment flowing through me immediately shatters though the moment Larry's voice rips through my thoughts, uttering excitedly, "It's just around the corner."

Apprehensively I gulp as I look around at everyone beginning to pair up. Stacie weaves her arm through the crook in Larry's, pulling him forcefully towards her. Maria grips the hand of a tall, lanky guy who came with her as they interlock their fingers, leaving behind one guy. His dark eyes meet mine as we both begin to take in each other's appearance. A thick coat of arrogance covers his stocky build. Lifting his round face towards me he tilts his head, giving me a sleazy expression as he slides his hand through his short dark hair. Crinkling up my nose in annoyed repugnance I gaze at him when suddenly he walks right past me, quickly catching up to Maria and her date. A boisterous laugh rolls out of them as they obviously are using me as the butt of their joke. Grabbing hold of my internal nerve I close my eyes briefly and proceed to follow slowly behind them all. I already want this horrific night to be over with and it has just started.

Every so often Larry turns around, giving me an apologetic smile. Stacie's forceful grip on Larry's arm controls his every action. She nearly drags him along, preventing him from slowing to my pace. I know he wants to involve me more, but Stacie is not about to allow him to acknowledge me any more than he has to.

I walk all alone in the distance as the rest of the group is laughing and having fun. As they turn the corner I suddenly hear loud gasps intermingled with several shrills of amazement. Quickly I round the corner, when my heart and body immediately stop. I begin trembling in fear and excitement.

There, parked in front of the club, is the same amazing car from earlier this week. Heavy weights of memories flood into my mind, pushing me firmly into the concrete. A looming vision of the dark-haired faceless man intermingles with the memory of my soul being invaded. Though the thick burden of my frame locks me here, my mind gravitates in excitement towards the car.

"Lauren, are you all right?" Larry asks sharply. Even though I can hear Larry, my thoughts remain imprisoned by this coincidental sighting, stopping me from answering him. "Lauren," Larry commands, shaking me out of my hypnotic state.

Suddenly I am acutely aware of everyone staring at me. I can hear a few rude snickers coming out of the girls. "Sorry," I utter softly. "It's just I think I saw this very car on the freeway earlier this week," I finally stutter, trying to hide my quivering voice.

Everyone's gaze quickly turns back towards the car. "You mean this car?" Larry questions emphatically, gesturing towards the illustrious car.

"Yes, that one," I defend ardently as I firmly point my finger at the same car. "It was just a strange experience I had that morning." My mind drifts off into deep thought as I continue, "I tried to see who the driver was, but I couldn't see his face. The whole time I could feel...this..." Coming to my senses I look up quickly, adding, "Nothing. It was just a strange experience."

"You don't know what kind of car this is?" Larry laughs.

Narrowing my eyes questionably I begin shaking my head in confusion, uttering, "No, should I?"

"Lauren, I doubt you will ever see this car again. I have never seen one before and you are lucky enough to have seen it twice in one week," he chortles softly.

"What is it?" I ask vaguely.

Larry's eyes gleam with excitement as the corner of his mouth turns up, revealing a slight maniacal smile like a proud father getting ready to brag about his son's talent. "It's a Bugatti Veyron," he gloats as he struts over to the car like he is the owner.

"A Bugatti what?" I question, still completely lost. Like telling me the name is going to make me all of a sudden understand. If it isn't a standard car, then forget it.

The pitch of his voice raises as the excitement pulsating through him intensifies the vibrations in his voice. A deflated expression drops over his face like I have disappointed him. Turning back towards the car he reaches out, nearly touching it as his open and pleading hand begins shaking slightly. Forcefully he elaborates for my benefit, "This is one of the most expensive cars around. It costs more than a million dollars, if you are even lucky enough to buy one."

My eyes double in size when I hear him utter the amount the car is worth. No wonder people were staring at it on the freeway. I think if I owned a car like this I would never take it out of the driveway, least of all in bumper-to-bumper San Francisco traffic. What kind of person would drive an exclusive car like this?

Electricity immediately races through my veins, igniting my skin, setting it ablaze. My mind floods with anticipation. For the first time tonight I am actually excited to go inside. A yearning desire calls to me from the inside like another half of a magnet pulling me towards it. The deep urge to find the mysterious stranger consumes my every thought. I don't care if it was just my imagination that morning. I have to put an end to my own personal mystery. I have to find him. Pulling myself together I instantly head inside.

Excitement flutters through me as I nearly run down the long, dark hallway leading into a large room of complex patterns of colors mixed with pulsing waves of bodies heaving to the thick beat. The pulsating music intensely rolls along the club floor, vibrating up my feet and into my body, causing my heart to pound with the same rhythmic pattern. Vivid colored lights dance rapidly throughout the room, making it very difficult to see anyone's face. The only opportunity to catch a glimpse of someone's facial features is if the yellow swirling lights stream across them.

The intense heat radiating off the overcrowded dance floor wraps around me like a thick, sticky blanket, making it hard to breathe. The bubbling floor rises and falls with the motion of bodies vigorously pulsating to the thunderous beat of the music. Several layers of small dance floors surround the large center floor, allowing girls to stand above everyone, prostituting their dance skills before all the male onlookers. A myriad of bodies intertwine suggestively, causing me to instinctively turn my head, looking away in disgust. No wonder Stacie and Maria are dressed so provocatively. The way everyone is dancing appears as if they belong in a bedroom, not on a dance floor. Shots of discouragement pierce my mind with the enormous task of finding an unknown mystery man in a sea of faceless strangers.

Stacie immediately grabs Larry's hand, pulling him swiftly to the dance floor. Next to follow are Maria and her date, leaving me now standing here next to the arrogant jerk I have no desire to dance with. Besides, I can never exhibit such a public display of private affection, I don't care how much I like a guy. As I turn around to inform him that it is okay if he wants to leave, I notice he is no longer standing by me. He has already left. Animosity clamps onto my spine, poisoning my thoughts and destroying my hopes. I had no desire to dance with him, but I didn't want to be left alone in a room full of faceless strangers either.

An unyielding loneliness begins to creep back into my dilapidated body, leaving me feeling brokenhearted once more. An eerie, yet familiar sense tickles my neck and scales down my spine, causing a chill to shiver through me. Tears begin to well up as I stand here all alone. I begin hastily weaving my way through the multitude of unknown people. They all seem to be carrying on in their jovial merriment, no one acknowledging the extreme distress I am in. Hastily I look around the overpopulated room for a quiet place, when out of the corner of my eye I notice a small table in the back of the room next to a large window overlooking the bright city lights. Firmly focusing on the table I walk over, sitting down as I stare dolefully out the window, trying to fight back the impending tears.

The tears begin to well up even more within my eyes, causing me to just want to leave as fast as I can. Exhaling forcefully, I jump up to leave when suddenly my heart starts hammering against my chest. This constant slamming sensation is not an unfamiliar one to me. Unlike the throbbing from the vibrations of the music, this is something I have experienced before… this is my intruder. Fluttering jolts of excitement pulsate within my stomach. Pulling all my nerves in I begin encapsulating the sensation, trapping it within me. I don't want this feeling to pass. I need it now more than ever. This intense sensation is not a violation. I now give whoever this person is permission to invade me.

Intently I gaze around the room, trying to see who the perpetrator is as the sensation gets more severe with every breath. An internal ripping is separating me from reality. A trembling electricity pulses through my veins, exhilarating my skin and igniting my mind. Only one thought rolls around within me – I want to see who is doing this. I know now this is not an accident, nor my overactive imagination causing this intense feeling.

I frantically shift my eyes back and forth like I am at a tennis match, scouring the room for any sign of the mystery man. I freeze as my wide eyes lock onto a striking man walking towards me. His long, graceful stride glides through the throngs of people as a palpable heat radiates off of him. An invisible cable line piercing through my soul links us together as my desire to see him is the gravitating power bringing him towards me. Everyone naturally moves out of his way like he is surrounded by an invisible force field. He walks through the sea of people untouched as his eyes now lock onto mine.

Excitement scales my spine, exploding within my mind, causing a tingling sensation to rush through me with the realization of who this is. This is the man from the freeway – the owner of the amazing car – the intruder of my being. Though the swirls of light prevent me from seeing him clearly I recognize his dark hair and strong jawline. His black form-fitting V-neck sweater molds to his physique perfectly, showing off his tall, thin, yet muscular physique. His sleeves are pushed up slightly, revealing his chiseled forearms. The veins in his arms thrust out slightly as they flow down the flexor and extensor muscles, accentuating his masculine appearance. Slowly I gaze down his body, trying to take in every detail I can. His well-defined torso merges perfectly into the strong curves of his hips. His black, slim-fitting slacks enhance his smooth, sensual walk. Every step he takes reveals his strong male endowments. His thigh muscles press against the thin black fabric, tightening the pants just enough to reveal his perfectly formed backside… as well as front side.

As he slides effortlessly past all the females in the crowd, I notice their heads hastily turn towards him as their gawking eyes pulsate in undulating desire. Though their stares are completely obvious he never once turns to acknowledge their noticeable yearnings for him. Ignoring their advances, he passes by them effortlessly as his eyes remain affixed to me. Disbelief swirls within my ignited frame like a loose live wire whipping in the wind. Gradually he inches his way closer to me, causing a tingling sensation to tickle the tips of my fingers. This has to be a dream. There is no way he can be walking towards me, a lonely loser stuck in my pathetic rut.

Keeping my eyes fixated on him I notice the swirling colored lights bouncing vividly off of his nearly black hair like an angelic halo of shimmering colors. As he inches his way closer I notice the tips of his thick, slicked-back hair delicately brushing across the bottoms of his fleshy ears. My breathing quickens as I take in every detail, devouring it within me. I need to see all of him, this mystery man who haunts my dreams and who has intruded on my innermost desires. Intently I try to visually rip through the darkness, attempting to see all the details of his face.

Giving in to my desire I take a slight step forward, struggling to ease my way closer to him, when suddenly he stops moving towards me. The shadowy darkness engulfing him amplifies as his eyes narrow in displeasure. His rigid frame holds motionless as he slightly shakes his head, denying me any further movement. The rising urge to see him completely consumes me, making it impossible to obey his command. Slowly I move forward again, when abruptly the bright yellow light crosses his face, illuminating his features. His chiseled structure is framed by his masculine square jaw, merging into his strong chin and forming a soft cleft. The muscles in his jaw quiver slightly as he firmly clenches down.

Scanning across his face I stop on his sumptuous, full lips, causing my stomach to quickly flip. His plump, pouty bottom lip hangs down slightly, sending a strange tingling sensation to rush up through my legs and into my mind, making me want to gingerly trace the bottom of his lips with my tongue. His candy apple mouth explodes from his pale white skin, giving him a near mythical appearance. The intense hypnotic power of his exquisite face is causing me to think in ways I would have never thought before. My soul trembles in delight as my mouth suddenly starts watering at his stunning appearance. He slightly parts his pouty lips, revealing a mischievous smile against a backdrop of gleaming white teeth.

He now appears to be beckoning me even closer. Wanting to fully comply with his sudden request, I start to proceed towards him when I catch sight of his piercing eyes. The unique intensifying color mystifies me, stopping me dead in my tracks. They almost appear to have an opaque aquamarine luster to them, like the shallow waters of the Indian Ocean. The outer edges of his mysterious translucent eyes hold a menacing virulence, causing a frightening shiver to rush up my spine with an impending warning.

His extremely long, dark eyelashes frame the almond shape of his eyes, making his eye color appear even more intense. As I gaze deeply into his mesmerizing eyes I notice the vast emptiness within them. His mystifying eyes are hollow and blank, but shimmering like polished glass. Eyes are the windows to the soul, but his eyes are not revealing any part of his.

Standing here motionless I am unsure if I should move forward or stay where I am. Part of me wants to proceed, while the other part wants to run away as fast as I can. But I can't run. I feel trapped in his hypnotic gaze. The more dominant part of me has no desire to leave yet. In fact, that part of my being is gravitating towards him like a highly charged magnet. The intense feelings of passion and fear are both present and colliding rapidly within me. I'm not sure which one will win out in the end.

I am paralyzed by his pulsating gaze while my feet feel like they are attached to the floor, making it nearly impossible to move. Suddenly the mysterious feeling rushes vigorously through my heart and chest, intensifying, making it extremely difficult to breathe.

Grasping firmly onto my chest I intently gaze into his eyes, pleading for him to stop. I have no idea what he is doing or how he is doing it, but I can't breathe and I know I am going to pass out at any moment. He keeps his gaze fixated on me as his eyes remain void of any emotion for what he is causing to tear through me, ripping my soul wide open.

Panic starts to rush violently over me as my breathing becomes more and more labored. The lack of oxygen I'm experiencing causes the colors in the room to fade, leaving my vision and body dancing on the edge of consciousness.

Out of my peripheral vision I notice everyone around me dancing in what appears to be fast motion. The wild streaks of blurry colors flash violently by me like rushing, painted wind. My whirling, terrified mind sinks deeper into the darkness, dragging me down into the murky lake of despair. My vision blackens as I begin drowning. I try to yell for someone to intervene and help me, but no sound escapes my mouth. I am completely trapped within his mesmerizing power. I am in trouble in a room full of people who are oblivious to my absolute plight. Struggling for breath, my weak body can't hold on much longer, fully resolving this is the end.

CHAPTER 5

An Alien Form of Myself

Darkness encases me, blocking out all signs of reality, leaving me feeling entirely alone. Echoing out of the penetrating obscurity I hear my name undulating through the blackness, like someone talking through a long narrow tunnel. With every struggling breath I take I slowly feel the strong vibrations of the music pulsate through the floor again, gradually resuming the once deafening volume. Reality gingerly seeps back into me as I'm able to break free from my imprisoning dream-like state.

Colors and shapes vividly return, shattering the darkness that had once consumed me. Everything around me shines with a bright pristine clarity like the murky veil over my life has finally been lifted. As consciousness presses back into me I am instantly aware of my gaze still locked within the stranger's. For the first time tonight I can see a glimpse of regret streaming from his ordinarily emotionless eyes, allowing me to witness his brief inexplicable guilt. A crack into his soul opens, allowing a tremendous amount of angst to pour out, flooding his stale eyes. Then instantly, without warning, the glance is gone like a light being turned off, blackening everything.

"Lauren, are you all right?" The thick, concerned voice pierces through my hypnotic trance. "You look like you are going to faint."

For the first time in a few heart stopping minutes, I am able to break the hypnotic grasp the stranger has had on me. As I hesitantly turn toward the concerned voice my legs begin quivering violently as my mind feels like it has been pumped full of helium. Larry quickly rushes to my side, carefully wrapping one arm around my waist, supporting my weight entirely. His eyes narrow as the furrow deepens with anxious anticipation. Confusion wraps vividly around my dazed mind. I have no idea what is going on or why he is firmly holding onto me.

The incomprehensible phenomenon which had consumed me dissipates now, leaving normalcy to creep back into me. Larry's arms remain feverishly wrapped around me, sending an uneasy heat to rush out of my stomach, boiling the epidermis layer of my skin. An alien fury seethes deep within me, igniting an unfamiliar rage. Yanking myself free from his grasp I turn to yell at him, when suddenly the vivid colors begin to fade, causing the room to spin rapidly. A dark, seeping cloud devours the outer edges of my tainted vision.

"Whoa, hold on Lauren, let's sit you down." Wrapping his arms around me again, he gingerly sits me on the nearest chair. "Maybe we should take you to the hospital."

Exhaling forcefully, I order, "No. Don't be ridiculous. I will be fine. Just let me catch my breath, that's all."

Slowly my vertigo subsides as the spinning gradually comes to a halt. The heavy rush causing my lightheadedness diminishes slightly, sending a stream of new energy to pulsate through me like fresh rain on a parched field. There is no need for him to take me to the hospital. I am feeling perfectly fine. I just got dizzy, that's all. He doesn't need to know the truth – hell, I don't even know the truth.

Lifting my head abruptly I glance over to where the mysterious guy had been standing, only to discover he is no longer there. Disappointment mixes with a flooding anger, forming a toxic concoction to rush through my perturbed body. "He left, how could he leave? He did this to me and now he should be the one to help me, not Larry," I mumble silently to myself.

Frustration runs rampant within me as I contemplate my undeniable attraction to the mysterious stranger – whom I should be frightened of. This enigma encapsulates my thoughts. The only thing I know is that I am undeniably drawn to him like a moth to a burning flame, but I can't seem to control myself. This undulating feeling is absolutely foreign to me. I have never felt this way before. I usually have no problem keeping people at a distance, but he is different.

As I sit here in confusion I notice Stacie and Maria rushing feverishly up to Larry and me. Relief is spread over their anxious faces, resembling the same concerned look Larry had on his face. "You found her," she utters joyfully. This is the first time Stacie has sounded excited or even relieved when speaking about me.

A small crowd of unwanted guests begins to hover over me, causing a rush of claustrophobia to surround me like a low-lying peninsula in high tide. Vibrating nerves surge up my spine, streaming across my shoulder as I gaze up at the insincere wretched group. Clenching my fists tightly I try to fight the flight response coursing through me. The only one who even possibly cares about me is Larry – but he's not the one I want around me either.

Bewilderment tickles my mind as something Stacie said tiptoes on my memory. Narrowing my eyes, I turn hesitantly toward Stacie, who now has positioned herself protectively next to Larry. Uttering reluctantly, I ask, "Stacie, what did you mean by he found me?" I was trying to sound as cordial as possible. A swift shiver unexpectedly rushes up my spine, causing the hair on the back of my neck to stand erect like my mind is not wanting to hear the answer.

"Lauren, no one knew where you were," she hisses with a smug, scrutinizing expression on her face.

Shaking my head rapidly I draw my eyebrows tightly together, trying to understand the stupidity of her statement. I have only been sitting here for a few minutes. "What do you mean? I've been back here the whole time. It's only been about ten minutes since you all left me." I quickly shoot the arrogant jerk a sharp glare. "You guys must have not looked very well," I snap, trying to hide the anger in my voice.

Unconsciously Stacie and Larry turn towards each other as a silent communication rolls between them. Their wide eyes and dropped jaws mirror each other's startled appearance. Silence saturates everyone's frozen bodies as I immediately scan their facial expressions, scrutinizing their every unspoken word. Their eyes pan back and forth at each other like the cat's eyes on a wooden clock. Nobody is willing to break the silence.

My heart rate increases, causing my palms to sweat slightly. "What? What is wrong with all of you?" I shout. The ravenous, unbridled anger quivers viciously within me. I start to stand up when Larry firmly, yet gently pushes me back to my seat.

Grabbing hold of a vacant chair he sits down next to me. Gently he puts his hand on my thigh as if he is preparing to give me some sort of grave message. As I gaze sharply down at his hand something ignites within me again, causing an angry shiver to rush up my spine. All I want to do is slap it off, when suddenly his soft eyes get very serious. "Lauren, you weren't gone for only ten minutes," he gently replies, "you were gone for over two hours."

The pounding of my heart intensifies as I slowly fall into distress. There has to be some sort of misunderstanding on their part. The experience I endured only lasted a few minutes, not a few hours. If it would have truly been over two hours, I would be dead by now. There is no way a person can survive for that long without breathing. They have to be wrong, there's got to be another reason.

Anxious energy curdles my stomach as my breathing starts coming faster, causing my arms to go slightly numb. The numb tingling sensation sends sharp pricks rushing vigorously throughout my hands. I have had a couple of panic attacks, so I am able to recognize what it feels like… and this is definitely one. Lifting my hands up to my chest I try slowing my breathing down, diminishing the effects of the attack. "Wait, I don't understand. When that guy…" Lifting my hand aggressively, I snap my finger towards the arrogant guy who came with them – I didn't know his name because no one, least of all him, had the decency to introduce us – "…disappeared, I came up here to sit down. The next thing I know you all are asking me if I am okay. It seriously was only about ten minutes. There is no possible way it could have been over two hours." I ramble off, purposefully leaving out the part about the mysterious stranger. I don't even know where to begin with that part when I'm not even quite sure what happened. I can just imagine the rumors they would say about me if I were to share the strange, yet erotic experience.

Larry gazes forcefully into my eyes, uttering fervently, "Yes, Lauren, it has been over two hours. Take a look." Shoving his hand deep into his pocket he pulls out his cell phone, handing it over to me. Reluctantly I look down at the large screen on his sleek phone. My heart drops as I stare at it. The glowing numbers sear through my eyes, piercing my mind as the reality is now placed in front of me. Though my vision tries to deny it, my astonished mind slowly encapsulates the intense reality of this bizarre fact. Rubbing my eyes vigorously I take a quick second look, noticing the time has not changed – it is still after midnight. I replay every detail of tonight's events rapidly within my mind as I try to understand where the past two hours have gone. The time just slipped away from me like sand flowing swiftly through open fingers. Forcefully I hold onto his phone, refusing to let go as my hand trembles violently around it.

"Lauren, we got here close to nine-thirty. I remember looking at the time just before Stacie grabbed me to go out and dance. I was dancing and having fun when I suddenly realized I hadn't seen you in a while. I began scouring the dance floor for you when I saw Toni," his eyes glance up, gesturing over to the arrogant jerk who left me standing in the middle of the dance club all alone. Finally, I have a name to put to the smug ass, a name that fits him perfectly. "Toni was out on the dance floor with some girl. I rushed over to him, asking if he had seen you anywhere."

Immediately Toni pushes his way in front of Larry, rudely cutting him off, attempting to affirm what had happened, "And I told him what happened." His shrilling ostentatious voice cuts through me like piercing needles, setting me off the instant he speaks. "I explained that I hadn't seen you since you left me."

Those words instantly shoot through me like a fiery dart straight out of hell, setting my already tingling frame ablaze. I left… him? The anger rises and falls within me like a witch's brew boiling over with toxic venom and eating away at the solid ground below. With every word he utters it increases the danger level within me.

Toni continues, adding fuel to my already raging fire, "I just told him you probably snuck off to the bar so you could get drunk. Or if you were lucky perhaps you found someone to run off with, doing who knows what in a dark corner somewhere." His low chortle vibrates in the center of his vocal chords, causing a crude growl to vibrate within his laugh. Similar snickers escape from Stacie and Maria as if an unspoken agreement is being passed through them.

The vile plague rushing through me continues to eat away at my emotional control. I'm not sure how much more I can take. He doesn't know me at all. To assume I am getting drunk or even worse – doing lewd acts with a guy I don't even know – is degrading.

My indignant thoughts begin concocting up all sorts of ways to curse him down to hell. I have no idea where all this rage is coming from. This sudden natural capacity for vehemence frightens even me. I need to try and control the unbridled anger welling up inside of me. Slowly I turn my attention back toward Larry. "Did you start looking for me then? Did you even come up here at all?" I press forcefully.

His eyes drop, gazing down at his hands while his knees begin bouncing intensely. "To be honest, we didn't look for you at first. When Toni told us what he thought you were doing, we just assumed he was probably right and you were off having fun somewhere," he adds defensively as his voice drops to a near whisper.

The now violent churning pot of rage boils over within me as I instantaneously jump to my feet, dropping Larry's phone to the floor. This time Larry can't hold me down. My muscles pulsate as a foreign substance takes possession over me. The ominous darkness ripples within me, enveloping me like a black shroud. Standing here I forcefully glare at everyone as I contemplate the events leading me to this rage. During the night I have had my breathing nearly come to a stop, my heart beat at some crazy rhythmic pattern, apparently have been sucked into some sort of time warp, and the man who caused all of this confusion has mysteriously disappeared. After going through all of this, I am not about to be accused of being an alcoholic slut by a jerk who doesn't even know my name.

Turning sharply, I look over at Toni, my eyes narrowed in angst as my face stiffens, causing my tight jaw to quiver. My thick acidic voice belts out, "You believed him!" Lifting my quivering hand, furiously I point at Toni. "He doesn't even know me. He didn't even have the decency to tell me he was going to find someone to dance with, he just up and left me. This guy has no idea of what type of girl I am – even if it bit him in his ass."

My penetrating glare sears deep into Toni's eyes as if they are deadly weapons. He frightfully recoils as he turns away from my vicious glare. "And by the way, Toni, I don't drink. So don't ever assume anything about me anymore," I utter in a low, smooth tone that cuts through the thick, sweltering air.

A heavy stillness presses down on everyone as they stare at me in utter shock. No one has ever seen or heard me do something like this before. I have no idea where all this anger is coming from, but somewhere deep within a hunger craves for more. I have lost my temper before with people, but never like this. It always comes across as a pathetic attempt at getting mad. Part of me wants to apologize, but the now dominant side of me is yearning for more. I need to leave before I say something else I will regret.

Everyone is frozen in silence like mannequins positioned frightfully in a haunted house. The deafening quiet speaks loud and clear as my cue to leave. Gathering whatever strength I have left I proceed to walk away from them, when once again there is a gentle tug on my arm. Closing my eyes firmly I take a deep, soothing breath in, and then reluctantly turn around to face my intruder.

Tender remorse flows out of Larry's shocked, yet compassionate eyes as he stands before me like a defeated, broken-down man. His sorrowful blue eyes burrow deep inside of me, diminishing the anger that appears to be burning out of control. "Lauren, I am sorry if we offended you in any way. We… I mean I, didn't mean to hurt you. I was truly worried – and still am – about you. You don't need to leave by yourself, please let me at least walk you to your car," he gently whispers.

His hand remains firmly wrapped around my arm like a father gently redirecting his child. The warmth of his hand radiates through my sleeve, soothing my temper. As I look deep into Larry's eyes I can see the sincere remorse flowing out of them. I can see the worry written on his face and feel the trembling grip not willing to let go. A sharp exhale escapes vigorously from my mouth as his genuine kindness pricks my conscience, causing me to rethink my decision to leave.

"Please," his voice is pleading genially. How can I be mad at him? He has just been trying to do the right thing all night long.

Just as I am about to agree to his gentle demands, I hear Stacie in the distance uttering in a low, yet piercing sarcastic voice, "She probably was just asleep the whole time. That's why she is completely oblivious to how long she was away from us. Then good old Larry happened to wake her up from her deep sleep, which is why she is such a bitch. We disturbed her beauty rest." Her shrilling voice breaks out into a boisterous cackle, causing the others to laugh hysterically along with her.

Her voice, though muted and soft, rushes through me like crashing waves against a crumbling rocky shoreline. Surging jolts of rage chafe my skin as it rolls over me again. I gaze upon Larry's oblivious expression streaming innocently across his face. He is either pretending he didn't hear her demeaning comment, or he is completely ignorant of the sly remark. Either way it does not matter anymore, the damage is already done. The once-tamed beast is again set free by Stacie's berating comment.

"Larry, thank you for offering, but I don't need or want you to walk with me. I'll be fine. I am a big girl," I strongly assure him.

Leaning in I wrap both my arms tightly around him, pressing my chest against his. Scanning my eyes viciously toward Stacie, our eyes lock firmly into a tight dueling gaze. Curling up the side of my mouth I give her a sinister smile as I pull him securely against me. Holding Larry against me I instantly feel his trepidation quivering hastily within my grasp. Stacie's smug expression quickly drops, exposing a vulnerable and deflated countenance at what she is having to witness. I can practically see the green envy-filled air pulsating out of her like toxic gas radiating from a dangerous plant. A deep, dark sense of accomplishment crawls up my spine, tingling throughout me.

Hesitantly he pushes me away. Tilting his head slightly he stares at me with a perplexed gaze. "Lauren, you're a hard person to read," he states, completely mystified by my constant swaying of emotions.

I have to agree with his perceptive statement. I am having a hard time figuring myself out. I'm not usually an angry and vindictive person. Everything I am doing tonight feels like an alien image of me.

Giving him the best crooked smile I can muster up, I ruefully add, "I think I am just tired and need to go home. I don't feel like myself either right now. This has been a long day for me and I am not used to this, that's all. I promise I'll be myself on Monday." Smiling, I add gently, "Thanks again, Larry."

As I get closer to the exit a violent chill runs up my spine, causing me to break out in goosebumps. I turn around to take Larry up on his offer to walk me to my car, but he is already standing with the group. My ridiculous pride consumes me. There is no way I can go over there after my obvious tantrum and explain to them, degradingly, how I am too terrified to walk to my car by myself. I would rather die than humiliate myself like that. Besides, I am just being ridiculous. I'll be fine. What can possibly go wrong?

CHAPTER 6

Between a Rock and a Hard Place

Hastily I escape the oppressive hot air permeating out of the dance club. As I flee into the cool night, the frigid air hits my face like sharp needles pressing through my skin, chilling me to my core. Wrapping my arms protectively around each other I try to shelter myself from the invading cool night air. Deeply I breathe in the chilly air as I vigilantly walk down the sidewalk, attempting to avoid the natural temptation of seeing if the amazing car is still parked in front. Innate curiosity flows rapidly through me, making it impossible for me to fight the urge to look. Turning quickly toward the now vacant spot, my heart sinks instantly with the realization that the stunning car does, in fact, belong to the mysterious man.

Waves of disappointment now rush over my body. I don't understand how he could have caused such excruciating pain within me. My mind begins spinning with doubt at the possibility of the mysterious stranger's ability to literally view my innermost desires -- only to then leave me feeling abandoned and a vacant shell of myself like I am someone else, something I have never been. A deep, burning rage appears to be eating away at me, leaving me a vexed and bitter form of who I was. What has he done to me? I will never be able to find out because he is gone. In a city this size the reality is I will never see him again.

The still night air engulfs my frame with an eerie hush, causing me to instinctively look around. Suddenly I realize how quiet and motionless it is tonight. I hadn't really noticed before how the street is ghostly still, like an abandoned city after an apocalypse. The appearance is a sharp contrast to my earlier descent down this same sidewalk just a few hours ago. The street which was booming with life earlier has now been infested with a penetrating silence. The intense quiet flows over me, instinctively setting every nerve within me on high alert. Unconsciously I increase my speed as the hollowness looming in the air presses down on me.

Gradually I scan the surrounding area like a hawk intently looking out for danger. My highly stimulated mind begins playing tricks on me, causing me to see things that are not actually there. The bright moonlight shining against the large buildings causes sinister shadows to stream frightfully across the ground. The dreadful appearance looks like giant hands ripping viciously at the protective light radiating off of the street, as if they are trying to snuff out the light around me. Other shadows appear to be reaching towards me, gesturing for me to go no further.

A cold breath of air tickles the back of my neck and slides down my spine, sending an anxious chill to quiver within me. Gripping hold of my internal strength I press on, rushing determinedly towards my car. Turning the corner of the ghostly street I can see the safety of my vehicle ahead, causing my panicked breathing to slowly resume its normal pace. Focusing intently on the safety of my car, I proceed to increase my speed, when suddenly a shudder races up my spine, causing the hairs on the back of my neck to stand straight up. A wave of terror blasts into my already overanxious mind. An intense sensation of someone watching me pierces my mind like glaring eyes waking me from a deep sleep. A sharp sting of vulnerable panic thumps in my chest as I feel the penetrating stare.

This intruding glare isn't the same phenomenon I have experienced before. The deep, almost seductive gaze I felt earlier left me wanting more. This sensation isn't piercing my soul but is violating my body, leaving me feeling dirty and repulsed like I have been defiled by a vagrant. These unseen gazing eyes flood my thoughts with intense fear that someone genuinely means to do me harm. Everything within me wants to scream, but it won't do me any good. There is no one on the street who will even hear it, let alone come to my aid. The street is as quiet as a graveyard tonight.

Slowing my breathing down I carefully listen for any noise around me, trying to identify who it is and where this person is located. Holding my breath, I begin to listen intently for any sounds echoing around me. Silence surrounds me as the wind whispers gently into my ear like rolling waves on a calm day. Holding my breath one more time I try to hear anything, but it is to no avail. It is just eerily silent. A sense of peace slowly washes through me as the still, silent air encapsulates my body. The culprit must be my overactive imagination that is causing me to feel this way.

Though there is silence all around, I am still on high alert from the assaulting sensation of being watched. Hesitantly I try one last time, taking in a deep inhalation while holding my breath. This time I close my eyes, listening carefully to any nearby noises. Pushing my focus through the whispers of the wind I suddenly hear something very different. In the near distance I can hear the uncanny sound of a set of footsteps coming from behind me. As I listen carefully an overpowering fear rushes up my spine with each awkward step this stranger takes. The weighted steps of the stranger slam against the sidewalk, as if the person is very large in stature. After every heavy thud there is a scraping or sliding sound against the pavement, like he is dragging a lame foot. This pursuer's pace is slightly faster than mine, causing an eerie feeling to race up my spine again.

Quivering adrenaline laced with a gut-wrenching panic rushes through me, causing my mind to be placed on high alert. Slowly I exhale as quietly as possible, trying to keep the sound of his footsteps within my mental grasp. This is not my imagination. I am unquestionably being hunted. Intense terror rips its way through me, consuming my awareness as I realize it's too late for me to turn around and head back to the club. I know my only hope is to get to the safety of my vehicle as fast as possible.

The sound of the perpetrator's heavy footsteps behind me echoes louder as he appears to be increasing his speed. Trepidation wraps around my back with a shivering sensation pressing against me, causing me to not turn around for fear of what I might see. Reacting to my gravitating pull towards the safety of my car, I increase my speed to a near run. My only hope is that I can outrun this obviously disadvantaged man. My thunderous heart slams within my throat as my terrified body runs on pure adrenaline.

As I'm about to give in to the foreboding thoughts, a rush of soothing pressure hits my chest, penetrating my heart then exploding within me with an infectious surge of reassurance. The familiar change to my breathing snuffs out the wailing banshee screaming within me. This welcome feeling takes on a new rapid pace, filling me with an exciting and yet protective edge, causing me to stop dead in my tracks. This inexplicable feeling I know is not coming from the pursuer that means me harm. This is from the beautiful stranger from earlier tonight. This radiating sensation I am familiar with is beginning to consume my entire being, melting into every smooth curve and crevasse. A sharp, searing edge chisels out of my pores with a benevolent warning as a sense of wrath vibrates within me. Though this emanating feeling takes over, strangely I have a sense of peace flowing down from the top of my head to the tips of my toes, like a gentle breeze whispering over me. This wrath is not meant for me, but for the perpetrator who is pursuing me like a game of cat and mouse. Hastily I look around for both the culprit that is terrifying me and the liberator who appears to be rescuing me from my imminent demise.

Anxiously I stand here in the middle of these two different, yet powerful sensations vacillating between these two choices while I quiver with uncontrolled fright. Frozen in my tracks I quickly gaze around, trying to find where either one is coming from. I know they are both undeniably here – I can still feel their penetrating gazes. Reality viciously wriggles throughout my brain as I realize I am caught in the middle of a rock and a hard place.

I remain completely paralyzed except for my hands which tremble uncontrollably. My shallow, quick breaths are causing me to become lightheaded. A conundrum of emotions spins rapidly within my mind. I have no idea if the perpetrator is still coming towards me, thus devouring me within his vile plans, or if the mysterious stranger is here to continue his attack. Closing my fists tightly I realize I have to get to my car, but my immobile frame is not cooperating with my desire to move.

My optimistic attitude deflates as the weight of the circumstance drops down on me. As all the optimism within me slowly starts to fade away I gaze up towards my car only to discover a possible glimmer of hope. There, just beside my car, is the sleek, black and plum colored car. Waves of relief mixed with trepidation crash upon my frightened back, eroding away my fears towards the hunter behind me. Widening my eyes I gaze upon the car, wondering if I will survive this, as sharp palpitations hammer against my chest. A heavy exhale rushes out of my quivering mouth – hopefully he is here to help me.

My heart flutters as a slight smile tugs at the corners of my lips. I lock my eyes onto the prospect standing before me. There next to the car is the tall, dark and mysterious man from the club. A turbulent swirl spins within my stomach, sending out throngs of buzzing bees, causing my legs to quiver. Everything within me wants to rush instantly over to him and fling my arms vigorously around his neck… but I don't know him – at all. Though a part of me is frightened by him, I can't deny the gravitating and familiar pull he has on me.

I slowly scan every part of his physique as he stands erect between my car and the passenger side of his car. His rigid arms hang straight and tense down onto either side of him. His tightly clenched fists quiver aggressively against his sides as his stiff figure remains motionless and unwavering. His stationary gaze remains fixed on something – or someone – behind me. His usual supple and voluptuous mouth is tightly clenched as he grits his teeth forcefully, causing his jaw to quiver in pulsating anger. His firm stance and chiseled, fierce features show signs of turbulence pulsing through him, but remarkably his eyes still remain blank like a poker player hiding his hand. He glares past me with a vacuous stare as if he is communicating his darkest thoughts with whoever is behind me.

I remain frozen in my tracks, completely paralyzed by the fear rushing within me. Uncertain surges of trepidation rush over me as to what choice I am now forced to make. Do I run toward the man who stirs an awakening deep within me, or do I take a chance and run from him and the pursuer hunting me? I'm not sure if I have the strength to make a decision for myself and I know beyond a doubt I don't have the strength to run from either of them.

As my mind contemplates my choices I hear my name suddenly cutting through the silence like thunder rolling in the still night air. A sense of relief suddenly rushes over me. Maybe I won't have to make a choice now. This has to be Larry calling out to me.

"Lauren!" The low, growling voice forcefully beckons me toward him.

My instant relief is shattered by the unfamiliar and smooth, low, growling tone. The sound is like velvet rushing through the wind. It gently glides across the air, consuming me like a warm blanket wrapping soothingly around me. It's not an angry sounding voice, but one of concern toward my safety. This is not Larry's gentile, soft spoken voice uttering my name, but a precise voice vibrating with extreme masculinity. He beckons towards me with a power that pierces my core, reawakening me. His velvety, yet powerful tone utters my name, giving special attention to every letter as if saying my name is sacred within his mouth.

His is the kind of voice that speaks with power laced with sensuality and conviction, resonating confidence in every syllable he utters. The low tone of his voice causes a slight growl to vibrate vigorously within his throat. The resonating soothing sound penetrates deep within my ears, igniting my body. Though I have never heard him before, there is a familiarity that rolls deep within my mind.

His voice cuts through the silence once again, this time with a demand, "Lauren, you need to come here, now!" A forceful power explodes out of him. It shoots through the cold night air, slamming into my soul with his growling and compelling demand as if he is giving me one last chance before an impending battle ensues. His intense gaze pleads with me to comply with his request. I know I have to go to him or there will be a consequence neither one of us will want. Without thinking I start running towards him.

As I approach, his intense glare begins to fade while his erect frame slowly deflates, causing a forceful exhale to escape through his now relaxed mouth. His eyes begin scanning over me like he is actively searching for any damage. He is scrutinizing me like a hostage who has been released over to the safety of an awaiting protector.

A churning, jittery energy residing in my stomach pulsates out like a dam breaking as I now stand just inches away from my self-prescribed protector. As I look up into his magnificent piercing light-blue eyes, extreme heat rushes up the back of my neck, causing my face to flush with heat. Wrapping my arms tightly around myself I stand here completely mesmerized by his absolute brilliant appearance. The swirling, bright colors of the club didn't fully allow me to witness his stunning features.

His extreme height towers over me, forcing me to have to lift my head to look into his hypnotic eyes. As I glance up at him, examining his every feature, his luscious lips part slightly, giving me a most glorious smile. His full and seductive lips part just enough to reveal his gleaming white teeth. Deep, penetrating dimples frame the edges of his glorious smile, causing my heart to instantly skip a beat. Though his smile is mesmerizing, there is a sinister edge dancing within the corners of his mouth, causing a quick chill to race up my spine.

For just a brief moment I am lost in his magnetic power, forgetting where I am and what has just occurred. Reality slowly presses back into my mind as the fear starts to crawl within me, causing the hairs on my neck to stand. I have no idea if the frightening pursuer is still following me or if this beautiful stranger standing before me has scared him off – this stranger who has intruded on my deepest desires and has eluded me tonight is now standing just inches away from my face.

I squeeze my arms even tighter against my stomach trying to control my quivering nerves that have been stretched to the limit tonight. In part due to the man who stands in front of me. I ran from one predator straight into the grasp of a man who caused me distress earlier tonight. Did I leave the fire just to run into the frying pan? I am not quite sure if I'm totally safe, yet something within me flutters, sending a vivid ray of peace all over me. Though there is a terrifying edge to him, the calm resonating within me is causing me to feel completely safe in his presence.

I grip onto my trembling hands, trying to hide the terrified deliberating swirling around in my head. His eyes quickly glance down upon my wringing hands, causing his face to soften. His eyes quickly snap back up, locking onto mine. Gingerly he tilts his head down toward mine, uttering softly, "I don't think you'll have to worry about him any more… look." Turning his head toward the street, he gestures with his eyes for me to look.

Gently turning my head, I notice a rather large, stout man now hobbling away from us. He has on a bulky and dirty trench coat that vaguely resembles the once-khaki color. His thick form fills out the coat, giving him a substantially large appearance. Bleak darkness oozes off of him, leaving a frightening trail within his wake. As he runs I notice how he favors his left leg more than his right, giving him a slight waddle. Suddenly he crosses just under a street light, causing something within his hand to shimmer. The flash from something metal in his hand flickers and the reality of what could have occurred sends my stomach to churning violently.

Turning nervously, I gaze up at the man who stands in front of me. His motionless eyes are affixed on the fleeing perpetrator, making sure he is completely gone. I want to feel some sort of relief and gratitude to this man for helping me, but I need to know who he is. At this point I am not completely sure if I am safe yet.

As my mind contemplates my predicament, the mysterious man turns abruptly and peers down upon me. His amazing crystal clear blue eyes pierce right through to the deepest part of me, causing my mind to go blank. I can't just stand here like an idiot, giving him all the power – I have to say something. "Is he gone?" I squeak out.

Wow, that was ingenious. Out of all the questions I have for him that is the only thing I could come up with? I know the answer to that stupid question. I saw him run away. Well, at least it's a question, so now he will have to answer it.

"Yes, he is gone," he reassures me in his velvety voice. Looking deeper into my eyes he adds, "And trust me, he is not coming back." His voice is a deep roar with a crisp firmness biting off each word, as if he knows something he's not willing to share with me.

Slowly lifting his hand up toward my face he gingerly tucks a loose strand of my dark hair behind my ear. Instinctively I jump back in fear until his thumb lightly strokes my cheek, causing my skin to heat up, melting me on the spot. My staggered breathing increases as my heart beats out some rapid rhythm. An unfamiliar yearning slithers up my spine, emitting a toxic venom of desire which feels like it's melting me. I try as hard as I can to keep my breathing quiet so he won't hear it. Whoever this is he is going to be the death of me. My psyche is not going to be able to handle anything else tonight.

Slowly I try to back up, attempting to break free from his intoxicating touch when he reacts to my movement, instantly dropping his hand. "I'm sorry. I didn't mean to frighten you," he adds apologetically.

"No, you didn't," I utter sheepishly. That is a lie. He does frighten me a little bit. Even though there's a part of me that yearns for him, there still is a voice within my head screaming at me to run as fast as I can and never look back. "I think I just need to sit down or something," I mutter weakly.

He instantly turns to his car, opening the passenger door for me. This is the car that earlier today I was trying so hard to see inside. Now here he is holding the door open for me to freely explore. I want to just run toward it, but I still have no idea who this person is.

I do know there are some questions I need answered. Like how in the hell does he know my name? And what happened to me tonight? I need to be safe first and not put myself in another dangerous position. "Thank you, but I can't sit in your car."

His eyes narrow as the furrow between his thick eyebrows deepens while he stands here holding the door open for me. He stares at me with a perplexing gaze upon his face as his firm stance remains motionless. "Didn't you just say you need to sit down? Here is a seat – now sit down," his smooth, hypnotic voice demands.

An immediate self-preservation explodes in my mind, giving me an alien courage. "No! You have no right to tell me what to do. You may have helped me, but that does not mean I am just going to get into your car. I don't know you at all. You could be just as dangerous as the man who left." An instant laugh rumbles in his throat while a small snort escapes through his nose like I'm missing an inside joke.

Ever since my experience tonight in the club, there is now a foreign aggressiveness looming within me. Here is a gorgeous man standing in front of me who just protected me from an almost incomprehensible tragedy, and I accuse him of being just as bad as – or worse – than the near attacker. He is just trying to be nice, but I have to be safe. I'm not sure if I can take my chances in trusting him yet. Before I can be sure about him I need some questions answered first.

Now that I obviously have the strength and courage, I have to ask him some questions. I take in a deep, cleansing breath, calming the sudden fire smoldering within me. I can't look up at his face or I will lose my nerve and not be able to talk. I will just sound like a bumbling idiot.

Exhaling softly, I clarify, "Look, I don't mean to sound ungrateful, because I'm truly appreciative for what you have done, but I'm just a little confused about a few things that happened tonight." I pause slightly to catch my breath, and then add, "I also really need some answers to my questions."

Just then I hear a car door slam, which causes me to jump slightly. Quickly I look up only to discover he has shut his passenger door and is now standing with his back to me. His hands are gripping the frame of the car, causing his fingers to tremble. The muscles in his smooth neck and jaw quiver rapidly from his taut jaw clenching down tightly. His wide shoulders rise as the muscles in his back tighten.

I can't be afraid now. I have to continue. Squeezing my hands into fists, I shove them forcefully into the pockets of my jeans. I know I have to ask him even if he gets mad. I need some answers. "First of all, I don't even know your name, but you somehow know mine. How is that?" I add, trying to catch my breath.

His hands let go of the car frame, dropping them swiftly to his side. His shoulders and back remain firm like a solid wall blocking me from seeing his face. My head spins while I try to remind myself to breathe. A tingling sensation saunters up my back as I nervously stand here for what feels like hours until he finally turns around. His tall, muscular figure reclines against his car as he folds his arms languidly. He gazes over at me as a sheepish grin slowly spreads across his face.

My heart starts racing again. This is not fair. He is using his good looks against me. My thoughts begin racing with illicit images as I gaze upon his statuesque physique. I mentally fight against the sensual images pulsating within me. Focusing on my goal I snap, "Are you just going to stand here or are you going to answer my question? If you're not going to answer it, then I'm going to leave." I look down ardently as a pregnant pause fills between us. "Thanks for helping me."

As I gaze up I discover that he is staring at me with a slight mischievous smile on his face. Trying as hard as I can to remain unaffected by his obvious charm, I quickly turn away from him and walk toward my car when suddenly there is a slight tug on my arm like he is delicately trying to stop me from leaving.

"You know, you're kind of cute when you're upset." A big smile spreads across his face, allowing me to now see his gleaming white teeth. His hand remains wrapped around my arm, sending searing heat to penetrate into me. My heart sinks completely and I forget what I was going to say.

Standing here in shock I am absolutely dumbfounded by the words vibrating out of his sumptuous mouth. Did he just call me cute? An unfamiliar heat rushes into my face, tainting my skin color a vibrant pink. His blazing liquid blue eyes flame with passion while his sumptuous mouth smiles wickedly at me. This is not fair, using his good looks against me. He is playing a game I cannot win.

Gripping onto my internal strength I look up at him forcefully, needing some answers. Dropping his hand from my arm he shoves it into his pocket. "You want to know my name?" he asks smoothly. His voice is slow with a captivating quality, tainted with a hidden meaning within his question.

"Yes…" Then with a quiet, timid voice I add, "Among other things."

"Well, I think I can answer that." A large, playful smile spreads across his face, causing deep dimples to form on his cheeks. Leaning once again up against his car he utters candidly, "My name is Donovan. Are you happy now?"

"I'm sort of happy – Donovan. Thank you for answering that easy question, but there is a second part I still need answered."

CHAPTER 7

Breathless

Silently he stands in the middle of this desolate parking lot, staring at me. It has to be close to one in the morning by now. There is an unnatural stillness looming in the air, making it hard to breathe. Though we are in the center of the city, there seems to be no life echoing in the stagnant surroundings, like an eerie calm before an impending storm. The only sounds resonating are the heavy breaths rushing through Donovan and my mouths, sending a nervous twinge to race up the nape of my neck.

Part of me does not want to ask the question and break the silence, but I know that I need some answers. "Donovan, how do you know my name?"

As I ask him the impending question I notice the sharp corner of his jaw begins to quiver as his muscles tighten back up. His languid posture quickly solidifies as he pulls himself up from his car. The muscles in his face quiver, causing his cheeks to appear as if they have a heartbeat of their own. Clenching his fists tightly he begins fidgeting over my sudden inquiry. "Can't you just be happy with knowing my name? There is not some mystery to it," he growls.

I stand here completely mystified as to why he is so upset with my simple question. "If there isn't a mystery, then just answer it. How do you know my name?" I add fervently.

A heavy sigh of defeat escapes out of his luxurious mouth. "I probably heard it tonight at the club, it's that easy." His eyes pierce right through mine as if he is trying to persuade me to believe him, while his erect torso gently quivers with pent up secrecy. I know there is more to his answer than what he is willing to divulge.

"Wait, did you just say you probably heard my name in the club?"

"Yes, and your point?" His voice is no longer silky smooth, there now is a crisp, jagged edge as he snaps out his response.

Instinctively reacting to his abrasiveness I flinch back as every muscle within me coils up into a tight mass. Though his words are not severe, his voice is laced with a fervent warning. I don't know Donovan at all and perhaps my prying questions will push him over an edge I will not want to witness. For all I know he can make what happened to me tonight in the club look like child's play.

A haunting curiosity battles within me. I may be getting myself into a dangerous situation, but I can't fight my desire to know the truth. "Did you definitely hear my name in the club or did you probably hear it?" My mocking voice resonates with a stern demand.

"What do you mean? I am confused. I already told you I heard your name in the club. What more do you want from me?"

"The truth… you didn't tell me you heard my name," I protest firmly as my muscles stiffen. "You said you probably did. Which one is it?"

Pivoting rapidly on his heels he turns away from me as he clenches his hands into tight, quivering fists. The muscles within his hands and forearms pulsate violently as if he were clutching a tremendous amount of weight within them. His pulsing muscles and protruding veins in his forearms immediately cause a déjà vu. These are the same arms from my dream that broke me free from my binding chains. My heartbeat rises to the base of my throat as shock rolls through my motionless body.

Slowly his tense hands gravitate up, shielding his face. Clasping his hands forcefully over his face he vigorously drags them through his thick layers of black silken glass as his hands grip tightly onto a large chunk of lustrous hair. Frustration consumes his once self-assured appearance as his shoulders slouch. "Lauren, I told you how I heard your name. Can't you just trust me?" he pleads weakly.

"I don't know you enough to trust you." Hesitating slightly, I add, "I want to trust you, but I don't know if I can yet. There are so many unexplained events that have happened, and I think you are deliberately hiding things from me."

"What do you want me to say, Lauren?" he sighs infuriatingly.

"I want the truth," I plead softly.

Vigorously he turns around, gazing deep into my eyes as he slowly starts to walk towards me. Locking his penetrating gaze onto me as his liquid blue eyes seem to peer right through me, prying open my soul for his pleasing benefit.

Reacting to the intense sensation being forced upon me, I slowly stagger backwards as he continues his fervent glare. Slowly he pursues me, pushing me back until my legs slam up against the back bumper of my car, pinning me vigorously against it. There is nowhere for me to escape. He now dominates the situation I stupidly put myself in. My heart pounds firmly against my chest as my breath quickens. A sense of doom washes over me as I press myself securely against my car. I have been put in a submissive position, having lost all control I had once obtained.

Slowly he continues walking towards me until his chiseled physique is just inches from mine, causing me to lie against the trunk of my car. Pursuing me even closer, his unyielding physique hovers deliberately over me as his eyes melt over me, filling my mind with his lust. My pounding heart hammers violently against my chest, sending me into a trembling state of panic. Every part of me is vulnerable to him. My body and soul are now on display for him to use or abuse.

His piercing eyes never waver in their intensity as his chiseled arms press vigorously on either side of my quivering frame. Laying his face down just inches from mine I can feel his warm, sweet breath pour over me. Donovan's mouth twitches as he venomously utters a feverish warning, "I don't think deep down in your soul, you really want to know the truth. You just want to keep living in your safe little dream world. Where there aren't things out there that you can't explain. Haven't you ever heard the warning – curiosity will kill the cat? You aren't ready to know the truth yet."

I lay here immobile on the trunk of my car as I try to catch my breath. My clammy hands press firmly against the cold metal of my car as a battle of emotions rage within me. Intense fear viciously resonates throughout me, causing tears to suddenly well up within my eyes. Quickly I force my eyes closed so that he will not get any pleasure from seeing me lose control. Clenching my eyes tightly closed I am able to focus all my attention on controlling my impending emotional meltdown. If he is going to force his way upon me I need to have the strength to defend myself. Slowly I feel the tears starting to subside as the fear rolls off me like a tsunami retreating back out into the ocean.

Feeling the trembling emotion within me slowly diminish, I gradually open my eyes again. Hesitantly I gaze up at his now shocked, almost repentant gaze, like he is disgusted with the monster within that reared its ugly head. The pained expression on his face reveals an inner torture.

Taking advantage of his slight weakness, I exhale softly. "Are you going to hurt me?" my voice cracks slightly as I ask in a pleading tone.

Donovan closes his eyes as tight as he possibly can, forcing the muscles around them to vibrate from the obvious strain he is placing on them. Slowly his eyes open as the muscles in his face soften and his consuming stance shrinks, revealing a calmer expression as if he is pleading with me to forgive him.

He hovers over me while he intently examines my frightened expression. Timidly he pushes himself away from the car, freeing me from the imprisoning hold he had on me. He shamefully turns and walks dejectedly toward his car. "I will never harm you in any way. You don't understand," he calmly states. A long, thick pause floats over him as if he is trying to choose his words very carefully. "I am sorry. Sorry for everything. This is entirely my fault. I will never be able to forgive myself. Maybe you should go." His voice is soft with a thick, buttery layer of regret rolling off of each word.

"What are you talking about? You haven't done anything unforgivable. I just want some simple questions answered, that's all. You are the one blowing this whole thing out of proportion."

"You don't understand, Lauren. I can't answer your questions yet."

"What do you mean, yet? I think I deserve to have some questions answered. I also think I deserve to know how tonight it felt like you were peering into my soul, causing me to have a two-hour lapse in time that I am not able to attest for," I ramble off.

Quickly Donovan turns around, looking at me questionably. "You feel things when I look at you?" he asks desperately.

"Yes," I utter softly, pulling myself free from the trunk of my car, placing myself in a less vulnerable position. Sitting up erect I position myself closer to the driver's side of the car in case he has another one of his temper tantrums.

Sensing my trepidation, he nimbly gives me a reassuring smile, letting me know that he will not hurt me. "What kind of things do you feel?" Donovan asks softly.

"What do you mean? Are you or are you not going to answer my questions?"

"Not yet, but I promise I will answer them soon, you will know when. But right now I need you to please tell me what you feel when I look at you." His voice is laced with a sincere, yet tender tone.

"You expect me to answer your question," I clarify.

"Please Lauren, answer the question."

"Why? You're not answering mine, why should I answer yours?" I snap, acting like a stubborn child.

Donovan suddenly walks over to me, causing me to immediately flinch away from the trunk of my car. "Lauren, I am not going to hurt you, I promise." His voice is silky smooth, laced with a seductive growl wrapping around each word as he gently nips at his moist, full bottom lip. Peering deep into my eyes he pleads softly, "Lauren, please." Despite the fright he gave me, there is an undeniable draw to him.

A warm sensation floods over me, causing a tingling sensation as he utters his gentle plea. It's getting harder to resist his requests. I am naturally drawn to him as if we are magnets being pulled toward each other.

Grunting in defeat I utter, "Fine, it probably is something ridiculous anyway. It's just that sometimes when you look at me it feels like my soul is being ripped open, like I am an open book for you to read. To tell you the truth, sometimes I can actually feel you reading it." Closing my eyes, I shake my head in angst as I hear myself uttering the ridiculous accusation, adding, "Then suddenly I can't breathe while my heart begins to race rapidly… that's it."

Gazing ruefully up at him, I notice a flat, expressionless appearance on his face. His blank gaze sends a wave of embarrassment rushing through me. I am not only offending him by these absurd accusations, but am possibly causing him to rethink my emotional stability.

Nervously I glance down at my intertwined fingers, weaving them anxiously into twisted tiny circles. I am too afraid to look up. I have no idea how he is reacting to my absurd accusation. He is either going to run for the hills thinking I am crazy or he is going to lose his temper again. Even though he did promise me he will never hurt me, I still am not sure if I can completely trust him. If the second case scenario happens I am prepared to jump into the driver's seat of my car.

"Lauren, please look at me," his low, smooth voice warmly utters as he methodically walks over to me, gingerly sitting down next to me. His penetrating gaze pours over me causing an insecurity, bidding me to look up at him. Instinctively I glance up causing our eyes to lock fiercely upon each other. Tremendous heat smolders around me encapsulating my body as his deep, piercing glare causes me to tremble in delight. My stomach flips as the heat permeating off of him envelops me.

Donovan utters softly, "When was the first time you felt like that?"

"It's silly isn't it? You must think I'm crazy," I sigh.

"I didn't say it was silly and I don't think you are crazy. On the contrary, I think you are smarter than you realize," he reassures me as his piercing blue eyes bore deeper into mine. "Once again, when was the first time you felt that way?"

I didn't have to think very hard. I know the exact time and place when I first had the invading sensation. "The first time was earlier this week on my way to work. I was stuck in traffic when I saw your car on the freeway. That was the first time I truly felt it," I add hesitantly.

His tranquil aqua blue eyes gaze intently into mine, causing my heart to beat out of control while my staggered breathing begins to increase. "Do you feel anything now?" he mutters softly.

I am definitely feeling something all right, but it is not what he is thinking. "No," I whisper softly.

My heart rate pounds out some unique rhythmic pattern while my stomach slowly starts churning with nervous undulating energy. There has never been a guy who has made me feel so anxious yet absolutely turned on at the same time.

My eyes remain locked within his penetrating gaze, when suddenly my heart nearly stops as I witness his glorious eyes transform right before me. His once crystal blue eyes slowly fade as if bleach is removing all the color from his irises, causing his eyes to go completely white. All the color has been stripped from his eyes except for extremely small pupils set right in the middle of the solid white backdrop. Jumping back in fear I begin to panic at the obvious transformation that has just occurred within him. My trembling body stiffens as I become paralyzed by fear.

I try to scream, when instantly my heart pounds rapidly out of control. Reaching my hand up to my chest I grab onto my shirt, forcefully trying to stop the thunderous slamming of my heart against my chest. Suddenly an intense feeling pulsates deep within me, exploding out of me like an erupting volcano. My soul is not just being opened up it is being forcefully torn wide open. My ragged breathing accelerates to a near pant as everything around me begins spinning violently out of control.

Gathering all my internal strength together I begin pleading forcefully for this invading sensation to stop. "Stop, please stop."

The pounding and ripping sensation consuming me instantly dissipates, leaving my ravenous body weak. My breathing gingerly returns to its normal healthy pace, causing me to take in deep, cleansing breaths. I look up at Donovan's face, only to discover his soft liquid blue eyes have returned, replacing the once ominous bleached white eyes.

"What did you do?" I whisper faintly.

A heavy sigh escapes Donovan's mouth as he dejectedly staggers toward his car, forcefully cupping his hands around his face. His broken down form melts against the side of his car, nearly becoming one with the car. His quivering hands grip tightly onto the back of his head as his arms squeeze down on him like a vice. A deep lament roars out of him, piercing straight into my heart. A thread of understanding weaves my heart to his. The anguish flowing out of him mirrors what I have been succumbing to for the past year. Wanting to know what just happened to me, I slowly walk over to Donovan, stopping just inches away, I cautiously plea, "Donovan, what did you do to me?"

Donovan's trembling hands clings to the side of his car as a vague hush rolls over him, refusing to acknowledge my question. Disbelief floods my overstimulated mind as I try to comprehend the inconceivable event I just witnessed. Though I am still terrified, I need him to answer me. Slowly I lift my hand towards his back when instantly I notice him tense back up.

"Don't touch me, Lauren," he protests softly, with an almost defeated edge to him.

I immediately drop my trembling hand, backing up slightly. A heavy sigh slithers out of my mouth as I look at Donovan's battered, yet rigid body. My mind begins spinning out of control with numerous questions. This wasn't my imagination, his eyes did transform in front of me. How can anyone cause the color of their eyes to disappear, only to reappear later? The insurmountable questions I have for Donovan just keep piling up.

Silence looms anxiously in the air until his buttery voice rips through the stillness. "Lauren, I don't understand how…" his voice trails off, causing the last part to become inaudible. Donovan quietly adds, "I am sorry, but I think you need to go – now."

Instantly my heart sinks. I still have a lot of questions that need answers and strangely I am not ready to go yet. Anyone in their right mind would have accepted his offer, but I must not be in my right mind. Something unexplainable still draws me to him and I can't run from him even if I want to. I have no idea if I will ever see him again if I leave and that is something I can't accept.

Though the experience was terrifying, surprisingly I am not afraid of him. "I don't want to leave. If you think I am afraid of you, you're wrong. I may not be able to explain what has happened, but I can't and I won't leave, yet."

"You need to leave. Trust me, once you know what has happened to you, you will not just be afraid of me, you will hate me," he growls in disgust.

"Why will I hate you?" Pausing slightly, I add sharply, "Donovan, please turn around and look at me."

Slowly he spins around facing me dead on, causing my heart to drop, mixing into the fluttering commotion of my stomach. Though his countenance echoes an internal pain as if he is being tortured, his flawless face remains unaffected, like a calm gentle brook gliding through a meadow.

"There, are you happy now?" There is a sarcastic edge to his voice.

"Yes, I am."

"Good, because you need to leave now." His voice is gruff and demanding, causing the inflections within him to increase.

"You have no right to tell me what to do, you're not my boss. I'm not going to leave," I snap loudly. A fierce anger taking up residence within me surfaces as if it is a constant fire festering in me, waiting to explode. The intrusive surge rushing through me appears to be fusing with my blood, making it harder to control.

"You're right, I am not your boss, but if you are not going to leave then I will," he snaps venomously.

It appears he is just as stubborn as I am. If I'm not going to leave then I am sure he will make good on his threat. I don't want to be left alone here, but most of all I don't want Donovan to leave yet. "I don't understand. Why all of a sudden do you want me to leave? What did I do?" Turning my back to him I inaudibly murmur, "I don't want you to leave me."

A tumultuous exhale bursts from his mouth with a deflated rebuttal, as if something I said bothers him, but I don't care. I don't want to leave yet and I definitely don't want him to leave either. "Please don't leave," I plead, turning back towards him.

Gazing up at him ruefully I notice his once brooding expression has melted away, revealing a renewed life, like the calm after a storm. Slowly Donovan walks towards me, placing his hands affectionately on my shoulders. Despite the cool night air, extreme heat emits off of his hands like a furnace radiating throughout my chilled body, instantly warming me up.

Slowly Donovan leans down, placing our faces just inches apart. My heart takes off like a jet engine as my shallow breathing quickens. My feet melt into the pavement while my heart beats so loud I am afraid he can hear the nearly audible thundering echoing within my chest.

The corner of his sumptuous mouth slowly turns up, forming the most perfect crooked smile. He raises a brow playfully as a gleam of amusement rolls across his face. A slight snicker escapes his sumptuous mouth. Blood rushes to my face, tainting my skin a ruddy color as a wave of insecurity floods my now embarrassed body. Deliberately I gaze down at the ground, trying to hide the vivid color consuming my face.

"Trust me, Lauren, you will see me again very soon, but for now you need to go. Believe me when I tell you that you did nothing wrong. It is what I have done that is selfish and wrong."

His hypnotic voice vibrates within my inner ear, compelling me to obey as if my agency has been seized, giving me no choice but to obey. Doubt envelops my mind like a thick blanket smothering out all reality. "How am I going to see you again? You don't know where I live or even have my phone number." Shaking my head vaguely I add, "Do you want my phone number?"

A deep sinister laugh bursts out of him, causing a jolt of anger to race through me like a live wire. The irritation I had just extinguished immediately boils over, sending sharp jolts to race in me. The consuming rage possesses my inner being like a virus. My trembling hands clench into tight fists while I growl intently, "What is so funny? Why are you laughing?"

Instantly he stops laughing as he warns me feverishly, "Don't lose your temper again."

A tumultuous whip of heat explodes within me, locking its target onto Donovan. This time the anger has a firm grasp on me, limiting my choices and my ability to control it. The scorching rage billowing within me intensifies with each episode I have. Reacting to my overwhelming rage, I shove Donovan forcefully away from me. "Don't tell me what to do in that calm, aggravatingly placating tone. I can lose my temper if I want to."

"Lauren, control it. Please. You need to fight it with everything you have," he warns with a coated sense of urgency laced over every word. Undisguised regret flashes across his face, while his eyes remain flat and emotionless.

Looking upon his immense guilt streaming across his twisted, morose face helps me to slowly gain control over the trembling fury pulsating throughout me. Slowly the anger dissipates, like Donovan has switched off the breaker feeding my rage. His hands gently grip onto my quivering shoulders until I begin regaining control.

"I am sorry. I don't know what is wrong with me," I mutter softly, completely mortified by my wretched display. Uttering weakly I add, "I think I have just had a very long and confusing night. I wouldn't blame you if you don't ever want to see me again. Maybe I should just go."

Slowly I start walking toward the driver's side of my car, when suddenly Donovan grabs hold of my arm, firmly stopping me in my tracks. A lascivious energy surges from his hand like a hot radiant stove, filling me with thick, anxious pleasure. Gently, yet deliberately, he spins me around so that our faces are just inches from each other. My heart pounds uncontrollably again as the heat resonating from his hand intensifies the quivering sensation I am succumbing to.

Donovan's aqua eyes liquefy with flames of intense passion, igniting a flutter from his closeness and desire causing my stomach to twist and turn with flapping butterflies. Gazing deep into my eyes he gradually leans in until his warm, soft cheek rests meekly against mine. The touch of his skin on mine instantly sets me ablaze. His sweet, warm breath heaves against my cheek, lightly rolling down my neck, causing a shiver to roll up my spine.

His ragged breathing becomes quicker and more forceful with every exhalation as my heated body shivers in exhilaration. My skin awakens as his warm breath washes over my neck, making the hair on my skin stand up in pure pleasure. His breath merges into my skin, tickling the passion within me, awakening a raging inferno I never knew existed.

My stuttering breath increases as his long, sensual fingers delicately stroke the exposed skin on my arms, causing goosebumps to appear. He deliberately slides his fingers up my arms until they stop forcefully on my shoulders. His strong hands firmly grasp onto my shoulders, digging his fingertips feverishly into them. Complete pleasure consumes my trembling form with every touch of his skin on mine.

Closing my eyes tightly I allow his touch to penetrate deep into my senses, sending pulsating electricity to saturate our highly sensitive bodies. Just when I think I can't handle any more, Donovan's firm, yet pliant mouth moves gently towards my ear. He drags his smooth, supple lips over my ear, tenderly tracing the outline of my earlobe, causing my breath to shudder with anticipation.

Softly exhaling a deep quivering sigh, he whispers breathlessly into my ear, "Lauren, trust me, I am not blowing you off, but I think it is best if you go home now. You have no idea how hard it is for me to control myself. I promise I will see you again…very soon. "

Closing my eyes even tighter, I lean forcefully against his warm – nearly hot – cheek. "Do I have to leave, now?" I mumble breathlessly. My staggered breathing is making it hard for me to talk.

"Yes," he utters firmly, pulling himself away from my cheek. The cool night air replaces the warmth that once resided there, leaving my skin feeling abandoned.

He gazes feverishly down at my face with his lustrous liquid blue eyes shimmering in the moonlight. Donovan's eyes bore deep within mine as he slowly leans down, pressing his soft, full lips lovingly against my forehead. The extreme warmth of Donovan's mouth penetrates my skin, nearly burning the surface and boiling my insides. He lingers on my forehead just long enough to make me feel as if I'm going to bursting into flames. His fingertips firmly dig into my shoulders, intensifying the sensation flowing throughout my body.

Deliberately I move closer into him, wanting more, when suddenly his sumptuous mouth pulls away from me, causing me to stumble. Donovan's firm hands support me from completely falling as he gently pushes me away from him, leaving me feeling cheated. Dizzily I gaze up into Donovan's stunning face, wanting more from him, when I notice the passion that once resided within him is now gone.

Relinquishing the firm hold he has on me, he pleads softly, "Please, Lauren, you need to go. Let's just say we… I mean I, am not known for my control. I have done enough damage for one night."

"What are you talking about? You haven't done any damage. If anything you have made me feel for the first time in over a year," I sharply add.

"I am going to only say this once and then I am saying goodnight. You need to leave." Donovan's rigid voice slowly darkens as he utters a fervent warning, "I *know* what you want and I know what I did. Trust me, when you figure it out you will hate me as much as I hate myself." Turning his back on me he quietly utters, "Goodnight, Lauren. Trust me, you will see me – soon."

He stands here with his rigid back to me as I hesitantly get into my car. He never once turns around to acknowledge me as I regretfully drive away. A lonely, empty feeling flows over me like

I'm leaving a huge part of my heart and soul behind, entrusted to Donovan's care. Driving down the street I gaze ruefully in my rearview mirror, hoping to catch a glimpse of him driving away, but as I look back I notice he is already gone. There is no sign of him or his car anywhere. My heart sinks as I realize I have no idea when – if ever – I will see him again.

CHAPTER 8

Reflection

Darkness envelops me like a creeping shadow impeding my sight. Everything around me is a blurry shade of grey as all of the crisp colors are replaced by the encroaching gloom of an obscure night. The chill of the air presses through me, causing my muscles to tremor violently. A hazy, disheveled fog consumes me as I gaze all around for some kind of clue as to where I am, only to discover I am standing alone on a long narrow path in the middle of nowhere. Hesitantly I look back, trying to ascertain how I got here but there is nothing around me but darkened trees everywhere. The large trees have been overtaken by thick draping moss hanging like ominous webs from every branch. Streams of silver light, caused by the moonlight, penetrate the thick darkness, gradually revealing the unfamiliar scenery around me.

Peering all around I notice several massive trees lining each side of my narrow path, creating a virtual fence and preventing anyone from straying off. The outstretched branches of the trees appear to be reaching their way up to the celestial sky, obstructing the moon's bright light. As the wind rushes through the air it causes the leaves and branches to dance in the moonlight, triggering a strobe light effect on the ground below.

The cool wind swirling through the air pierces through me like millions of tiny icicles attacking my trembling body. A vulnerable shiver rolls up my spine, causing me to instinctively wrap my arms tightly around myself, rubbing my arms vigorously. Feeling the touch of my cold skin against my hands I discover that I am wearing very little in the way of adequate clothing.

I glance down at myself, eyeing the racy clothing item I have on. My eyes widen while my brows stitch together in astonishment. I'm only wearing a long, black silk nightgown. Shaking my head slightly in dismay I begin examining every detail of my exposed figure and the unfamiliar piece of clothing on me. The scarcely-there nightgown clings tightly to my torso while exposing areas of breasts I never reveal – least of all out in the middle of nowhere. The bottom half of the silken lingerie is extremely long and loose, flowing effortlessly in the wind, making the swirling fabric difficult to walk in. As it wraps vigorously around my legs I nearly trip and fall several times. Bending down to release the fabric from my legs, I notice I'm not wearing any shoes either.

The gravel path below my feet feels like jagged rocks puncturing through my flesh. Still I continue down the path though my tumultuous fear intensifies, begging me to stop. I am a vulnerable mess out in the middle of an unfamiliar path, nearly naked, with no idea of how I got here. Every part of me is hurting from the intense cold and the excruciating pain caused by the gravel. I want to cry out in anguish, but I can't. No matter how much agony the rocks cause my feet, I have to keep walking.

A thick layer of mist blankets the ground below me, making it tremendously hard to see where I am stepping. My only way out of this frightful situation is to continue following the narrow path I have been mysteriously placed on. I need to find shelter as soon as possible before the intrusive chill of the night air devours me.

The further along the path I get, the thinner the spacing between the trees, igniting a sense of relief within me. The mist billows up against something, stopping it from continuing. Gingerly the fog gives way, revealing a dark archaic stone wall at the end of the path and stopping me from continuing. This squat wall is covered with a heavily laden amount of moss and mold feverishly growing from the constant exposure to the moist environment. The primitive wall looks as if years of neglect have eroded any sign of vitality from it. The wall appears to be encircling a small clearing within its protective grasp. A narrow entrance into the clearing is flanked by two massive eroding columns.

A yearning tug within my gut pulls me towards the narrow entrance. As I stand suspiciously in front of the entrance I glance up at the massive cement columns, examining the blackened chiseled features. The large pillars tower over me like guards protecting their fortress, causing me to begin debating if I should continue. Closing my eyes tightly I take in a deep, cleansing breath as I proceed to step through the opening. Instantly a sigh of relief flows through me as my feet hit the ground just beyond the wall. The harsh terrain that was once penetrating my feet is now gone, being replaced by a soft, supple surface soothing my aching soles... I am now on grass. Not just any grass, but thick, plush grass that has just recently been mowed. A breath of reprieve shudders through me as I realize someone has to be close enough to maintain this lush lawn.

The mist is now invading this area, making it hard to see where I am walking. Trying to make some sense of my surroundings I begin examining everything around me when I notice several solid formations sticking up out of the fog. I walk toward one of the concrete objects jutting out of the fog like the top of a building. As I examine the rough edges of this large rectangular object, my mind instantly shudders in horror. This is not just any object. This is a large headstone. Walking closer I attempt to get any information from it, but heavy amounts of mold and moss grow all over, blocking out any identifying features. The corners of the headstone are all cracked with large chunks having eroded away over time. Turning around I notice more headstones protruding out of the mist, causing the hair on the back of my neck to stand rigid in fear.

"What am I doing in a cemetery?" I breathlessly utter. Not only am I completely lost wearing a thin unfamiliar nightgown, but I am lost in one of the creepiest places to be at night. Panic electrifies my overstimulated mind as I try to comprehend how I got here and how I am going to get out of this situation.

Frantically I look all around for a way out when a piercing sound cuts through the fog, stopping me in my tracks. The haunting sobs of a man resonating in the distance fill the cemetery with a heavy weight of grief. The man's deep agonizing cry has a gravitating pull on me. Turning away from my natural instinct to leave as quickly as possible, I proceed to walk towards the weeping sobs of the anguished man. It's as if my mind has no control over what my body is now doing.

Standing just inches away from the source of the tortured sound is an elderly man crumpled up at the base of a headstone. Frantically I peer down attempting to see who he is, but his shaggy grey hair is covering his face. His piercing cries fire out of him like arrows penetrating my heart, duplicating the sorrow within me.

Bending down to console him, I utter compassionately, "Hello. Sir, are you all right?"

The mysterious old man remains sitting here wailing, completely oblivious to my declaration of concern towards his plight. His unaffected figure lingers here curled up next to the headstone, completely ignoring me altogether as if I wasn't even standing here, like I am a ghost haunting his pain. Bending down on my haunches I attempt to get his attention when suddenly I catch sight of the name inscribed on the headstone. I spring back in unrequited horror. There, carved into the hard ancient stone, reads the name "Donovan." Stammering back to my feet I attempt to read the last name, but the thick layer of moss is preventing me from reading it.

A vibration radiating from the ground surges up my bare feet, pulsating up my entire body. My surroundings slowly spin like I am stuck on an unruly merry-go-round, causing my vision to fade slightly. I look toward where the old man was, only to discover he is no longer there. As I anxiously gaze around the abandoned cemetery, the mist that is encircling me begins aggressively bubbling up, covering everything. The thick, swirling fog encompasses me entirely with its blinding grey mist, blocking everything from my sight.

The shrouding fog dissipates like shattered glass, revealing a giant mirror where Donovan's headstone once resided. Complete confusion invades my mind as I gradually proceed over to the mystifying mirror that is curiously standing in the middle of a cemetery. As I approach the mirror I can see my image reflecting boldly within it. The extreme inappropriateness of the long revealing nightgown creeps wildly into my mind as my eyes widen, leaving me feeling self-conscious and exposed. My silver-dollar eyes absorb the bizarre reflection in front of me. Though the girl standing in the mirror resembles me, her dark aura appears to mute my countenance. Gingerly lifting my hand towards the mirror I slowly trace the outline of my mirage, examining my face. A deep ache in the pit of my belly presses out as I gaze at my reflection in horror, realizing it is really me. As I look up my gaze locks onto the eyes reflecting back at me, sending a tremor of disquiet to envelop me. My once vibrant blue color has completely disappeared, leaving my eyes a sinister white color except for just a small dark pupil in the center of my eyes. The abomination staring back at me sends me into an unyielding attack of jitters. Numbing panic takes over me as I cling tightly onto the edges of the mirror. Violently I scream out, "NO! NO!"

At that very moment of complete and utter despair, my eyelids rip open, revealing the calm sanctuary of my secure room. The blazing sun shoots through my windows, causing my eyes to ache. Instinctively I squint, trying to block out the intrusive bright light. My breathing quickens as I fearfully gaze around my room, making sure I'm not standing in the middle of a dilapidated cemetery.

Though I'm fully aware that it was all a dream, my mind is having a hard time breaking free from the effects of the terrifying experience. Hesitantly I lift the covers, expecting to find myself wearing a black revealing nightgown. A heavy sigh of relief vibrates out of my mouth as I notice my wrinkled jeans and shirt from last night. The mild tremor pulsating throughout me slowly dissipates, allowing my heart rate to resume a normal pace.

Vaguely I remember the details as to how I got home, and even how I wound up in bed, but the rest of the night was a nightmare mirroring a fearful reality I had no idea existed. I gaze out my window while my mind starts replaying every lucid detail of last night. I can still feel Donovan's warm, soft skin firmly pressed up against my cheek as his sweet breath tumbles down my neck, sending shivers racing vigorously down my spine again.

Picturing Donovan's face in my mind I begin seeing his haunting transforming eyes reflect in everything around me. The lustrous blue sky mimics the translucent shimmer of his unforgettable eyes. I can still feel their piercing gaze seeping deep into my soul, revealing my inner thoughts. My heart rate repeats its faster pace as I recall the terrifying transformation of Donovan's eyes right in front of me. A shiver vibrates up my spine, exploding over my torso as I wonder how something like that could occur.

Refusing to get up I turn away from the glaring window, fully wanting to give in to my thoughts of Donovan. My exhausted body is completely rundown, but I can't allow myself to fall asleep. The fear from last night's dream still haunts my every action. Instantly I fling my feeble legs out of the cumbersome covers. As I sit here on the edge of my bed my head suddenly begins throbbing violently, causing the walls in my room to spin in swirling circles. Quickly I throw myself back down before I fall over. My hammering head and aching muscles feel as though I am suffering from a hangover, but I didn't have anything to drink last night. The only explanation for this ragged feeling is the overindulgence of heightened emotions my brain was put through during the night.

Lying in my bed I slowly watch the spinning walls around me come to a steady halt like a sick rollercoaster ending its torturous ride. Finally I convince myself to attempt getting up again, but this time I will have to do it a lot slower. Grabbing my blanket in my hands I firmly wrap it around myself as I slowly proceed to sit up. Gingerly I sit here on the edge of the bed while my quivering legs steady themselves.

Slowly I stand up, causing my legs to tremble under the extreme weight I am putting on them like they are unwilling to cooperate with me. I have no idea where I am going. I just know I can't stay here in my bed any longer. I have to keep my mind busy so I won't think about Donovan any more. Thinking about him will only heighten my level of depression. I know he said that I will see him again, but I don't understand how. He doesn't have my phone number or even know where I live. The reality is last night was a unique situation which will most likely never happen again.

Delicately I walk out onto my balcony as the cool morning air washes over my damp skin. Tightly wrapping my blanket around me I take in a deep breath, allowing the fresh air to invigorate my inner soul. The cool morning air floods my entire frame with rejuvenating strength, calming the rising trepidation within me.

I watch as the cool breeze blows in several light gray clouds, dotting the crisp, clear blue sky like invading soldiers setting rank against the bright morning light. As I look out into the horizon I can see the looming black clouds gradually blowing in. The breeze carrying the impending storm has a crisp, cold edge, causing a quick shiver to race up my spine as it tangos with the cool wind over any exposed skin.

Wrapping my blanket firmly around me I quickly head back inside when suddenly I hear music echoing from my bedroom. The muffled music instantly brings my mind back to reality. I quickly walk back into my room, trying to figure out where the song is coming from. Standing in the middle of my room I gaze all around, attempting to locate the haunting organ music playing on an annoying loop. My eyes narrow, deepening the furrow between them as a conundrum of speculations flood my mind. Why in the world is there an ominous organ playing in my room?

Suddenly I catch sight of the irritating cell phone William gave me illuminating next to my bed. Shaking my head slightly I let out a breathy growl as I rush over to grab the phone. Pausing in front of it, my heart rate spikes and my stomach flips with anticipation that this could possibly be Donovan. Wrapping my clammy hand around the phone I look down with a scowl as my hopes disintegrate. There sprawled across the large screen is the name Bill.

William always wanted me to call him Bill. But to me, that has never been his name. My dad would call him Bill, but I have never been fond of that name. It's like a cheap imitation suit trying to pass off as the real thing. I don't understand how a name so plain can come from an elegant sounding one. If you are going to shorten it then why not Will – but Bill – ugh.

I gaze at the name on the screen as a severe disappointment pushes down on my already heavy and dilapidated body. A full sigh escapes through my pouting lips, causing my cheeks to inflate slightly as I think of the one person I wish had my number. A fiery wave of anger and depression instantly flows over me like a consuming tidal wave, engulfing my every thought. I need to stop before I succumb to the deep despair I am heading into. He is gone and there is nothing I can do about it. My questions for Donovan will remain unanswered.

Shaking my head vigorously I answer the phone as upbeat as I can, "Hi, William."

"Good morning, Lauren," he states excitedly. His perky voice resonates through the phone. He sounds annoyingly chipper for eight o'clock in the morning. What is up his sleeve?

"Good morning… Bill," I add sarcastically, placing heavy emphasis on his name.

"Ah, you saw my name on your phone. I know you don't like to call me Bill, but it would have taken me too long to punch in William. I am not tech savvy like all you young kids." There is a pregnant pause, and then he adds, "So… how do you like the ringtone choice? It's not too ridiculous, is it?" he states sheepishly.

I don't want to hurt his feelings, he did give me the phone, but why in the hell would he choose such a creepy ringtone? "Um…well…can't say it would have been my first choice," I utter too eagerly. Trying to change the subject I add, "William, is there a reason why you are calling me early on a Saturday morning?"

"Yes," he mumbles out while his voice slowly takes on a suspicious tone. "Your mom is leaving on another one of her long trips." An uncomfortable pause presses through the phone, causing the air within my room to thicken. "I am just thinking how it would be fun for all of us to get together for a brunch at my house." He quickly adds, "So what do you think? Will you come over to my house this morning for a get together?" He almost seems to beg.

Poor William, for years he has been trying, with little success, to force my mother and me to get along. It's about as easy for us to coexist congenially as putting fire and ice together. One inadvertently will destroy the other. This has been our dysfunctional relationship for as long as I can remember. I think William believes he can instantly improve the sour relationship we have formed. Perhaps subconsciously he feels he owes it to my father to bring us together. Why William feels responsible for our relationship is beyond me. It was not my father's or even William's fault my mother cares more for her social life than she has ever cared for me.

My father tried to overcompensate for my mother's obvious lack of parental bonding by spending an extreme amount of quality time with me. Which I believe heightened her jealousy towards me. William is not only attempting to do the same thing, but I believe he is also trying to honor my father's wishes by undertaking a nearly impossible task. I know William's heart is in the right place, but this is something even he can't fix. My mother's undulating resentment towards me was formed the day I was born. It doesn't surprise me though that William is giving it another try before my mom, once again, leaves on one of her self-indulging road trips.

Everything within me wants to reply with a resounding no, but I can't hurt him or let him down. I owe it to William. He has been my surrogate father, stepping into the vacant shoes left by the sudden death of my father. Besides, deep down I don't want to give up either, she is my mother. I need to give her the benefit of the doubt and let her leave on a good note.

"Yes, William, I'll come. What time do you want me there?" I ask, trying to hide the anguish in my voice.

"You know you are welcome here anytime, but I'm planning on eating around ten o'clock, so you will need to be here a little before then."

"That gives me very little time. I'll come over as soon as I get dressed."

Looking down at my clothes I realize that technically I am still dressed, just in the same thing I wore last night. I don't think he will appreciate me showing up looking like a ragged mess, wearing what I passed out in. Quickly I ask, "What time is my mother planning on being there?" This way I have the exact time I have to work with.

"She should be here any time. She is so excited to get together before she leaves." He futilely attempts to exaggerate the animated tone in his voice, but he can't fool me. I know the real reason for her enthusiasm and it's sure as hell not to see me. She would never miss an opportunity to brag about what she is doing. This is the kind of day my mother loves, a narcissistic celebration.

I huff quietly at his lame assumption that my mother would actually be thrilled to see me. "Yes, I am sure she is excited," I add sarcastically. "Well then, I will just get myself ready and come on over."

"Oh, I almost forgot, Lauren. Yesterday I overheard Larry asking you to go dancing with everyone. Did you end up going with them last night? I mean, you are usually up earlier than this, so hopefully that means you had a fun night." His voice spins around the word fun with a breathy chortle, respectfully adding, "You deserve it. You haven't done anything since…well, in a year."

A disconsolate moan vibrates within my chest as the disappointment I was able to bury once again consumes my entire being. I don't know how to answer him without completely losing control again. This is the last thing I want to talk to him about. It's not because I don't want him to know, but I don't really understand it myself. How do I explain all the strange and mysterious things that have happened to me?

A conundrum of emotions spins viciously within my mind as I contemplate the events that have happened to me. I am not sure the word *fun* is the right term to describe last night. I think some more appropriate words to describe it would have to be: strange, scary, erotic and confusing, but definitely not fun.

Forcing down the knot building up in my throat, I utter fervently, "Yes, I did go out last night with some of the co-workers. It was an interesting night – and that's all I am going to say about it right now."

I hear him exhale softly over the phone as he tenderly expresses, "You know Lauren, you can tell me anything." His gentle, pleading voice echoes softly into my ear, resonating over my quivering frame like a warm, soothing blanket firmly enveloping my dilapidated body.

I know I can tell him anything, but I can't right now. Hesitation flows heavily from my breath as I pause slightly, not knowing completely where to begin or if I truly want to explain last night. "Yes, I know I can, but..."

"Don't worry, Lauren. You can tell me whenever you're ready to, okay?" he interrupts softly.

The pressure of how, or even what I was going to say is now gone. I slowly relax as a restoring breath rolls out of me. "Thanks. I will be talking to you soon – trust me."

"Okay. Well, I'd better hang up with you. Your mom is going to be here soon and you need to get dressed, right?" he teases, as he skillfully changes the subject.

"Yes, I do. Do you want me to bring anything?" I ask.

"No, just bring yourself. See you soon," he chuckles softly as he hangs up the phone.

CHAPTER 9

Crimson

Slowly I turn onto William's long, narrow, tree-lined driveway as my heart begins nervously beating for some strange reason. Tightly gripping onto my steering wheel with my clammy hands I slowly maneuver through his tree-lined drive. The slim, tall trees line both sides of his private road, blocking his house from my vision. As I drive deeper into his property the trees seem to open up, revealing William's large home like a beacon reminding me of the only home I have left. There, standing like a great welcoming symbol for me, is his enormous intricately carved Spanish fountain positioned in the center of his circular drive.

William's home is a large single story ranch style house that was built in the late sixties, but he had the entire inside completely gutted and renovated. The front of his house is laden with several large ceiling-to-floor windows, allowing for breathtaking views of the countryside and the sun to permeate throughout the house.

A large front porch runs the full length of his house with several cozy furniture pieces positioned perfectly for outdoor entertaining. Hanging from the rafters under the porch is a huge swing laden with pillows, making it appear more like a floating bed than a typical porch swing. From the comfort of William's swing I am usually found sitting as I watch the impending storm clouds form ranks in an attacking motion around the mysterious lone Mt. Diablo in the distance.

The tires of my car crackle against the small gravel rocks positioned protectively over his dusty driveway. I am sure I'm not the only one who can hear my tires rolling across the gravel road. The noise of an approaching car can be heard echoing all through William's house. Pulling around his circular drive I catch sight of my mother and William sitting comfortably on the swing. Instantly William gazes up at me with a large mischievous smile spreading victoriously across his face as he appears to be frolicking in his obvious victory of bringing my mother and me together, but the day is not over yet. Gazing up at him I give him a playful smile in return as I slowly park my car.

Walking over to me he utters enthusiastically, "Lauren, I am so glad you came early. I was afraid you were going to come just in time to eat. Now this means we can all visit while the quiche is still in the oven." A calculating smile spreads victoriously across his face. This is exactly what he planned for. I honestly hope for his sake it ends as well as he expects it to.

Gazing over at my mother I notice her stiff proper figure still sitting on the porch swing with a flat suspicious expression strumming across her face. Giving her a slight smile I respectfully mumble, "Hi mom."

Her eyes narrow as she responds smugly, "Hi sweetie. Are you feeling okay today? You don't look very good." Her eyes dance over me with disdain. "Pardon my expression, but you look like you have been to hell and back."

"Naomi, stop. I think she looks beautiful," he protests, giving her a sharp disapproving glance.

I am grateful that William chimed in, but he is being ridiculous, I know I have a natural but simple beauty. But my personal image of myself lately has hit a rock bottom and I don't see it changing anytime soon. "William, thank you for saying that about me, but I have to disagree with you," I object kindly.

For him to say I look beautiful – after a night of no sleep – is a bit absurd. He doesn't need to go overboard in trying to make his point to my mother. Beautiful is not the word I would use to describe myself right now. Though my features and body structure have been described as a delicate and stunning daisy, I have never felt like I can compete with all the roses around me. My dad used to tell me being a daisy in a field of identical roses makes me the breathtaking one in the room. But today I don't feel very beautiful.

"Well, I do think you look beautiful today. Your eyes in that shirt look stunning. They almost appear to jump right off your face in an explosion of dazzling blue."

Instantly my mom stands up and proceeds to storm off towards her car like a disappointed child who didn't get the reaction she was intending. I highly doubt my mother thought William was going to reprimand her in front of me, least of all disagree with her by saying that I look beautiful. It appears my mother's self-inflated ego has taken a hit.

Though my mother's statement was completely rude and malicious toward me I don't want her to leave, especially after all the work William has done for us. Rushing toward her car I catch up to her, offering my hand in peace before she leaves. As I approach my mother, her rigid chest is already in her car leaning over the driver's seat.

Forcefully I grab hold of the open door, trying to prevent her from closing it and leaving. "Mom, please don't leave. If it means anything I want you to stay," I beg.

"Don't be such a drama queen, Lauren," she snaps as she begins to pull herself out of the car. As she turns around and faces me I notice a thick pile of travel brochures and magazines about Europe positioned precariously within her hands. "Good, since you don't want me to go, why don't you just make yourself useful and carry these for me," she adds arrogantly.

Raising the stack of heavy papers over my hands, she persists to drop them aggressively towards me. Instantly my hands break free from the tight grip I have on her car, catching the stack of magazines just before they fall to the ground. I lose my balance slightly as I stumble forward trying to prevent the stack – and me – from falling. Shocked, I gaze up at her in disbelief only to notice her smug, arrogant smile gleaming down at me. A corner of her mouth purses up in a slight satisfied pleasure.

"Nice catch." Patting me on the shoulder she suddenly leans down just inches away from my ear. "You know, you do look like hell. Almost like you were out all night partying. And we both know that's not possible," she utters inaudibly in my ear as a quiet laugh escapes out of her thin mouth. Her warm breath hits my face like a punch from a heavyweight boxer as it penetrates my heart and encapsulates my body with sorrow tainted with rage. Instantly she gets up and brazenly walks away from me, leaving me standing here in complete shock. I watch as she cheerfully walks over to William, who is blissfully unaware of what she has just said. If he had heard he would have lost it on her, but she knows what she is doing. If I say something to him she will just deny it and I will be the one left looking like a brat. She is manipulating the situation and by the looks of her strut she is reveling in her obvious success.

Numbing waves of disappointment and hurt ripple within my mind. How can a mother be like this to her own flesh and blood? I tried to put my hand out to her in peace, but all she could do was bite it. All I have ever wanted was a relationship with her, but she has never had any time for me. Perhaps it's because I don't fit into her stamp of the perfect daughter. One she can brag to her friends about on how I am married to a successful doctor, have two point five children, live in a big house with a white picket fence, and completely engulf myself in the social scene of this town. Maybe if I was more like that she would finally want to be my mother and would be proud of me. I don't know if she has ever loved me or if she has only ever resented me for the relationship I had with my father. In my father's eyes I was his princess and that never went over very well with my mother. Perhaps subconsciously she blames me for the sour relationship they had.

All my moral reasoning dissipates as I watch her parading away from me. A shockwave of fury intertwined with disappointment builds viciously inside of me like an uncontrolled cocktail of gasoline and fire mixing in me. An instant flash of white light explodes within my soul, engulfing my entire consciousness. My thunderous heart violently pounds against my chest as my breathing quickens, intensifying the situation. My overstimulated mind is basking in the loss of control I am succumbing to.

Slowly I viciously walk towards my mother as the pent-up rage inside me gradually consumes all my humanity, leaving a fiery rage simmering within its wake. Suddenly everything around me turns a vivid shade of red, like a bright crimson film is covering my eyes, tainting my vision. The red oozes off of everything except in the very center, where my heartless mother stands in bright vibrant colors. This is something I have never experienced before. I have heard of seeing red, but I didn't think it was possible to actually see everything transform into a bright shade of red.

Though rage pulsates through my veins like a live wire racing in my body, surprisingly my mind and my actions remain in absolute control. All my senses are on high alert, causing me to be much more aware of my surroundings. I can feel the energy in the air as if it is soft feathers gently caressing every nerve ending on my highly sensitive skin. Though part of me is frightened at what is happening, another part is reveling in the consuming power I am gradually succumbing to.

As my mother and William walk into the house, I notice her arm link around William's. Narrowing my eyes I begin to take in her every movement as I nearly gaze right through her. Suddenly her shrill voice echoes through my head with a clarity I have never heard before. I begin following them into the house, focusing in on her every word. The background noise dissipates, leaving her voice the only sound I can hear. Everything around me is still tinted a flaming red color – except for my mom – while my highly acute mind remains on high alert.

As I get closer to my mother the sound intensifies as if her words are screaming in my head uttering, "I want you William. I have always been physically attracted to you, even when Max was alive."

Disbelief washes through my highly suggestive mind. Why would my mother tell William that? I know my mother is aggressive, but this is ridiculous. I'm not about to allow her destructive paws anywhere near him. She is not going to ruin him if I have anything to say about it.

"Mother, how dare you say that to him." My voice is harsh and low as the words fire from my mouth.

She quickly spins around, glaring at me with silver dollar eyes. Her mouth mimics a baby bird at feeding time, wide open in shock. Confusion streams across her face as she stammers in response, "Lauren, what are you talking about? What is wrong with talking to him about Europe?"

"Don't play games with me anymore. I am sick of it. I heard what you said to William and I'll be damned if I let you sink your paws into him." An acidic edge vibrates off of every word, cutting through the stillness in the air.

"I am not playing games with you. I didn't say anything to him other than my vacation plans."

"Don't lie," I snap back.

The room glows a crimson red as the trembling anger within me intensifies, making it appear as if everything is on fire. Surprisingly though, my actions and thoughts remain under complete control. My heightened mind is acutely aware of the exact words I heard my mother say. This is not my vivid imagination playing tricks on me. There is no doubt in my mind what my mother's shrilling voice uttered.

"I heard you tell William that you are physically attracted to him. What mom, you can't just wait until I go back home before you make your sentiments known? You had to make sure I heard it, didn't you? You manipulated my father and I am not going to allow you to manipulate William as well. You have been playing cruel games with me my whole life and it's going to end now," I utter forcefully.

My mother remains frozen like I am Medusa turning her supple body into petrified stone. Her wide eyes and gaping mouth vividly etches the sincere shock into her face.

Slowly William walks over to me with a piercing disappointment on his face. His stern jaw vibrates as his thin lips press firmly against each other, causing a slight frown to appear. His once joyful countenance now quivers with shock and disappointment. His berating glance sends a cold chill to race through me, instantly extinguishing the fire raging within my soul.

"Lauren, your mother said nothing of the kind. We were just talking about her trip to Europe. That was all – and I mean all – she said. Your accusations are rude and uncalled for." His eyes bore deep into mine as if he is searching for some answers. "Why are you acting this way? This behavior is not like you."

Gradually the bright crimson color invading my sight slowly dissipates like smoke clearing a room, revealing vivid normal colors of everything around me. The intense anger and high alert consuming me slowly diminishes. An extreme amount of remorse rushes throughout my thoughts like cold muddy water flowing through me, leaving me feeling grimy inside. Shards of anguish and regret rip through me, causing stinging pain to pierce through me. The guilt is eating away at me like toxic acid ripping through my entire being, leaving just a dysfunctional shell in its wake. Intense sorrow radiates out of me, causing tears to explode forcefully from my eyes. I slowly quiver with regret as I fall into a full-fledged meltdown. Collapsing onto William's couch I moan weakly, "Oh mother, I am so sorry. I don't know what is wrong with me. I feel like I am going crazy."

The intense crying I have succumbed to makes it almost impossible for me to speak clearly. My tortuous guilt won't allow me to look at either of them for fear their berating expressions will intensify the excruciating guilt I am already in. Grabbing one of the pillows from the sofa I vigorously throw it over my face, trying to hide my extreme shame and embarrassment. My muffled voice is weak as I murmur into the pillow, "I don't know what is wrong with me. I'm hearing things and experiencing things that aren't normal. I feel like I'm going crazy and I took my frustrations out on you. Please mom, forgive me. I am so sorry. This was the last thing I wanted to happen before you left."

Suddenly the couch cushion sinks down next to me, causing me to roll towards the intruding person. A warm, gentle hand slowly strokes my back like a caring parent lovingly calming their disconsolate child. This is not my mother's hand. This is a strong, beefy hand with a rough sandpaper feel to it. William's rough skin gently catches on the cotton fibers of my t-shirt as he affectionately strokes my back. Feeling his warm, soothing touch opens the floodgates of my tears even more. They soak the pillow I had forcefully placed around my face as I attempt to muffle the sound of my heartbreaking sobs.

"What is going on, Lauren? Are you in some sort of trouble or something? Please talk to us, let us help you." His voice is gentle and calm like a warm blanket pouring over me. His low hypnotic tone soothes the storm within me. For just a brief moment I feel like I am talking to my father, allowing me to feel like everything is going to be okay – but deep down I know it won't be.

Gingerly I lift the pillow, revealing my shamed face as I turn towards William. His dark eyes are narrow, causing the furrow between them to deepen. The life lines around his eyes intensify, making him appear as if he has gained ten years. His eyes softly glisten from tears he seems to be holding back from the distress he feels for me. His expression pierces through me like a painful dart nailing the center of my heart.

Turning towards my mother I attempt to give her an apologetic glance when I notice her standing here motionless – in shock. A guilty glimmer rushes through her wide eyes like a child getting caught eating a cookie from the cookie jar. I examine her questionably as she gazes over the top of my head, staring out into space, refusing to look at me.

I must have cut her too deep this time. Gazing up at her respectfully, I stammer, "Mom, please look at me."

Blinking several times my mom finally peers down at me, but it is just a surface glance. She only looks at me for a brief moment then quickly glances over to William. "William…" There is a slight pause as if she doesn't want to acknowledge my presence, adding, "…Lauren. I think I really need to go. Thank you for everything, William."

William shoots up and immediately walks over to my mother. "Naomi, please stay."

My mom isn't the one who needs to leave – I am. It is my gratuitous behavior that caused this uncomfortable situation. "Mom, please don't leave. I am the problem here, not you. Let me be the one to leave. This is my fault anyway."

Reluctantly she walks over to me, gazing down at me warmly. Her morose expression stains her face like bloody war wounds that have left scars. I stare regretfully into her sorrow-filled eyes, when all of a sudden she bends down and affectionately kisses the top of my forehead. This shocking display of affection leaves me sitting here completely stunned by her gentle reaction.

"Lauren, I haven't been on my best behavior either. You did say some things that hurt but they are true, and as far as the other thing you said – well, I don't quite understand how…" Her voice trails off like she is speaking to the wind, unsure or unwilling to entirely explain what she is thinking.

I know my mom is not telling me everything, but at this point I'm lucky she is even willing to talk to me. Looking up at my mom I plead softly, "Mom, I am so sorry for everything I accused you of. It was out of line and completely false." A sharp chortle reverberates from my mother, causing me to lose my train of thought. Shaking my head slightly I add, "Please don't leave yet."

"I need to, we will talk later." She looks at me, her eyes deep with hesitation as if she wants to ask me something, but can't. Turning toward William she gives him a coy smile as she utters softly, "William, thank you so much for everything. When I get back maybe we can try this again, hopefully with a better outcome."

"Really Naomi, you don't need to leave," William asks gently.

"Yes I do, but thank you for trying to do this." She gives a plastic smile. "Promise me we will do this again when I get back."

"I promise," William utters fervently.

I follow them out to the front porch as William continues to walk my mother to her car. I proceed to dejectedly throw myself onto the awaiting comfort of his porch swing. Curling up into a tight upright fetal position I dolefully lay my head against the edge of the swing, gazing up at Mt. Diablo and wishing this horrific day was over. At that moment something deep inside of me quivers with fear as if it is warning me that this long, dreadful day is just beginning.

CHAPTER 10

Mt. Diablo

Heavy regret and complete bewilderment washes over me as I sit here on William's porch swing. Gently I lay my head up against the supporting rope while I stare mindlessly into the numbing vast space. My dilapidated muscles are extremely weak and exhausted from the giant temper tantrum I had. It is taking all of my energy just to make the swing move the slightest bit.

My weakened body slowly seeps into the soothing motion of William's swing while I contemplate my inappropriate display toward my mother and the fiery rage that had ignited a foreign monster within me. Suddenly a sharp jolt of the swing interrupts the soothing rhythmic pattern I was able to create. Weakly I turn my head only to discover William now sitting right next to me gazing questionably into my face. "Okay, your mom is now gone so… talk," he demands.

An audible exhale escapes out of my mouth as I turn regretfully towards the visual safety of the lone mountain. I can't face him right now. The extreme disappointment streaming across his face stings right through me like piercing knives slicing me. I know he wants some answers for my behavior, but I don't have anything for him yet. I still have no idea why I acted that way or how I could have heard my mother saying those things to William when obviously she never did. How am I supposed to tell William that I think I am having a nervous breakdown?

"Lauren, I'm not going to make you talk to me now if you don't want to, but you will have to explain your actions to me at a later date," he barks. His voice drops to a low throaty growl, causing my frame to stiffen. His resolute tone snaps with a firm demand, making me aware of how I will have to adhere to his condition.

Sitting clear at the other end of the swing William gazes pensively up at Mt. Diablo. His body is positioned defensively away from mine. We both sit here in silence swinging slowly back and forth. Tightly I hold onto one of the pillows as I intently watch the now encroaching storm clouds form tight ranks around the mountain. The ominous clouds slowly engulf Mt. Diablo like a destructive tidal wave rapidly pouring over the unsuspecting mountain. The dark clouds begin their penetrating attack on the once visible mountain with heaving black force. The dark swirling mass of energy rushes vehemently over the tip, covering its peak from all viewing eyes.

"What are you so intently looking at, Lauren?" he questions gently. His once sharp rebuking tone has completely dissipated, leaving a buttery smooth and relaxed pitch to now flow out of him.

"Nothing really, I am just watching the clouds form around Mt. Diablo," I utter weakly. My limp body melts into the swing while my soul feels exhausted, like I have just been dragged through hot fiery coals. I don't even have the strength to turn towards William.

"Have you ever heard the legend of how Mt. Diablo got its name?" he asks cheerfully, trying to distract me and lighten my dismal mood.

I have lived here my entire life and I can honestly say I never knew there was a story behind its name. "No, I never have heard the story before, but I have a feeling I am going to hear it now," I respond with as much cheer as my weakened state can muster up. I am not really interested in hearing it, but at this point a change in subject might be exactly what I need.

Slowly I turn to look at him when suddenly I notice a huge mischievous smile spread eagerly across his face like he is getting ready to tell a group of campers a terrifying ghost story. He starts rubbing his hands vigorously together in a roguish way as his eyes now gleam with mischief.

"If you think you are going to frighten me, I hate to tell you, you're not. I am too old and too tired to be frightened," I warn with a thick frankness coating my voice.

"Oh, really? We shall see." He starts laughing in a maniacal kind of way.

"You are so weird. Are you going to tell me the story or not?" I snap.

"Hiss – retract your claws you grump. Lighten up a little. I am just having fun." He rubs his hands briskly together adding, "Are you ready then?"

He leans back against the swing and gazes up at the mountain. Resting my head comfortably against a pillow I watch the clouds continue to form around the mountain as I ready myself for his story.

William's voice lowers slightly, taking on a dark, almost reverent tone. "Well, the folklore begins in 1805 when this area was home to the Chupcan Indians. Though this was their territory the Spanish military, believing the Chupcan Indians were less than human, was sent to round up all the Indians and obtain their land.

"The Spanish military set out on a cool, cloudy day, much like today, where the ominous clouds completely covered the tip of the mountain. The Chupcan Indians' village was near the base of the mountain in a nearby thicket. Spanish scouts were sent out to locate the exact location of the village. When the Spanish soldiers discovered the village of the Chupcan people they knew this was their opportunity to capture the village and obtain custody over the land."

His voice drops even deeper as a low growl forms in the base of his throat, continuing, "That night the Spanish military completely surrounded the village, deciding to wait until sunrise to make their attack. They had their strict orders to completely annihilate all the men while attempting to capture as many women and children as they could to sell them into slavery. It was to be an all-out massacre, leaving nothing of the village.

"During the night the Spanish army set their attack plan in motion, completely surrounding the village. There was no possible way for the Indians to be able to escape.

"That night a thick, dense fog rolled in, settling across the ground. The thick fog engulfed the entire area, making it hard for the Spanish soldiers to see anything. They were not prepared for fog that seemed to encompass the entire area with a silver cloak. The heavy blinding mist made it difficult for the Spanish to see very well, so to compensate for the lack of visibility the soldiers linked their arms together, forming a solid barrier. This was to insure that the Indians could not sneak past them during the night under the shroud of the blinding dense fog.

"The next morning the fog dissipated, allowing the Spanish military to proceed forcefully with their plan – capturing and killing the Chupcan people in the village."

William's arm thrusts forward as if he is wielding a sword, adding now forcefully, "They rushed in, weapons drawn, ready to attack, only to discover the entire village was no longer there. They had vanished, supposedly into thin air. There was not a single sign of a village ever existing there. It had just completely disappeared. The Spanish military was absolutely shocked at how an entire village, teepees and all, could just simply disappear through their solid barrier."

Interrupting William, I state facetiously, "That's it, William? You have no idea what scary is. That's not a scary story." I grimace at his feeble attempt.

"That wasn't the end of the story, Lauren. You interrupted me. I was just getting to the good part."

"Sorry, go ahead then," I utter timidly. William was right though, telling me this story is definitely improving my mood.

"Now, where was I before you so rudely interrupted me?" He gives me a quick mischievous wink, then proceeds where he left off, "Oh yes, the Spanish military discovered the entire village had disappeared during the night without any conceivable way of doing so. As they walked through the abandoned village one soldier noticed a white man standing in the center of the once thriving village. He was tall and slender with sharp, strong features to his face.

"The soldier ran to his captain yelling that there was a man left standing in the center of the vacant field, but he was not an

Indian, nor Spaniard – he was a white man. The Spanish captain ran with the soldier to see who this mysterious person was.

"As the captain got closer to the stranger his heart began to beat out of control and his breathing increased to a rapid pace. He suddenly felt like he couldn't breathe, like all the air was being pushed out of him and his thundering heart was going to jump out of his chest."

Instantly my back stiffens and I jolt straight up as William describes the terrifying feeling that came over the Spanish captain. It is as if William is describing the exact scenario I experienced when I was with Donovan. A sick twinge in my stomach rises, making me want to stop William from continuing the story, but I need to know the rest. Who was the mysterious person who stood in the middle of the Indian village? Perhaps this folklore can help solve my own mystery.

William's voice is now laced with a dark edge as he leans over me with a bleak mask over his face. His eyes are gleaming with mischief as a corner of his mouth rises in pleasure at my obvious rigid posture.

"As he got closer to confront this frightful personage he noticed his eyes were clear. There was absolutely no color to them except for a small black pupil in the center. This stranger seemed to stare right into the soul of the captain.

"The captain of the army couldn't breathe and for just a moment he thought his life was going to be taken by this obvious monster. He grabbed on to his cross which hung around his neck. Then, he called out to God to help him escape from this evil who was trying to destroy him. Suddenly the captain was able to breathe and the pain in his chest vanished. When the captain looked up, the man had a menacing smile on his face."

My heart drops to the base of my throat, causing an audible gulp. This can't be possible. Donovan's eyes did the same exact thing. He has given me no explanation for why his eyes transformed in front of me. And at times I can feel Donovan peering into my soul, like a voyeur playing with my thoughts and intentions. The hairs on my arms stand straight up in warning. A cold chill runs through my veins as he continues the story.

"The captain began running away yelling El Diablo! El Diablo!" William shouts at the top of his lungs, causing me to jump back in fear. "The rest of the soldiers followed behind their captain, running away from this obvious devil they believed came out of the mountain and allowed the Chupcan Indians to escape during the night. Because of the mysterious devil, it was many years before any Spaniard would ever lay a foot on that unhallowed ground. They feared the devil would come back and finish off what he couldn't do that day – claim their souls and drag them down to hell."

William's ominous voice reverts back to his normal tone as he begins laughing at his lame attempt at telling a scary story. "How did you like the story? Crazy isn't it? To think something so bizarre like that could happen is ridiculous. That is just one of the crazy folklores behind Mt. Diablo's name. I bet the truth is some plain story."

I lack the strength to answer him because I remain paralyzed by the fear rushing through me. The anxious twinge churning inside of me is making me feel sick to my stomach as my mind wraps around the possible reality and existence of demons. Perhaps my life has been altered by an ominous being I never believed in. I thought this story was going to distract me, but instead it has made me even more terrified and confused by my recent experience.

"Lauren," William utters forcefully, snapping me out of my trance. "Was my story that boring for you?"

"No, on the contrary, you have no idea how terrified I am." My voice slightly trembles, causing me to stammer out the words.

"I didn't mean to frighten you. You do know it's just a story...don't you?"

I don't know if I can correctly answer him, because I'm not completely convinced it is just a story. After my similar experience with Donovan this folklore is my only explanation for solving this mystery. Maybe if he would have told me the story a long time ago, even several days ago, I would be laughing at him instead of trembling in fear. It's as if everything I believe in has been thrown out a window.

"William, can I ask you a question?" I ask softly as I gaze pensively up at Mt. Diablo.

"Sure, anything you would like."

"Do you believe in the devil or that there can actually be demons out there?" I whisper reluctantly as I turn to face William, hoping to catch his reaction to my blatant question.

William's eyes instantly transform from a shimmering brilliance to a flat, hollow look of frustration. His once playful amusement he seemed to revel in is now devoured by a dark, sincere expression tainting his face. Sliding his hand slowly to his mouth William thoughtfully drums his fingers against his lips. His pensive eyes narrow, stitching his brow together in a gaze of deep contemplation. A sharp disconsolate moan escapes out of William's taut mouth as he utters firmly again, "Lauren, it is just a story."

"Yes, you have already told me that, but do you think maybe part of it could have been true? That perhaps there was a devil or demon with clear eyes that traded the Chupcan peoples' freedom for something more sinister?" I clarify.

He peers at me with scrutinizing eyes as he examines every searing expression on my face. A full term pause presses around us as a glimmer of discovery shines within his hazel eyes. He responds respectfully, "I do believe in a devil and even in demons, but as for helping the Chupcan Indians -- I don't believe in that." His eyes seem to hide some sort of deep pain oozing out of the carved lines around his eyes, masking the truth behind his cracked wall.

I press the subject even further, needing a deeper answer than what he is willing to share with me. "Why? If you believe in demons, why don't you believe that part of the story?"

"I just don't," he hisses like a viper as he springs to his feet. Impatiently he paces back and forth while his ragged breathing causes his rigid shoulders to quiver. Exhaling softly he gradually calms himself down. Turning towards me, William utters firmly as if he is trying to convince me of his truth, "Besides, I don't believe the devil or even demons, for that fact, have a body. I believe they are just evil spirits."

Though his trembling voice causes me to have some doubts to the sincerity of what he said, William does have a valid point about demons only being spirits. If demons are only spirits then Donovan cannot be one because he has a tangible body of flesh. I felt his warm and magnificent skin against mine as his sweet, fiery breath vibrated down my neck. He is not a spirit – but what if not all demons are spirits? Is there such a thing as a trapped soul who still has his body but is a slave to the evil one?

A cold chill races up my spine, tickling the back of my neck and sending a shiver of excitement to dance on the back of my neck like a marathon runner who has the finish line in sight. I now know where I need to go and get some answers. Jumping to my feet I stand just inches away from him, "William, thank you for the story. It was, let's just say… interesting. I think I am going to head home now, though. I have a lot of things I need to do." I'm lying to him, knowing there is only one thing I need to do right now – go to the top of Mt. Diablo. Up there I hope to find some answers. Electricity races through my veins, causing my legs to twitch in anticipation of leaving.

"Are you sure you don't want to hang out any longer? You haven't eaten yet," his voice pleads.

"No, I really do need to go. Thank you for everything." Walking over to him I give William a tight, grateful hug, whispering into his ear, "Thank you." I then softly kiss his cheek.

I cannot look at William's face because the intense desire of what I need to do completely consumes my entire being. I don't want his compassionate gaze to cause me to rethink what I am about to do. Hastily I proceed to my car as I feel the cool air beating against my skin. The sharp, cool waves of the piercing wind hit me with such force that I realize the imminent storm is now hammering the top of the mountain. Looking up at Mt. Diablo I notice the clouds have completely engulfed the summit. My muscles tremble uncontrollably as my mind attempts to persuade my body to follow through with this crazy idea. There is only one place I need to go for some answers and I am not about to let the approaching storm stop me.

CHAPTER 11

The Terrifying Truth

I arrive at Mt. Diablo State Park with plenty of time left until they close the protective gates to the lower parking lot. The upper parking lot is closed off due to the heavy rain. From where I'm parked it's an easy walk up to the summit museum, but the rain is making it extremely difficult to see. It is as if Mother Nature is doing everything within her power to stop me from reaching the summit. Though the rain is falling like shattered glass from heaven, I have to do this. There is no other place I know of that can answer my burning questions. Even if William's story was just folklore there are too many similarities between it and what I have experienced. This mountain and its shroud of mystery is the only place I know that can possibly answer my questions.

As I open the car door the brisk air and icy rain hits me like stinging darts, penetrating the skin of my face. The startling cold snaps some sense into my mind like a bucket of ice water being thrown on me. The shock to my system causes me for a brief moment to wonder what the hell I am doing here.

This is absolutely ridiculous. How can I possibly think Donovan is some kind of demon or an evil entity? I don't believe in devils – or demons, for that matter. My father taught me there are only good or bad people in the world and it is our choice how we will act. No demons, no angels, just people. We never attended a church, because my father saw too many of his friends professing to be religious on Sunday while living a completely opposite life every other day of the week. At this particular moment though, I wish we would have gone to a church. It would have given me at least a basic background into what kind of sinister situation I am possibly dealing with – if anything. As of now I am heading into the unknown with no understanding of what I might be blindly walking into.

Whether this is a stupid idea or not, I need to do this for my own sanity. If I don't, I'll just keep letting my delusional thoughts haunt my mind. I need to find out who or what Donovan is and what is going on with me. I have never experienced anything like what happened at William's house today. The invading rage that consumed not only my mind but also my vision, brought my innocence to its knees, making me feel like darkness was devouring me. The now incessant burning blackness within me seems to be intensifying. It creeps out of the recesses of my mind like unattended embers waiting for a chance to ignite a rage within me that is nearly impossible to control.

The rain pelts my exposed skin as the droplets stream down my arms, tickling the surface, causing a quick shudder to vibrate through me. Taking in a deep breath I close my car door firmly as I stare at the soaked path in front of me, knowing the moment I begin this journey there will be no turning back – in more ways than one. There is no quick getaway once I get to the top of Mt. Diablo. I will be at the mercy of whatever is going to happen – if anything at all. Shoving my hands vigorously into the pockets of my jeans I take in a soothing deep breath as I step onto the path that is not my golden brick road, but a muddy trail that hopefully leads to the man behind the curtain.

To my surprise the path is easier than I had anticipated. Despite the torrential rain washing over me like a flowing waterfall from above. It's an absolutely beautiful day. The trees are all coated with their vibrant spring leaves vividly resonating off all the branches as they dance magnificently in the wind. The leaves are spotless, unscathed by the dirt and pollution swirling within the air, allowing their virgin green color to shine. The plush grass mimics the sparkling leaves with a brilliant green color. The grass rolls magnificently down the mountainside like green silk sheets rippling in the wind. Scattered beautifully throughout the grass are colorful wildflowers and Poppies sprinkled everywhere. The bright orange color of the California Poppies shimmers like gold against the virgin green grass and leaves.

The constant flow of the rain is giving everything, including me, a shower. Large droplets drip from my soaked hair and roll down my face, making it hard to see. My thunderous heartbeat and vigorous blood flow is keeping me surprisingly warm despite my sopping clothes. My nerves are on fire with the disquiet pulsating viciously through my body. I push my drenched curls out of my face, allowing me to see the green patina rooftop of the summit museum up ahead.

The large museum sits at the edge on the point of the mountain. The intricate stonework alludes to a castle-like appearance rather than a monument building. The green patina of the copper roof calls out to me like an eerie cadence vibrating through the wind. My pace instinctually speeds up, matching the call as my excitement and anticipation increase for what may lie ahead of me.

My heart pounds uncontrollably as if it is going to take flight out of my chest. A shallow pant like an overheated dog takes over my breathing, making me feel slightly lightheaded. I have mentally prepared myself for some kind of answers, but the realist part of me is expecting there to be nothing up here. I will have walked through this ridiculous downpour for nothing.

As I barely clear the corner of the observation deck which has a 365-degree view, I notice there is no one here but me. It appears I'm the only idiot who is willing to traverse the element show that Mother Nature is putting on today. Standing on the edge of the observation deck I anxiously look all around me, when I catch something out of the corner of my eye moving towards me. Quickly I turn to see what it is when immediately my legs collapse, causing me to drop aggressively to the ground. Complete disbelief washes over me, causing me to go completely numb as I sit here on the ground like a petrified log, hardened and frozen with fear. This isn't possible. How did he know I was going to be here?

"Lauren, are you all right?" Donovan yells as he runs over to me. He quickly stretches out his hands as if to help me up.

Instinctively I scurry back away from him, pressing my defenseless back against the damp stone railing. Out of all the possible scenarios running through my mind this was the last thing I expected. My senses are on high alert, allowing me to feel every drop of the cold rain hammering against my skin like water droplets on a hot skillet. Coiling up into a tight ball I ready myself for a possible attack. I lock my eyes questionably onto his, as if pleading with him for some answers.

Walking up here my only desire was to get some answers as to what is going on with me and who or what Donovan is. I just thought perhaps I would read more about the Chupcan Indian folklore, or at the very least I might have found someone up here who may have had a personal experience with the paranormal.

Sitting here motionless on the ground I allow my fear to completely paralyze me. Everything around me seems to be moving in slow motion. Even the raindrops hit the ground at a gingerly pace, allowing me to witness every exploding droplet in detail. Though everything around me moves at a lethargic pace my mind is spinning at a hyper speed. I begin reenacting every scenario for my escape, but every one of them has Donovan quickly overpowering me. The hike back to where I'm parked is too far away and I highly doubt my legs have the strength to carry me down the mountain.

As my mind replays my drive here and parking my car, there was absolutely no evidence when I got out of my car that anyone other than me was going to be up here. I would have noticed his amazing car in the parking lot, but there was nothing there. My thunderous heartbeat vibrates viciously against my chest, making me feel like I am going to pass out at any moment. Slowly I scan down to Donovan's outstretched hand and instantly realize I am in a very dangerous predicament with a man I barely know and definitely do not trust.

He drops his hand down to his side, taking a defensive step backwards. His stunning face quickly transforms from a concerned look to one of irritation and disappointment. He gazes pensively down at me with his piercing eyes, sending a warm shiver to race up my back. His nearly black hair falls delicately against his milky smooth face. The pouring rain flows heavily down his silken hair, causing small streams to roll down his chiseled nose and land on his sumptuous mouth. Breathlessly I gaze up at Donovan as he towers over me, causing my ragged breathing to intensify with a wicked combination of desire and dread. His drenched black t-shirt clings tightly to his torso, emphasizing every muscular detail rippling effortlessly from his chest, exposing every hill, valley and washboard etched into his chiseled chest. My pathetic and vivid imagination betrays me as it recalls every detail of Donovan's body hovering over mine and his taunting lips that were against my ear. A toxic concoction of fear and lust spinning rapidly within my mind causes a strange sensation of pleasure to climb up my spine.

He stands here in the rain in all black like a gorgeous model ripped from the pages of a magazine, while I on the other hand feel like a ridiculous drowned rat. Twinges of excitement start to flow within me, snuffing out the fear that once resided viciously within me. Though there is something mysterious and frightening about Donovan, I can't deny the gravitating pull he has on me.

Donovan's eyes stitch together as his head drops slightly, uttering quietly, "Lauren, I am sorry if I frightened you. You don't need to be afraid of me. Remember, I told you I will never hurt you."

Donovan stands here gazing down at me with his emotionless eyes as his rigid body remains frozen, neither one of us willing to move. Suddenly a rare glimpse of emotion races across his face like a shooting star in the dark night, revealing an agonized expression. Abruptly he turns his back to me, instantly hiding the glimpse I was given. His voice darkens to a smooth, haunting tone as he pleads, "Lauren, why are you here?"

There didn't seem to be a question in what he said, but more of a plea, as if he is trying to remind me of why I decided to come to Mt. Diablo – now – in the rain, even. A deep flicker of courage ignites within me and rises to the surface, causing me to feel like a gladiator who is standing before a frightening lion. Hardening my chin and trying to hide my quivering voice, I add, "What do you mean, why am I here? Why are you here?"

Feeling the cold, wet ground seeping through me I realize I have to get up. I can't sit down here on the ground in a submissive position. I have to put myself in a less vulnerable situation by not allowing him to tower over me. As I start to stand up Donovan walks over to me to help me up. Immediately I raise one of my hands, stopping him from coming any closer. The only thing I want from him at this point is some answers – starting with why he is here.

Reacting to my abrasive gesture he reluctantly backs up, giving me the space I desire. Both of us stand here in the pouring rain silently staring at each other. I need to know why he is here, yet I can barely think. His raw sexuality and extreme good looks cause me to go tongue-tied and brain dead. This is the first time

I'm able to fully examine him in the daylight. My heart begins vigorously racing against my chest like a team of wild horses fighting to be released from their imprisoning cage. An intense desire for him trembles within me, reigniting the pilot light constantly burning within me now.

As I try to grab hold of the uncontrollable desire racing through me, I catch sight of Donovan's face. Though my brain doesn't seem to be working, it appears that I have the upper hand right now. His slumped posture and broken down expression reveals some sort of internal torture he is going through. If I'm going to get any answers I need to act now, while I have a chance. I need to take advantage of the position I am in and not relinquish my obvious power here.

He needs to answer my questions first this time. Last night he called all the shots because I was sucked into his absolute beauty, but I can't let it happen again. This time he is going to answer my questions first if he wants me to answer his at all.

Unwavering power rushes through me like a protective armor, shielding me from any impending blows. In an instant I have gone from being terrified to feeling like I have some control in this situation. I have no idea where this tenacious strength is coming from, but I like it. I'm fed up with this whirlwind I have been sucked into, all I want is some simple answers.

"Donovan," I inhale slightly after saying his name. Firmly resolute in my position, I demand, "You need to answer my question first this time." Then sighing, I add respectfully, "Please."

"Lauren, by answering my question, you will receive the answers you want from me." He stands here looking into my eyes, pleading with me to think about what he is saying.

"That makes no sense, Donovan. By answering *your* question first how will I be answering mine? That's a bunch of bullshit. You just don't want to respond to any of my questions," I yell. He is playing mind games with me and I'm not going to take it.

"Lauren, think about it, please," he pleads again. "You need to figure this out on your own." Donovan cautiously makes his way towards me until his seductive physique is just within a few inches of mine, causing my breathing to vibrate anxiously in anticipation. This time I don't try to stop him. My mind goes completely blank. This isn't the type of retribution I was expecting from Donovan. I thought for sure he was going to be angry with me for forcefully standing up to him, but instead his tender hands land gently on my shoulders. Heat radiates from his hands, warming me up as he gazes respectfully into my eyes, uttering soothingly, "Why did you come here? What are you seeking, Lauren?"

My mind is swimming in a murky sea of confusion. How can answering his stupid question answer mine? I don't understand why I have to figure this out on my own. Can't he just answer my simple question?

Soothing warmth emanates out of his hands like heating pads and rolls down my spine, infusing peace into every muscle and relaxing my tense shoulders. Though I want his hands to stay where they are as long as possible, I know I will not be able to focus on the task at hand if his touch remains on me.

As I back away from his enticing hold on me, his hands once again drop effortlessly to his side. Turning my back toward him I walk over to the edge of the observation deck, gazing bewilderingly at the breathtaking views below. The rain slowly dissipates as the swirling ominous clouds start ripping apart, casting streaming translucent sunbeams onto the valley below. Vibrant colors burst from the valley floor as the rays of light ignite the freshly washed scenery.

I stare out at the valley trying to picture in my mind the story William told me. Gazing down into the thicket where the Chupcan village must have been, I try to imagine how this sinister demon allowed the Chupcan Indians to escape the Spanish military. And how the general saw this man who had no color to his eyes, causing him to run away yelling, "El Diablo" – the devil.

Swirls of confusion vividly race through my mind as to the possible reality of a frightening world I never believed existed. Deep within the pit of my stomach I can feel the quivering heat of fear radiating out, bubbling viciously just under the surface of my skin. As I replay the fearful events from last night, the trembling anxiety swelling within me intensifies. I can still picture Donovan's eyes as they frightfully transformed in front of me. Can Donovan be the same sinister demon William spoke of in the folklore? Immediately my mind recalls the information William shared with me on how demons are just evil spirits and Donovan is not a spirit. I know Donovan has a body of flesh – I have felt his tangible, warm and supple skin pressed firmly against mine.

"What are you thinking about, Lauren?" Again he is not posing a question but merely wanting me to add a voice to my thoughts. "Have you come up with an answer yet?" he intently prods.

His low and rumbling voice now echoes from right behind me, causing an eerie tinge to shudder through me. He had discreetly walked up to me, causing our bodies to nearly touch. His warm, sweet breath now softly pours down on me like heat from the warm sun. I breathe in his dark, rich earthy smell – like wild Redwoods and mountain ferns just before a summer shower. It seeps deep into my soul, instantly releasing the quivering energy rolling beneath my skin, causing me to vibrate uncontrollably.

Donovan wraps both of his firm arms around me, trying to control the violent shaking I am succumbing to. Reluctantly he utters, "Lauren, maybe we should leave so you can go someplace and get warm."

"No, I'm just fine. You are not about to leave me yet," I reply with more zeal than I intended.

"But you are shivering," he states as he wraps his arms even tighter around me.

"I'll be fine, t-t-trust me," I utter morosely, trying to hide the pleasure pulsating through me from his touch.

An intense amount of heat begins flowing fervently from him, permeating deep into my center causing me to internally ignite, warming me deep within. The temperature seems to heat up as his arms tighten around me. Donovan's warm, seductive frame nearly engulfs me, protecting my saturated, trembling body from the cool penetrating air. Gently I caress the back of his warm silken hand with the tips of my fingers, trying to convince my imaginative brain that Donovan is really not an evil spirit. The muscles in his strong hand pulsate vigorously against the tips of my fingers. My hand gently caresses his soft, supple skin while extreme heat radiates off of him. It's as if his skin houses an internal furnace raging inside of him, exuding heat out of every pore. How can I think he is a demon when I can feel his sensual build up against me right now?

"Lauren, tell me why you are touching my hand right now?" His voice is once again pleading with me in a calm, quiet and buttery tone. No matter how hard I try I can't seem to fight his low, soothing voice. His pleading words resonate deep within me, compelling me to answer him even if it means Donovan will be offended or upset with my ridiculous assumptions.

Exhaling forcefully, I reluctantly answer his plea, "I had to feel for myself that you are…" I hesitate slightly, then quietly utter, "…real."

"What do you mean, *real*?" he states calmly.

"That you are flesh, not…" Quivering fear consumes my vocal cords, making it extremely difficult to continue. A long silence tears through us while I mentally choose my words carefully. It's absolutely ridiculous that I am even thinking he can possibly be an evil spirit.

My overanxious nerves quake against the firm, muscular grip he is holding on me. Suddenly I feel the muscles in his arms tighten up around me as a loud exhale forcefully exudes out of his mouth, uttering the frightful words for me. "That I am not an evil spirit." His veiled voice remains flat though I detect a slight relieved tone in his breath, like I had just removed a huge weight off his shoulders.

This time it's me who is tensing up like I have just been hit by a bolt of lightning. My body instantly freezes as I stand here locked in his solid grasp, gazing fearfully out into the distance. How could he have known what I was about to say? How did he know I was making sure he wasn't a spirit?

Do I play off what he has just uttered like a joke or do I confront him dead on about it? Just then I hear him sigh again and release a slight laugh at the same time. "Lauren, not all of us are spirits. Some have bodies too, you know," he taunts in a creepy, yet serious tone.

"What? What are you telling me?" I whimper weakly, feeling the tears frightfully pool up within me. Nervous energy bubbles viciously within my stomach, causing me to feel like I'm going to be sick. The trembling in my muscles intensifies. I'm not sure if I want to hear the answer.

"I told you if you figured out why you are here you would know why I am here." His flat voice lacks any emotion in his words while his rigid arms continue to hold a firm and unyielding grasp around me.

Extreme panic consumes my imprisoned body as I realize I have no idea what he wants from me. My arms suddenly react defensively to what he has just confirmed. Instantly I aggressively try to push myself away from him. I writhe in Donovan's constricting grip, attempting everything within my power to break free from the abnormally strong grasp he has on me. Instantly I start kicking and screaming, but the harder I try to pry myself away, the stronger his hold on me intensifies.

"Let go of me, Donovan. Let me go," I plead with him in near hysterics.

"No, you need to hear me out first. I promise I won't hurt you," he implores. His voice is firm but calm at the same time.

There isn't an ounce of weariness or strain to his voice. I doubt he is even using all of his strength to restrain me.

"I don't need to do anything first. You are telling me to trust you when you have given me no reason to believe you. I don't even know who or what you really are. Let me go!" I yell at the top of my lungs.

My nearly exhausted body is trying everything within my meager power to break free from him, but his strength is unnatural like I am trying to break out of a solid concrete fortress. I am doing more damage to myself than to him. There is absolutely no hope in me escaping his grasp. I'm not strong enough to break free. Here I stand in a sinister man's grasp, completely vulnerable and alone, with no way for help or escape. Even if there is somebody up here, I highly doubt they would be able to win a battle against a possible monster.

"Please Lauren, if I let you go will you just hear me out? Then you can leave if you want to," he pleads.

At this point I have no other option but to agree to his demands. I'm a prisoner within his grasp and there is no way I can escape. I know somehow I need to get up the courage to just listen to him. If I just listen to him then he promised I can go.

Relaxing my muscles, I slowly give in to his request, relinquishing my incessant attempts at trying to break free from his solid grasp. As I give in to his unyielding demands my mind begins flooding with thoughts of my imminent demise, which totally terrifies me. My tears that have been pooling up feverishly within pour out uncontrollably, streaming down my quivering face like a rushing river consuming everything within its path. Uncontrolled terror rips through me, causing fear to flood into every crevasse of my trembling body.

Slowly I feel the muscles within his arms starting to relax their iron grip. He slowly releases the tight grip he held on me. He pushes his warm torso away from me, allowing the cool air to wash over me, completely extinguishing the heat that once warmed me internally. Chills roll through me, causing me to break out in goosebumps. I stand here in trembling fear, debating whether or not to turn around and face him. Digging deep within my soul for some sort of strength, I finally get up the courage to turn around and confront Donovan. As I spin around Donovan is no longer standing behind me. Intently I look all around to see where he has gone, when suddenly I notice he is now sitting on the ground with his back up against the stone wall of the railing. His head is bowed down with his face buried dejectedly in his hands. His tormented appearance gives very little up, but I suspect there is more going on within his head than he is willing to divulge.

Numbly I stand here completely baffled by the feelings rolling around in my head. Part of me is so angry I want to go over and kick him when he is down. Yet there is another part of me that feels sorry for him, like an injured lion. As hard as I try not to feel sorry for him I can't stop myself. The gravitating pull towards him is intense, but the possibility of being bitten is a reality. A lion can't help but bite, it is in his nature. I am not sure what is in Donovan's nature – yet.

I know he needs to tell me something, but I'm terrified of what that something could be. Whatever it is he needs to tell me it can't be any worse than what he has already alluded to. Deep down I know things are never going to be the same again.

"Lauren, I can't look at you right now. Feeling your pain at this moment is torturing me enough. If I look at you… well, let's just say I can't allow myself that kind of pain," he murmurs into his hands.

"So does that mean I can go now?" I snap. The instant I utter those words I regret it. For some strange reason I'm not quite sure if I want to leave yet.

"No, not yet. I have to tell you everything first. Then I promise you can go," he sighs.

Lifting his head up out of his hands he places his chin despondently on his fingertips. Trying to avoid my emotional meltdown that is vividly present on my face he stares thoughtfully out into the distance. "Lauren, if you could only ask me one question, what would it be?" His voice sounds weak yet direct and to the point.

"Are you saying I can ask you anything and you will answer it?"

He looks straight into my eyes as our gazes lock. Though his eyes are emotionally void, the soft lines around his eyes deepen, etching his chiseled features into a tortured pain. His brow narrows, deepening the furrow between his eyes. For just a brief moment as his eyes bore deep into mine, I could have sworn I felt his unimaginable torment racing throughout his slumped and dejected frame. An immense amount of sadness and regret pours out of his dispirited facial features, a shattered glass left in sharp pieces on the floor. His slumped shoulders appear as if he is bearing the burdens and sufferings of many people.

My mind pierces through his hard outer shell, allowing me to feel two distinct cadences streaming out of him, overpowering all the other burdens he carries. One is a searing regret for what he has done to me; and the other powerful emotion flowing through him is for someone who at one time meant the world to him but destroyed his life. The excruciating pain pouring out of him hits me like an avalanche flowing over me, causing me to collapse up against the same portion of the stone wall Donovan is leaning against. Donovan is sincerely a tortured soul, whether by his own choices or innocently thrown into it I will find out – soon.

Quickly he turns his head away from me, damming off the flow of his pain as if he knows he is causing me some sort of agony. A sudden realization flows over me. He wanted me to feel his unbearable agony so I will understand that he is not a thoughtless monster reveling in the torture of others. He is completely tormented by everything he has done or will do to anyone. This brief look into his pain causes my heart to instantly break for him. This is not what he wants to be.

"Lauren, I am giving you a chance to ask me one question, any – one – question," he promises.

"So you are only going to let me ask one question. That is not fair, Donovan. One question is going to lead to another and another. So you are telling me you are going to only answer the first one," I whine.

Wrapping my arms tightly around myself I start rubbing my hands vigorously back and forth against my arms. This is the first time all day I am actually feeling chilled to the bone. The cool breeze is blowing through my wet clothes like natural air conditioning.

Donovan peers over at me with examining eyes. "Lauren, you're getting too cold, maybe we should do this later," he demands.

Great, I knew he was going to notice me trying to get warm. I don't want to leave yet. I am finally going to get an answer to at least one of my questions. "No," I utter firmly. "You said I can ask any question and you promised to answer it. I'm not leaving until I have an answer from you," I reply forcefully.

"Are you sure you are ready for the answer?" he states with a riotous smile.

"Ready or not, I have to have an answer."

Donovan turns towards me as he lifts one arm up to the edge of the wall, pulling himself up to a standing position, preparing himself for the impending question. Gazing up at Donovan I realize I liked it better when he was sitting down on the ground. He is so much taller than me that his height intimidates me, along with everything else about him.

"Lauren, choose your question wisely. You only get one." A slight twisted smile spreads across his face as he utters his warning. Hopefully that means he will answer all my questions, but in case he doesn't I'd better make it a good one.

All the questions I want answers to begin flooding through my mind like a freight train racing vigorously down a mountainside. Different thoughts flow through my head, like: Why can I feel him peering into my soul; what happened to me in the club; why were there two hours unaccounted for; and how can his eyes go completely clear sometimes? As I think about all these questions none of them seem to answer the real burning question. If I truly only have one question – I know what it is going to be.

"What exactly are you? Are you some sort of a demon or something like that?" I spit it out so fast my mind has no chance to actually take in what I had just asked. I can't believe I actually just asked Donovan if he is a demon. It is too late to take it back. I have to ask the question, he has not given me a solid answer yet as to what he actually is. I know my answer is soon coming.

His face and body remain pleasantly even, unaffected by my question. Is he mad or offended? I am not sure if he thinks I'm insane or if he knows I have hit the nail on the head. He is not about to let me see or feel any of his emotions now. I'm going to have to patiently wait for his answer.

Donovan leans up against the wall, his face void of any expression. Stillness looms in the air while I wait impatiently for him to acknowledge my question. The silence is almost deafening when suddenly he turns his head abruptly and looks at me. A slight crooked smile gleams on his face – the first positive emotion he has exhibited since he mysteriously showed up on the mountain. A good sign… I hope.

"You know Lauren, that was two questions, not one," he specifies with a slight smirk on his face.

"No, it wasn't." I have to think for a moment. I mumbled the question so fast that I don't remember what I said. I asked him what he is, if he is a demon or something. I guess technically it was two questions. Leave it to him to find some reason to void out our agreement. Pushing my wet hair out of my face, I contend sheepishly, "Okay, so technically it was two questions, but they go hand in hand, Donovan. So in a way it was kind of one question. Are you going to argue or answer the question?"

The fear is still vividly resonating from my face along with the bloodshot eyes from my crying session I had just gone through. The tears that had been streaming down my face are barely beginning to dry. Despite all the trepidation I'm having about this whole situation I am able to gather my strength and hold firm to making him answer my question.

His smile starts to slowly dissipate from his face. The smile that was a source of brief comfort for me is now gone. It has been replaced by a morose, yet agonized appearance. "Yes," his voice is low and buttery smooth.

"Yes, what? Yes, you will answer the question, or yes, you are a demon?" I specify, not sure I am ready to hear the answer.

Looking at me intently Donovan's eyes bore deep into mine. His hands slowly lift up to his face, morosely covering his eyes then dragging them aggressively up until his hands fiercely rummage through his hair. Grabbing onto a handful of wet hair he feverishly clamps onto it while letting out a disconsolate moan. Still holding onto his hair like a safety net he turns reluctantly toward me, uttering, "Yes to both." He admits, "I am answering your question right now. I am, in fact, a demon. Technically demons are spirits, for the most part. In my case and in several others, we are more of a…" There is a thoughtful pause, "… I guess you would call it an enslaved soul."

His voice is calm and gentle-sounding like he is simply explaining the ABCs to an innocent child. There is no anger or guile in his voice. He is just uttering a simple fact as soothingly and calmly as possible.

Ravenous anxiety instantly consumes me, causing my fear to race frantically through my veins. It is one thing to think Donovan could possibly be a demon, but it is a whole other ball game to have the scenario actually come true.

I can see Donovan's mouth moving but there is no noise or words coming out of him. All I can hear is a deep thunderous pounding in my ears like I am drowning in a stormy sea. Quivering convulsions roll over me, causing me to become numb as my breathing increases. Slowly the colors fade and darkness creeps across my vision while gravity presses down on my tingling body. Next thing I know, Donovan is at my side sitting me on the ground, gently pressing my head between my knees. Gradually my hearing begins to come back as the lightheadedness slowly dissipates, leaving me feeling weak.

"Lauren, are you all right? Do I need to take you to a doctor?" he asks in a concerned tone of voice.

My eyes widen in surprise as I turn and look at him owlishly. Can he even take me to the doctor? He's a demon. Even if he is capable of taking me, what would I tell the doctor? "Oh, I am fine, doctor. I just passed out because I found out the guy of my dreams is a damn demon," I think to myself.

"Lauren, I can take you to the doctor. I do have a body of flesh, you have felt it," he utters as if he knows what I am thinking.

"Mm-hmm, sure. Then what do I tell him – that I nearly passed out when I found out you are a demon?" I murmur sarcastically.

Just saying it out loud makes me feel sick to my stomach. I can feel the vomit in my throat rising. At any moment I'm going to lose it. "Oh crap, I think I am going to be sick. Move…" I jump up as fast as I can and lean over the side of the stone wall. I hang here weakly over the side feeling completely awful. I am so glad I didn't eat anything at William's house or else I would have lost it all right here in front of Donovan. As I lay my overheated cheek firmly against the cool, wet stone wall I can almost hear the sizzle from my overheated flesh as it relinquishes my quivering emotions engulfing me.

"Lauren, I am truly sorry for everything I have done to you. This is my fault entirely." His voice is soft as his eyes close tightly in torturous pain. "I told you last night when you find out what I have done, you will hate me as much as I hate myself."

Laying here against the cool wall I begin contemplating his statement. What has he done to me? I know there is definitely something wrong with me. I am having a hard time controlling my temper, which has never been a problem before. Lifting my cheek free from the cool stones I gaze up at Donovan, aggressively asking, "What do you mean? Have you done something to me? There is more to this scenario and you need to tell me now."

Donovan wraps his arms tightly around his legs and rests his chin on the tops of his knees, murmuring into the air, "I don't know if you can handle the rest right now. It's not going to get any better, I promise you."

CHAPTER 12

Enslaved by My Desires

The nervous bubbling sensation that had curdled my stomach is gone now, leaving just a sour taste in my mouth. Lifting my head up off of the cool wall, I gaze out at the trees and valley below. Everything around me appears to be spinning out of control like I am stuck on a giant merry-go-round. I hold onto the wall for balance as I slide my quivering back down the rock facing until my butt lands firmly on the ground.

Leaning up against the wall I slowly feel my strength start to return. Turning forcefully toward Donovan I stammer out, "Donovan, it doesn't matter if I can handle it or not. I have a right to know what you have done to me."

Donovan's head tilts slightly as his clear blue eyes examine every part of me in a scrutinizing manner, as if he were a psychiatrist determining my mental status. His eyes seem to pour all over me, searching every detail of my figure. His surreptitious gaze feels as if it is penetrating my clothes like x-ray vision. The insecurity within my mind thickens like molasses as I wonder if he is looking deep within my mind for any reason not to divulge what he has done to me.

I narrow my eyes, expelling a lethal look. Hissing in a strong, persuasive tone I add, "Donovan, you can't make the decision for me. It's not your choice if I can handle it or not. I have a right to know what is going on with me. If you are worried about me – don't. I promise I will be fine. I'm done freaking out."

"I don't know what you are talking about. Yes, I am worried about you, but I wasn't going to make any decision for you. What gave you that idea?" His response is indignant with a hint of confusion spiraling within his deep, breathy voice.

The bewilderment shadowing his face causes deep lines to etch into the supple skin around his eyes, unaffecting his deep penetrating focus on me. I stammer out, "Well, for starters it's the way you are staring at me. It's like you are examining me, making sure I can handle it or not."

"Well, you are wrong," he utters curtly. A pregnant pause lingers between us as his eyes remain fixated on me, then he adds hesitantly, "That is not why I am '*examining*' you." A slight coy smile pulls up on the corners of his full lips as it spreads fiercely across his face. A glimmer of embarrassment twinkles just under the watery surface of his shallow blue eyes.

"If I'm wrong, then what are you thinking?" I utter in confusion.

As he looks deep into my eyes he softly bites the inside of his bottom lip, tugging on the soft, supple skin as he tries fighting back a suspicious smile. He shakes his head quickly as if he is blocking out an inappropriate image. He gives me a gentle nod, making me feel like I'm missing some inside joke that is somehow centered on me.

"I will have to answer that at a later date – not now," he states amusedly as a slight laugh rolls out of his full supple mouth, sounding low like a guttural growl rather than a laugh.

"Why?"

"Well, because it has nothing to do with what we are talking about," he utters coyly as a timid smile brilliantly spreads across his face.

"You promise you will tell me later?" I utter timidly, realizing there was a hidden innuendo to what he had said.

"Yes, I promise." Then he adds nearly inaudibly, "Perhaps I will even show you."

There is no hidden insinuation to what he said. I can feel the lusting heat radiating out of him like a wildfire threatening to devour me. My eyes instinctively gravitate toward his mystifying and luscious mouth as I frantically watch him continue biting on his bottom lip. My undulating mind quivers with shocks of electricity as his mouth holds me hostage in erotic thoughts. My unbridled emotions run on autopilot like I have lost all control over them. Searing passion bursts through me like a giant hurricane rushing into my heart and expanding to every part of me. A heavy pant consumes my breathing as I fight back the urge to lean over and bite onto his bottom lip. Just the thought of having his supple lip between mine causes a herd of wild horses to explode within my stomach, sending twinges of aftershocks to roll down my thighs.

Confusion washes over me as to why I'm feeling this way. My uncontrolled thoughts are not reacting the way I need them to. I should be mad or even scared, but I definitely shouldn't be turned on. This is ridiculous. Closing my eyes I try not to look at his sumptuous mouth anymore. Shaking my head vigorously, I attempt to get the burning sensual image of his seductively full lips out of my mind.

"Lauren, do you want to hear everything or not?" he asks seriously, trying to change the subject.

Immediately the tantalizing image burning in my mind is gone, snapping me right back to the horrifying reality I'm completely engulfed in. Opening my eyes, I slowly gaze at his face and not his hypnotic mouth. A gentle, sympathetic expression veils his once overtly sexual appearance, giving him an almost youthful and timid quality. The amused, yet embarrassed expression Donovan has streaming across his face causes my heart rate to accelerate as he gives me a smug look. Prickling terror washes down me as I grimace at the possibility that he knew what I desired to do to him. Swallowing the knot lodged in my throat, I utter breathlessly, "Sorry, what did you say?"

He enunciates each word slowly and precisely so I will understand what he is asking me, "Do – you – want to – hear – everything?"

Donovan's face gleams while he asks the question. Resting his elbow on his knee, Donovan lays his square jaw and cheek firmly in the palm of his hand. Donovan consciously nibbles at the nail of his little finger instead of his bottom lip. Instantly he looks up at me, giving me an over-exaggerated wink.

A fearful shudder rushes up my spine as I anxiously stare at his mischievous face. Please just let him be flirting with me and not that he knows why I was staring at his mouth. Nervously my mind starts spinning with incredulous thoughts. I am reading way too much into his simple wink. I need to just calm down. There is no possible way he knows what I was thinking. I didn't say anything out loud and I definitely didn't act on my desire.

Trying to control my thoughts so I can listen to what he needs to divulge, I pretend to wipe the excess water off my eyes as I discreetly slap my face, knocking some sort of sense back into me. "Yes, I do. Sorry, I am ready now."

His face immediately transforms from a smiling expression to a serious form in just a matter of seconds, switching his emotions off like a light switch. Mirroring his expression, mine takes a tumble down to depths of darkness as I realize this is going to be bad. I feel like I'm stuck on an emotional roller coaster I have no control over. I'm constantly rising up to extreme heights, then plummeting down to the deepest darkest depths of utter misery.

He spins completely around so that he is now facing me straight on, he now has the ability to examine my every reaction. I am sure he wants to make sure I will not get sick again or even worse, fall into a total mental breakdown. I feel like he thinks I'm this frail and weak person. But in reality I'm extremely strong. It's just not every day you come across a demon or an enslaved soul, as he put it.

"You have to do me a favor though," he asks.

I don't want to agree to something until I know what the favor is. "What is it?"

"You need to listen to the whole thing. Don't interrupt me until I am done telling you everything. There will be a few points where you will want to say something, but please just wait until the end. This is going to be hard enough for me to say and I will not be able to get through it if you are constantly interrupting me," he orders timidly.

"What if I have a question about something? You are telling me I can't ask it. That's not right." Irritation rushes through my perturbed mind as once again he is calling all the shots. It's taking everything within me to remain calm, which lately is almost impossible.

"There is no doubt you are going to have a lot of questions. I just need to get through everything, then I promise you I will respond to all of your unanswered questions," he clarifies.

Leaning forward up against my thighs I wrap my arms tightly around my legs, resting my chin on the tops of my knees. Deep down I know I'm going to have to agree to his demands if I want to hear the truth. I just hope he will keep his promise.

As I look up at him I notice he has moved and he too is leaning up against his thighs, resting his chin firmly on the tops of his knees. He is now straight across from me so that our knees are slightly touching each other. Placing his face just inches away from mine he wraps his arms around his legs tightly. Cautiously, with the tips of his fingers he tenderly, yet securely grabs onto my fingers. His long, strong fingers anxiously caress mine as if my hand is a worry stone that he can timidly take his nervous energy out on. His gentle touch on my fingers causes my heart to nearly beat audibly. Though his sudden touch excites me, a sense of peace floods my mind, eradicating the fear that wants to take control of me, allowing me to hear the truth.

Reluctantly I concede, gazing firmly into his clear blue eyes, "All right, I will do my very best to just listen."

Looking up he gives me a beautiful, encouraging smile. "Thank you. Don't worry, I will keep my part of the bargain also. I will answer anything and everything – later, I promise." There is firmness to his voice as he reassures me calmly.

He holds onto my fingers even tighter as if he is making sure I won't leave. I have yet to return the sentiment, leaving my fingers to dangle weakly, not sure of my emotions yet. Resting my chin against my knee I gaze off to the side, trying not to look at his distracting face. Suddenly I hear a loud sigh as he utters softly, "Lauren, to answer your very first question again. Yes, I am what you would call an enslaved soul. My body and my soul were lost in total servitude to higher demons. Because I gave it willingly I still have my body, but it is also in bondage. I am stuck serving a sentence that – let's just say, is for a very long time.

"It happened many years ago. Trust me when I say this was the last thing I ever wanted, but someone had to do it." His dark, thick voice weakens as his words trail off, like there is more to his story than he is willing to share with me at this time.

His dark, thick tone vibrates with regret and a tremendous amount of pain cutting off the breath to every word. As he bites through the words with a bitter disgust, his tone alludes to the fact that he is possibly serving someone else's sentence.

"There are true demons out there, Lauren, but they do not have bodies unless they possess them. They do, however, have names and definite personalities. You don't ever want to mess with them. There is not even an ounce of good left in them. Their only purpose is to collect as many souls as possible. Actually, that is what we are all trained to do. For me it is a little easier. I have a body that gains peoples' trust. I can easily find their desire then give it to them." His voice is dark and full of resentment as he speaks about these people. It's as if he has no pity for them, like they deserve what they get. They made their choice, where he had no choice in the matter.

His voice deepens as he growls out the rest, "Once they have their desires they are enslaved by the very things they once coveted. The things they wanted so desperately they would do anything for – except of course their own hard work – now those things bind them to hell."

"But, how..." Lifting my head up off my knee I stitch my brow together, deepening the furrow between my eyes as I utter in confusion, "How can you know what they want and how are you capable of giving it to them?"

He also lifts his head up, eyes firm while his liquid blue color solidifies with indignation, adding reprovingly, "Lauren, you promised."

Meeting his gaze head-on I wrinkle my nose apologetically, uttering, "I'm sorry. Go ahead."

Instantly I lay my cheek back onto my knee, hiding my face from his penetrating eyes. I can't have him see the fear streaming across my face from all the creepy things he is uttering. I'm not just afraid of him, but I'm also terrified about the viable and lethal spirit demons. If Donovan knows I exist, so do the spirit demons. This is a foreign world to me, something that only existed – or so I thought – in my nightmares. I can recall a time when I snuck off to my friend's church, curious of what went on behind all the closed doors. During the sermon I heard the minister say, "Be careful what you do so the devil won't possess your souls, dragging you down to hell." I remember arguing with him afterwards about how it was wrong to scare his congregation into being good, it doesn't bring trust. But now I will never argue with a minister ever again – it is all true.

Suddenly I feel Donovan grab onto my hand even tighter as if he is preparing me for what he is about to divulge. The extreme heat from his hand begins to intensify, radiating out like sizzling coals off of a burning fire. My fingers feel like little sausages cooking and blistering. Gingerly I wiggle my fingers, trying to allow the cool air to seep between our hands, hopefully stopping the heat from scorching my hand. Donovan suddenly loosens his tight smoldering grip, allowing the outside air to extinguish the searing heat.

Giving me an apologetic smile, he continues, "It is easy for us to find out what people want, Lauren. Most people don't ever go after their dreams because they don't know what their true desires are. Well, as demons we can sense or see…" He shoots me a quick surreptitious glance, continuing, "… what everyone's true desires are and feed on them. I know exactly what people want, I can see every malicious, seductive or enticing act."

Instantly I look up only to notice Donovan is now gazing at me intently. My heart starts pounding rapidly, causing my face to flush a hot pink color. The heat continues filling my face and pouring down my spine with a sudden realization. He knows all of my passionate desires I have had and will have for him. They play out in his mind like some seedy movie for him to enjoy – his own personal adult channel.

Giving me a quick, penetrating glance he then, with a beguiling smile, adds, "It is like my mind is full of all these strangers' own personal movies. Sometimes I wish I could just shut it off. But other times, I do have to admit, they are truly entertaining to view." He gives me a quick teasing smile, then immediately looks down at our intertwined hands, continuing, "When we know what they sincerely want, we can offer it to them, until that desire has them completely enslaved by it. Before they know it their souls are gone. It is almost always something to do with the seven sins: lust, greed, gluttony, envy, wrath, sloth and of course, pride which cometh before the final fall to hell."

His voice thickens with disgust as he stares pensively down at my fingers, delicately twirling my fingers within the tips of his. "The interesting thing is whatever I want, I get. If I want a fast car, money or lust I can get it. We are immune to the chains that bind humans to hell because we are already there." He pauses briefly, adding sarcastically, "Lauren, I don't actually have a house there, you know."

I quickly glance up at Donovan, noticing his large smile spreading across his face. It reveals his perfectly white teeth against his crimson mouth. He is attempting to lighten the mood, but it isn't going to work. The reality of what I have been sucked into presses down on me like a vise, crushing all hope out of me.

He must have noticed my unresponsive gesture to his quick humor because he adds explanatorily, "I was just speaking metaphorically. Our souls are already damned." He gives me a quick smile. I am not able to return his smile. I don't think it's funny that he is damned at all. Looking at him I form my mouth into a tight line, laying my head back down on my knees.

He gently sighs, adding, "Well, I should clarify something first. I am not technically immune to the consequences of acting on my desires. I have more to lose than the spirit demons do – I can lose my eternal body. Every time I give in to my desires I risk losing not just my soul, but me – completely. When I say completely, I mean it," he repeats strongly. "I wouldn't be able to sit here talking to you right now. I would be full of guile, so much so that all I would want is your soul to be in hell. There would be nothing left of me. I would be entirely evil.

"Lauren, I am holding onto whatever humanity I have left in me. As long as I have some kind of hope that there is a way out of this, I can't give up. I may be an enslaved servant of evil, but that does not mean I am evil. Please try to understand, I was once a decent person and that person still exists somewhere within me. It is something I have to fight daily, not giving in to my physical desires." His fingers grip tightly onto mine as a heavy sigh rushes through his mouth. "There is one desire I will always regret having." His nearly inaudible voice seems to echo in my mind with a loud intensity, "You – You are my desire."

My slouching posture springs straight up as I gaze at him with wide owl eyes. What does that mean for me? My head feels like it is swimming in debris-filled water, making it hard for my thoughts to stay afloat. Chills race up and down my spine like an electrical circuit in my veins has just switched on. The hairs on the back of my neck stand erect as the murky water in my mind slowly becomes transparent. I have a very bad feeling I'm about to hear what he has done to me.

"Lauren, you were not my desire – at first. I was sent to give you your desire then capture your soul."

I push down a thick audible gulp as I hear him utter the terrifying reality. I can't be hearing him correctly. Did he just say he was sent to take my soul? Shivers move up my shoulders like breathy fingers tickling the surface of my skin. The imaginary fingers press down on my shoulders, seeping into my chest, squeezing my heart and taking over my quivering, catatonic body.

"You will be surprised to know I have already given you one of your desires… and no, it is not what you think," he says sheepishly, giving me another one of his coy, yet mischievous smiles. I stare blankly as the words he says hum like he is standing at the end of a long tunnel.

Donovan's face quickly transforms into a dark, sinister gaze. "Lauren, several days ago you were on the phone with your mother. When she was telling you about her new trip she was planning and you wanted off the phone…"

"How did…" He quickly looks up again, giving me a stern look. Raising my hand instantly I place it over my mouth. I had broken my promise yet again, but I don't care. How did he know about that conversation? Instant scenarios start flooding my mind as to how Donovan could have known this information. Perhaps my mother knows Donovan, but that would mean she knows what Donovan is and that's not possible. My mother is a horrible mom, but not an evil person who deals with demons… but I'm a good person too, so why am I in this situation?

"Lauren, are you going to listen?" he demands in a sharp, snappy voice.

"Yes, I'm going to listen, but just to warn you, my list of questions is building up quickly," I answer, my voice sounding barbed, yet confident while internally I am a mess.

Rolling his eyes impatiently, he utters hastily, "I know they are piling up. I wouldn't have expected anything less. Now, please let me finish? I am almost done."

I give Donovan a forced smile, letting him know he can now continue. But he doesn't smile back. As his gaze drops, his shoulders and posture deflate like an old helium balloon shrinking. "During the phone conversation with your mother you said, and I quote 'something, help me.' There soon came a knock at your mother's door."

I know I told him I wouldn't get sick again, but this is too much. He is repeating the exact words I said to my mother and he wasn't anywhere in my house. A sharp sensation drills into my abdomen, causing it to toss and turn as the anxiety of what I'm hearing curdles my stomach. This time I really am going to be sick.

"Lauren, when she stated she needed to go, you wished you could have thanked the person for saving you." Peering deep into my eyes, Donovan utters firmly in a tight rigid voice, "You can thank me now."

I jump to my feet, ripping my hand away from his. My breathing intensifies to a quick shallow pace. I begin pacing back and forth, shaking my numbing hands rapidly, attempting to get some feeling back in them. I hastily mumble out every thought flooding my mind, "How can this be? This can't be real. I don't understand how he could have even known I was going to want help. How did he know where my mom lived or that she was even going to call me? And who sent him to do this to me?" I am ranting incoherently without making any verbal sense as I fall deeper into an abyss. "I am such an idiot to believe someone like him would ever like me. I am a gullible bad judge of character who naïvely believed that he liked me. And for the first time in over a year I was beginning to feel alive, but I'm just another assignment for him to drag down to hell. Well, he has successfully done his job. I'm in hell, right now!"

"Lauren, stop," he snaps back as he grabs me in his arms, locking them around me like a vise and stopping me from my hysterical rambling and pacing. "I know what you are feeling right now and it is not true. I told you that you would want to interrupt me several times, but you can't. You haven't heard the whole story yet. Don't assume anything about me without hearing the whole thing first. Please calm down, please. It is important you don't lose your temper." His tense, solid arms hold onto me tightly while he pleads with me in a low and firm voice.

His calm, soothing voice is speaking to me as if he were a counselor talking me through a rough situation. The deep, rumbling hypnotic tone filters from my over-anxious mind, easing the tense rage bubbling viciously within me. Softly he presses my head against his chest, engulfing my trembling torso with his strong, warm arms. He begins stroking the back of my head, attempting to calm me down while his other arm wraps tightly around my waist.

I completely let go of all my strength as my exhausted body goes limp in Donovan's arm. The muscles in Donovan's arm tighten up as he grips onto me, supporting my entire dead weight in just one arm. Closing my eyes tightly I try to fight back the tears that once again threaten to consume me.

"Lauren, yes, someone did send me for you, but when I peered into your soul on the freeway, I saw something different in you. You had no guile or lust searing within you, your soul was innocent. All you wanted was to change your situation after the tragic…" he clears his throat forcefully, continuing, "… demise of your father. Instantly the empty void within me filled with an unimaginable craving to see you again. I was a parched man who was gazing at a cool, dripping glass of ice water. All I wanted was to devour you completely, quenching the unyielding emptiness within me.

"Lauren, I knew you were going to be at the club that night and I had to see you again. When you arrived with your friends I saw you and a deep, yearning urge washed over me. I had to take you. As I gazed deep into your eyes I felt something I hadn't felt in a long time." His husky, rumbling voice lowers to an almost inaudible whisper. His arms tighten around me, pressing me into his chest. I melt into him, forming an unbreakable bond.

"I wanted you to be mine and no one else's. I knew the guy who was with you that night longed to be with you and I was not about to let him have you," he growls as his arm instinctively tightens up around me.

My mind begins to replay the events of the night and who this mysterious guy was who wanted me. He can't be talking about Larry. Larry was with Stacie that night – not me. There is absolutely no fire between him and me. I'm just a charity case in his eyes. Narrowing my eyes I proceed to correct his assumption by informing him of what really happened, "Donovan you are being ridiculous. Larry didn't want me. Besides, he was with someone else that night."

"Trust me. I know what I am talking about. Remember, I know what his true desire is and it is not for the other girl," he firmly corrects. "His deep yearning for you is what stirred up an intense anger within me. When I lose control it is very dangerous for me and everyone involved, but I couldn't allow him to have you. I needed to make you mine. A gushing want ignited within me as all my thoughts told me to take you, to make you all mine so he could never have you."

His voice drops to a near whisper, making it hard for me to hear him. He quietly continues, "I couldn't fight it, the feeling was too overpowering. I knew I was not strong enough to stop this temptation myself. I was going to lose this internal battle and you now have to be the one to pay the price for my lack of control."

"What did you do to me, Donovan?" I growl the demanding words. My voice is thick as I choke out the words. A sinister edge to my voice slices out of me – even frightening me. I try to look up at him but his grip on me tightens around my chest, locking me firmly against him. The harder I push away from him, the stronger he holds me against him.

Bending down close to my ear he softly whispers into it, emphasizing each word slowly and methodically, "I took you – or shall I say, I took your soul." His voice is breathy like an ocean breeze whispering against my face. He audibly exhales a soft sigh from his mouth as it washes down my quivering back.

The uncontrollable rage which constantly burns within me is now seeping out of my pores like a toxic gas spewing dangerous venom everywhere. My enraged muscles quiver violently against the firm, enveloping grasp Donovan has on me. Placing my trembling hands on his firm chest, I forcefully push as hard as I can against him. Reacting to my frantic demand he instantly flings open his arms, freeing me from his imprisoning hold. Backing away from him I look into his soft, blue tortured eyes. "You are telling me you damned my soul? Why!" I cry out. "How could you do this to me? This is my soul, not yours to take," I desperately plead.

"I tried, but I couldn't help it. I know it sounds like an excuse, but this is my nature now. And after it happened the guy who caused my jealousy rushed over to your aid. I looked into your eyes and instantly regretted it, but it was too late," he mutters with guilt. "My jealousy once again appeared as I watched the same guy take care of you. All because I selfishly acted upon my own desires, which now enslaves you and damns me even more." He shamefully utters, "I promise you, Lauren, I will fix this – somehow. Even if it means I have to go to Lucius himself and beg for your soul to be freed. I will do it."

"You had no right to take it. I'm innocent, remember?" I clarify in a barbed tone. As my physique tightens my lethal gaze seems to rip him apart, causing him to back away from me.

"You're right, I can't just take it. Not without at least a small amount of your consent, which you did give," he sighs.

Rippling waves of anger rush through me, causing my muscles to pulsate as if electrical shocks are shooting violently through me. I never gave him permission to condemn my soul. I had no idea what he is and if I would have known I would have run far from him. Curling my fingers into a tight fist, gripping down until my knuckles are white, I swing forcefully at his jaw. His hand instantly snaps up, stopping my fist just inches away from his taut jaw. Instant pain shoots through my knuckles like I have slammed my fist against a brick wall, not his hand. Biting down on my tongue I try to hide the immense pain pulsating in my hand. Closing my eyes tightly, I push down the writhing sensation threatening to take over me.

His large hand wraps firmly around my fist, holding my hand prisoner. My frame shakes internally with violent hysterics as my dark voice shrieks forcefully, "How dare you say I gave you permission to destroy my life?"

His eyes intensely look at me. "I didn't say you gave me verbal permission, Lauren," he clarifies, still holding onto my fist. "You gave me permission with your thoughts and desire you have for me. I just took that small opportunity and acted on it. You desire me and I want you." He bends down and gently presses his lips to the back of my hand. Heat from his warm lips penetrates my skin, soothing the throbbing pain. "Is your hand all right?"

Ripping my hand away from his, I gaze up at him with a toxic mixture of anger and lust, snapping, "I'm fine." As I protectively grab hold of my hand I notice a slight smile creep into the corner of his mouth. I gulp audibly, fully aware he is right. I had -- and still do have -- a desire for him. Whispering, I add, "You acted on my lust for you."

Immediately I recall what Donovan said about granting people their desires until it completely destroys them, but was my desire for him really an opportunity for him to take me? I don't see how lusting after him is so bad. My heart instantly sinks as I remember the sins he talked about earlier. "My lust for you is one of the seven sins," I whisper softly as I gaze at him with a flat, livid expression on my face.

He didn't take my soul unjustifiably. He definitely had justification. There is no way I can get out of this. I am on a slippery slope with no way off. No matter what I do it is going to lead me down to hell.

"Yes, I acted on your lust for me, but I promise you if I have to condemn myself to a deeper pit of hell to free you, I will do it. This is entirely my fault, not yours." His weak, breathy voice rolls through the cold mist like smoke from a dragon, sweeping over my skin with his tortuous remorse.

Gazing deep into his emotionless eyes I notice a glimpse of grief beginning to rip through the shimmering glass walls of his flat, inexpressive eyes. As angry as I am, the darkest part of me is still captivated by him. I want so badly to hate him, but I can't. I have no idea what he has and still is going through. What he did to me is the type of act he detests with every fiber of his body. To sentence someone he cares about to an imprisoned life like his is the strongest form of wickedness.

Slowly I walk away from him as my spinning mind tries to make sense out of all this uncertainty. Mindlessly I stare out into the distance, wondering why all this mayhem is happening to me when all I wanted was a better life. I guess I need to be more careful of what I wish for – it just may come true. My heart quickens as I realize this unbelievable situation I am in is due to me. Even though I knew there was something scary about Donovan, I wouldn't listen to my inner voice. All I want is him. My heart and soul yearns for him like a missing piece in a complicated puzzle. Wrapping my arms around myself I begin rubbing my arms, trying to fight back the fearful shivers rippling through me. The gravitational pull I feel toward Donovan is undeniable. I was – and still am – completely enamored by him and no matter how hard I try, everything keeps telling me to stay with him.

"Donovan, it's not all your fault. I'm the one who wanted a change and yes, I want you too," I state coyly as I cover my eyes, completely horrified about what I just admitted. Every emotion imaginable is running rampant throughout my beaten down body and soul. My emotions feel like they are stuck on a teeter-totter, constantly going up and down.

"You did nothing wrong, Lauren. It is perfectly normal for you to want your life to be different. And it is also normal to be attracted to someone. It is just not normal or right for me to desire those things. I lost my right to those things a long time ago." He pauses slightly, then murmurs, "Now, so have you."

"What do you mean by that? Are you telling me I no longer have a right to feel passion for anything anymore?" I cry.

"Not exactly."

The heat from Donovan washes over my back as he walks towards me. His strong hand securely wraps around my arm, gently spinning me around so he can see my face. My hands remain firmly placed over my eyes to block him from peering into them. I am too afraid to look at him right now. I can't allow him to see the smoldering desire that I still have for him.

Donovan slowly places his hands carefully on my arms, allowing the heat of his hands to flood through me like a hot breeze. His searing fingertips lightly slide their way up towards my shielding hands, causing my overexcited skin to suddenly explode with goosebumps. The speed of my ragged breathing increases with every affectionate glide of his delicate fingertips. Instantly my unbridled desire for him explodes with a trembling moan that escapes forcefully from me.

He wraps his hands around mine gently while softly pulling them away from my shielded eyes. His voice is low and velvety smooth, "Lauren, open your eyes."

Though I am not completely ready to look at Donovan, I know I can't just stand here with my eyes closed. I have to look at him. As I slowly open my eyes my thunderous heart just about stops. Donovan's face is within inches of mine, staring at me. His liquid blue eyes are filled with an indescribable amount of passion swimming vibrantly within them. Looking at his ravenous, passion-filled eyes, my stomach flutters with overwhelming excitement. Searing heat from the pit of my stomach radiates out like a giant explosion, forcefully sending waves of uncontrolled passion pulsating within my veins.

"Lauren, trust me, you can still feel passion. In fact, you will feel it with more intensity than you have ever experienced before. The difference is you can't ever completely give in to it." A heavy sigh rolls out of his plush lips as he clarifies, "What I mean is you can't let it cause you to lose total control."

A live wire of pulsating energy rushes through my body, getting ready to explode out of me at any moment. His warm hands on my skin trigger my heart to beat rapidly as the intense passion within me begins to overflow. The untamed pilot light constantly burning within me simmers silently, waiting to ignite whatever emotion I have at that moment. With all this emotional craziness no wonder I am teeter-tottering on the edge of insanity lately. I'm feeling everything flooding through me at an emotionally charged level.

Suddenly his hands drop from mine as he backs away slightly. The expression on his face quickly transforms before me as a dark aura snuffs out the passion that had been flaming within his eyes. The countenance on his face burns with a fervent caution. "I need to warn you," he implores in a deep, husky voice, "remember how I explained if I lose control and completely give in to my desires it puts me closer to entirely losing myself? The same goes for you now. Lauren, you can experience desire and every other emotion. You just can't entirely give in to them." He warns, "It is important you don't lose your temper. It will be easier for you to lose control, to get extremely angry at any little thing. When you completely give in to temptation things around you will start to look different. Colors may change, become distorted or even vibrant, but your thoughts will remain completely aware of everything."

My heart instantly stops while my stomach violently twists and turns. Fear slithers down my spine and gradually wraps around my ribs as I tremble internally, causing my knees to buckle.

"Lauren, are you okay?" Donovan utters as he rushes over to my side.

"I don't know if I am." Cupping my hands around my cheeks I add weakly, "Earlier today I experienced something like you described when I lost my temper with my mother. Extreme anger rushed through me as I stood there staring at her. Then suddenly everything around me turned a bright shade of red." I look up at Donovan with wide doe eyes, reluctantly continuing, "There in the middle of the red scene stood my mother in full vibrant color. The strangest thing happened next. I could have sworn I heard my mother talking crudely, but when I confronted her about it she looked dumbfounded – even denying my accusations. It felt like I was going crazy."

A stream of horror shoots across Donovan's flawless face, causing me to stiffen in fear. "Lauren, you didn't go crazy. You did hear your mother. It just wasn't her voice you heard though, it was her inner desires," he frowns with concern.

"Wait, are you telling me I heard my mother's true desires of her heart?" I utter in shock.

"Yes, you allowed yourself to delve deep enough into the darkness where you were able to hear your mother's true intention. That usually takes time before you can do it without completely losing yourself in the process. I am surprised you were able to stop yourself." Donovan sighs in disbelief as he bends down and gazes forcefully into my eyes. "Promise me you will control your emotions," he begs.

"I promise," I reply gently as a numbing sensation pricks the tips of my fingers.

My oversaturated mind swirls around the validity of what had happened to me. The frightening reality of what could have transpired is visible on Donovan's mesmerizing and hypnotic face. Each of his facial features are taut as the corners of his jaw quiver beneath his supple skin. The thick, nearly tangible air swirls around us as I visually take in his masculine presence. Though I could stay here with Donovan indefinitely, I'm not sure how much more my heart can endure.

"Donovan, I'm exhausted from all the information you have divulged. I need to go home and think things through – right now. I don't know how much more I can take. I feel like I'm going to pass out any moment."

"I understand, but…would you mind if I drive you home?" he asks as he gazes upon my silver-dollar-sized eyes, quickly adding, "I promise I won't talk at all. I will just drive you home." His eyelids lower as he hesitantly watches his wringing hands. A nervous air swirls around us as he adds softly, "Call me old fashioned, but I was raised to make sure the girl I am with gets home safely."

A gentle jolt quickly flips within my stomach as I fight back a coy smile. No matter what Donovan is or has done, his gentle voice and soothing expression cuts through me like a hot knife through butter. I know Donovan, deep down, is truly a gentle soul.

Peering deep into his beautiful, clear blue eyes I agree softly, "All right. I am not sure if I'm mentally capable of driving anyway."

A huge, brilliant smile spreads across his face revealing his perfectly white teeth. "Thank you," he utters gratefully. Gazing into my eyes he walks slowly up to me, sliding the backs of his fingers gently down my arm like he is stroking a delicate flower. His fingers lightly encircle the tips of mine. Gently he grabs hold of my hand and lifts it to his mouth, softly pressing the back of my hand against his warm lips. His lips linger there long enough for me to feel a slight burning sensation. He lifts his eyes toward me as he gives me an affectionate smile, adding in a low, husky tone, "Let's go."

He lowers my hand but still holds onto it as we silently walk toward the path leading down to my car. No matter who he is or what he has done I know I will never want him to leave me. Now that I have felt him in my life, if he were to leave there would be a huge void in my soul. The gravitating pull we have on each other is strong, like two worlds have collided forcefully together leaving an inextricable imprint, a void only the source of its impression can fill. The two worlds will never be the same again, like I know I will never be the same. Donovan has left a permanent impression on me that only he can fill.

I have no idea what is going to happen next, but I know he will do everything in his power to save me. And in return I am going to do everything in my meager power to save him.

Resting my head against the window of my car I gaze out, watching all the trees and scenery fly past me. The rushing surroundings begin melting into each other, erasing all the sharp lines. A kaleidoscope of streaming colors blend into one another until the vivid shades gradually fade into thick blackness as the humming silence lulls me into a deep, hypnotic sleep.

CHAPTER 13

$$\infty$$

Suspicious

A flickering of light penetrates my thin eyelids, causing me to squint as I push back the intrusive signs of daylight. Prying my heavy eyelids open I begin cautiously looking all around my room as I try to remember how I got into my bed last night. No matter how hard I try to remember, a shroud of mystery hovers over my mind. Donovan has no idea where I live and I know I didn't tell him how to get to my house. The last thing I remember was getting into the passenger side of my car as Donovan told me to lay back and rest. The only sounds echoing around me were the roar of the engine and an occasional sigh escaping from Donovan's firm, yet plump mouth.

My stomach flips with excitement as I scan my room for any sign of Donovan. Firmly I call out, "Donovan, are you here?"

I lay here quietly in my bed as I wait for Donovan to hopefully respond, but instead deafening silence ripples through my stagnant room. Donovan is gone again, leaving me alone with many unanswered questions. A heavy weight of sadness encircles my heart like hungry vultures readying themselves for a feasting frenzy.

My mind tries to recall every detail as to how I got in my apartment last night, but a void vibrates within my mind forcing me to surrender to the reality that I may never know. Slowly I get up from my bed, feeling the weight of everything I went through pressing down on me like a car crusher reducing my height. With every step I take my heavy feet slam against the floor with a loud thud as I attempt to make my way to the bathroom, hobbling like an old lady. Every step I take sends sharp pain running up and down my legs.

I gaze at the bathroom mirror expecting to see some monster image of myself staring back at me, but to my pleasant surprise it is just me and not a clear-eyed demon in the reflection. Carefully I examine every detail of my pale, lifeless face reflecting back at me. The hollow, almost emaciated expression on my face takes me aback. My sunken eyes and hollow cheeks accentuate my haggard, run-down appearance, causing me to utter in disgust, "Gosh Lauren, you look horrible."

My weak and tattered body feels and looks like I have been dragged through mud. Needing to wash off the grime from yesterday's rain, I start to peel off my dirty clothes. My jeans cling to my legs like stiff cardboard, unwilling to release their firm grip on me. As I strip the layers of unwanted memories from off myself, I slowly begin to feel life flow back into me.

Turning the shower water to as hot as I can possible take it, I quickly jump in, allowing the steaming water to breathe life back into me. The water gently showers onto my face, cascading down my back, relaxing every muscle within me. Standing here under the water I allow it to wash off the muck, stress, and confusion from yesterday. It slowly enlivens every part of my disheveled body as I soak in the healing water, feeling slightly normal again.

Stepping out of the shower I notice the swirling steam from the hot water fill the entire space. The steam covers everything in my bathroom with a thick layer of moisture. Grabbing my towel, I wrap it vigorously around me as I walk over to the mirror – and jump back in fear. There scribbled into the fog on the mirror, are the words *I am sorry*. The drip marks from where Donovan's fingers had touched the mirror are still oozing down like teardrops falling from every letter. My heart instantly speeds up as I stare at the vivid evidence dripping in front of me that he was just here. Grabbing tightly onto my towel I run out into my bedroom, looking all around the room for Donovan.

"Donovan, are you here?" I yell. Holding onto the towel I slowly walk out into the front room. An eerie silence looms in my apartment, causing a chill to race up my spine. "Donovan, please, if you are here, answer me," I shout as I wait quietly in my living room for some kind of movement or answer.

I can see my damp, nearly exposed chest moving to the beat of my heart as I stand here in just my towel. Cold shivers race through me as water droplets from my wet hair stream down my back. With every minute that passes, my somewhat exposed skin shivers against the cold morning air. I can't just stand here waiting for an answer that obviously isn't coming.

I stomp back to the bathroom as I stare at the dripping message written on the mirror. Lifting my hand, I furiously swipe the image away. Disappointment and anger build up within me as I gaze at my reflection in the mirror. Searing temptation rushes through me, beguiling me to give in to the rage. Suddenly I remember Donovan's warning about not losing my temper or I will lose myself in the process. Not wanting my reflection to be like the one from my dream, I close my eyes, taking in a deep, cleansing breath, extinguishing the palpable rage flowing within me.

As I open my eyes the quivering anger that rolled within me is now under control. Though the raging temptation has subsided, my mind is still on high alert. Walking out of the bathroom, trembling fear rushes through me. I sincerely have no desire to be here any longer. There has to be somewhere I can go where I don't have to be completely alone.

The penetrating silence of my apartment pierces through me with a heavy reminder of being abandoned. I need to hear some kind of noise. Suddenly, as if out of nowhere, the stillness is shattered by a familiar, yet annoying organ tune. This infuriating tune sends a chill racing up my spine. I have got to change the creepy organ ringtone to my phone, especially after what I now know.

Running over to my phone I answer it as quickly as possible, "Hello."

"Lauren, are you all right? You sound winded, like you can't catch your breath." His voice is low and thick with concern as each word flows heavily through the phone.

"Yes, I'm fine, William. I was in the shower when the phone rang – that's all." That part is true. He doesn't need to know the rest of why I'm breathless.

"Lauren, I just called to check on you. I have been worried about you. You left my house so suddenly and I have been trying to call you since you ran off yesterday."

"You have? I've had my phone with me the whole time. It didn't ring once. Trust me, I would have answered it if it did." I honestly did not hear the phone ring at all. My mind was otherwise occupied yesterday. Even if the phone rang I probably wouldn't have heard it. I'm not sure if I had reception up on the mountain or not.

I cling to my only hope of warmth, my saturated towel, as I stand in the middle of my room, freezing cold. My trembling milky white skin breaks out in goosebumps as I quickly jump into my bed, needing to get warm as quickly as possible. Throwing my large down comforter over me I curl myself into a large cocoon awaiting transformation. The heat from my comforter radiates throughout my chilled body.

William suddenly is silent, causing me to wonder what is going through his overprotective head. Laying here in my bed I start replaying in my mind what I said to see if I accidentally let something slip out that I shouldn't have.

"Lauren, the only reason your phone would not work is if you had travelled outside the area. Where did you go when you left my house in such a hurry?" His voice has a sharp, rebuking edge to it, wanting some answers and wanting them now. This is not the peaceful, gentle William I am used to.

"What do you mean? I didn't go anywhere." My voice is quivering as I try to make my words sound convincing, but I'm not sure if I am able to hide the insincerity coating my tongue. I have never lied to William before, but I have no other choice – this is my hell, not his. The truth could put him in danger. What do I tell him? 'Oh, by the way, the legend you told me is true. I did in fact go up to Mt. Diablo to meet a demon I am totally infatuated with. To make matters worse, I think he might have possibly turned me into a demon as well.' He will put me in a psych ward if I tell him the truth.

Just saying the words in my head sounds absolutely ridiculous. There is no way I can tell him the truth. If he thought I was going crazy before, he would believe that I am completely losing my mind. I cannot tell William there are real demons out there searching and waiting to capture our souls. I have to keep it a secret, it is hard enough for me to believe or even understand.

"Well, Lauren, I thought that…" there is a slight hesitation in his voice like he isn't quite sure how to say it, "… that after I told you the story of Mt. Diablo, you had left to go up to that damn mountain to find out for yourself."

Instantly I deflate like a popped balloon as I drop my shoulders and exhale all of my breath. My mind swirls in shock, causing me to even forget to breathe. How did he know I was even thinking of doing that? I gave him no reason to think I would ever believe his story. I never told him about my experience with Donovan and how his eyes had gone completely clear like the devils in the story. Why would he immediately assume that scenario?

An uneasy stillness looms on the phone like silent wings encircling us, causing a nervous discomfort to rush over me. No matter how hard I try to minimize the situation in my head I can't hide my sincere shock at how he figured it out. Scavenging my completely mystified mind for any clue as to how he knew what I had done, I begin wondering for a moment if William genuinely believes the fable. Perhaps he has had some kind of supernatural or demonic experience that has tainted his view of the world – like me. My stomach instantly turns with the preposterous thought that

William has dealt with demons before. My overactive brain is vigorously at work again, attempting to convince me of a situation that is completely irrational. The most likely scenario is he just had a lucky guess.

William's deep, crisp voice interrupts my thoughts, "Lauren, it wouldn't have been safe for you to go up there yesterday."

Trying to choke out the word, I utter softly, "Why?"

"Well, first of all, the rain was horrible up there. I could tell from my front porch it was pouring up there. That kind of condition doesn't make it easy or even safe for hiking to the summit." His once stern tone is replaced with a quiet, calm and aloof attitude that appears to mask his real concern as if he is hiding something he is not willing to divulge.

A thick hesitancy rolls from his voice like a hot, breathy refrain climbing out of the phone and piercing my soul. He has only shared his first concern, now I need to hear his second reason of why it was dangerous for me to go up there. I know somewhere within that illustrious reason holds his true disquiet. "William, what is the second reason?"

"What do you mean?" His voice cracks like something is pressing down on his vocal chords as he squeaks out his answer.

He is lucky we are both on the phone, because I can read his face like a giant billboard. He is a horrible liar, which honestly is a great quality of his. Even though I'm not standing in front of him I can hear his trembling voice vibrating through the phone.

A wicked thought writhes within my heart, slithering into my mind. I now have the ability to search his soul and find out what he is really thinking… but I will have to pay the ultimate price… my eternal soul. I have to trust Donovan though, and not react on my carnal needs. I will have to go about this the hard way – simply ask him. I just hope he will be more honest with me than I am being with him.

"Sorry, William, you are a horrible liar. You said 'first of all.' That means there is a second reason why I shouldn't go up there."

He lets out a heavy sigh as he utters hesitantly, "You know, Lauren, it was just a story… it's not true." Though William's voice is gelatinous with a persuasive tone, I can hear vibrating around the borders of his voice a sense of apprehension.

My burning question rushes out of my mouth before I even have a chance to control myself. "So you are saying you don't believe in devils?" I bark in contempt. "But – what if the story is true? What if there are clear-eyed devils or demons amongst us?" I try to restrain my impertinent attitude I am succumbing to, but I'm unsuccessful.

Wrapping my comforter even tighter around me I ready myself for some kind of retribution, but there is nothing but a pregnant silence lingering between us. My veins pulsate with nervous energy as I wait in silence for some kind of answer.

"Lauren, what I do or do not believe in is not a subject I wish to discuss over the phone," he snaps. His voice takes on an unfamiliar fierce cadence as he speaks in a reprimanding way. "If you wish to talk with me about it – respectfully and in person – then and only then will I answer any of your questions."

His sterile voice strikes me like sharp arrows ripping through to my very center, causing me to tremble with regret. I should have never talked to him in a disrespectful way, but I couldn't help it. Controlling my unyielding reaction to things around me is going to be harder than I had originally thought. I have already offended William, who is the closest thing to a father I have left. If I can't bridle my riotous emotions then I'm not going to last much longer.

The penitent sorrow crushes down on me like an avalanche of heavy boulders slamming against my chest. A sudden flash of loneliness tickles the rough edges of my tattered mind as I gaze around my abandoned room. The well of uncontrolled tears bursts through my protective floodgates, flowing effortlessly down my cheeks. I am left all alone to deal with this literal hell I am in. Staying here in my apartment – with all that has transpired – terrifies me to my very center. I don't want to be alone right now. My heart cries out for my father, but that can no longer be.

I cry out for the next best thing. "William, I'm sorry for talking so rudely towards you," I humbly mutter. "I'm going through something I don't understand and I need a father right now." I try to hide the sound of my tears in my voice, but I am sure he hears the desperation within me. "Do you mind if I come out to your house?"

"Lauren, you know you're always welcome here any time. I would love for you to come back out here." He exhales softly. Then his voice takes on a somber, respectful tone. "And if you need to talk, I may not be your father, but you can always talk to me. You know I think of you as my daughter."

Hearing him utter those words reinflates my heart and is exactly what I need to hear. My tears flow freely from my eyes, increasing in speed as they pour down my face, saturating my once dry skin. I know deep down he thinks of me as a daughter, but hearing it during my time of need pierces into my soul, giving me the strength I need to fight for my humanity and salvation.

"Thank you, William," I sigh. "You don't know how much it means to me to hear you say that right now."

"Lauren, I will always be here for you and will do anything for you… anything," he whispers with sincere conviction. I know that he would do anything for me, but I hope he will never have to. It would kill me if he ever had to suffer on my behalf.

CHAPTER 14

Fire

The morning sun has not yet engulfed the silver light of the twilight sky. Staring into the shimmering dusk air I sit languidly on William's porch swing, gently swaying in the cool dawn air. The comforter from William's guest bed is tightly wrapped around me, prohibiting the brisk morning air from hitting my skin. Curling up into a tight ball I keep replaying the bizarre events that have altered my life and my innocent world drastically.

William was kind enough to allow me to sleep at his house last night. I was such a mess yesterday I did not want to go back to my apartment by myself. I know he is concerned with what is going on with me, but I couldn't talk much about it yesterday. He wanted some questions answered, but I didn't know how to answer his onslaught of questions. Instead of talking to him he allowed me to spend the day curled up in a ball on this very spot where I now still reside. The only time I moved was to convince William I was going to bed, but I couldn't sleep. I spent most of the night yearning for a respite that only Donovan can provide. Leaving me a message written in steam on my mirror does not constitute as remaining with me. Feeling fatigued and abandoned by Donovan, I return to the comfort of William's porch swing, staring up at the mountain that has answered many of my veiled questions.

Reluctantly I gaze up at Mt. Diablo as the rising sun transforms the mountain into a beacon of blazing glory. I remain transfixed at this now glowing mountain as my mind impeccably replays the events that transpired on the summit with great detail. My skin hums in delight as I recall the touch of Donovan's fingers on my skin. A shiver tickles my neck at just the mere memory of his skin on mine.

Wrapping the comforter even tighter around me I close my eyes as I recall every little detail about him: his dark hair falling effortlessly against his velvety cream skin; his piercing blue eyes that stare deep into my soul like an open window; his sculpted strong face, chiseled physique, and velvety smooth husky voice that will forever be burned into my heart. As I remember his soft, supple, full lips touching my skin, my body instantly bursts into flames of passion for him. No matter who or what Donovan is, I am forever changed by him. There is now a void within me like a great black hole only he can fill. A wicked smile pulls on the corner of my mouth as I begin to imagine lustful images of

Donovan. My lucid fantasy is interrupted by a vision of clear, malicious eyes staring into my soul. The reality of who Donovan is shatters my lascivious thoughts.

I attempt to convince my forsaken mind that this is some imaginary nightmare I have concocted and not my reality now. The sensation of being abandoned creeps back into my mind. Though it has only been two days, it feels like an eternity since I have seen Donovan.

Slowly I open my eyes, breaking free from my frustrating memories only to notice the brilliant sunrise causing everything to glow a bright orange in color. The gleaming vivid colors ignite everything around me with blazing vibrant warmth. The sun awakens the glistening scenery with a clear new day. Just as the sun has given everything around me a new day, I too feel like a sunrise has occurred within me. I was in the stale darkness of my pathetic boring life, but now there has been something set ablaze within me. For the first time I feel alive.

The morning breeze gently sways the swing, softly rocking me into a deeper state of relaxation. For the first time all night exhaustion begins to take over me. The quiet peaceful sounds of the morning begin to lull me into a tranquil sleep when suddenly the discreet creaking sound of a door echoes from behind me.

"Lauren, have you been out here all night?" he mumbles in a hoarse voice.

Gingerly I turn towards William who is now standing behind me, examining my entangled mess on his swing. Dark circles encompass his eyes and his worn-down face looks as if he has had even less sleep than I – if that is at all possible. The five o'clock shadow forming last night now covers the bottom half of his face with thick salt and pepper stubble. His usually combed hair is going in every direction, a complete indication of how restless his night was.

"Did I wake you?" I utter apologetically in a dry, thick voice.

"No. I have been up for quite a while." No matter how hard William tries exaggerating his tone I can hear the exhaustion straining in his groggy voice.

My eyes scan his interesting morning wardrobe, examining his mismatched details. His dark blue and red flannel plaid pajama bottoms are paired with a tattered bulky light grey sweatshirt. Peering down at his feet I notice he is wearing the same black dress socks from the night before. I try to swallow the laughter forming in the base of my throat, but a small snicker sneaks out through my nose. Instantly he shoots me a sardonic gaze as his brows stitch together, deepening the furrow between his eyes and exaggerating his gaze.

Looking me up and down with the same scrutinizing gaze, he utters, "I wouldn't be so quick to laugh at me. Have you taken a good look in the mirror this morning? You're pretty comical-looking yourself."

Pressing my hands against my completely disheveled hair I try to flatten the unruly pieces standing straight up. I'm sure my appearance is just as much of an indicator as to how my night fared as his appearance is to me. We look like two peas in a very exhausted pod.

"I wouldn't worry about it now. You have plenty of time to put yourself together before you go to work," he quietly mutters.

Crap. I completely forgot it is Monday. I've been so preoccupied with what has transpired over the past few days I haven't stopped to realize what day it is. I haven't had a good night's sleep in days. The intense exhaustion pressing down on my ragged body and consuming my brain is causing me to move in a state of slow motion. There is no way I am going to be able to work, least of all today.

My eyes spring open like a blinking owl as the muscles in my face tighten in shock like I have just witnessed a ghost. William's face drops in a harsh, disapproving gaze as he lets out a throaty sigh. Gripping onto the blanket tighter I lower my chin onto my clenched fists, hoping William won't ask any exploratory questions – but my hope shatters. I hear his slow, yet intense walk moving towards me. His socks drag against the wood decking like sandpaper rubbing forcefully against a rough surface. Trying to fight the urge to look up at him I begin to bury my head even more into my fists, when suddenly the porch swing rocks violently. The movement of the swing nearly causes my relaxed frame to tumble right out of it.

"Lauren, are you not going in to work today?" he asks point blank.

He may be my honorary father but he is also my boss, and the fact that I'm not planning on going to work today is not going to be easy for him to accept. Knowing he is going to be upset with me I slowly lift my head, uttering softly, "No. Actually, I'm hoping to use a sick day today."

William stares straight ahead with empty, unresponsive eyes as his deflated shoulders instantly freeze. Methodically he slowly pushes the porch swing back and forth, sliding his feet gently along the ground while shaking his head in a questionable fashion.

"William, are you upset with me for asking for the day off?" I quietly ask.

Pursing his lips tightly together he exhales a quick, sarcastic laugh through his strong nose like I am missing an inside joke. "Lauren, I'm not upset that you are asking for the day off. I'm..." His voice trails off slightly like there is more to say, but he isn't sure how to say it.

William's eyebrows darn themselves together, emphasizing the thick scowl racing across his rigid face. He continues to stare blankly straight ahead as his taut jaw quivers slightly. The palpable silence radiates off of him, causing my stomach to flip. I can tell he wants to say something more, but he is unsure how to verbalize his thoughts.

Gradually the rocking motion of the swing slows until it comes to a complete stop. Turning toward William I notice he has been examining me, scrutinizing my every detail.

"What is wrong, William?" I nervously plead.

"Lauren, are we going to keep avoiding the elephant in the room or are you going to finally talk to me?" he insists.

A thick knot lodges forcefully within my throat as my heart starts racing rapidly against my chest. A tingling fire pulses through my veins, causing me to instantly sweat. I thought for sure he wasn't going to ask me any more questions. That he was just going to let me go to him when I am ready to talk, but I guess that is not the case. Pretending I don't understand what he means, I utter sheepishly, "What are you talking about?"

"Lauren, don't play games with me," he demands. "You know exactly what I mean. If you are going to ask for the day off then I think I'm entitled to know the truth. What is going on with you?"

His voice slices through me like razor blades tearing open my protective shield, causing tears to pool up. I whimper, "William, I don't know how or if I can tell you."

William turns his eyes quickly toward Mt. Diablo, staring up at it in revolting disgust. Flinching back in anger he utters coarsely as the words hiss through his taut lips, "This is all because of that damn mountain and stupid story – isn't it?"

Reacting to his harsh words I close my eyes as tight as possible, causing my tears to stream down. His sharp words pierce through me like stinging needles. Coiling up into a tight ball under my blanket I grimace at his thundering remark. Fear rips through me as I instantly realize I have no idea how to answer his question. Trying to avoid his question I hide my face from William's penetrating gaze.

"Lauren, answer me," he demands in a thick, harsh tone. His thunderous voice echoes through the air, causing me to flinch in his direction. This is a whole new situation for me. I'm not sure how to respond to his berating tone.

The muscles in his taut jaw quiver viciously from his teeth clenching against each other. His sharp pursed mouth forms a rigid immovable thin line across his face. It appears I have hit upon an extremely sore subject I never knew existed.

Silent tension looms in the air like thick smoke forming a tangible barrier between us. I need to answer him – immediately. "Yes," I whimper, trying to gain some control in my voice.

A severe exhale explodes out of William's mouth. "Oh, Lauren… what have you done?" he protests weakly. A dark deflated expression washes over his face, leaving his slumped, quivering expression echoing with internal pain. A single teardrop escapes from his tightly closed eyes as he fights back a mysterious emotion surging within him.

He utters in a broken-down voice, "Please tell me you didn't go up to that damn Mt. Diablo yesterday, attempting to seek out answers you have no right prying into. Please…please Lauren, tell me you didn't."

The pain I had felt earlier is nothing compared to the pain I'm obviously causing him now. The anguish consuming him burns into my deepest soul, causing me excruciating pain like I am being burned alive. A deep, unexplained disappointment oozes out of his pores like thick sweat sending off toxic gases – nearly destroying me with pain. The unimaginable throbbing I'm succumbing to rips through my soul like a shredder, tearing me apart. How can going up to a mountain upset him so much? What is he not telling me? Trying to stop the pain from killing me, I reach up and grab hold of my chest forcefully. My tears are flowing so hard it is almost impossible for me to talk.

"Lauren, please tell me?" he utters in a weak, raspy voice.

"Yes. Yes, I did," I whisper. "Why is that so wrong, William? Why are you so upset and hurting so bad? Where is this pain coming from?" I strain in a quivering breathy tone.

He slowly lifts his large muscular hand, gently covering his eyes. He lowers his head against his hand as a large heavy sigh escapes out of him. "Not again, God. Please, not again. I can't handle it if I lost her too. I know it was his fault, but this is now *my* fault. I should have never planted the information in her head," he whimpers breathlessly.

An immense amount of confusion pours over me like a giant tidal wave crushing all the pain residing within me. Demanding to know what he is talking about, I utter fervently, "What the hell are you spouting off about? What do you mean lose me too?" The knot in my throat lodges near my windpipe, causing my voice to lower in intensity. "Lose me to what? And who else did you lose to this mysterious thing?"

"It's nothing. You just should have never gone up there – that's all," he stutters breathlessly.

"I don't understand why you are so upset. I did nothing wrong. You were the one who told me the stupid story. You also said yourself you don't believe in the fable." Gazing intently into his eyes, I question firmly, "What are you hiding from me? Tell me."

He turns abruptly toward me, revealing the throbbing agony written all over his face. Suddenly he stands up and hastily walks away from me as he stares up at Mt. Diablo, presumably cursing at it with his harsh dark eyes. Turning suddenly toward me he gazes down at me with a soft, compassionate expression on his face stating, "Lauren, you're right. I shouldn't be so upset with you. You can have the day off. I will excuse it." He turns towards his front door and mutters softly, "I need to get ready for work though. I have a busy day ahead of me."

"Oh, no you don't, William. You need to answer my questions. What is going on with you? You're not going to run away from me," I snap forcefully. Jumping up from the swing I anxiously walk over to William. Still holding onto my blanket for security, I plead feverishly, "Please, William, tell me."

"There is nothing wrong. I'm just exhausted and blew everything out of proportion – that's all."

"That's bullshit. You're not telling me the truth. What are you hiding from me? Please William, tell me what you know. Trust me, after what I have gone through the past few days I can handle anything," I cry.

Lifting his hand to my face he gently touches my cheek, whispering softly, "You have your secrets you aren't ready to share with me yet and I have mine."

"I will tell you all of my secrets if you want, but please, I need to know yours," I whimper.

"Someday our secrets will be explained, but for now we both have some things to figure out first."

"Why?"

Bending down he softly kisses my forehead. "Trust me."

A vague hush comes over me as I gingerly watch William disappear into his house. Standing here motionless I stare up at the mountain that has forever changed my life. A heavy weight of regret fills me, causing a dizziness to consume me. Walking over to the porch swing I throw myself onto it. Tears stream down my face as I numbingly stare out into the distance, allowing my heavy frame to seep into the corner of the swing.

William rushes out of the house as he hastily throws on the last items of clothing. Turning toward me and giving me a quick attempt at a smile, he runs towards his car. Silently I watch as his car speeds down the gravel road, fading into the distance and leaving me in its silent wake. Anxious adrenaline starts pulsating through my motionless body. Needing some sort of release from this rushing energy I start gazing around for an escape. William's lush pasture seems to summon me to enter its soothing retreat. Answering its beck and call I head out towards the awaiting field, bringing my blanket with me for comfort.

The soft spring grass against my bare feet feels like a spongy cloud rippling beneath my clenching toes. The plush grass and warm sun invigorates my drained body. Removing the blanket from me, I gently spread it out onto the soft mound. Sitting on my now restful spot, I slowly feel the anxious energy shedding off of me like a snake shedding its dead skin. I allow the pain and loneliness I am feeling to penetrate my tattered mind. Wrapping my arms tightly around my bent knees as I rest my cheek against the tops of my knees, I suddenly feel an intense warmth radiating from behind me. I attempt to whirl around when I notice legs from someone sitting behind me slowly wrap around my sedentary hips and pretzel wrapped legs. Instantly I start to jump up when the person's hands pull me back down.

"It's just me, Lauren," Donovan utters softly as his hands remain tightly wrapped around my shoulders, keeping me from getting up.

"What… how in the hell did you know where I was going to be?" I snap as I try to subdue the fear vibrating within my voice.

"Lauren, it's not hard to find you. Remember, I am able to locate whatever my desire is." Clearing his throat softly, he almost warns, "We also know where each other are, at all times." His voice lowers to a disheartened tone, "Are you trying to hide from me? If you are I can leave if you would like." He slowly starts to get up from behind me.

Grabbing onto his hands that are still resting on me I try to stop him from getting up. "No – please don't go. I'm glad you found me," I add breathlessly. Having his body so close to mine causes tingles to pulsate through my veins, causing the hairs on the back of my neck to stand erect. Though I don't want him to move, there are so many unanswered questions I need answered and I can't do it with him so close to me. Nervously I start fiddling with the blanket below us trying to think of how to ask him these questions.

"Lauren, what do you want to ask me?" he asks hesitantly as he rakes his hand through his dark, thick hair.

"What do you mean?" I try to hide the surprise in my voice.

Suddenly a loud, low laugh escapes from his moist, plump lips. "Lauren, do you remember anything I told you the other day?" he asks sarcastically. "You can't hide your desires from me. I know everything you desire – everything. So go ahead and ask me or would you like me to just answer it?" he states with a wicked smile.

I spin around so that we are now face to face. His piercing blue eyes remain locked onto me as he places his hands behind his back, slightly reclining, leaning against his muscular arms. His legs remain on either side of me as he gives me a slight snicker. I can tell by his amused expression he is having way too much fun with my uneasiness. I don't know how, but I am going to have to learn to guard my desires around him a lot better.

Peering at him I utter forcefully, "Donovan, that is not fair. You have to give me some sort of privacy with my thoughts."

His smile widens slightly in triumph. "Lauren, I don't read thoughts," he clarifies. "I see people's desires in my head at the very moment they want it. Right now I know what you truly want." Suddenly a beautiful, yet mischievous smile spreads across his face. "I have way too much fun seeing your desires," he teases.

I can feel the embarrassment setting in as the blood rushes to my face, causing a flush to crawl up my neck and taint my cheeks a vibrant red. My thoughts I can learn to control, but my desires, they are a different story. "Donovan, that is still not fair. I can't see your desires – yet."

His smile immediately dissipates as his face transforms into a dark and serious expression. His once relaxed physique is now erect as he peers forcefully into my eyes. "And you won't ever be able to – I will make sure of it. I am not going to allow my desires to damn you. Trust me. I am fixing this," he utters in a quick fervent voice.

A heavy weight of regret quivers within his trembling strong hands. Slowly I wrap my hands around his while I caress the backs of them with my thumbs. The muscles within his hands pulsate, feeling like rippling silk beneath my thumbs. Gazing up at his face I watch as a flutter of gratification ripples across his chiseled features. Donovan's warm, sweet breath increases in speed while his eyes remain tightly closed in pleasure. My thunderous heart hammers against my chest as I mumble softly, "I don't want you to fix it if it means you will leave me."

His eyes snap open, peering deep into mine. "Lauren, I will not abandon you. Now that I found you I will do everything within my power not to leave you, but I will not let you become a monster." His gravelly voice exaggerates the statement as if he is not just trying to convince me, but himself.

Just a few minutes ago my main desire was very different, but now all I can think about is how he is going to fix this situation without my heart being scarred in the process. I can't have him just save me. I need him to save us both. I have no idea why there is a gravitating pull towards him, but I am going to have fun figuring out why.

Donovan gently squeezes my hand while peering into my eyes. An unspoken word streams between us of his unyielding desire to fix this. I don't quite understand what he is up against, but I know the ardent task is going to be nearly impossible.

Using his strong legs around me Donovan presses me closer to him, purposefully sliding his body against mine. Lifting my hand up to his sumptuous mouth, he slowly presses his lips affectionately against it. His lips linger against the back of my hand long enough for me to feel heat from his mouth increasing, causing a burning sensation against my skin. The sting doesn't hurt. In fact, the arousing flutter causes my stomach to flip and cry out for more. A broken exhale slowly vibrates out of my mouth as I take in every carnal sensation, causing the tingling feeling in my stomach to drop lower. My thunderous heart beats a million miles an hour in anticipation of what is to come.

His arms wrap around my back, gently drawing me up against his rippling chest. His hand presses firmly onto the small of my back, gripping my shirt aggressively in his hand as if he is trying not to lose control. His shaky breathing intensifies in speed as he moves his moist, pliable mouth slowly up my arm.

Donovan's full lips linger on each spot just long enough for me to feel the scorching heat from his mouth against my skin. Gradually his mouth makes its way up my arm to the base of my neck. Donovan gingerly lets go of my arm as sensual waves of passion instantly erupt within me, causing me to feel like fire is flowing through my veins.

His mouth is just inches from my ear, allowing me to hear and feel his jagged breathing against the hollow of my neck. The heat from his breath exhales delicately against the nape of my neck, sending shivers racing up and down my spine. A deep control coats his staggered breathing, like he is doing everything within his power not to become a slave to his desires. Instantly he presses his plump lips, not so gently against my neck, causing a sharp gasp to explode from my mouth. Pulling me firmly against his chest he lifts me up so that we are both now perched on our knees. His firm, yet trembling hand releases the tight grip on my shirt, anxiously making its way up my back.

"Lauren, this is what I was thinking about on Mt. Diablo. Remember I said I would tell or show you what I was thinking?" he stammers breathlessly against my neck.

A deep hunger rises within me like fresh meat being placed in front of a starving lion. Instinctively I wrap both my arms tightly around Donovan. Using all my strength I pull him forcefully against my trembling body. Donovan's mouth begins lightly skimming across the nape of my neck, burning me along the way as if his mouth is a torch leaving singe marks against my supple skin. The intense sensation coursing through me causes my rapid breathing to vibrate out of control.

His moist, soft tongue lightly traces my jawline until it reaches my ear. Delicately he moves his tongue slowly across the base of my earlobe. A wave of intense heat forming in the pit of my stomach suddenly explodes out, filling me with trembling gratification. A tickling sensation quivers into my thighs while I remain frozen in complete pleasure. I hold my breath, enjoying every sensation he is giving me.

"Breathe Lauren, don't forget to breathe," he quietly moans into my ear. Uttering a breathless warning he adds, "And don't forget to stay in complete control."

"It's easy for you to say," I exhale softly.

His strong hand firmly makes its way up my back until it is buried deep within my hair. Gently he grabs onto a handful of my hair as he murmurs into my ear, "Trust me, this is not easy for me."

Slowly Donovan's mouth begins to move across my cheek until it is just inches away from my mine. His mouth lingers there, causing an uncontrolled sensation to build up like a dam getting ready to burst. His skilled teasing is building up a tidal wave of pleasure, taking aim on him. Intense anticipation rushes through me with the realization of where he is heading. I'm not sure how much longer I'm going to be able to hang on. The only thing stopping me from attacking him is the mere pleasure I'm enjoying reveling in right now. My heart is pounding out an erratic rhythm while my skin seems to ignite with every touch of his mouth.

Donovan was not joking when he said I will feel everything stronger now. I don't know how much more I can handle, yet I have no desire to stop him.

Donovan wraps his hands around my head, tilting me slightly away from him as he stares deep into my eyes. The overwhelming sensation of him gazing into my soul rips through me as he observes the ravenous desire I have for him. A brief, sardonic smile spreads across his face. Then suddenly, without a word, he presses his lips feverishly against mine.

His soft, sumptuous lips rhythmically move with uncontrolled passion across my mouth as his powerful kiss consumes me in burning desire. The flames of passion between us ignite into a full-fledged inferno, setting my soul on fire. The heat of passion wells up within my mouth, spilling down my throat and causing the burn to engulf me. My toes curl under as I attempt to contain the buzzing passion within me. Aggressively I twist my hands into his dark silky hair while our lips merge together in complete ecstasy.

His wet tongue sensually traces the shape of my bottom lip, causing a low, disembodied growl to vibrate out of my throat and merge with a forceful exhale. My knees instantly buckle beneath me. Donovan flexes his arm tightly around my upper torso, stopping me from falling. Though my collapse has broken my intimate concentration, his lips never cease in their undulating intensity. While holding onto me tightly in his arm he begins lightly pulling on my hair, causing my head to tilt back, exposing my neck for his strong, palpable mouth to enjoy. My lips may have been pulled free from his, but his mouth remains attached to my neck. Insistently, yet gently Donovan's lips stroke my neck while he slowly lays me back. Gripping onto Donovan he lays me onto the blanket, supporting our entire weight in just one arm. A husky, uneven moan expels out of his mouth, causing my frame to quiver in delight.

My ragged breathing increases as I coil my hands vigorously through his hair. A low, raspy groan shudders from Donovan as he carefully lowers his body onto mine. His defined stomach rises and falls against mine, causing our bodies to melt into each other. The intensity in his kiss transforms, taking on an aggressive edge. Donovan's sweltering hands slide along my arms until they reach mine. Firmly grasping onto them he abruptly raises my hands above my head – holding them securely there.

Donovan's irregular breathing increases as he continues to kiss my neck passionately. The heat radiating from him intensifies, burning through my clothes like I have a hot furnace on top of me. Needing some sort of cool air to wash over my overheated body, I attempt to free my hands from his burning grasp – but they won't budge. It is no use trying to pull them free. He is so much stronger than I am. I begin panting and writhing beneath him, attempting to get his attention when suddenly I catch sight of his slightly opened eyes.

Gasping in fear I stare in horror. His frightening eyes are not void of color like before, this time they are solid black, like coal. Dark, oozing night encompasses the once brilliant shade of blue that existed within his eyes. The consuming power of darkness is overtaking him. Aggressively I push against Donovan as hard as I can, uttering forcefully, "Donovan, stop!"

His mouth continues to move across my neck with an unclaimed fervor. Pleading gently with him I utter again, "Donovan, please stop. You are losing control. Please – I need you to remain with me. I can't completely lose you now." I whisper intently, "You promised."

A sharp vibration shudders through him like an electrical jolt. Donovan instantly rolls off of me, throwing his arms incredulously over his face as he shudders in disgust. I attempt to console him, but his shoulder recoils from my touch.

"Lauren, please don't." His low voice is weak and broken.

"Why? It's not your fault," I answer sympathetically, trying to ease his guilt.

Turning sharply toward me he fiercely removes his hands from his face. "Look at me," he orders coldly. "Look at the evil within me."

A malicious mask has transformed Donovan's face, concealing his once soft, gentle nature. Darkness now cloaks his face with black shadows secreting from his skin. The central hub to all the darkness is coming from his frightening eyes. A sinister, coal-black color has completely devoured the blue. Black veins ooze from his eyes like syrupy streams seeping down his face. His facial muscles quiver violently as if the disturbing black veins cause him pain.

My heart palpitations increase as I gasp violently at the malevolence running rampant over his once magnificent features. For the first time I'm able to see the grotesque evil that lies within him. His black eyes remain locked onto me as I jump back in complete horror at the obvious monster he has become.

Quickly Donovan turns away, throwing his hands once again over his face. He spits out in revulsion, "Lauren, this is my fault. I am a monster. Literally I am the definition of a monster – a demon." He quietly hisses, "I am so sorry."

His dilapidated voice rips into my heart, causing a heavy vise to crush down on it, nearly squashing it. Thick, salty tears slowly well up within me as I watch his quivering body deflate in self-loathing. This dark existence isn't the life he asked for, but one he is now innocently forced to serve.

An aching knot in my chest radiates out with a longing to comfort him. Gradually I scoot closer to him, wrapping my arm around him again, attempting to comfort the disgust burning within him. Donovan tenses up as he tries to roll away from my touch. Tightening my grip, I hold onto him with all of my strength.

"Lauren…"

"Stop," I demand in a sharp voice. "Donovan, I know who you are and – to be honest – what I am now." He stiffens in reaction to my statement. "I chose to kiss you. You didn't force me. Donovan, I want you as much, if not more than you want me." Chortling softly, I add, "I guess I have better control than you."

"Lauren, you need to stop trying to make me feel better, it is not going to work. I don't blame you if you are terrified of me," he whispers as a soothing lull washes over him.

"Donovan, for someone who can see people's desires, you truly suck at it." Biting down on my lip, I add, "And you sure know how to ruin the mood with your brooding attitude."

Spinning around so that our faces are just inches away, he snaps back questionably, "What are you talking about?"

The dark, encompassing evil within his eyes has completely dissipated, leaving Donovan's soft crystal clear blue. The thick dark streams of black stains that had surrounded his eyes are now just a faint horrific memory in my mind. Donovan gazes over at me with his breathtaking face just inches away, making it extremely hard to think, let alone talk. I stare at his chiseled, strong face as he glances at me forebodingly, causing a deep furrow to form between his piercing blue eyes.

My vision locks on to his hypnotic lips, causing my mouth to water slightly like I'm staring at a juicy, yet poisonous apple being offered to me. I begin recalling every lascivious moment his mouth was on me, causing the flutters in my stomach to take flight with passion. My heart begins beating erratically as I stare at his moist, plump lips. My now constantly changing emotions grip hold of me causing me to only think about having his lips back on me.

"Lauren, it's not going to happen," he states flatly.

Shaking my head rapidly I force the enticing image out of my mind. "See, this is what I mean," I grumble. Pulling my arm away from him I instantly sit straight up, completely disappointed with what he said. "You can see what I want, yet you don't understand that all I want is you – completely."

"Lauren, it is too much temptation. It's not worth losing our souls over," he replies sourly.

"I know."

"Then what do you mean?"

Looking down at my hands I nervously twist them around, trying to get up the nerve to say what I need without sounding pathetic. "I don't want you to leave me."

I notice Donovan's hand gingerly streaming across the tips of my fingers. Staring down at our hands I watch as his thumb lovingly strokes the trepidation from me. Suddenly his warm, smooth hand presses gently underneath my chin, forcing me to look up at him. His thumb slowly caresses my jaw as he softly responds, "Is that what you think? That I am going to leave you?"

A soothing heat in the pit of my stomach radiates out as I gaze into his crystal blue eyes. My voice betrays me, forcing me to have to nod in response. Gripping onto my pants I begin wringing them nervously between my fingers, waiting for his response.

"Lauren, I already told you I will not abandon you…"

Suddenly, as if out of nowhere, he turns abruptly toward William's house, staring at it intently. When he turns back in my direction the tender expression on his face has now been replaced by annoyance. Boring his eyes deep into mine he quickly lifts my hand to his mouth as he softly kisses it. "Lauren, I need to go, but I promise we will continue this conversation soon."

Pulling my hand from his, I sigh, "What? You just said you wouldn't leave me."

Smiling curtly, he corrects, "I said I wouldn't abandon you. I will have to leave you every now and then, you know." His smile instantly fades, "This is one of those times I need to leave you."

Echoing from the distance I hear a low voice call out anxiously, "Lauren, are you out there?"

Frantically I gaze in the direction of William's house. "What time is it? He can't be home yet." Feverishly I begin to jump up when Donovan immediately grabs my arm, lightly tugging me down.

"Wait until I leave, please," he asks respectfully.

"But I don't want you to leave. I'll just grab my things and then we can go back to my place and… continue our conversation." I hear my mouth utter the words, but in the back corner of my mind I know otherwise.

"I can't, Lauren. I have to leave." A slight snicker instantly appears on his face, causing me to growl in frustration.

His smile widens. "I am not laughing at you." He turns to face William's front porch again, then turning back to me with the same smirk on his face, he moans, "I think you should answer him though, before he comes out here looking for you."

Giving Donovan a questionable gaze, I immediately oblige. "Yes William, I'm out here. I'll be right there," I yell impatiently.

"There, are you happy now?" I snap, slightly annoyed.

Protesting his obvious change in mood I begin to stand up when he fervently grabs my arm and pulls me down, causing me to land on his lap. Wrapping both of his arms securely around me he holds me there. His strong hands gradually slide up my back until they are entangled in my hair once again. His smoldering eyes intently look into me, causing my heart to speed out of control – again. I thought he said no more.

His mouth is just inches away from me as he whispers, "Lauren, before I leave I need to ask you something."

"Anything." My mind is so lost in his scorching gaze I will agree to almost anything.

"I want to take you somewhere." Donovan's face lights up with excitement. "So can I officially ask you out on a date for this Friday?"

My eyes light up as a brilliant smile spreads across my face. With no hesitation I quickly reply, trying to hide the excitement in my voice, "Yes."

Suddenly he leans in, firmly pressing his lips to mine as they move in synchronized bliss. His kiss, though passionate, lacks the uncontrolled edge like before. I can feel that he is doing everything within his power to not lose control. The constant heat formed in my belly slowly oozes into my veins, causing me to aggressively pull him towards me. Hastily he presses me slightly away, trying to calm his ragged breathing down.

He breathlessly stammers out, "Remember you have a date with me on Friday. Don't go accepting another one – okay?"

"What? That is a stupid question. I don't think you need to worry. No one will ask me out," I respond, slightly confused. A mischievous smirk appears on his face like he is aware of something that is going to transpire.

Effortlessly he lifts me up, uttering softly, "You need to go."

Frustration washes through me as I bend down and aggressively grab the blanket now crumpled up on the soft grass. "See you soon, Lauren," Donovan echoes as if his voice is speaking miles away. Quickly I turn to say goodbye when I notice that he is gone. I begin frantically gazing all around trying to see where he went, but he is nowhere to be seen. It's like he vanished into thin air – a ghost in the darkness – leaving me standing here all alone with only the mere hope that I will see him again.

William's low, rumbling voice suddenly cuts through the silent air. "Lauren, where are you? I know you are out there somewhere. Are you coming or am I going to have to come out there and get you?"

"I'm coming," I hastily shout.

Gripping the blanket tightly in my hand I begin running toward William when I notice a look of horror streaming across his face. His eyes scan my neck and arms in complete shock. "Lauren, what the hell happened to you?"

Completely taken aback by his statement I gaze at him in confusion. "What do you mean? Nothing happened to me."

"Look at your arm and neck." He points with a scrutinizing finger. "This is not nothing, Lauren. You look like you have a horrible splotchy sunburn."

As I look down at my arm I notice it is covered in red burn marks everywhere Donovan's mouth touched. If my arm is this bad I can just imagine how my neck looks. There is no way I am going to be able to explain what happened to me. Taking the easy way out, I decide to use William's scenario.

"I put sunscreen on, but I guess I didn't do a very good job," I utter quickly, hoping he will believe me.

"I should say you did a lousy job." A deep line creases his brow as he slowly scans me up and down with a scowling look of wariness in his eyes. William's eyes transform to a sharp, cold look as he turns abruptly and walks into the house.

I look longingly back at the field where Donovan and I laid together. Hopefully he will keep his promise for Friday, but this is going to be a long week.

CHAPTER 15

∞

A Long Week

My monotonous week feels like it is dragging on as I robotically move throughout the ins and outs of my daily work. Hypnotically I stare down at the massive pile of paperwork that has built up over the past few days. No matter how hard I try to get my work done, I can't seem to get my mind to focus on anything other than Donovan and what has transpired between us. My overactive mind obsessively replays every tantalizing image of Donovan. I can still feel his penetrating blue eyes rush through me while his rumbling, gruff voice vibrates deep within me. Just simply thinking about him causes my stomach to turn in unbridled excitement. His sudden disappearing act has left me all alone to deal with the reality of what has been forced upon me and my constant fluctuating emotions.

"Hi, Lauren. How are you today?" A kind voice rips through the silence.

Even though my mind is deep in thought I still know this voice without needing to look up. There are only two people in the entire office who will say hi, let alone talk to me. I have successfully scared off everyone else. And the one person I could always lean on is beginning to be afraid of me... or for me. Ever since this weekend when William found out I had gone up to Mt. Diablo our relationship has been strained. He hasn't talked to me at all, let alone about what has transpired between us. Until he is ready to tell me what he knows – I can't tell him what I am. This gentle voice behind me is the only person who has been kind enough to still talk to me.

"I am surviving. How about you, Larry?" I utter flatly, trying to hide the robotic nature I'm trapped in.

Turning towards Larry I notice he is leaning up against the corner of my tiny cubicle with his arms folded against his chest. He is earnestly gazing at me with a kind, nonjudgmental smile on his face. Since my erratic behavior last Friday and then my subsequent absence from work on Monday, Larry has been checking in on me every day. Asking how I'm doing is usually followed by an, 'Is there anything I can do for you?' question.

I wish I could talk to him, or more importantly – William – about what is happening to me, but I can't. Whatever he is hiding from me must be consuming him, because he has been too preoccupied this week to even notice what people in the office are saying about me.

Stacie and her office gang have had fun spreading rumors, exaggerating the scenario that happened to me last week. She has been telling everyone how mentally unstable I am. The only person who has been willing to stand up for me is Larry. He has undeniably changed the opinion I had formed about him. He is not the arrogant office stud I had initially thought, but a compassionate, honest guy. He could have been like everyone else in the office, ignoring me like I have a deathly scourge while at the same time rudely talking about me behind my back…but he didn't. Instead he took a higher road and revealed to me what his true colors are.

"I'm doing fine, Lauren. Is there anything I can do for you today?" he asks in a low, quiet voice, bringing a quick smile to my face.

"No thank you, Larry. I'm fine," I gently respond.

"All right then, if you need anything just let me know," he utters dejectedly.

He proceeds to dolefully walk away from me like I'd ripped a hole in him. A sharp pain of regret shoots through me as I watch Larry, who has taken so much crap for me, walk away rejected once again. "Wait, if you aren't going anywhere for lunch today… hmm …would you like to eat with me in the break room?" I stammer out shyly.

"What… you want to eat lunch with me, today?"

"Yes," I add hesitantly.

The nape of my neck begins sweating as his rigid, stunned body stands motionless before me. Larry shoves his hands into his pockets as he gingerly walks closer to me with a brilliant smile spreading across his face. Leaning down inches away from me, he whispers softly, "I would love to, but you know who else eats in the break room, don't you?" He nods his head impishly towards Stacie's desk.

"Yes, but Stacie will just have to deal with it – won't she?" I snap haughtily.

Giving me a quick, comforting smile Larry gently shakes his head in agreement as he turns towards his desk that sits amidst the maze of cubicles. A twinge of regret suddenly washes over me as I turn back toward my stark cubicle. There is no way Larry, or myself, will be able to escape the tortuous aftermath that will come from this event. Larry has gotten backlash from Stacie for backing me and not her. Everyone in the office is having fun believing the lies Stacie has been telling them. If they're all running from me now I can only imagine what would happen if everyone knew what really happened that night and who I am now. Trying to suppress the dread consuming me I instantly immerse myself in the heaps of neglected paperwork.

Nervously I stare at the large black and white clock on the wall as it seems to be screaming that it is lunch time. Reluctantly I walk into the crowded, sterile lunch room, gazing around for Larry. A still hush rolls over the once boisterous room as everyone's scrutinizing eyes instantly turn in my direction. A light shimmer of sweat coats my forehead as I try to ignore all the gawking stares. Gazing around the room I notice Larry, perched at a back corner table giving me the only smiling face in the entire room.

Of course Larry would have to choose the table in the back. Now I have to walk by Stacie and her group of inhospitable cronies to get to him. Reaching deep inside of me for my inner strength, I slowly proceed to cut through the crowd of staring faces like Moses walking through the parted Red Sea. I don't even have to ask one person to move, they shift out of my way automatically.

Everyone's eyes stay glued to me as I make my way slowly back to Larry. His comforting face is the only thing preventing me from losing it. I know that Stacie hates me, but this kind of alienation is going too far.

Grabbing hold of the chair across from him I sit down, slowly looking over at him, ruefully uttering softly, "Maybe this isn't the best idea."

"Just ignore them – I do," he roars loud enough for everyone to hear his disapproving voice. Larry snaps his head towards Stacie, giving her a quick, rebuking glare of disgust. Softly turning back to me he utters with a reassuring smile, "Shall we eat?"

Wings of silence envelop me as I poke and prod at my salad like it is an alien creature I am dissecting. I intently try to listen in on the deep grumbling echoing behind me. The sea of unrelenting waves of insults vibrates from behind me like a wrecking ball crashing through my protective shield. My quivering white fingers tightly clutch around my fork as I take my anger out on my poor awaiting salad.

"So how is your salad?" Larry asks warmly as his incredulous eyes scrutinize my transparent reaction to what is taking place around me.

"Huh… what did you say?" I mindlessly utter.

"Lauren, we can leave if you want to."

"No, I'll be fine," I object weakly, trying to convince not just him, but also myself. Staring down at my destroyed salad I coyly add, "Larry, may I ask you a stupid question?"

"Sure."

I stare down at my hands as I continue torturing my plastic fork. Nervously twirling a piece of lettuce around, I ask dubiously, "How old are you?"

His eyes instantly narrow, revealing several deep creases in his forehead nearly forming a perfect staircase stepping down to his bewildered expression. "That may be out of the blue, but it's not a stupid question." A quirky smile gleams across his face as he adds, "I'm twenty-one. Why?"

"Wow, you seem older than that," I respond in surprise. His face suddenly drops as his eyebrows stitch together and his once sweet smile dissolves.

I notice his crushed expression, instantly causing me to drop my fork. Leaning in slightly I quickly respond, trying to explain myself, "I didn't mean it as a bad thing. I meant it as a compliment. You seem – well – more mature than the rest of the idiots here."

His sharp creases on his brow slowly relax as he shrugs innocently, "Thanks, I guess."

The constant rumbling murmurs, like a group of motorcycles, suddenly stop. A thick air of abhorrence swirls up from behind me. Chills race up my neck as I sense peering eyes ripping through my spine. I can sense Stacie's heated anger rolling ferociously up my back, tickling the back of my neck. Palpable silence looms all around me like she had been listening the entire time and isn't pleased with my statement.

A sharp exhale of disgust rips from Stacie's mouth, shattering the thick, suspended silence in the air. Stacie deliberately leans back in her chair, nearly hitting mine, making sure I can hear her loud and clear but preventing Larry from hearing. "What is Larry doing bottom feeding? Does he feel like he needs to be doing charity work with her?" Stacie slithers out.

A low praising rumble instantly breaks loose from all the eager participants encircling the table behind me. Maria's pompous voice hisses through the air like a snake slithering around me. "I would have thought for sure her psychotic episode last weekend would have scared him away – but I guess not. Larry really must be hard up. She's not even pretty."

A low, arrogant voice chimes in on the berating taking place behind me, "Why do you think I walked away from her at the club? You both blow her away. She's second class compared to your sexy bodies." A shrill of laughter and self-gloating echoes from the girls.

Stacie proclaims in a sharp, cold voice, "That psychotic bitch, who does she think she is? She's trying to play on Larry's sympathetic nature."

Her stabbing words burn into the deepest part of my soul, causing thick flames of irritation to run through my veins like a live wire ready to short out at any moment. A sharp jolt of anger rushes through me with every word escaping from their mouths. Grabbing tightly onto the edge of the table I attempt to fight back the blazing temper bubbling within me. Trembling waves vibrating within my hands cause my fingers to literally rip at the underbelly of the table. Flakes of particle board drop onto my lap like brown snowflakes.

A dark urge to release my overwhelming anger on Stacie suddenly washes over me. The heat pulsating in my core intensifies, flowing through me with a craving to hurt her. A yearning emanates out of every pore on my skin like an evil toxic gas. My trembling thoughts teeter on the knife's edge of embracing uncontrolled desire. Gritting my teeth tightly I begin trying to fight the unyielding force within me. I can't let my temper go to the point of seeing red again. Donovan warned me that my soul will be utterly gone if I give in to my desires completely. My anger strengthens as I think about Donovan and how he has left me to fend for myself. Staring down at the table I'm secretively destroying, my heart begins pounding out of control when suddenly a loud, harsh voice cuts through my morbid thoughts.

"Stacie, shut the hell up," Larry roars. "How dare you talk to her like that? What the hell has she ever done to you?" Standing up abruptly, Larry forcefully pushes his chair back so quickly it causes the metal feet to scrape against the floor with a high pitched screeching sound. The piercing sound rips through my ears, causing me to break out in tingling goosebumps, ripping me free from the imprisoning rage I was succumbing to.

"Lauren, you don't have to listen to this shit any longer. If you want we can go eat outside," he hisses, still glaring at Stacie.

The raging furnace within me diminishes as my coiled, trembling body unwinds. I stare up at Larry gratefully, explaining, "Thank you Larry, but I think I'm done with lunch." Looking down at my now mutilated salad, I add respectfully, "Maybe we can do this some other time."

Hastily I leave the horrific effects of the lunch room behind me as I head back to my desk. The rumbling commotion of arguing erupts viciously behind me as I walk out the door. Larry's deep, thundering voice cuts through the sea of turmoil, instantly hushing them while he gives them all a vicious berating. A shocked hush hangs over the break room until the silence is interrupted by Larry storming out.

Sitting at my desk I blindly stare at the blank wall, trying to gain some composure. My consuming anger is completely gone, leaving only fear and regret now in its wake. My mind instantly replays the horrific situation I was just in. An overwhelming desire to flee from this tortuous place, like a frog jumping out of boiling water, comes over me. Looking up again at the clock on the wall I watch as the hands slowly move, counting down the minutes until work is over. Time feels like it is going at a snail's pace, but a brief sense of exhilaration washes over me as I realize this long and exhausting week is nearly finished.

Grabbing hold of my last paper of the day I begin filling it out when the sensation of someone standing behind me crawls up my spine, causing the hair on the back of my neck to rise. Reacting to the intruding feeling I quickly spin around, noticing Larry standing just inches behind me. Jumping back slightly I breathlessly snap, "Larry, you scared me. How long have you been standing there?"

His eyes tighten slightly in response. "Not long." He starts fidgeting with his hands as he sways apprehensively back and forth and utters sweetly, "Lauren, I'm so sorry about what happened today."

"Don't worry about it, I'm fine." I smile politely. "Thank you for sticking up for me, though."

He continues to sway anxiously as he nonchalantly wipes his hands on his nicely form-fitting khakis. An almost pasty expression rips across his face. Trying to break the nervous energy forming between us I quickly turn around and grab my purse so I can finally go home. I can hear Larry's ragged breathing as he anxiously fidgets with his car keys, waiting for me to face him. Turning back around I face Larry as I darn my eyebrows together. Giving him a bewildered look I utter, "I hope you have a great weekend. I'll see you on Monday."

I head down the staircase to leave. As I proceed to get closer to the large glass exit doors I notice Larry has been following me. "Larry, if you are worried about me getting to my car safely I think I am able to manage it just fine." Shoving my hand deep into my purse I begin to blindly search through the chaos of my unorganized purse for my keys.

"That's not why I'm following you." He sighs deeply. "I want to ask you something." He hesitantly grabs hold of my shoulder, gently stopping me in my tracks. Despondently I stare at the large glass exit door which holds my freedom from this horrific week, realizing I was just inches away from my escape – until Larry had to stop me.

His eyes shift side to side as he refuses to look at me. His hand suddenly starts trembling on my shoulder as he turns and looks at me. "Um… Lauren, I am wondering…Well…you said today at lunch that we should try getting together again and…" His voice slightly cracks, causing his fair skin to flush a deep crimson color.

Oh no, he's not going to ask me out – is he? I was just trying to be nice to him today for defending me – that's all.

"Well, I'm wondering if you would like to go out tonight?" He softly bites on his bottom lip as he almost seems to hold his breath. Why do I make him nervous? I'm nothing special.

My body instantly deflates like a ruptured balloon as I stand here mindlessly staring at him with a gaping mouth. I didn't realize I had inadvertently set the stage for him to ask me out. How could I have been so stupid? I didn't mean to lead him on in any sort of way. Brainlessly I attempt to come up with an excuse as to why I can't go on a date, allowing me to let him down easily. The last thing I want to do is hurt him – or worse, anger him. He is the only person right now who is willing to talk to me at work. Larry is a great guy, but my life is a mess. I can't drag a nice guy through the hell I'm literally living in right now.

Like an idiot I stand here in front of him, completely tongue-tied. Frantically I move my hand around in my purse, entirely unaware of what I am looking for. Staring down at my purse I mindlessly begin mumbling incoherent crap. "Um…

well… uh…" What in the heck am I looking for? Panic washes over me as my empty mind refuses to cooperate with me. I have no idea what I am aggressively searching for, but I refuse to quit. Entirely flustered by the awkward situation I gaze furiously into my purse, avoiding any eye contact with him.

"Lauren, I know it's kind of short notice, but I thought it could be fun to go out tonight – just as friends," he specifies softly, trying to ease the tension. "Besides, you need a diversion after the crap you went through today."

A rush of guilt rolls over me as I hear his soft voice echo in the hall, forcing me to relinquish my frenzied search for whatever it is I'm looking for. Slowly I gaze up at Larry's kind, gentle face as I silently stare into his dark blue eyes. His face drops slightly as he anxiously waits for my answer. I can cut the uneasy energy streaming between us with a knife. Shoving his hands deep into his pockets, Larry impatiently starts to tap his foot against the stained linoleum floor. A bright light instantly enlightens my dark, deserted brain. Keys, that's what I was looking for. Purposefully this time, I reach my hand into my purse and remove my keys, holding onto them like a security blanket.

"Well, Lauren, what do you say? Do you want to go out tonight?" he utters in a calm, low voice, cutting through the silence.

What harm can come from one date? Donovan's probably not even going to show up anyway. Turning my head slightly I gaze out the large glass door that leads to my freedom, which now seems to elude me. A fiery glow from the setting sun reflects off the windshields of all the cars and pierces through the glass door like millions of laser beams. The intense blaze burns into my heart, causing it to beat out of control. A rush of heat charges through my veins, setting all my nerve endings on fire. A chill slithers its way up my spine, triggering the hair on the back of my neck to stand up in exhilaration. Frantically I begin looking all around, entirely aware of why I am feeling this way.

Everything that Larry and I have been talking about immediately dissipates from my mind. I rush over to the large glass door as I anxiously peer out into the parking lot. The glare produced by the setting sun streams through the window, stinging my eyes and making it difficult to see anything. Reacting to the bright, glaring sun I squint slightly as I look all around trying to see Donovan's car. As I frantically gaze at the narrow rows of parked cars I suddenly notice a tall, slender figure leaning up against the driver's side of my car. He leans back against my car with his arms folded tightly against his chest and his legs crossed effortlessly. Undulating heat pours through me with anticipation. I have been waiting all week to see Donovan and now it appears he is finally here.

Though everything within me validates my assumption, I need to make sure by witnessing his glorious face with my own two eyes. Peering through the thick glass door, I penetrate its translucent shield with my desire to see his face. A thick, gravitating force converses between us as Donovan slowly turns towards me, revealing his stunning face. He stands there gazing back at me, when suddenly a brilliant roguish smile stretches across his face, triggering a sharp tug within my heart. Swirls of butterflies take flight within my stomach, causing a tumult of energy to explode out of my quivering body. Surges of heated goosebumps ripple on my highly sensitive skin as I stare excitedly upon him.

I gaze upon Donovan's brilliant appearance, trying to take in every stunning detail. His striking dark hair frames his face delicately, as if each piece has been strategically placed to enhance the sharp features of his chiseled face. A black tight-fitting sweater clings to his rippling torso, accentuating every curve and line of his lean, yet remarkable build. His black sweater and dark hair is a striking contrast to the color of his aqua blue eyes, causing the color to jump out in stunning brilliance.

An exuberant smile instantly appears on my face as I energetically begin to reach for the door. Grabbing hold of the doorknob a sudden wave of regret presses down upon me as my mind is abruptly aware of Larry standing directly behind me. Holding the doorknob tightly within my hand I slowly turn towards Larry. He is now inches away from me, firmly standing erect as his emotionless face stares out the window, glaring threateningly at Donovan.

"Who is that, Lauren?" he whispers, slightly annoyed by Donovan's' presence.

Timidly I gaze up at Larry's face, softly replying, "He's um…" I hesitate slightly, not sure what to call Donovan. He's not technically my boyfriend – if a demon even can be one – but he's not just a friend, either. I stammer out the best description, "Someone I have been seeing."

Staring into Larry's eyes I watch as the spark that was once in them completely dissipates, revealing only disappointment laced with impending questions. Guilt creeps up into me as the excitement that has been rushing through me dissipates, leaving my slumped body deflated as I realize I am going to have to turn Larry down. My thunderous heart beats against my tight chest as I stand here between what feels like two opposing sides of a heart wrenching spectrum. I don't want to hurt Larry – he has been my champion this week. But that is it – he is just a friend. My heart and soul belong to someone else and there is no way I can deny it. The high I was feeling is replaced by an immense amount of grief as Larry peers down at me with a look of disappointment. I don't need to say anything. A silent visual communication passes between us.

"When did you meet him?" he asks softly, turning his gaze back to Donovan.

My trembling hand fiddles with the handle on the door as I softly answer him, "I met him last weekend."

"Was it when we were at the club?" His voice lowers deep into his chest as he rumbles in surprise.

Why should he even care when I met Donovan? It's not like it's any of his business. Deep irritation slowly bubbles up, causing me to snap out my response, "Sort of. I guess."

"How?" he huffs as his eyes deepen with a cold, dark glare. "Did you run off with him in the club like Toni had suggested?"

A hot chill races up my spine as my hand instantly releases my tight grip on the door knob. Anger and disappointment rips through me like a wild tiger tearing away at the calm that was once inside of me. Everything he said today means nothing now. I thought he believed me, but apparently he believes all the asses at work instead. I rumble out with a thick, acidic edge coating my response, "You jerk. I don't need to explain anything to you. I have already told you what happened in the club, and if you don't believe me that's not my problem. I thought we were building a friendship, but obviously I am wrong."

Turning sharply, I forcefully grab onto the handle of the large glass door, attempting to flee from this hellhole I work in, when suddenly there is a gentle tug on my arm. "Lauren, I'm sorry. I did – and still do – believe you. You're right, I am being a jerk." He pauses slightly as he clears his throat, "There is just something about that guy I just don't trust."

Letting out a forceful exhale, I stare out the large glass door only to discover Donovan is now glaring at the situation I am in. A livid expression washes over him as he stares vehemently at us. Obviously Donovan is acutely aware of what is going on between Larry and me. Breathlessly I watch as a vicious expression streams across his face and pours down his taut form, giving me the impression that he is about ready to barge in and rescue me.

Hastily I give Donovan a reassuring look as I utter forcefully to Larry, "Thank you for caring, but I'm not your concern. I will be perfectly fine." Flinging the door open I add intently, "Good night Larry."

With every step closer to Donovan the stress from my week sheds off my body like a snake breaking free from its lifeless skin. Leaving my disastrous day in the dust I nearly run towards Donovan in anticipation. Bubbling heat of nervous energy pulsates within the pit of my stomach as I gravitate even closer to him. Standing inches away from Donovan I breathlessly stare at him as he intently examines my every detail. What does he see in me? Like Toni said, I am second rate. He glances down at me as a coy smile streams across his face, chasing away his once austere expression.

"Lauren, I told you not to go accepting another date," he utters, slightly laughing.

The excitement I am feeling slightly dissipates as I look at him harshly in response to what he said. "What do you mean, I can't go accepting another date? I haven't heard from you in days. I thought for sure you weren't even going to show up," I state abruptly. I position myself defensively in front of him with my arms tightly entwined around my abdomen.

Complete bewilderment rinses away his joyful expression as he states gently, "Lauren, why would you think I wouldn't show up? I couldn't wait to see you again."

I repeat sardonically, "Why wouldn't I think that…where have you been? I haven't heard from you all week. You just abandoned me to deal with my new reality on my own, leaving me feeling insecure and alone." I weakly look down at my tightly entangled arms, uttering softly, "I thought for sure you had come to your senses, leaving me like all the other souls you have entrapped."

A soft, regretful moan escapes fiercely out of him. He reaches over and apologetically caresses the back of my hand. "Lauren, I did not, nor will I ever abandon you. I wanted to call, but I…" His voice quietly trails off like he is hiding something from me. He violently shakes his head back and forth as if he is forcing an unpleasant memory out of his mind. Looking down at me he gently gazes into my eyes. "Trust me, I covet you way too much to ever leave. My eternal hunger for you runs thick within my veins. You are now part of my blood, body and soul. You are the vice I never want to repent of. And that bastard Toni has no idea what he is talking about. You are sexy and beautiful, definitely not second rate." He looks intently into my eyes, adding firmly, "Your soul, though, will not be entrapped for long. I promise you."

His words shatter my defensive shield as they pierce my heart with a severe amount of heat. Warmth radiates out from my heart with an overwhelming amount of inexplicable joy, causing my rigid frame to slowly relax. Donovan's hand tenderly caresses away the last bit of trepidation. A deep sigh of relief rolls out of me, taking with it all my fears as I slowly peer up at his gentle face. His amazing blue eyes gaze unremittingly down at my face, piercing through to my very soul. His crystal blue eyes liquefy as if the dark windows to his soul remain open to me, allowing me the privilege to peer in and see his inner desires.

The door to his deep soul now is wide open for me to gaze in, allowing me to know for the first time what he truly feels for me. A flood of passion permeates my heart until I cannot contain it any longer. The heat originating from his passion pours out of my heart, filling me until it floods every hidden corner of my body. I embrace every intense part of it, not wanting the overwhelming sensation to stop.

Crystal clear images flash in my head, blocking my vision like I'm watching a movie only we can see. These images are not my memories or thoughts. These pictures are not seen through my eyes, but through Donovan's. I suddenly see myself standing in the corner of the crowded night club. Sorrow fills my being as I'm allowed to feel the tremendous regret he had for taking my soul.

Darkness fades that scene as light instantly reveals the situation in the dark parking lot. An overwhelming need to protect me from the perpetrator who meant me harm instantly fills my vision. A chill races up my spine, gripping onto all the nerves and crippling me as I see clearly the pursuer's intensions for me. The reality of what could have happened if Donovan wasn't there causes my stomach to curdle. Donovan must be sensing my fear because the image in my mind instantly dissipates, allowing the sensation of passion to replace the fear I had been feeling.

His desires immediately take me in a new direction as my body suddenly starts shuddering. I see my face clearly in my mind as he replays him kissing me, causing my breathing to quicken with pleasure. Warm flowing swells formed in my core surge out, causing me to hold my breath while my thighs tingle in pleasure.

Our souls seem to be colliding together, intertwining, becoming one being. This amazing gift from Donovan intensifies my pull towards him. Needing to know more about him, an inflexible urge rushes through me wanting to delve deeper into his soul and memories. Deciding to take advantage of this opportunity I search deeper into his eyes for more information about him. Abruptly the vision of us dissipates and I no longer can see my face clearly within my mind. The awareness of passion I was enveloped in is now replaced by a tremendous amount of grief laced with intense anger and disappointment. A heavy weight pushes down on my heart like it is going to break at any moment.

Uncontrollable tears well up within my eyes when suddenly I can see – as clear as can be – an older man slouched by a headstone, crying. The scene holds an eerie familiarity to it. I have seen this man before – in my dream. Needing answers, I attempt to focus in on the man when instantly everything is gone.

"Lauren, I allowed you to see a brief glimpse into the way I feel about you and that's it. I will share my secrets with you when I feel the time is right," he states sharply.

Slightly taken aback by the rebuking tone ripping through his voice, I drop my hand quickly away from his. I probably did go too far but I still have so many unanswered questions and this, to me, was a perfect way to get them answered. "Donovan, I'm sorry, but I want – no, I need to know what really happened to you," I murmur unapologetically.

A pregnant pause lingers between us as he closes his eyes. He exhales sharply as he looks down at me with a tortured expression on his face. "Lauren, this is my hell, not yours. What's done is done. There is nothing you can do about it now."

Gently I press my hand against his smooth cheek. Closing his eyes, he tenderly leans his cheek against my hand. Turning his head slightly he presses his lips lightly against my palm. "Please, Donovan, let me in. It may be your hell, but it doesn't mean you have to live it all alone. Remember I am now blood of your blood," I remind him emphatically.

He gently wraps his hands around my wrist, pulling my hand away from his cheek. Holding it inches away from his face he softly strokes my fingers. His eyes are affixed to the belly of my hand, as if he is a palm reader studying every line in it, completely lost in deep thought.

"Donovan, please, I think I have a right to know." I take a step closer to him, causing there to be no voided space between our bodies. A thrashing amount of trepidation oozes out of him like heat from a forest fire.

Lifting my hand to his mouth he lovingly kisses the back of it. "Lauren, you want me to tell you all about my life?" I nod my head softly in response. "Okay," he agrees hesitantly. "But I am not going to tell you." His eyes glance all around the parking lot and up into the windows of the offices above us, then immediately gaze back down at me with a liberating expression streaming across his face. "I am going to show you, but first I think we need to take your car home."

CHAPTER 16

Velocity

My trembling hand attempts to unlock my stubborn front door as anxious, untamed energy exudes out of me. The uneasy energy forming in the pit of my stomach now explodes out of me like an atomic blast. Anticipation for what is in store for me governs my every action, making it hard to do even the simplest act – like unlocking my stupid front door. Sheer embarrassment at my attempts at my lock causes me to get flustered. A dominant stream of amusement oozes out of Donovan as he enjoys watching me struggle to keep my mental composure. His close proximity to me is not allowing my mind or hand to work efficiently. The only things running through my mind are lascivious thoughts of Donovan and several curse words. Aggressively I continue jiggling the key in the lock, trying to open my door, but no matter how hard I try it won't open.

"Do you need some help with that?" he sarcastically states.

"No. I think I'm capable of opening my own front door…thank you," I snap in frustration. Shoving the key forcefully into the lock, I vigorously twist and turn the key. "Open, you stupid door." The humiliation swirling in my stomach suddenly morphs into an angry fit of rage. Gazing forcefully at my front door I frantically kick it in complete irritation. "Damn it. What is wrong with this stupid thing? Why won't you open up – you damn thing."

Suddenly Donovan's warm fingers gently envelop my quivering arm, instantly extinguishing the irrational surge of anger flowing through me. Calmly he slides them down my arm until they rest on the top of my hand, which is still gripping the doorknob. His more muscular hand gently envelops mine as he lightly squeezes it against the doorknob. I feel heat slowly building like a kiln baking everything beneath it, penetrating deep into me until I feel like our hands are becoming one. Though there is an immense amount of heat, there is no pain associated with it. Our fiery hands seem to be pulsating through the doorknob. Suddenly Donovan turns my hand and the handle at the same time, instantly causing the door to fling open.

"There, is that better? We can now get into your house," he utters in a pretentious tone.

Denial washes over my frozen body as I peer down at my still overheated hand. "How did you do that?" I reply weakly.

"Do what?" he slyly responds.

"Donovan, you said you were going to tell or show me everything. Don't start lying now," I huff firmly.

A husky exhale rolls out of his mouth as he looks at me with a conceding expression on his face. "You're right, the truth starts now."

Firmly I gaze up at his beautiful face as I inhale deeply, adding, "Okay, since you're ready to be honest, is that how you brought me into my apartment last weekend?"

A wide, beautiful smile spreads across his face, causing his eyes to glimmer with excitement. "Yes, except I didn't use your hand to help me open the door."

"So if you didn't use my hand – where was I then?" I inquire, slightly confused.

"Well, technically I don't need your hand to do that. As far as last week goes, remember you fell asleep in the car? So I carried you into your apartment. I couldn't just leave you in the car – fast asleep. I didn't want to wake you, either. It was easier to let you in this way than having to deal with your keys. You were completely out the entire time I carried you in and put you to bed."

"Wait, you put me in my bed?" I query, attempting to wrap my head around it.

"Yes, but I didn't change your clothes, if you remember. I was a perfect gentleman," he reassures me.

A timid uneasiness washes over me as I gingerly ask, "Did you stay the whole night or did you leave?"

Donovan's eyes bore deep into mine as his hand slides up my arm, causing chills to crawl up my neck. Gently his hand skims up my neck until it rests lovingly under my chin. Lifting my chin so our eyes meet he utters vehemently, "I stayed the entire night. I left after you were done with your shower. I needed to make sure you weren't going to have a nervous breakdown from all the information I sprang on you."

"I was perfectly fine. I wouldn't have had a nervous breakdown," I add overzealously, trying not to just reassure Donovan, but also myself.

"Yes, but the nightmare you were having did not reassure me." His liquid eyes pour over me, soaking my mind with a heavy amount of passion laced with regret.

Donovan leans down, resting his forehead against mine. His warm, sweet breath tickles my face as it gently caresses my highly sensitive skin, flowing down over me. Wrapping his hand tightly around my waist he pulls me securely against his firm physique. Anticipation explodes within my heart, causing my skin to tingle feverishly. My craggy breathing increases as my thunderous heart pounds aggressively within me, sending echoing waves of pressure to build in my ears.

"I would have been fine," I mumble breathlessly.

He doesn't respond to my comment, forcing a palpable silence to roll over me as he holds me firmly against him. Throbbing gushes of desire quiver within me and cause my erratic breathing to flood over my moist, trembling full lips. Donovan's smooth, steady breath pours over me, filling my senses with his warm, earthy smell like he is unaffected by the fervor between us. Extreme heat exudes from his skin as he slides closer to my ear. His warm breath rains over me, caressing my ear as he whispers into it, "Lauren, are you ready to leave?"

A terrifying rush shoots down my now rigid body. "What do you mean?"

Pressing his cheek securely against mine, he utters, "Remember, I am going to answer all your questions, but if I am going to do so we need to leave – now."

"Leave? Am I driving or is your car here?" I naively ask, still slightly confused and nervous about what is going to happen.

A thick, breathy laugh heaves out of Donovan, forcing him to pull slightly away from me. In confusion I look up at Donovan's face – which now holds a mischievous appearance – uttering, "Did I say something wrong?"

"No, not at all." The smile on his face increases, exposing his deep dimples. "It's just – we're not taking a car. We are going to go a much faster way." He snickers like he is hiding something.

"What do you mean?"

A spark suddenly ignites within him, releasing an instant wave of relief as his eyes burn deep into my soul. The muscles within his arms tighten, embracing me in his iron grasp. Suddenly, without warning, he firmly presses his lips onto mine, kissing me feverishly. His searing hand slides down my arm until it reaches my keys. Grasping onto them he gently removes them from my hand, tossing them into my apartment.

Donovan's mouth envelops mine as a surge of heat swirls aggressively within his mouth and rushes into mine, penetrating my throat. Hot air cascades vigorously down my throat, scorching the supple edges as it burns its way into me. This kiss is very different. It lacks the uncontrolled edge like before. It's as if his mouth is only pressing firmly against mine, filling me with this indescribable heat.

The muscles in his arms tighten around me, locking me firmly against his. Instantly a spinning sensation rushes over me as if I'm twirling out of control. The velocity of the air increases with a swift burst of speed. Hastening wind envelops me like I have been sucked into the outer edges of a cyclone. An uneasiness forming in the pit of my stomach causes a sensation of motion sickness to consume me. Panic races through my veins, forcing me to open my eyes to try and understand the phenomenon I'm experiencing. My thunderous heart starts beating rapidly as I discover a whirling kaleidoscope of colors racing all around me. The whirling movement of melting colors fades effortlessly into a blob of unrecognizable shapes and forms. My muscles tense up as I grip onto Donovan's sweater. Shockwaves of terror push through my immobile body as I anxiously try to pull myself free from

Donovan's tight grasp. My useless attempt is to no avail. I might as well be pushing against a brick wall.

Slightly lifting his mouth off of mine, Donovan groans firmly, "Close your eyes, Lauren."

Tenderly, yet deliberately Donovan instantly places his luscious lips back on mine, compelling the heat from his mouth to once again penetrate deep into me. The fire pulsating through me intensifies. Donovan tightens his grip around me, forcing my now limp body to press firmly against his in a protective gesture.

Immediately I obey his demand, closing my eyes tightly as I try to fight back the nausea and fear bubbling up within me. Though I no longer can see the smears of colors, I can feel the rushing air circling all around me. Other than the wind enveloping us, there is no other sensation of our swift movement. My feet feel as if they are still firmly planted on a solid surface.

The air around me suddenly transforms from its crisp, cool edge to a thick, sticky sensation. The hot, dense air pushes down on me like a heavy weight, making it difficult to breathe. The outside air now mimics the fiery furnace emitting out of me. This heavy, sticky wind has a different sensation to it than the cool, crisp air in Clayton.

As my pragmatist mind attempts to thwart the validity of what is actually occurring, the thickly encompassing wind instantly slows to a calm, steady breeze. A hot, humid layer of air now engulfs me like a smothering blanket, instantly causing a shimmering layer of sweat to bead up. Donovan loosens his iron grip on me as a sharp exhale slowly escapes from him, filling my mouth with a final burst of heat. The fear I was successfully suppressing now bubbles to the surface as Donovan slightly pulls his mouth away from mine.

"Lauren, you can open your eyes now, it's over," he calmly whispers in my ear.

I don't want to open my eyes, but my curiosity of where I am or what has happened consumes me. Burying my head firmly into his chest I reluctantly whimper, "I'm not sure if I can."

Holding me against his firm chest he carefully strokes the back of my head as he rests his chin firmly on the top of mine. "Lauren, I am sorry. Are you sick?"

"No. I don't think I can open my eyes yet," I state weakly.

"Why?" he utters, with an apprehensive edge to his question.

Sighing softly, I press my head into his firm, muscular chest. "I'm afraid."

"Are you afraid of me?" he hesitantly asks.

"No," I quickly snap reassuringly. "I'm afraid to see where we are. If I open my eyes I will have to confront the validity of what has occurred, and I don't think I can do that."

Kissing the top of my head he gently pleads, "Lauren, please open your eyes."

His breathless plea envelops my apprehensive mind with a warm, reassuring comfort, giving me the strength I need to confront this frightening scenario. Reluctantly I obey his soothing request and slowly pull myself away from his brawny chest, allowing the humid air to press between us. As I pull myself away from his firm grip my weakened legs collapse beneath me.

Flexing his arms firmly around me he stops me instantly in mid-fall, uttering with a thick layer of concern in his voice, "Are you all right?"

"I'm fine, I think I got a little dizzy, that's all," I state flatly, trying to hide the embarrassment in my voice.

A soft laugh escapes from Donovan, causing an irritating chill to race up my spine. "Do you want me to look or not?" I snap.

Seizing the courage that beats under the surface of my skin, I forcefully push myself away from Donovan's protective grasp. Swallowing all of my fear which is sitting like a lump in my throat, I slowly take in a deep, cleansing breath. Dense darkness caused by the deep night sky prevents me from focusing in on anything. Peering intently into the strange, deep-black night I struggle to make out any familiar form to my surroundings. Slowly shapes and images in front of me begin to take on a willowy form as my eyes gradually adjust to the darkness.

The full moon slices through the dark night with beams of shimmering light, igniting everything around me with a silvery glow. I stare out with wide eyes and gaping mouth at the foreign scenery I'm standing in the midst of. I watch in astonishment as the moonbeams dance delicately over the ripples of what appears to be a large body of water. The gray glow of steam swirling off of the water pours onto the ground like waves of sticky moisture invading everything. Slowly I gaze all around me, attempting to convince my mind of the inconceivable. Many beautiful, substantial live oak trees dot the surrounding area, creating an ancient, eerie atmosphere. Their firm, almost regal appearance towers over us as if we are intruding on their existence. The branches of these trees reach out in great lengths, stretching in a multitude of directions. These regal trees are infested by an immense amount of moss draping from the branches like sheer green curtains.

A thin layer of fog blankets the ground beneath the splendid trees, casting a sinister green glow all around us. The sweltering night air mixed with the steaming humidity forms an invading fog. The slithering fog slowly undulates along the ground, attacking the bases of the majestic trees as the mist bubbles and rises in triumph. It covers the ground in a nearly hostile warning for all to stay back.

Disbelief attacks my bewildered eyes as I scan my surroundings for any sign as to where I might be. Suddenly I catch sight of a long, narrow gravel road in the distance. The road is flanked by two straight rows of large cypress trees standing erect in an almost rigid style of military stance. Instead of their branches reaching towards us they stretch up to the heavens as if they are pleading to the skies on our account.

Heavy clumps of moss cling tightly to the upstretched branches also as they dance delicately in the humid night air. The thick moisture rippling in the atmosphere feeds the constant need of the invading moss as it consumes every tree with its delicate devouring power.

A familiar, yet haunting feeling is awakened within me by these erect guards lining the narrow gravel road. Straining my eyes, I attempt to see down this straight and narrow path, fully expecting to find an old graveyard at the end. But to my surprise, positioned gracefully at the end of the road is a large white plantation house. Massive stone columns flank the front of the house, extending up past the second story. Placed protectively behind these eight solid columns are two oversized porches.

The bottom deck is obviously used to greet all who enter this grand establishment. Every detail is used to ensure a traditional southern front porch. A large porch swing positioned by the front door hangs delicately by two thick chains. I can hear the soft, gentle rattle from the chains as the swing gently sways in the balmy breeze. To the side of the large black door is a small iron tea table set, with a white linen tablecloth thrown delicately over the top of the table. Set around the elegant table are four intricate white cast-iron chairs which are laden with heavy amounts of rust from the constant exposure to the intense humidity. Acting as a shimmering backdrop to the inviting porch are several ceiling-to-floor windows framed with large black shutters.

The terrace above the porch is just as impressive, with its oversized windows and shutters. Two large French doors on the second floor terrace are open slightly, allowing the sweet, balmy, fragrant air to fill the rooms beyond its boundaries.

In amazement I turn towards Donovan, only to discover he is intently gazing upon the magnificent house. His flat eyes suddenly fill with a strong amount of regret as he stares longingly at the grand house. I whisper, trying to match the silence looming in the air, "Donovan, where are we?"

"We are in Mandeville, Louisiana." His voice breaks slightly as he quietly adds, "This is my home town and that is my family's house."

A heavy thud drops into the basement portion of my stomach as my sand-dollar size eyes turn towards the large house. I take in every serene detail, trying to imagine his family life here. Suddenly a woman walks out onto the upper terrace, standing there gazing contemplatively into the distant grounds. The moonlight streams down on her like a spotlight from heaven, lighting her entire face with an angelic glow. An intense yearning explodes within me, causing me to proceed aimlessly towards the mysterious woman.

The moonlight pours over her with a shimmering glow, revealing every detail on her face. Her striking chiseled features are accentuated by delicate age lines positioned gracefully throughout her face. The balmy night breeze causes her long salt and peppered hair to lightly dance against the moonbeams, heightening the streams of grey swirling within her dark hair. Gazing upon this elegant woman's face, I notice her striking eyes and the years of pain etched deep into them. This pain almost mimics the eternal torment written all over Donovan's face. Even from a distance the striking resemblance between this older woman and Donovan are uncanny.

A warm sensation radiating from behind me envelops me like a warm blanket. Reacting to the feeling, I instantly turn around only to discover Donovan now standing behind me, gazing intently up at the woman. His face immediately drops as he hastily pulls me back towards the protective darkness of the cypress trees.

"Donovan, is she a family member? Don't you want to see her?" I ask naively, confused at why he is hiding from her. "Who is that woman? Is she your mother?"

"No," he sighs. His eyes remain fixated on the now mysterious woman.

"Donovan, if she isn't your mother then who is she?" A surge of regret instantly rolls up my spine. For some strange reason I'm not sure if I'm ready to hear the answer.

A regrettable exhale rushes through his mouth. "That is my sister." His eyes pierce deep into mine. "That is my… younger sister," he clarifies hesitantly.

Confusion fills my already saturated mind as I gaze up once more at the woman, scrutinizing her every feature. Straining my eyes I attempt to make her appear younger, but no matter how hard I try there is no denying the validity of her age.

"Donovan, you must be going blind. That woman can't be your younger sister, there is no possible way. She is probably a good forty years older than you," I force out brazenly.

Moving within inches of me, he tightly wraps one arm securely around me. Donovan gazes deep into my eyes as if he is assessing my emotional status. Obviously seeing nothing alarming in my face, he utters softly, "Lauren, I am four years older than my sister… so technically that makes me…" He hesitates slightly as his eyes roll up like he is calculating numbers in his head, then he continues, "Sixty-seven years old."

A wave of trembling horror races through me, causing my legs to buckle beneath me. Obviously prepared for this type of reaction, Donovan's engulfing arm immediately flexes against my torso, stopping me from falling to the ground. His secure arm holds onto me as my quivering and shocked body dangles weightlessly within his firm grasp.

Feeling a wave of nausea roll over me, I utter breathlessly, "Donovan, I think I need to sit…" Before I am able to finish my sentence my legs suddenly swing up into his awaiting arms. The motion is so quick and effortless on his part, like he is only lifting a small ragdoll. Holding me naturally within his firm grasp he carries me over to a large dead branch lying across the misty ground, only inches away from the private gravel road. Softly he places me onto the fallen branch as my overwhelmed body seals onto the thick bark.

Feverishly grasping onto the branch for some sort of support, my fingers easily dig into the spongy texture of the bark like it was made of dense foam. The constant exposure to the sweltering damp environment has completely destroyed this once resilient solid branch. It has been transformed into a weak and defenseless shell of what it once was. Lifting my head up toward the tops of the trees I begin pleading for some kind of sanity to return. Pressing my fingers deeper into the malleable bark I suddenly can feel the firm, pure core of the tree, unscathed by the tumultuous environment surrounding it.

Digging deep into my solid core I gather whatever pathetic internal strength I have left as I look up at Donovan. Sitting next to me, his dejected physique slumps onto the branch as his firm hands encompass his face. Slowly I examine his strong muscular hands quivering over his breathtaking face. I slowly observe his every detail, scrutinizing his youthful appearance. "Donovan," I utter weakly. "How is that possible? You don't look a day over twenty-three."

Instantly dropping his hands, he begins intertwining his fingers roughly. "I was twenty-two years old when I started serving this sentence. So physically I am still twenty-two, but technically I am sixty-seven years old."

A heavy sigh presses out of me as I try to understand the logistics of what he is saying, muttering, "I'm confused. If you were twenty-two when it happened, why haven't you aged?"

"We…" His eyes instantly flash deep into mine. "I mean – enslaved souls. You will soon not be a part of this equation." He gazes reassuringly upon me. "I am not subject to the same laws or regulations that humans have on them, those rules do not apply to us."

Glaring deep into his emotionless eyes I try to gather any information out of them, but his shallow eyes are not betraying him. "Donovan, what do you mean by laws and regulations?" I mutter in uncertainty. My voice is thick and a higher pitch than usual as my vocal chords seem to be compressing down on any air escaping me. "Do you mean government laws or laws of nature?"

A sharp, boisterous laugh escapes out of him, making me feel like once again I'm missing out on an inside joke. "What is so funny?" I protest, almost too loud as the constant fire within me ignites like gasoline being thrown on it.

His laughter promptly stops as he gives me an apologetic look. "I'm sorry. I didn't mean to upset you." He lifts his hand and tenderly pushes a loose, wavy strand of my brown hair behind my ear while his thumb traces soft little circles on the top of my cheekbone. Gazing deep into my eyes, he utters, "Remember, don't lose your temper."

His seducing touch instantly extinguishes the uncontrolled fire burning within me. Still feeling the bubbling irritation, I lightly lean against his hand as I ask softly, "Donovan, why did you laugh at me?"

A gentle sigh escapes his moist mouth as he places both of his hands firmly on the sides of my face. Holding my face securely in the palms of his hands he gazes deep into my eyes. My heart starts pounding out an irregular rhythm as I look intently upon his mesmerizing face. His liquid blue eyes pierce deep into mine, sending shivers of lust, formed in my thighs, to fill my entire body.

"Lauren, I did not, nor will I ever laugh at you," he states fervently. "I merely laughed at the thought of the government ever trying to stop us, when most of the time they are in bed with us." He pauses slightly when I instantly notice a crooked smile appear on his face. "Figuratively speaking, that is." He adds fervently, "Lauren, the government has no power over us and neither do the laws of nature."

I stare deep into his hypnotic gaze as a dense weight of bewilderment rips through me. "What do you mean by laws of nature?"

"Time, gravity and all of the above do not affect us the same way. Demons are not subject to these laws."

His eyes don't move from my face as I try to soak in what he is simply stating to me. I replay events in my mind, trying to understand it all. If time doesn't mean the same to him, that explains how we arrived in Louisiana from Clayton in what felt like only mere moments. There are many more unexplained situations where it appears as if he disappeared into thin air or appeared out of nowhere.

He must be noticing that I am beginning to put two and two together, because his hands release their secure grip on my face. Donovan's fingers slide lightly down my arm as if his fingertips are silky down feathers timidly brushing across my skin, causing shivers of bliss to run vibrantly up my spine. I inhale sharply, trying to keep my focus on what's at hand.

Gazing intently at Donovan's face I try to keep my mind in focus. "Are you telling me you can time travel?" I stammer out. My voice is still quivering from his tantalizing touch.

Reacting to the trembling in my voice, an alluring smile spreads gloriously across his face. His fingertips stop their enticing journey down my arm, resting delicately on the backs of my hands. He gazes melodically at my face, reassuring me that he is not going to laugh at me.

Smiling gently, he responds to my question, "Not exactly. To time travel still requires you to obey the basic laws of time, but for us it works by our thoughts or our desires. If I think of something or someone…" He winks at me slightly, "… and intently focus only on that image, within seconds I am there. So it is not technically time travel, because time doesn't exist for me. That is why I don't age. Time doesn't have a firm hold on me as it does with humans."

"Wait, Donovan, are you saying you are not human?" I mutter quickly.

"I am what you would call unique, both human and demon. There are many like me that still have their bodies, but that does not make them human. On the contrary, they are the total opposite. They have completely embraced the iniquitous side, making them much more malevolent than any spirit demon. As long as I hold onto whatever humanity I have left, I will not become a complete monster."

The hairs on my arms rise up in fear as he speaks of these insidious beings that have completely embraced the wickedness inside of them. "Donovan, why are they more dangerous than the spirit demons? Time must not affect them either."

Firmly he gazes up at me. "First of all, Lauren, you need to understand something. It isn't only – they – who are dangerous. I am in that same category as they are. Just because I am holding on to whatever decency I have left doesn't mean I won't eventually slip, giving in to the malicious side of me." His voice is thick with a deep warning, adding, "What you don't understand is that it is not simply time that has no effect on us. That's not what makes us dangerous."

"What do you mean?" I question softly as a tingling sensation crawls up my spine like millions of spiders pouring over my back.

"Lauren, nothing has an effect on us. We can control all the elements surrounding us, bending them to our will. If I wanted to, I could pick up a car like it is merely a tinker toy and throw it across a field."

Panic presses down on my lungs, causing all the air to push out of me. I watch the resolute expression roll across his face like he is reveling in his power. I have not seen this side of Donovan before. Though he is simply being honest, there is a firm, vicious edge flowing through him.

"How is that possible?" I utter in amazement as the tingling sensation wraps around my ribs.

"The only way I can describe it is, when you were younger did you ever swim in a pool and try to pick up your father or a larger person?"

My eyes narrow as my brow presses together in confusion. "Yes, but how does swimming in a pool have anything to do with what we are talking about?" I state reluctantly.

A half-hearted smile appears as he adds, "A lot. Do you remember how buoyant your father felt? And how you were able to carry him around the pool with almost no effort on your part, yet he was probably three times your weight? That is how it works for us. Everything is nearly weightless. It takes no effort on our part to carry or throw something that is even ten times our mass."

Donovan sits motionless while his hands rest gently on the backs of mine, waiting for some kind of response from me. His once straight posture now reflects his mind-set. His shoulders slump forward in a defeatist attitude. I can tell by his disconsolate broken-down body he is wondering if I'm going to run away from him, kicking and screaming in fear.

Turning my hands over so that our palms are against each other, I wrap my fingers tightly around his hands, holding onto them firmly. "Donovan, you don't scare me. I know you will never hurt me. I have complete faith in you," I state fervently, reassuring him that I'm not afraid of him – in any way.

"Lauren, you are absolutely right, I will never hurt you, but you shouldn't have so much faith in me. Faith is meant for those with hope and I don't have any hope left," he grumbles softly.

Slowly I slide along the spongy branch until I am only inches away from his dejected body. His eyes still stare down at my hands as he refuses to meet my gaze. "Donovan, there is always hope."

His eyes spring up quickly, holding a searing intensity within his gaze. "You are right. There is hope for you. I have already communicated with Lucius on your behalf. As for me it is too late. I am serving my sentence. Fighting for me is a battle we will both lose."

A sharp, stabbing pain quivers through me as he whispers the frightening name he communicated with about me. I have heard him mention the name before, but simply the utterance of the name sends cold shivers across my shoulders. "Donovan, who is Lucius? You mentioned him when we were up on Mt. Diablo. Is he…" A lump lodges in my throat, stopping me from continuing. Fear is stopping me from saying who I think it is. I never believed in the devil, but now I believe in anything.

"No, to answer your question, Lucius is not the devil," he replies reassuringly. "It may sound funny, but as demons we don't randomly run around without any order. There is, I suppose you can call it, our checks and balances. Lucius is – I guess you can say – my boss. He is like me though. He still has his body, but he has embraced the evil completely."

Though I can hear Donovan speaking, my mind instantly goes into autopilot. Vibrating streams of fear ripple through my veins as Donovan explains the logistics to the working order of Hell. The more he talks about it, the more my terror bubbles to the surface at the horror of knowing there is an all-encompassing demon out there that isn't too happy with Donovan for trying to free my soul. This menacing demon is now fully aware of me. How am I going to be safe with this sinister being hot on my trail?

My legs begin to tingle violently with a numbing feeling as the thoughts flood my mind. All of a sudden I hear a crashing sound like rocks slamming into each other violently. Slowly I gaze all around trying to see where the sound is coming from, only to discover that my legs are ferociously vibrating. Peering down at them I immediately discover my entire frame is wildly trembling in fear. The crashing sound echoing loudly in my ears actually is my teeth savagely slamming against each other.

Donovan suddenly wraps his arms tightly around me, trying to control the unimaginable trembling I have succumbed to. Holding onto me tightly he softly touches the back of my head as he whispers in my ear, "Lauren, you will be fine. I will never let anything happen to you. You are safe with me. Lucius will never harm you while I am around."

Quickly my head snaps up as I react to what he just said. Feverishly I ask, with an immense amount of trepidation in my voice, "And what about when you are not around? He knows that you are trying to free my soul. What if he personally comes after me when you are not around?"

His hand securely wraps around the back of my head as he lightly presses my cheek against his muscular chest. He holds me there firmly as if he is trying to convince himself that nothing is going to ever happen to me. Delicately he presses his lips against the top of my head, kissing me softly. "I will never leave you then. I can't let anything happen to you. You have been through too much already." An edge of fear ripples through his words. I know we are in for a real fight.

"Lauren," his voice is so soft that it is a breathy whisper against my head. "Can we take a break for a while? I will still answer all your questions, but I think we need to stop for a little while."

Even though I know he is trying to change the subject, what he is asking makes sense. My head is beginning to throb from all the information that has been thrown at me. I need some time to process everything.

"What do you want to do?" I ask hesitantly.

"Well, I was thinking that we can perhaps get some food since you haven't eaten yet. It is almost midnight and you must be starving."

I have no desire to move from the security of his enveloping arms. It feels safe to be in his arms, like nothing can get to me, but I am starving and I need to eat soon. I have been so inundated by everything happening to me that I haven't noticed my growling stomach until he mentioned food. The gurgling instantly turns within me. I suck my stomach in tightly, trying to mute the obtrusive noises of my growling stomach. "I think food is a good idea," I quickly add, trying to get him to forget my stomach growl. "Where do you want to eat?"

"Since we are so close it would be fun to eat in New Orleans."

Lifting my head away from the security of his magnificent chest I gaze reluctantly upon his strong face. From this angle his nose gives a perfect anchor to his masculine face. "How are we going to get there?" I whisper fearfully. "Please tell me it's not going to be the same way we arrived here." I shudder, remembering what it felt like.

A glorious smile spreads across his face instantly. "It will be over before you even know it," he boasts.

His arms wrap tightly around my waist as he holds onto me firmly against his solid chest. Gently lifting my chin so our faces are now merely inches away from each other, he then gazes into my eyes. My heart begins pounding out of control again. I hunger for his kisses, but what is about to transpire I can do without. Donovan knows what I desire because instantly his lips press against mine. The heat from his mouth permeates my skin. This time his kiss is not in control, his tongue explores my mouth as I answer back with the same exploration. Fluttering wings in my stomach take flight as I lose myself within his kiss. Closing my eyes tightly I fully give in to my own desires, softly biting his bottom full lip, causing a low moan to roll out of him. Entangling my hands forcefully into his I grip onto a handful of his silky smooth hair, pressing his head firmly against mine.

The world I once knew has been forever changed. I have no idea what is going to happen next, but I know it will never be the same again. No matter what he is I need him in my life, and it appears that he needs me in his.

CHAPTER 17

Sacrifice

We stand impatiently in front of a long row of ornately decorated buildings with neon signs scattered everywhere overhead, trying to decide where to eat. My oversaturated mind is having a hard time determining what I'm in the mood for when the only thing I want is to have Donovan's sumptuous mouth back on me.

Donovan has walked me up and down Bourbon Street several times in a useless attempt to find something for me to eat, but nothing is sounding good. I can tell by his occasional breathy growls I'm beginning to irritate him. Every time he suggests something my eyes focus intently on his luxurious lips, causing me to lose my train of thought.

I have never had this much uncontrolled desire around Donovan before. Perhaps what is heightening my aroused sensation is the highly sexually charged atmosphere oozing all around me. Bourbon Street seems to have an overpowering element of desire to it. The dim lights scattered above the sidewalks mix with the erotic beat of music swirling vividly throughout the thick, hot air. There are occasional windows with barely dressed women placed suggestively in them, attracting the seedy men looking for an erotic experience. The sticky sweltering air seems to be making the girls around here dress in things that leave very little to one's imagination. These scantily dressed girls are standing out in front of the bars dancing provocatively, causing the atmosphere around me to heat up in every way possible.

As I walk through the crowds of people, their overwhelming desires excreting from their bodies profusely pour deep into my soul. Combining their yearnings to my already heightened sensory state causes a sexual cocktail to swirl deep inside of me. Sweat droplets run down the back of my neck, tickling the epidermis layer of the skin, causing a pleasurable exhale to escape from me. My breathing deepens as I inhale the thick, sensual air, causing my body and thoughts to want to fall into a hypnotic trance. Taking in a deep, cleansing breath I struggle to resist the overpowering yearning raging deep within my soul. My heart mirrors the sensual beat of the music while my body heat is matching the stimulating and arousing excitement in the air.

"Lauren, focus. What do you want to eat?" Donovan firmly grumbles, attempting to snap me out of my hypnotic state.

His moist lips appear to be beckoning me, this time though my will is spent and I'm happy to oblige with their request. Standing up on my tiptoes I press my sweltering figure firmly against Donovan's. Leaning in I begin softly stroking the surface of his lips with mine, occasionally using my tongue to trace their plump outline. My jagged breath exhales softly into his, causing his eyes to close in enjoyment. My hands slowly explore the firm ripples of his back muscles as they make their way down to the sweeping arch of his lower back. My trembling fingers now are inches away from his well-curved bottom – wanting more – needing more. I press my lips firmly against his as our mouths dance to an undulating rhythm. My tongue begins exploring his mouth, tasting the sweetness of it. A surge rushes through me as I give in to the hunger raging deep within me. Lightly I stroke his back with the tips of my fingers as my hands make their way up to his thick, silky hair. A husky, deep moan rumbles in his chest as it mixes with his breathy exhale. Weaving my fingers vigorously throughout his soft hair, I grab onto a large handful and pull him forcefully into me. The intense desire within me is building into a full inferno. This is a side of me neither of us is familiar with.

His trembling hands trace up my arms until they reach mine, intertwined in his dark hair. Knitting his fingers firmly into mine he grips onto them tightly. In a split second he pulls my hands abruptly out of his hair and firmly places them at my sides.

Tearing his mouth away from mine he breathlessly sighs, "Lauren, stop." His voice is firm, yet a thin layer of remorse coats his deep tone. "I should not have brought you here. This is way too much sensation overload for you right now."

"What do you mean? What did I do wrong?" I probe despondently.

"You were fully giving in to your desires," he winces. "You were allowing the alluring stimulation around us to affect you. You need to guard yourself better by focusing on trying to ignore these tantalizing images and cravings of others."

Abruptly I yank my hands free from his, intently snapping, "You're saying I only kissed you because of the enticing environment around me?"

"No. I am saying you were surrendering to your desires. Something you would have never done if you weren't so easily tempted by the erotic environment and the tempting images of those around us. Remember what I said, you now can sense the desires of those around you. Your soul now craves those temptations. You cannot act on it or you will lose your humanity. You know what they say: The good spirits go to bed at midnight." He smiles slightly, trying to lighten the mood.

"What is so wrong with kissing you, Donovan?" I try to hiding the disappointment in my voice triggered by his obvious rejection.

Leaning down he presses his forehead gently against mine as he reaches down and lovingly grabs hold of my hand. "Kissing me is not wrong, but completely giving in to the craving is. Please understand that I did not reject you. If you think I did, then for that I am deeply sorry. I love when you kiss me. But I can't have you lose your soul over me, especially when I am so close to having it released," he whispers timidly.

The raging fire burning inside of me dissipates, leaving only a small flicker that now constantly smolders in me like a pilot light ready to ignite again. Instantly I become aware of my uncontrolled actions I freely exhibited for all to see. The realization of what I had almost allowed myself to do sends a wave of guilt crashing over me. Tears slowly well up in my eyes. Closing them tightly I try to fight the tears from spilling over and streaming onto my cheeks.

"Donovan, I'm so sorry." I sniffle weakly, wiping any evidence of crying off of my face.

"Well, I guess we are even now."

I glance up at him with a gush of confusion spreading over my moistened face. "What do you mean?"

"Remember you stopped me from losing my control with you? So I suppose we should both probably be more careful with our sensual desires towards each other. No more public places where arousing temptations are running rampant for you." Donovan winks while giving me a mischievous smirk.

I try my best to reciprocate the same positive sentiment he is showing me, but nothing in me is able to conjure up a smile. My state of despair isn't allowing me to respond with any joyful expression.

His arms wrap around me as he pulls me tightly against him. Bending down, Donovan kisses the top of my head reassuringly, stating, "Lauren, don't worry about it so much. If it makes you feel any better, I was thinking the same thing. It was just a matter of time until I pounced on you."

"Donovan, stop trying to make me feel better."

"Lauren, I'm not joking. The only thing stopping me from attacking you was that I was getting slightly irritated with your indecisiveness on what you wanted to eat." He adds sarcastically, "So are you still undecided or can we get you something to eat now?"

Pulling away from the secure grip he has on me, I gaze up at him dubiously. "Are you hungry? Because I think I have lost my appetite."

"Actually Lauren, I am never hungry," he states frankly.

My brows pull together tightly as my eyes narrow, deepening the furrow lines. "You don't need to eat?"

Peering all around us he makes sure no one is listening. "Lauren, remember I am not subject to the same rules of nature as you. I don't need food to survive." Winking at me slightly he bends down, kissing my forehead again. "I do eat though, but only because I enjoy the taste of food, not because I need to."

Just when I thought he couldn't surprise me anymore he goes and astounds me again. I know he said the laws of nature don't apply to him, but no matter how many times he tells me I don't think it will really sink in.

A slight laugh escapes from his enticing mouth as he gives me a demure, yet comforting smile. "Don't overthink it, Lauren, it will only give you a headache again."

Releasing his compassionate embrace on me, he grabs onto my hand firmly as he intentionally leads me out of the overcrowded street. We hastily cut through the crowds with no hesitation as he weaves his way toward a definite destination. Naturally, everyone moves out of his way without even a single 'excuse me' mentioned.

"Donovan, where are we going?" I demand.

"I know a place not too far with a slightly better atmosphere where we can talk without you or I being tempted by the attacking images of others."

We sit outside under the large covered patio of a quaint café which is away from the rowdy congestion of Bourbon Street. Though the café is crowded – even at nearly one o'clock in the morning – Donovan had no problem getting us a quiet table in the corner of the patio facing Jackson Square Park. I don't think Donovan has ever had a problem getting anything. All he has to do is smile at the maître d', causing the poor girl to become butter in his steamy hands.

The atmosphere at the café is different than Bourbon Street. There is still a crowd here, but it is not the rowdy, highly sexualized environment we just escaped from. The people here seem to be more interested in the food and surroundings than finding their next conquest for the night.

Calmness embraces me as I stare out at the grand castle-like cathedral sitting on the outer edge of the park. The people on the street move joyfully to the lively, vibrant music playing in the background. The pessimistic thoughts that once lingered deep within me have entirely dissipated.

Several street performers are scattered around the area, filling the balmy air with music even at this hour of the night. As I gaze around at the performers, one in particular catches my eye. A slender, elderly black gentleman with silvery gray hair and scruffy beard dances effortlessly in front of me. He vigorously taps to the lively music playing on the street as his tattered clothing swirls fluently around him. The energy expelling from his aging body is incredible as he allows the music to surge within him. The ragged man's tapping completely seizes the attention of all the onlookers as he dances freely on the street. Every ounce of energy he has is being put into his performance, yet I can barely hear the sound exuding from his ragged shoes.

As the song ends the crowd that had formed around this elderly man erupts in enthusiastic cheers. I continue to watch as the exhausted man sits down on the edge of the curb. Slowly he removes his shoes, turning them over. To my astonishment I notice that the bottoms of his dilapidated shoes are entirely filled with thumb tacks. No wonder I couldn't hear the tapping sound. This poor man was throwing everything he has into making those tacks sound like tap shoes. His overwhelming desire to do everything within his power to provide for his family presses into my mind. Sorrow envelops my shoulders like a sweltering blanket in this heat, causing my heart to throb for this poor soul.

Donovan's hand suddenly slides onto mine, grabbing onto mine gently as he whispers, "What are you thinking, Lauren?"

Turning towards Donovan, I plead softly, "That man, I know what he wants. Can't you give it to him?"

"Lauren, his heart is in the right place. He is doing what he can to provide for his family. Would you want to damn that man's soul for simply a few bites of porridge?"

"No – not at all, but my heart is breaking for him," I state grudgingly as I gaze over at the tattered man who is now replacing the broken tacks in his shredded shoes. "What can we do for him?"

Gently Donovan presses his plump lips onto the top of my hand as he utters softly against it, "Let him dance. If we get involved he will lose all of his joy and desire to dance. He is not only earning money for his family, Lauren, he is also giving happiness to those who watch him. Look around you."

I glance all around, noticing all the happy smiling faces walking away from the entertaining scene the older gentleman has provided for them. "Lauren, take that away and many people would be affected by the loss of one humble man. Even the simplest effort can have the largest impact."

As I turn back towards Donovan I see him through new eyes. I have been mainly focusing on his appearance like an immature school girl crush, but there is so much more to him. A deep well of benevolence lies just beneath his surface. I don't see a sinister demon sitting in front of me. His compassion for this tattered man's soul is something you don't find even in mankind. How can this person, whose sole purpose is to capture peoples' souls, be full of compassion? I know Donovan didn't want to be this monster, but why would anyone, least of all him, accept this eternal servitude to an evil faction?

I begin tracing the eternity symbol on the back of his hand as I try to smooth out the incomprehensible gaze on my face. "Donovan, can I ask you a question?"

"Lauren – you know you can ask me anything," he answers reassuringly.

Looking down at my thumb that is now tracing the veins on the back of his muscular hand, I whisper hesitantly, "How did you end up –" A long, awkward pause flows through us. Even though I know Donovan is a demon, I'm struggling to say that horrid word.

As I gaze sheepishly up at Donovan I discover he has an amused expression streaming across his face. He appears to be having way too much fun watching me squirm in my uneasiness. Slowly he leans in inches away from my face and utters softly, "Do you mean, how did I end up a demon?"

Gazing into his crystal blue eyes I bite the edge of my bottom lip as I reply subtly, "Yes."

A weak sigh slips through his mouth as he reclines back in his chair. "Do you really want to know?"

"Yes, Donovan, I do." I instinctively lean in, placing my elbows on the table and resting my chin firmly onto the palms of my hands.

Donovan looks away from me as he surveys the action surrounding the park. Intertwining his fingers he places his prayerful hands in his lap. "You know, Lauren, when I was younger this was where my friends and I would hang out. We loved coming here and occasionally, depending on our mood, would entertain the tourists like our older friend over there."

"What…you would street perform?" I blow out a breath in surprise at what he divulged. My gaping mouth and wide eyes reinforce my disbelief.

"You know, I wasn't always this serious. I was young and free once." He shrugs in regret while raking his hand through his hair.

Wiping the sweat off of my forehead I remember this was once someone who had his entire life in front of him. He has been robbed of his life and dreams by whatever circumstance imprisoned him. "What would you do on the street?"

A quirky, child-like smile appears, making me want to imaginarily play with him. He pushes his sleeves up just above his forearms as a soft laugh echoes out of him, making me want to laugh also. "My friends and I had a stupid garage band that, depending on how bored we were, would play on the street here." He grabs a spoon from the table, twirling it between his fingers as he quickly shakes his head. "Remember, Lauren, this was a different time when every teenager secretly wanted to be a rock star."

"Oh, that's right. I keep forgetting that you are an old man. Do you need me to get you a walker?" I sneer sarcastically, trying to hide my disbelief with humor. Quickly changing the subject back, I add, "Did you play an instrument or sing?"

A blast of air pushes through his nose, giving the sound of a quick laugh. A coy smile spreads across his face as he adjusts slightly in his chair. I realize he is completely aware of what I am doing, by ignoring my snide comment and deciding to only answer my last question. "My sister and I both play the guitar and sing.

My sister Dominique, the one you saw tonight, can play almost any instrument and is an amazing musician. We were both raised with music deeply woven into our lives. My mother was an accomplished piano player." His sparkly face deflates slightly as he leans against the table. Resting an elbow on the table he lays his cheek against the palm of his hand. His voice takes on a near reverent tone as he speaks about his mother, showing me that this is where his tragedy stems from.

Needing to find out more information about his family, I pry even deeper with my question, "Were you close to your family?"

His gaze turns from the street back to me, focusing on my face intently. His eyes don't waver from my mine. "Lauren, we were your poster family for how things should be. My sister and I were best friends. Wherever I went, she was there, too. My mother and father had an epic eternal love which set an example of what I desired in a relationship. So to answer your question, yes, we were an extremely close family."

"I don't understand, Donovan, if you were the perfect family how did you end up being damned?" I ask as I gulp down a large amount of water, trying to replace the fluid I'm sweating out.

His soft, child-like expression instantly tightens, shattering his soft features as his eyes transform from peaceful remembrance to one of sorrow and anger. "All great things must come to an end, which is true in my family's case."

"What happened?" I whisper as I cup the ice-cold drink in my hand, allowing the chill to soothe the heat raining down on me.

As I gaze into his eyes I notice the void inside of them as if he is staring right through me as he begins to relive a torturous memory. "My mother – the most loving, gentle and giving person you could imagine – was diagnosed with breast cancer soon after my twenty-second birthday. You need to understand, in those days a diagnosis like this was basically a death sentence. Her cancer was so advanced that she was given only a few months to live. Our family was mortified. My mother was the heart – and truly the home – of the family. You see, the house you saw tonight is in fact my mother's ancestral home. It has been in her family for several generations. My father couldn't simply up and move when my mother died to try and escape the painful memory of her. He would be continually haunted by her eternal presence seeping from the walls of the house, constantly reminding him of his excruciating loss.

My father, after my mother's diagnosis, changed from a fun, lively and energetic man into a bitter, withdrawn and extremely depressed man. He couldn't imagine why God would take away the love of his life. The man I always viewed as strong became more and more despondent as he seemed to sink into a full-fledged deep depression. Though my mother's cancer treatments weakened her physically, my father's depression weakened him spiritually. My sister and I began to worry immensely about our father. With every slip closer to death my mother got, it appeared that my father's anger with God and the world intensified." His voice thickens with an acidic edge to it as he speaks of his father's intense anger. Extreme pressure from his hand causes the spoon he has been fiddling with to twist into an unrecognizable object. Nonchalantly I reach over to grab hold of his hand, when immediately I pull away. The heat expelling off of him nearly burns me.

Grabbing hold of my hand with his now cool fingers, he lifts it to his mouth, kisses it apologetically, uttering in response, "Sorry."

"Don't worry about it, Donovan," I mutter kindly. "I am sorry for interrupting; you can continue if you like."

Smiling my favorite crooked smile, he expresses flatly, "It's not that I like talking about this, but I need to. You need to understand why I am in this situation and why it is always important to control your anger." Then he adds fervently, "You see, when anger or rage takes over, the desire to do the right things gets distorted. That was the case with my father. He no longer wanted to do things the honorable way. He didn't want to believe what the doctors were saying. Accepting my mother's eventual demise was not an option for him anymore. He began searching in dark places for another way out of this looming situation. In a town like this, trust me, evil doesn't have to search hard to find you. Apparently my father's desire spoke very loudly to an awaiting, sinuous demon." His voice became dark, causing a shuddering chill to race up my spine. My trembling hand is causing the water goblet to shake violently in my hand. Releasing the glass, I bury my hands under the table, trying to hide my obvious fear.

"I found out what my father was planning on doing, so I followed him to where he was meeting this creature. When I arrived, my father stood there in front of a tall, thin man whose thick black hair was slicked back tightly. As the moonlight reflected on his gleaming hair it appeared to resemble a black halo on the top of his head. His eyes were completely black with dark, vein-like circles encompassing them as if he had been given two intense black eyes. I stood there terrified by this tall menacing being."

My heart falls to the pit of my stomach as I remember how Donovan's face took on the same dark, sinister appearance. For a brief moment I can empathize with how he must have felt seeing that monster standing in front of his father.

He shifts slightly in his chair as he leans in closer to me. A disgusted anger quivers within his taut lips as his thick voice is laced with ire. "When my father discovered I had intruded in on his meeting with this ominous individual, he began yelling at me to leave immediately. I tried to stop him from proceeding with this insane proposal, but to my chagrin the deed had already been done. He had traded his soul for my mother's cure from the debilitating cancer that was eating away at her."

Donovan's eyes peer deep into mine and for a brief moment our souls connect, exposing the great sacrifice he freely did. I can see the tremendous love he held for his parents and the willingness to do anything for them. My breathing slows to a faint steady rhythm as my body deflates into the chair then refills with an enormous amount of sorrow. He gave up his life so that his parents could remain together. My tears pour from the soft barrier of my eyes and sting my skin faintly as they stream down my cheeks. The salty droplets suspend themselves from my plump bottom lip. Donovan reaches over and tenderly wipes away all the tears from off of my mouth. His thumb continues to trace my lip passionately as he gives me a coy smile.

Pulling his hand away and placing it on the table he continues, "Lauren, I couldn't allow my father and mother to be apart from each other. The sinister being allowed me to go in my father's place."

"Your father allowed that?" I utter sharply, horrified by a father allowing such an act.

"No, he put up a large fight, but in the end I won the argument." His voice is weak as if there is more to the argument than he is willing to share.

"Why isn't he trying to find you and release you, Donovan?" My voice cracks slightly from the emotional trauma I am having.

His eyes narrow as he gazes deeper into mine. It's as if he is about to give me information that transcends the situation between his father and him, like he is speaking directly to me. "Lauren, when your soul is released freely by a proxy, then your memory of the entire situation is erased. It is masqueraded as if that person has died a tragic death. The kind of death where usually there is no body found or it is destroyed beyond recognition." He strokes my cheek with his soft fingers, pushing a stray strand of hair behind my ear. I lean against his hand slightly as I absorb his soothing touch. "Obviously you can feel that I still have my body, Lauren. They only do that for pretense purposes. So my father has no recollection of what transpired between himself, Lucius and me. The only thing he believes is that I died in a terrible car crash."

I interrupt again in surprise as my stiff muscles freeze in response to the name he just uttered. "Lucius was the demon that your father made the deal with?"

"Yes."

"And your father truly has no recollection of what happened…why?"

"So he would not spend his whole life searching for me. In a way it's a form of compassion and self-preservation. It allows the person to be able to go on with their life without fear or torturing themselves."

"Lauren, the tragedy of this whole situation is not me. My father traded his soul, or now mine, for my mother's cancer to disappear – which it did – but two months later my mother died of a sudden heart attack. My father had to bury his son and his wife in less than three months. He has never been the same since. He has been allowed to live a long and sad life. As for my wonderful innocent sister, Dominique, she has had to take care of everything, including our now very old father.

"Donovan, that isn't right. You lost your soul so your mother would live. Since he didn't keep his promise you should be allowed to go free," I groan as I grab hold of his hand in excitement, realizing I may have discovered a way to help him.

"Slow down, Lauren. Lucius did keep his promise. My father asked that my mother be cured from her cancer, not that she would live. Demons are very crafty. They don't want to give you what you want. When you make a bargain with a demon you need to be very specific in what you ask for. They will search for any way to get what they want but not truly give you what you want."

My hand slowly releases his in despair as my immediate hope crumbles before me. Reclining back in my chair despondently and letting out a heavy sigh, I begin contemplating all that he has been through. For the past nearly forty years he's had to serve a sentence for something that he not only didn't do, but also never came to fruition. He was simply trying to be a loving and honorable son by allowing his parents to stay together, but the conniving Lucius had other plans.

The churning anguish in the pit of my stomach radiates into my heart, causing it to ache for him. Though Donovan's father lost him and his mother so close together, he at least has no memory of what actually occurred. Donovan, on the other hand, can recall every agonizing detail as he is eternally tortured for it. "Donovan, I am so sorry."

"Lauren, I didn't tell you this so that you would feel sorry for me. I don't want you to hurt over me. I knew completely what I was getting involved in. I want to share with you everything to do with my life, the good parts, and the bad parts." A slight growling laugh escapes from him. "It seems I have more bad to share than good," he utters flatly.

"I disagree. You have a lot of good to share. There are a lot of noble qualities still left in you. You must be hated in the demonic world for not fully embracing the evil side of you."

A loud, boisterous laugh escapes vigorously out of Donovan, causing his square shoulders to shake. He lifts his head up slightly as several of the customers sitting near us gaze in our direction. The melancholy mood that was looming over us instantly rips away with one simple joyous sound. His low, rumbling laugh is hypnotic as I watch a side of Donovan I rarely see hit center stage. His volume reaches a heightened level as I anxiously gaze around the café.

"Donovan, please be quiet," I command, looking around us.

"Lauren, don't worry. I know what all their desires are and trust me, they have no interest in us, but if you are done with your beignets, I think we should go," he laughs quieter.

Dubiously I gaze down at the powdered-sugar laden beignets, completely forgetting they were even there. I have been so engrossed by Donovan's story. Pushing my plate away I hastily add, "No, I think I am done. Where are we going?"

"Don't worry, we are not traveling yet."

"Yet," I reluctantly repeat.

A brilliant smile spreads across his face as he pulls my chair out for me, allowing me to stand up easily from the table. Throwing a small wad of cash on the table, he grabs hold of my hand and pulls me up to him as he pushes my chair back in. Ignoring my statement, he adds, "I thought we could go sit down in the park somewhere quiet."

"Is that a safe thing to do at night?" I ask hesitantly.

A sharp crease between his brows deepens and his eyes narrow with a debatable expression rolling through them. "Do you honestly believe we need to be afraid? Have you forgotten who you are with? I am deadlier than anyone out there. Who you need to be afraid of is me, but it seems I can't convince you of that." A cynical smile glints as he gives me a quick wink. Gripping tightly onto my hand he pulls me towards the exit as a serious tone washes over him. Wrapping his arm around me he pulls me tightly against his side, adding, "Nothing – I mean nothing – will hurt you. I promise."

"Donovan, can I ask why you were laughing so hard back there?"

Donovan affectionately kisses the top of my head. "I didn't mean to laugh so hard. It's just you have no idea how much I am hated. No one, least of all Lucius, thought I would be strong enough to last this long. Though I have lost everything, I still have my freedom to choose, and strength is something you can choose." His voice trails off to a near whisper. "Who knows how much longer I will be able to last, though?"

I wrap both of my arms tightly around his waist, allowing him to fit into mine like a delicately sculpted statue, each part of us benefiting the other. If it's a battle for his soul that is required, then I'm not about to let him lose. If it's going to take everything within my power to help then so be it, I am willing and able to fight for him.

We both silently walk, holding on to each other until we reach the resting ragged tap dancer. Donovan stops pensively in front of the tattered, struggling man. We stand here in front of the gentleman for what feels like an eternity. Nervously my mind begins racing because I have no idea what Donovan is thinking. I know he is firm about not wanting to grant this man his desire, thus damning his soul, but I'm not sure if Donovan is able to fight the yearning within him.

Squeezing my arms tightly around Donovan I hope my touch will help solidify his possible internal struggle. He must have sensed my fear because he gently kisses the top of my head as if he is reassuring me that he is in complete control. Sliding his hand into the pocket of his jeans, he pulls out all the remaining money he has left over from the café. Holding it tightly in his hand he walks respectfully toward the tattered man. Holding the money out politely towards him, he utters, "Sir, here you go."

The man's eyes gleam with gratitude for this generous contribution. "Tank yous kind sir. God bless yous," he utters in a thick, deep southern accent. His voice is groggy and hoarse as if he has been gargling with sand. As he smiles his shielding lips part, revealing several missing teeth. And as for the ones still hanging on, they are coated with yellow stains and brown remnants of tobacco. Though his teeth are lacking in general hygiene, his smile is glorious, melting away all stereotypical assumptions.

The man lifts his arm to retrieve the money, revealing the skeletal appearance caused by a severely malnourished diet. As the man's dirty, worn-out hand weakly grasps hold of the money, Donovan firmly grasps onto his hand, respectfully adding, "No sir, thank you. Please remember to work hard and always dance."

Donovan releases the man's hand as we slowly walk away. "Well, Lauren, if I wasn't hated before, trust me, that ought to put the final nail in my coffin." A mischievous smile spreads across his face as a sense of fear runs through my thoughts.

"Donovan, will you get in trouble for that?"

"Lauren, that is the least of what I have done. Shit will soon hit the fan, that is for sure. And if I were you I wouldn't want to be anywhere in that room when the shit starts flying," he warns.

We sit down quietly on the lightly damp grass as his arms and legs envelop my whole being. Though this has been an emotional night I don't want it to end. Donovan has revealed so much to me, allowing me to see who he truly is. He's not – nor will I let him become – the monster he sacrificed himself to be.

Exhaustion from the emotional night slowly weighs heavily over me like a soothing blanket, causing me to seep against Donovan's torso. His arms wrap around as I rest my hands on his slightly bent thighs. The humid night air soaks into me, causing my skin to mirror the sweltering temperature. As I stare pensively up at the stars my exhausted mind begins playing tricks on me. The stars up above start to appear as if they are all shooting stars, flying rapidly throughout the dark night sky. The gentle ringing of lively music plays in the distance.

Donovan lays his cheek firmly down on top of my head as he pulls me into him tighter. The heat from his sweet breath caresses me, pushing me into a deeper state of relaxation. His breathing is soft and steady as his fingertips gently stroke my arm. The quiet relaxation after the emotional night lulls me deeper into a tranquil sleep which I can't seem to fight.

CHAPTER 18

Invitation

Warm, bright light penetrates forcefully through my eyelids. Grabbing the covers that are placed impeccably on top of me, I vigorously heave them over my head. Turning irritably, trying to hide from the meddlesome sun, I instantly roll on top of something.

"What the…" I begin hurling my covers feverishly off of me. "Donovan!" I yell, frantically looking all around. "Where am I?" I wrap the sheet around me, completely unaware of where I am or what is going on. The last thing I remember is sitting on the grass in New Orleans, leaning up against Donovan as I tiredly gazed up at the stars.

Hysterically I pull the sheet away from me, making sure I am clothed. Grateful, I discover I'm still wearing the same outfit from last night.

A boisterous laugh escapes out of Donovan. "Lauren, do you honestly think I would have taken advantage of you? You were completely passed out last night – or technically, this morning."

I glance down sheepishly at Donovan who is lying, incredibly, on my bed. My heart begins pounding as I stare at this absolutely magnificent-looking man. His dark, striking hair looks unscathed by the obvious rough night we had, as his brilliant blue eyes gaze up at me with deep compassion, causing my heart to instantly flutter in response. Still clinging tightly to the sheet that is woven securely around me, I utter softly, "Donovan, what happened? How did I end up here – was it all a dream?"

He sighs softly. "No, it wasn't a dream." He pats the top of the pillow next to him, beckoning me to lie back down by him. All too eager to yield to his request, I instantly lay back down in the crook of his muscular arm as he cups my head gently. Lifting his head up slightly, he rests it against his fingertips. His piercing blue eyes gaze down at me, melting my apprehension.

"When you collapsed last night from sheer exhaustion, I took the opportunity to take you home."

"How?" I muse.

A brilliant smile spreads across his face. "Did you honestly forget how we arrived in New Orleans?"

"No," I groan. "I can still feel the queasiness in my stomach. I'm merely wondering how you did it if I was asleep."

"It is actually easier when you are asleep. You don't panic." He smiles widely. "By the way, don't throw your extra pillows off your bed anymore."

Twisting myself towards him, which tightens up the cocoon effect the sheet is causing me, I press my eyes together, uttering questionably, "Why? I don't use the extra pillows."

"But I will." A wicked smile spreads, causing a taunting glimpse to sparkle in his eyes.

Wrapping his hand affectionately around my face, he stares passionately into my eyes. Donovan slowly bends down, caressing my face with his full, sumptuous mouth, causing my stomach to flip in delight. His warm, moist mouth releases a deep tingling sensation down my legs that explodes out through my toes. He gradually moves his mouth towards my ear as he hovers partially over me. "Lauren, I may be a demon, which prohibits me from feeling genuine emotions, but I do know what love looks like and feels like. My parents set that example for me," he whispers wistfully.

I slightly pull away, looking up at him with wide eyes and a gaping mouth as my heart prepares for me to hear the unfathomable. "What are you saying, Donovan?"

"Lauren, I wish I could fully experience the emotion I am feeling for you, but as a demon I am not allowed to feel love. The only reason I can experience anything virtuous is because I am trying to retain my morality."

A single tear rolls down my cheek as I lay motionless beneath his nearly hovering physique. Delicately he brushes my tear away with his thumb as he looks longingly into my eyes. His eyes bore deep into me. "I have never felt this way for anyone, even before I became this monster."

Lifting my hand gingerly I brush my fingers thoughtfully across his cheek. My thumb delicately skims the curves of his mouth as his tongue intimately licks the tip of it. His eyes close tightly as a soft exhale presses out of him. His breath falls over my face, letting me breathe in his sweet, aromatic scent. "Donovan, I know what I'm feeling. This is new for me too," I utter softly. "I have never felt this way before, but I too was taught by my father what unconditional love is."

Donovan's eyes immediately widen at the mention of my father as his arms stiffen up around me.

"Did I say something wrong?" I sigh ruefully.

Noticing my frantic expression, he groans regrettably, "No, not at all. You did nothing wrong." He bends down inches away from my face. "Lauren," he whispers. My name rolls through the air like butterflies rippling down on me, landing delicately on my skin. "I – I love you. Please, no matter what happens, remember that," he pleads. His words tickle my skin like feathers, causing goosebumps to spread over me.

My mouth parts slightly as I attempt to give him the same sentiment, but before I'm able to utter the words he feverishly presses his mouth to mine. Gripping tightly onto him I pull him firmly down onto me as our lips move in simultaneous bliss. My tongue explores his mouth as he responds likewise, probing and mixing our love for each other. I can taste his warm, sweet air exuding from his mouth, enveloping every part of my body as my blood feels like it's going to boil from the heat pulsating through it.

Our jagged breathing intensifies, causing a frenzy to rip through us as our kiss transforms from a want to need. Aggressively I rip at the back of his shirt, trying to touch the one thing that has been eluding me – his bare skin. Ripping his shirt free I exhale joyfully as my hands finally touch his smooth, hot back. I slowly skim the surface of his skin with the tips of my fingers, feeling his muscles quivering beneath my touch. A staggered moan breathlessly escapes from his mouth as his teeth softly bite onto my bottom lip. Holding my lip captive in his mouth he proceeds to draw it in, sucking tenderly on it, causing me to writhe in pleasure. An inner tickling sensation in my gut gravitates into my thighs as I arch my back in satisfaction. Responding to my gesture, he ardently answers it as he moves his kisses slightly lower, onto my neck. The husky, growling sound he is making sends a quivering sensation to spin rapidly within my stomach. Searing passion formed in the pit of my belly radiates out like a live wire exploding out of my fingertips and toes. Trying to hold the pleasure in, I curl my toes tightly as I exhale audibly.

His mouth moves gradually down my neck as he kisses the soft surface of my décolletage while his hands trace the outline of my thighs. The fire surging in me begins to expand as our bodies rhythmically move together. Reaching down I begin aggressively pulling and tugging at the imprisoning sheet still wrapped tightly around me. I lift my hips slightly as I continue yanking on the sheet. Donovan's hand suddenly slides down my arm, firmly grabbing hold of my hand.

A forceful sigh rushes out of me as I plead, "Please, Donovan, don't make us stop."

Gingerly he pulls my hand free from the sheet. "Lauren –" He groans softly against my neck, "… you are the strongest temptation I have ever experienced. We have to stop." His breathless voice is weak as if he has run a marathon.

"Donovan, you can't stop now," I huff in disappointment. I feel like he has just loosened the cork of a champagne bottle but refuses to take it completely out.

"Lauren, I have to, and so do you," he emphasizes softly.

Wanting more, I gaze passionately into his eyes as I arch my back, pressing my chest firmly against his. He reaches up quickly, grabbing hold of my hand, adding forcefully this time, "Lauren, I am serious, I need to stop before I completely lose it and attack you." A livid edge taints his voice.

I smile mercilessly, discovering that possibly I have the upper hand in getting what I want. Teasing, "There is nothing wrong with that. You can attack me if you like. I will allow it."

His eyes bore deep into me, staring at me with a displeased expression. "Lauren!" he snaps severely. "Enough is enough, it is over."

Instinctively I flinch back at the harsh, thick tone that is now within his voice. He has never said my name in a callous way before. His berating voice snaps me out of my attempt at seducing him. Pushing him off of me, I roll forcefully over onto my side. "You are a damn tease. It's probably best if you leave – now."

A low sigh escapes weakly out of him as he tenderly wraps his hand around me. "You are right, it is probably best if I left, but I can't…no, I won't leave. Lauren, I am sorry for yelling, but we needed to stop," he groans apologetically.

"Donovan, I simply wanted to show you how much I love you," I whimper. My ego has taken a pretty good beating at this point.

"Lauren, don't you see? That is why I stopped. To show you how much I love you."

I turn abruptly, facing him straight on. How can rejecting me again translate as loving me? "I don't understand."

"Giving in to our natural desire would be an easy thing to do, but we would completely lose ourselves in the process. By denying that innate desire I am showing you that I find you and your soul too valuable to lose. I know it is frustrating, but soon you will be free to embrace passion completely."

"And what about you? Will you be able to experience our love completely?"

A soft, yet disappointing rush of air pushes through him as he embraces me. Burying my head deep into his firm chest, I utter timidly, "Donovan, I love you."

Bending down, he gingerly kisses the top of my head then quietly mumbles against my hair, "I hope you will always remember how much I have loved you."

Silently we lay here embracing each other, when suddenly the stillness is shattered by the intrusive, haunting organ song on my cell phone. Donovan begins laughing hysterically. "What a perfect song you chose for your cell phone. There's nothing like a haunting tune to remind you that you're living in a horror movie," he snickers sarcastically. "Was it done consciously?"

"I didn't choose it, William did." I laugh impulsively to his vigorous chuckle.

"What? Why would he choose that song?" His boisterous laugh abruptly ends.

"I don't know, perhaps he was just being funny. Why?" I'm slightly bewildered by his reaction.

The song continues to play, each time getting louder and louder, hammering down on top of him each frightening note. "I think you should answer the phone." He hastily hands the phone over to me.

I have no idea where this aloofness is coming from. He has shared so much of himself with me this weekend, but now it seems he is hiding something else from me.

I gaze up at Donovan dubiously as he holds my phone frantically in front of me. Reluctantly I take the phone and answer it. "Hello," I huff.

"Good afternoon, Lauren." William's voice is cheery and polite sounding.

Instantly I freeze when he declares, "Good afternoon." It can't be the afternoon yet – can it? Immediately I sit up, gawking frantically over Donovan's shoulder at my clock. Rubbing my eyes vigorously I look again in shock. I can't believe my eyes -- it is three-fifteen in the afternoon. I muster up all of the energy I can as I exaggerate my upbeat voice. "Good afternoon, William."

"I am wondering if you would like to come out here for dinner tonight?"

"Um…well…" I look over at Donovan who is laying here incredulously staring up at the ceiling like white paint is a masterpiece. "Well, William, I sort of met someone and –"

He interrupts hastily, "I know, Lauren, I saw him yesterday in the parking lot. I am actually hoping that the both of you can come out."

"What? You would like the both of us to come out…why?" Anxiously I turn towards Donovan who is now sitting up on the edge of my bed, staring straight ahead. Donovan doesn't acknowledge anything that is being uttered, which has me completely terrified.

"I would like to meet the guy who has captured your interest, is that such a bad thing?" William specifies politely. His voice seems to be hiding a deeper agenda I'm unable to figure out.

Donovan's eyes tighten as his taut jaw begins quivering slightly. He is still immobile, unwilling to look at me. There is more to this scenario than either one of them are willing to share with me. My nervous heart pounds violently against my chest.

"Lauren, are you there?" William questions feverishly.

"Yes, I'm here. Sorry, I was just thinking." My head is spinning, actually. Why is William so concerned with meeting Donovan, and why is Donovan reacting like this?

"Well, do you think you both can come out tonight?" He asks impatiently.

"Yes, we will be there," I moan reluctantly. "What time would you like us out there?"

"Be here by five-o'clock. See you both soon."

"See you then, William."

Holding my phone firmly in my hand I turn gradually towards Donovan, only to discover he is now standing impatiently by my bedroom door. His eyes are tightly closed, causing a deep line to crease between them. His right hand is firmly holding onto his chin as his head shakes vigorously back in forth in complete dismay. Faintly he incoherently rambles off something over and over. The only thing I'm able to recognize are the words 'how' and 'remember.'

"Donovan, what is going on? There is something you're not willing to share with me." Fear suddenly creeps into my conscience. "Donovan, do you know William?" I grimace.

Donovan's head snaps up instantly to my question. "Lauren, I need to go. I will be back to pick you up at a quarter to five."

"Wait, you are leaving? Why?" I mutter weakly.

Walking gingerly over to my side he kneels down inches in front of me. "Lauren, I have to take care of something. Don't worry, everything will be all right." His voice is reassuring, yet I know he and William are keeping something horrible from me.

CHAPTER 19

Recollection

The deathly silence in the car as we drive down the road towards William's house is like we are part of a funeral procession. Nervously I gaze all around, trying to think of something to break the silence looming between us. As I look around I notice the nonchalant simplicity of the car we are in. The car that Donovan picked me up in is a subdued version of the million-dollar car he was in a few weeks ago. This is instead a fully-loaded silver Mercedes. "Donovan, where is your other car?"

A crooked smile dances briefly across his face. "I didn't think it would be a good idea to draw more attention to myself. That is the last thing I need right now. Besides, technically that car is not mine."

"If it's not your car, then whose is it?" I ask, surprised.

Turning towards me he feverishly gazes into my eyes. "Remember, we can have whatever we want, whenever we need it, and I needed it to grab your attention. A simple Mercedes was not going to get your attention on the busy freeway."

Looking out the front window I suddenly realize what I'm about to bring into William's house. Donovan has instantly brought reality to the forefront of my mind. I'm not bringing a typical boyfriend home to meet the family – he is in fact a demon – hell, so am I now. How am I going to get through this night without William finding out who and what he actually is? Am I putting William's soul in peril by being around a demon that will be able to read his deepest, darkest desires? I hope and pray that Donovan will be able to suppress giving William what he desires, thus capturing his soul.

Instantly my heart pounds ferociously against my chest as we drive silently down William's driveway. My hands begin twisting and turning in my skirt as my nerves rise to the base of my neck and take center stage in my stomach. The anticipation I am feeling causes the acid to churn violently within me, making me feel sick. There is no possible way I'm going to be eating tonight.

We stop directly in front of William's front door. As I stare at the door the urge to tell Donovan to turn around and drive away rises to the surface. Gripping my hand tightly around the handle of the car door, I take a deep, cleansing breath in as I push down the urge to run. Holding tightly onto the handle I refuse to let go.

"Lauren, we need to get out of the car. This needs to happen," he utters dubiously.

Flinching back suddenly, I ask, "What needs to happen?"

"Let's go." He opens the door, avoiding my question as he hastily gets out of the car.

"Donovan. Stop. Tell me what is going to happen," I snap feverishly.

He keeps on ignoring me as he opens my door, motioning me to get out of the car. Reluctantly I obey and stand up, causing the nerves that have been bubbling in my stomach to travel down to my legs which nearly give out on me. Quickly I grab onto the frame of his car for support. I have no idea what is going to happen, but obviously Donovan knows something is about to take place.

Donovan rushes over to me, wrapping his arm around my waist for support. Gingerly he proceeds to pull me away from the car as we slowly head towards the door. I notice out of my peripheral vision the porch swing hanging there like an ominous reminder of where my journey to Donovan began. My world turned upside down here, staring up at Mt. Diablo as William shared the Legend of the Mountain. To William, he shared some far-fetched folklore, but here we are today allowing the same being to enter his safe and unsuspecting home.

I glower feverishly at the swing, completely unaware of William now standing firmly at the front door. His taut jaw and dark, firm eyes glare incessantly at Donovan. Donovan's crystal blue eyes match William's intensity as Donovan's arm tightens up around me. There is an unspoken word passing fervently between them. Glancing back and forth between them I'm now totally convinced that they know each other. Gritting my teeth together tightly I proceed ardently forward, dragging Donovan in behind me.

I stand vehemently within inches of William's face, snapping rudely, "Okay, what the hell is going on here?"

"Lauren, I should have told you…" Donovan whispers.

"You have no right to tell her anything. What the hell are you doing, driving the final nail in her coffin?" William growls. His eyes narrow to a thin slit as a deep canyon forms between them, giving him a fierce expression. He stares at Donovan with a thick hatred as rage pours from his skin like a deadly disease. The berating look on his face tears a hole into my soul. This is not merely anger that is exuding out of his every pore, but an intense amount of pain mixed into the cocktail.

"Lauren, what am I going to tell your mother when she gets back?"

"Like my mother even cares what I do. She only cares about her social life," I snap.

"William, you have no idea what is going on here. Don't start damning me or anyone else before you know what is actually going on," Donovan gnashes back.

"Ha! That's funny. I don't think you need my help in that area," he chuckles forcefully. "Lauren, don't listen to him. No matter how much he tries to tell you that your father was an idiot, he was the greatest…"

"William, please stop," Donovan sharply interrupts.

"Stop," I yell forcefully. Inhaling deeply, I try to make sense of this incredulous conversation between them. They both freeze as they stare at me, astonished by my loud outburst. "What is going on? How in the hell do you both know each other and what does my father have to do with this?" I turn and glance anxiously at William. "Please answer me. I know our relationship has been strained since you found out I went up to the mountain, but please no more secrets," I plead.

His anguished eyes turn hesitantly toward Donovan. "She doesn't know, does she?"

"No," Donovan states smoothly.

"Know what? Will one of you please tell me what is going on here?"

"Lauren, maybe we should take this inside. Don't you think so, William?" Donovan motions hesitantly towards the front door. The tension between them is thick enough you can nearly see the rippling waves of unbridled rage flowing between them.

William reluctantly nods, wary to let Donovan enter his house. Donovan gingerly slides his fingertips down my arm, slowly reaching for my hand. Reacting to the anger and confusion pulsating through me feverishly, I yank my hand away. I notice a gleaming, satisfied smile dance briefly across William's face in reaction.

As I walk into his house the aroma filling the air lacks anything edible. I begin looking all around, only to discover there are no place settings on the table, nor any sign that he was planning on having us over to eat. This was a sham to get us here.

"William, you didn't plan on having us over for dinner, did you?" I hiss.

"No, he didn't plan on us coming over for dinner. He wanted to get us over here so he could talk to me –"

"Quiet! I think she asked me the question – not you," William snaps out.

"Enough, we are inside now, so someone talk." The fear I have been experiencing now is being replaced by an intense adrenaline rush pulsing through my veins. I begin pacing back and forth, unable to control my anxiety bubbling up to the surface. Donovan walks over to my side, completely aware that my anger is nearing the boiling point. He strokes the back of my hand with the tips of his fingers, trying to calm the fire raging feverishly within me. Any other time his touch would have extinguished the blaze raging in me, but now it's simply adding fuel to my fire. I know they are both hiding things from me and I need the lies to end here, tonight.

Responding to my aggravation, Donovan pleads with William, "I know you want answers, William. I swear I will tell you everything you want to know, but only if we can do it in private."

"What… no. Donovan, I have a right to know how you both know each other."

"Lauren, I will tell you everything, just not now. You need to gain control first. If you hear it all right now with how out of control you are, you may go to the point of no return," he warns softly.

Turning towards William he frantically pleads, "Please, there is a lot I want to talk to you about, but we need to do it privately – right now."

Inhaling deeply, he looks over at me, attempting a smile as he sees my obvious distress. Turning methodically toward Donovan, his eyes pierce directly into Donovan like he is being forced to relive a horrible nightmare. Donovan drops his head repentantly, glancing regrettably down at the floor. "Fine, Donovan, you can have your wish. Let's go talk in my office."

Refusing to be left out, I vigorously begin to follow them. The office doors are positioned exactly at the end of the wide hallway. What forms the wide hallway is a set of extra-large double doors leading into his office. Originally the space was intended to be used as an oversized master suite, but William felt he had no use for a master suite. He did, on the other hand, have need of a large office space, so converted the room to fit his needs.

William pushes open the substantial door and proceeds to walk sorrowfully in. Donovan turns abruptly towards me, gently placing his hand up in a halting motion. "This is where you stop."

"Donovan, this isn't fair. I have a right to know. He is my family and you are…" My voice begins to crack.

He gingerly places his hand compassionately on the side of my cheek. Staring firmly into my eyes, he fervently states, "Lauren, I promise you I will tell you everything. I only need to talk to William first without you getting overly upset."

William grunts roughly in disgust as he reacts agitatedly towards Donovan touching me. "Enough, can we please get this over with? You wanted to talk to me privately, so let's do it."

William walks between Donovan and me, closing the door firmly behind him. I gaze furiously at the oversized barrier that blocks me from seeing or hearing anything. Lingering here in front of the door I frantically try to fight my innate desire to kick the door down, but I know I can't. Placing my hands firmly against the door I chant a mantra to myself, 'Don't lose your temper, don't lose your temper.' Slowly I can feel the anger shed off of me like a heavy, itchy blanket gradually being removed.

Turning around I face the spacious hall that leads to the living room. Slowly I start pacing back and forth, trying to release the nervous energy building up within me. If I don't release this unbridled energy I'm going to burst like a dam after a heavy flood.

Surges of tingling sensations pulse through my nerve endings like I'm being electrocuted.

Methodically I pace the long hallway as I drum my fingers vigorously against the palms of my hands. Suddenly I catch sight of a plethora of photos from William's life hanging all over the wall. The collage of memories hangs like a beacon in front of me. Pensively I gaze at all the pictures that show a timeline of his life. There are pictures of his ancestors mixed in with more recent memories. Hiding in the abundance of pictures are multiple pictures of my family. Framing the whole scene in an almost respectful way are pictures of my father. All the photos on the wall are delicately placed in matching frames – but one. This unique picture looks as if it has gone through the wringer. The wrinkled photo is a picture of my father and me out on William's front porch. We were sitting on the porch swing together with my arms wrapped vigorously around his neck.

I have forgotten all about that day, perhaps my mind has deliberately shoved it out of my memory. The horrifying days that followed superseded any joy I had felt previously. The tragic loss of my father only a few days after this photo was taken robbed me of any joyful memory during that time. Why would William mutilate the last photo taken of his best friend?

Reaching up, I softly caress the glass that protects the last memory of my father from the harsh elements. As my fingers trace the lines in my father's face, I try to remember every detail from that day. So much of how my father died remains a mystery. I have tried on many occasions to recall what happened, but the more I try, the more my mind shuts down. It's as if my subconscious is trying to protect me from any further meltdown. Like my mind has simply blocked out the details for my own sanity.

As I delicately stroke the image I notice something strange about my father's expression. To my chagrin my father wasn't smiling. In fact, he appears anxious, as if he was frightened about something. The shocking expression on my father's face confuses me. This has to be a mistake. Inching my way closer I try to make out the details in the picture. Wherever the crumpling marks are, they leave an area void of any color, only the white paper behind the image remains.

Vigorously I focus on his face when suddenly I notice the red in his eyes, as if he had been crying. What could have happened that day? Why would my father be crying? Instantly I close my eyes, fiercely trying to get my subconscious to remember anything at all about that day. 'Think, Lauren, think.' What happened that day?

The only thing I can remember is when William asked to speak with my father briefly in his office, but that wasn't out of the ordinary. They did things like that all the time. They would pretend like they needed to talk when in actuality they would be hiding out from me and my mom.

There has to be something else I am missing. Pure frustration wraps around my mind as I push myself to remember, but nothing is coming to fruition. Why can't I remember? I know something went horribly wrong that day.

Deep in the pit of my stomach a nervous, sharp twinge shoots violently through me, causing me to double over in pain. Reacting to the pain I grab onto my stomach as I let out a low, growling moan. At that very instant the large office door flings open aggressively. Immediately I feel the presence of someone rushing vehemently to my side. "Lauren, are you all right?" Donovan asks frantically. His arms wrap around me, engulfing my entire waist in his grasp.

Gingerly I stand back up, still grasping onto my stomach as Donovan's hands remain tightly wrapped around me for support. I gaze up at Donovan with a bewildered expression rolling down my face. They can't possibly be done with their conversation yet. It hasn't been that long. Pressing my brow tightly together, I utter weakly, "Donovan, what are you doing out here? How long were you both in there?"

"About forty-five minutes, why?"

Snapping my head up I stare up at him in complete shock. "There's no way you were in there for that long." Looking frantically around me I notice that William is nowhere in sight. "Donovan, where is William?"

"He is still in his office." Regret rolls heavily from his voice, causing me to turn towards William's office. The door is left slightly ajar, allowing me to catch a slight glimpse in. My heart is pounding as I apprehensively stare through the gap in the door.

William's desk is placed directly in the center of the large room, allowing me a clear view of where he is sitting. To my dismay I notice William hunched over, lying dejectedly down on his desk. His fingers are weaved together tightly on top of his head as his arms work like a vise, aggressively squeezing against his head. Extreme anguish exudes off of his tortured body, filling the room with intense sorrow. His face remains firmly planted against his desk. Though the door is open he does not look up even once to acknowledge my solemn gaze.

Heavy guilt pierces every fiber of my core as his extreme remorse beckons to me. Acting on instinct I quickly lung forward, but instantly something stops me dead in my tracks. Donovan's arms which have been firmly wrapped around me now hold me like a prisoner.

"Donovan, let go of me. He needs me," I growl. I begin to violently fight against his strong hold like I'm struggling against an iron cage. It doesn't matter to him how much I fight, I'm weightless in his grasp. Though I know my feeble attempts of breaking his grasp are useless, I have to try. "Please, Donovan. He is like a father to me. He needs me," I plead.

"No, Lauren, he doesn't need you right now."

"Yes, he does, look at him." I motion with my head towards the broken down figure slumped dejectedly on his desk.

"Lauren, he has a lot to think about right now. He doesn't need you to lose control over him," he warns firmly.

Turning sharply towards Donovan I bore my eyes deep into his. "You have no right to tell me what he needs right now."

"Get her out of here, Donovan," William yells sharply from his office. Immediately I turn towards the aching voice, only to discover William still slumped over his desk with his head engulfed in the vise of his arms.

"William, please, I don't want to go," I whimper.

His arms release their firm grasp on his head. Pressing his hands firmly against the top of his desk he vigorously pushes his head up. His eyes look like they are swollen and red from the immense amount of pain he is experiencing. Though I haven't seen this much grief on him before, there is something familiar in his expression. I glance quickly back at the picture of my father. Instantly I realize the expression on William's face resembles the expression of my father's – in the photo. I gaze back at William, this time noticing not only the sadness, but the fear in his eyes. "William."

He interrupts sharply, "Lauren, Donovan is right, you need to go – now. I will be fine, don't worry. We will talk later. I promise." He tries reassuring me, but something in his voice contradicts what he is saying and I know things will never be the same again.

Donovan instantly leads me out of William's house as the sorrow engulfs my breaking heart. An overwhelming loss rushes over me, causing tears to freely flow down my face. Silently Donovan drives me home while I lay my head forcefully against the window of his car. The pain resonating in me seeps deeper into my body, dragging me into a dark, desolate state of despair.

CHAPTER 20

The Calm Before the Storm

A heavy weight of blackness engulfs me like an eclipse over my soul as I lay here in my bed crying. Donovan lovingly pets the back of my head attempting to soothe away my pain, but even his touch isn't taking it away. My mind is replaying the tortured expression on William's face as I reluctantly walked out his door. The visual stimulation feeding my horrified memory intensifies my tears. Wrapping my arms vigorously around my saturated pillow, I hold onto it tightly for some sort of support.

Suddenly I feel Donovan's warm arms wrap around me, securely holding me tightly. Delicately he kisses the back of my head as he softly whispers into my hair, "Lauren, I am sorry, but all will be right soon."

My body is fatigued from the emotional breakdown, leaving me no energy to respond to his comment. The ever-flowing well of tears slowly begins to dry out as exhaustion starts to take a firm grasp on me. I lay here in a fetal position, fighting to stay awake as I stare out into my dark room. The moonlight streams intricate shadows across the walls. Through my irritated and cloudy eyes I watch as the moonlit shadows dance vigorously through the dark night. Heavy tranquility cascades over me like a warm breeze washing over my disheveled soul. Intense relaxation pushes me deeper into the mattress like I weigh a thousand pounds. Donovan's fingertips gingerly trace the outline of my torso, soothing me deeper into a state of heavy relaxation. His warm fingers wash the last bit of trepidation from my mind, allowing me to give in to my exhaustion. Sleep envelops my heavy form as the darkness stretches its blinding hold over me.

A bright looming light, what feels like minutes later, washes feverishly over my aching muscles, chasing away the dark that was allowing me to sleep. Unconsciously I tighten my eyes trying to block out the impending daylight, causing the raw, tender lining around my eyes to burn. Everything within me hurts. The extreme crying episode I indulged in last night left me weak and sore.

On impulse I reach for one of my vacant pillows and aggressively throw it over my head. If my burning eyes are not able to block out the intruding sunlight then this ought to work.

"How long are you planning on sleeping?" Donovan's low, buttery smooth voice beckons me from across my room. His voice is so unobtrusive, a sharp contrast to the unwelcoming brilliance of the sunlight.

Reluctantly I remove the barrier protecting my eyes from the harsh sunlight as I attempt to open my eyes – only to discover the sleep from my dry tears has sealed my eyes shut. Slowly I struggle, trying to open my eyes. Then almost in a ripping motion, like Velcro pulling apart my eyes slowly open. The burn of the bright sunlight causes my eyes to instinctively close again. Squinting tightly, I try to block out the irritation inflicted by the severe light. Slowly, one eye at a time, I begin to pry my eyes. Gazing around my bright room I discover that this is not the muted morning sun I typically wake up to.

Rubbing the heavy sleep from my eyes I turn towards the direction of where Donovan's voice came from. There, sitting in the corner of my room on my oversized chair, is Donovan intently watching over me. Instantly I am taken aback by his faultlessly carved appearance. I take in every detail as he quietly sits, gazing at me with a bewildered expression on his face – which suddenly catches me by surprise.

"What time is it?" I croak. My voice cracks several times in my attempt to speak coherently.

"It is almost two o'clock in the afternoon," he answers gingerly as if he is breaking some devastating news to me.

It is nearly two o'clock and I still feel exhausted, like I didn't get any sleep last night. Rubbing my eyes vigorously, I try to get them to focus when suddenly I realize Donovan has a clean, refreshed appearance. I utter in surprise, "Donovan, you left?"

"Briefly this morning – that's all. I didn't leave until you were finally asleep," he reassures.

"You didn't sleep at all?"

"No rest for the wicked." Noticing the strange expression on my face he adds, "Lauren, I enjoy sleeping, but I don't need to. Remember, I don't fall under the same laws of nature as humans. Besides nighttime are demons' busiest times."

"You are human," I state innocently under my breath. Quickly changing the subject I ask, "Okay, then what time did I finally fall asleep?"

The expression on his face suddenly turns as if he is remembering some tragedy. "You finally fell asleep around four in the morning. I was beginning to worry about you. I didn't think you were ever going to stop crying," he grimaced.

Looking sharply at Donovan, I whisper breathlessly, "William. He knows who you are and what has happened to me – doesn't he?"

Springing out of the chair, he rushes nervously over to my side. "Lauren, why don't you wake up a little bit first before you get yourself all worked up again. Besides, I thought you and I might get out of here today."

"Donovan, you said yesterday you would tell me what William and you talked about. I am a part of this scenario whether you like it or not."

His eyes flinch instantly in response to what I stated. There is some sort of underlying expression racing quickly across his face. Donovan's face in general hides all signs of emotion, but I have been able to ascertain certain glimpses of feelings in his eyes. This one I'm having a hard time figuring out. Does he truly want to get out of here or is he merely trying to avoid answering my questions?

"Yesterday you wouldn't allow me to participate in your conversation for fear that I would lose control. Well, I'm in complete control right now – so why are you avoiding the issue?"

"Lauren, I am not avoiding anything. I just want to give us a break from all of this chaos for a little while." He gingerly sits down next to me, reaching for my hand which is still gripping on to my pillow for support. Donovan pries my hand free from the tight grasp on my pillow then places my hand firmly in his. The heat from his hand pulsates through my skin, setting it ablaze. My heart begins beating erratically as his crystal blue eyes melt through my livid exterior. This isn't fair. He is using his extreme good looks against me. My will crumbles beneath his touch, causing me to be completely in his power – and he knows it.

"Don't you think we deserve a break, even if it is only for a few hours? I told you that I will tell you everything – so trust me.

First though, can we have a nice night?" he pleads as his smooth, velvety voice rolls out of his hypnotic mouth.

"What about William?" I breathlessly utter. A heavy sigh rushes vigorously through Donovan's plump lips. His haunting, clear blue eyes close tightly as he instantly goes rigid. I moan fervently, "Donovan, I can't abandon William while he is suffering. All I could think about last night was the tortured expression on his face. What kind of person would I be if I abandoned him like this?"

His eyes slowly open as he utters in defeat, "Fine, but first before you talk to William I have to go into the city to take care of some business. When I am done I'll come and get you, then we can go to William's."

My eyes flicker dubiously at the mention of business. It's not like he is a stockbroker or anything like that – he's a demon. So what is he actually going to be doing? I question him suspiciously, "What business?"

He smiles ruefully, "I only need to take care of something, that's all."

"I'm coming with you. You are not going to leave me here alone." A silky layer of force coats my gelatinous voice.

"No. You are not coming with me," he sternly clarifies. "But perhaps afterwards we can do something before we go to William's."

Leaning towards him I gaze intently into his eyes as my breathing quickens, adding insistently, "I am going even if I have to force my way. You're not leaving me alone after all the shit that has happened to me. I'm going – do you hear me?"

He vehemently rakes his hand through his hair as a heavy sigh pushes out of him. "Fine, but you are staying in the car – understand?"

"I guess that will suffice," I utter eagerly, trying to hide my satisfaction.

His strong protective attitude intensifies his masculine sexuality, causing my pink cheeks to betray me. I can't seem to stop the embarrassing flood of emotions constantly running through my thoughts, causing my face to flush. When will this overzealous reaction end? Every time I gaze into his piercing blue eyes all I want to do is attack him. My emotions are hardwired to my desires. The more frustrated or angry I feel, the more my desire for him gets out of hand.

Donovan slowly slides his fingertips up my arm, tracing every line and indentation on my biceps. His intense eyes pierce through me as a mischievous smile spreads sharply across his face. My heart begins pounding audibly in reaction to his velvety touch, sending hot waves of embarrassment to crawl over my face. Donovan moves slowly towards me, inch by aching inch. His eyes never waver from mine, locking me into a passionate game of chicken. The fire within me ignites into a full inferno towards him.

My irregular breathing starts accelerating, making it difficult to breathe. Tilting his head within inches of my ear he exhales softly, causing his sweet, hot breath to tickle my neck. "Lauren, I think you need to go and take a cold shower," he whispers against the nape of my neck.

I flinch back, completely piqued by his statement. I glare up at him only to discover he is smiling from ear to ear, completely overjoyed by his triumphant enticement. Balling my hand into a tight fist I firmly punch his arm as hard as I can – completely aware that he barely felt it, but I don't care. It is the principle that matters. I utter harshly, "Donovan. You are a complete tease. That is not fair." Annoyed, I stand up quickly and storm towards the bathroom to get ready. As I stomp ferociously away like a silly child who has been caught stealing a cookie, I can hear Donovan's hysterical laughter bellowing enthusiastically in the background.

"Ugh, you are not funny," I snap.

"I think it is extremely funny." He chuckles as I slam the door fiercely behind me. Though he is laughing, somewhere deep in the back of my mind it feels like this is the calm before an impending storm.

Silently I sit here in the car, still brooding from earlier. He was absolutely right about the shower though, it made me feel so much better – but I'm not about to give him the satisfaction of knowing that. As I look over at Donovan's face I discover he still has an elated smile streaming across his face. I know he is still reveling in his apparent victory in teasing me earlier. "Donovan, you know it wasn't fair of you to tease me like that," I berate exaggeratedly.

He picks up my hand and gingerly brings it up to his mouth, kissing it. "Yeah, I know, but you do have to admit it was kind of funny." He chuckles softly in the back of his throat this time.

Seeing the joy on his face is contagious, causing me to relax and laugh at his obvious triumph over my uncontrolled passion for him. He holds onto my hand tightly as he drives – my car this time – into the city. This is the kind of moment we both have been waiting for… a moment of feeling and being normal. Something of which both of us have been robbed.

A feeling of nostalgia rolls around in my head, tickling the surface of my skin as I stare out of the passenger side window. This is the first time I have been in the passenger seat of my father's car since his death. I used to ride in the front seat staring out of the sunroof at all the tall skyscrapers as my father would drive through the city. Instinctively I tilt my head up and gaze up out of the sunroof at the city buildings towering over us like enormous guards. The setting sun shimmers off the windows of the buildings with vibrant red and orange colors, setting them ablaze.

As we drive deeper into the gleaming city the fiery lights rippling off of the buildings above fade, replacing everything with a dark and dirty feeling. The muted colors and grimy cement structures now replace the vibrant financial district we were in. The deeper we venture into the belly of the city, the queasier my stomach feels. This is a side of town I am completely unfamiliar with. The seediness seems to ooze from every sidewalk, crevice and alley. As the darkness of the night devours the daylight, all sorts of interesting people begin slithering out of the woodwork and onto the streets. The sinful cravings leaching out of the night-dwellers are like a black plague covering everything. Their desires, for some strange reason though, don't penetrate my soul like the ones in New Orleans did. Perhaps it is because these people are already fully immersing themselves in their darkest desires. They don't need any help from demons to get to hell – they are doing a great job heading there on their own.

Gazing around at all the darkness I instinctually squeeze Donovan's hand tightly in fear of where we are going. If this isn't hell, it feels pretty close to it. I'm beginning to wonder why I insisted on coming along with him. If I only knew that I was going to be traveling into a deep abyss I probably wouldn't have.

"Lauren, you will be fine. There is nothing to worry about. I won't let anything happen to you," he reassures me, squeezing my hand tenderly. "This won't take long, I promise."

The car slows as Donovan pulls over to the side of the street and comes to a complete stop. We park just down the street from an old stone structure that is flanked tightly between two enormous glass buildings. This odd archaic building with its stone engravings and protective gargoyles perched high above the entrance seems out of place in this seedy area of the city.

"Donovan, you are not about to leave me alone in the car," I protest feverishly, holding firmly onto his hand.

"Lauren, trust me, you will be safer in the car than where I am going." His voice is sharp as if he is giving me a harsh warning.

"I don't care. You are not leaving me here alone. I'm not going to sit in this car by myself with these creepy people all around me. Where is your chivalry?" I hiss, looking out the window of my car at the obvious deals going on right in front of me.

A heavy sigh blasts through his mouth. "Fine, but you cannot go into the room with me…no matter what."

He quickly gets out of the car and proceeds to walk over to my side. Hesitantly I get out, pushing my back aggressively against the exterior of the passenger door. Waiting nervously for Donovan I stand defensively as I witness several illegal acts happening inches away from my face. Though it is barely after sunset the overwhelming darkness engulfing this place appears as if it's making an attack on me. I feel like I am stuck in the middle of a scary movie where the innocent victim is left standing alone in a dark alley as a plethora of predators' eyes watch her every move.

Silently I scan my surroundings when I catch sight of a dark vagrant staring at me, scrutinizing my figure with sleazy mouth gestures. The slimy onlooker's eyes stare right through me, making me feel completely violated. Instinctively I push myself further up against the car door for protection. Donovan instantly rushes over to my side, wrapping his arm protectively around my waist, pulling me against his side. Turning sharply toward the sinister observer, he immediately shoots him a vicious gaze. As I glare up at his rebuking look, I notice that his eyes are not the peaceful blue anymore. The ominous clear eyes which I had witnessed before are now piercing into the sordid man's soul, executing a comeuppance. In reaction to his obvious fear, the grimy vagrant immediately turns his attention away from me.

Donovan slowly bends his head down. "Are you sure you don't want to stay in the car where it is safe? Trust me, no one will bother you – now." His gruff voice holds a deep plea within his tone.

Not uttering a word, I wrap my arms tightly around his waist, holding on for what feels like my life. My eyes remain affixed to the roaming streetwalkers as I lean my head securely against his chest. He kisses the top of my head reassuringly as we proceed down the street towards the ancient stone building.

The dirty sidewalk is filled with all sorts of disreputable-looking people loitering in front of all the closed or abandoned office spaces. There is a thick, musky smell mixed with alcohol and a sour, rotten aroma whirling all around me, causing a quick shudder to rush through me. Darkness spreads across the area like an impending disease slithering down the dismal street. Street lamps are nearly nonexistent here and what few are stationed sporadically around have tragically met their demise. The source of their light has been destroyed, allowing the darkness to fully take over.

We haven't walked very far when a loud, piercing shrill escapes from one of the sordid streetwalkers. "Donovan, where have you been?" the female temptress asks in a slow, haunting voice.

Her piercing tone sends shivers racing violently down my spine, wrapping around my ribcage. The scary, yet regal voice doesn't coincide with the ragged appearance of the lady of the night. The tall woman's long, ratty brunette hair looks as if it hasn't been brushed in months. The bright pink and blue make-up she has plastered on her face looks as if a little girl has painted it on for her. Her dirty tattered clothes leave very little to the imagination, with a deep plunging neckline and a barely-there skirt.

Donovan freezes instantly in front of the ragged lady. He bows his head slightly as if she is a member of a royal family, muttering softly, "Lilith."

"Donovan." Her tongue makes a disappointed snapping sound against the roof of her mouth as she shakes her head in angst towards him. I can hear a distinct clicking sound of what I can only assume is a large tongue-piercing slapping viciously against her teeth. Instantly the nasty sound makes me feel sick as I picture the piercing in my head. Disappointment rolls through my mind as to how this seedy woman can know Donovan. The idea of them together races disturbingly through my mind, sending disgusting chills to rush up my spine. I flinch slightly away from him in reaction to my distressing thoughts.

Donovan pulls me tightly back into his gripping arms and against his rigid torso as he hastily walks past her. His speed increases with some feverish determination. Wild theories shoot through my mind as to why he is swiftly moving away from the obvious prostitute. Is he embarrassed that he knows her, or perhaps it is something she said that upset him?

"Donovan, who is that woman?" I question breathlessly as my mere human legs are having a difficult time keeping up with him.

"Nobody," he utters sharply, quickening his pace.

Though the speed he is walking is beginning to give me a side-ache, I am not disputing this pace. The faster we get there, the quicker we can get out of this hellhole. We are getting closer to the awaiting architectural building I can only assume is our destination. Suddenly, as if out of nowhere, the piercing female's voice echoes his name from the dark shadows on the sidewalk.

"Donovan, we need to talk," she hisses violently from a dark crevice below us.

Donovan's speed decreases to a near stop as I gaze around looking for the bothersome whore. Looking all around me I discover she is nowhere near us. In fact, she is about fifty feet behind, standing in the same spot we had just left her. A bewildered expression now masks her face as if she has no memory of where she is. Complete confusion washes over me as I turn back to where the voice is now coming from. Instantly, out of the corner of my eye I notice a dark, creepy shadow slithering gracefully into the hovering darkness where the shrilling, piercing voice echoes from.

"Donovan, you know you can't run from us, we are everywhere," the now acidic voice growls. A strange figure walks out of the darkness beneath an awning hanging over the entrance to an abandoned office space. I jump back in complete shock as the individual slowly clears the dark shadows. To my horror this is not the streetwalker at all, in fact this is not even a female. The shrilling female's voice appears to be coming from a despondent and ragged homeless man. As he gets closer to us I notice he is wearing a long, ratty, gray trench coat hanging barely above his ankles. The entire bottom half of his coat is encrusted in mud and grime. His scruffy ashen beard envelops his face like a dingy grey rag.

As the dirty, shabby man slithers gracefully towards us like a seductive runway model, he gazes severely at Donovan with a vacant look in his eyes. "Donovan," the scruffy man utters in a piercing female's voice.

"AAAAH!" I scream. The man's voice exudes the same haunting female tone instead of a typical masculine sound. It's as if the innocent man is being used as a puppet for some sinister being. His body is there, but something evil is controlling him.

"Lauren, try to be quiet," Donovan warns, yet I can hear fear vibrating deep within his voice. His is not the same kind of fear as mine though, but a deeper understanding of who this is and what it means for us.

There is no doubt this is the same iniquitous voice that had been exuding out of the prostitute's – just moments ago. Only now this shrilling tone is expelling out of the homeless man's mouth. I can feel myself beginning to panic as my breathing intensifies. Donovan's arms tighten their grip on me as he pulls me forcefully away from the encroaching evil buried deep within the poor, disheveled man.

"Donovan, what was that?" My trembling voice quivers vigorously against my chattering teeth as I realize I am falling deeper into a state of panic.

Donovan's eyes shift side to side, defensively scanning our surroundings as we proceed apprehensively down the dirty sidewalk. "Remember what I told you about demons that don't have a body? These sinuous beings are evil spirits that have power to –" his firm voice stops instantaneously as if he is aware of something approaching.

"Donovan, you don't want to get me mad, do you?" The now livid voice echoes from an approaching petite, yet voluptuous blonde woman. Her body is painted with heavy amounts of sordid tattoos, hiding the skin tone she was born with. Her black jeans and black tank-top mirror the dark countenance consuming her as if some sinister being has muted the internal light residing deep within her.

"No, Lilith, I would never want to do that," Donovan utters apologetically. This is the same frightening name he respectfully uttered towards the prostitute. Complete terror vibrates vehemently within me as I tightly hold on to Donovan for support. A horrifying nightmare has invaded my reality, sending me into a dark and disturbing place. Why did I have to be so stubborn and insist on going with him? Why couldn't I have stayed in the car like he had suggested? I would have been far safer in the car than being put in this dark, treacherous situation.

"Donovan, Darius has been summoning you for some time now. You aren't avoiding us now – are you?" The sinuous voice echoes out of the petite woman's crimson, unnaturally plump lips.

"No, I wouldn't dare ignore Darius. I have simply been busy, that's all," he purrs almost reverently. The muscles within him coil under my enveloping arms like a compressed spring ready to explode, as if he is preparing for a defensive strike.

The petite woman's emotionless eyes scan in my direction, studying my every detail. "I can tell," she hisses each word out, little by little with her high-pitched shrill.

"Leave her out of this," he growls sharply, shoving me protectively behind his shielding body.

"SILENCE!" Lilith rebukes forcefully. "You know she can't be left out of this. This is entirely about her and her family."

Her unexpected berating tone thuds violently throughout the air, causing me to flinch back in intense horror. Donovan tightens up his grip on me as he adjusts defensively in preparation for an impending attack. Instinctively I look all around, trying to see if there is anyone watching this situation as it unfolds. To my horror everyone is parading along as if nothing is happening. They are either blind or too afraid to get involved.

As I brace myself against Donovan's back preparing for a fight, I can't help but wonder who this menacing being is. How is she able to transfer her dark aura from person to person nearly seamlessly? Her shrieking voice seems to come out of nowhere, haunting our every move.

"Please, Lilith, this is why I am on my way to Darius right now. There is another option in the works that can solve this whole situation," he pleads fervently, still holding his defensive stance.

Lilith peers at me as a slight smirk spreads vulgarly across her prisoner's face. "Fine, Donovan, I think Darius would love to hear this alternative." She gawks ruefully at Donovan, adding in a disturbing manner, "Besides, I know Darius would love to meet her. After all, he already knows her –"

"No. He can't. Let me talk to Darius – alone," Donovan roars angrily.

"Enough, Donovan. My patience has run out." The tattooed girl's once chocolate-brown eyes instantly turn black as coal. Not even the whites of her eyes are visible. Her terrorizing eyes sink deep into their sockets, leaving dark sinister circles around them. "One more outburst and you will regret it." She slithers within just a few inches of Donovan, causing his muscles to coil even tighter. Her hand slides up onto Donovan's cheek, placing it threateningly on his face. My heart is about to stop at any moment as I witness this iniquitous display of power. The occupied figure stands up on her toes, leaning in and giving Donovan a mischievous warning. "I like you, Donovan, but don't think for a moment I will have a problem destroying you. Now shall we proceed or is this going to have to get ugly?" she mocks darkly, slapping his cheek as she stares down at me with her black-as-coal eyes.

He nods hesitantly, relaxing his tightly coiled muscles as he dejectedly proceeds to follow Lilith towards the ornate cement building. Some sort of ominous understanding must have passed silently between them in order for Donovan to simply give up so quickly.

Donovan presses me tightly against him as we proceed down the sidewalk. I can feel the heavy weight of my feet with every step I take. I gaze up at Donovan's stone face as he stares straight ahead at the approaching building.

"Donovan, who is she?" I whisper.

Leaning down he softly speaks against my head, "Physically I have no idea. Spiritually she is a very powerful and ancient demon. Remember, spirit demons have the power to possess those around them as long as they are already submersed in evil activities. Around here she has no problem finding a willing body to take over. Lilith is the kind of demon you don't fight unless you are ready to suffer. The kind of torture she can inflict on your soul – well, you would wish your spirit could die." He pauses briefly, as if he is trying to get the unspeakable image out of his mind.

"Donovan, then who is Darius? Is he a spirit demon like Lilith, or is he like you?" I whisper against his chest.

"He still has his body, if that's what you are asking, but he is definitely not like me. He is not fighting to hold onto his humanity. He sold it ages ago along with his soul," he grumbles.

"But I thought Lucius is who you deal with."

"He is."

"Then who is Darius?" I repeat, slightly confused at why Donovan is going to him. I turn faintly toward Lilith, making sure she isn't going to turn around and berate us for talking.

"Think of it this way. Darius is like the Assistant Manager. He has worked in the organization long enough to have earned that position. While Lucius – he is more like the Manager, and so on down the corporate chain to hell."

My heart begins pounding again with the impending reality of what I am about to walk into. My trepidation exudes from every fiber and corner of my mind. Donovan looks down and seeing the fear imprinted on my face, he pulls me closer to him, adding regretfully, "I am sorry, Lauren. I should have never brought you along. I was hoping to avoid this situation, but it is now too late." He pauses briefly, then adds fervently, "No matter what is said tonight, please remember I have always loved you…please remember that." His eyes blaze as if he is attempting to brand the words into my mind.

"I promise," I repeat.

We arrive in front of the entrance to the dark ancient building. As my eyes scan up the exterior outer wall I notice a pair of intricately carved gargoyles sitting on the edge of a ledge in a protective stance. Fear shoots violently through me while I stare into their peering eyes as if they warn me of the impending danger awaiting me. The eyes of the gargoyles seem to follow me as I timidly walk through the entrance. As I'm staring up at them I instantly hear the sound of a thick, heavy door being pushed open. The petite-framed woman thrusts the massive door open with very little effort. Obviously it is Lilith's strength allowing the woman's occupied frame to be able to push the heavy door open effortlessly.

Silently we walk into a large room that is surprisingly bright for how dark it is outside. Substantial two-story columns flank the outer rims of the enormous room, which is backed by equally impressive windows. Brown, muted yellow, and off-white tiles form an intricate pattern of a large star in the center of the floor. The vast entry room is completely vacant. Not a single stitch of furniture is anywhere.

As I hesitantly gaze around the empty space I notice a tall figure looming in the corner of the enormous room. His dark presence fills the entire space with his baleful gloom. Sinuously he walks, step by slow step, until he reaches the center of the wide open area. This all-encompassing person must be the Darius that Lilith and Donovan mentioned.

CHAPER 21

Wrath

The heart-pounding terror subsides slightly as my eyes behold Darius. He isn't at all what I was expecting him to be. My mind had pictured a frightening monster, but that is not what stands before us.

Physically he appears a lot like Donovan, tall and surprisingly good looking, but their coloring is completely opposite. Darius has light blonde hair with a modern short style, which in a weird way is surprisingly odd. A black athletic-fit long sleeve t-shirt clings to his torso, enhancing his tall, well-built frame. His appearance looks absolutely typical, not at all like the sinister demon I was expecting to see before me. As I peer deeper upon his creamy white face I am taken aback by his shocking eyes. They are completely white, other than small pupils in the center of his eyes, like the irises have been entirely bleached out. Donovan's eyes have done the same thing before, but only when he is peering into someone's soul. Fearing Darius will know my desires and use them against me, I instantly try to block my desires from him.

"Donovan, I am so glad Lilith found you. I was beginning to get worried about you," he hums facetiously.

His low, precise voice cuts at every word, yet it still has a velvety tone that softens the harsh edges. His face holds an innocent appearance to it, yet I can tell by Donovan's body language he is someone to fear.

Lilith rushes arrogantly over to Darius's side, gleaming at her obvious triumphant victory in capturing Donovan. "He said he was on his way to see you, if you can believe that," she hisses. Her loud, shrieking voice echoes violently throughout the barren room.

"Is that true, Donovan?" he smoothly asks, slowly emphasizing every word.

"Yes, I was coming to talk to you about a certain situation."

Darius's piercing eyes scan instantly down Donovan until they rest feverishly upon me. He interrupts sharply, crooking his head side to side as if he is cracking his neck. "Ah, Donovan, you brought Lauren here," he mutters in pleasure.

Hearing my name uttered through Darius's dark, nearly black mouth causes my fear to instantly hit a full raging boil. Everything within me starts quaking rapidly, causing me to feel lightheaded. If Donovan wasn't supporting my entire weight in his arm, I would undoubtedly collapse on the floor in absolute terror.

"Darius," Donovan nearly shouts, pulling Darius's attention back up to him. "I don't mean any disrespect, but can we please talk alone?"

Darius's eyes widen as he crooks his neck to the side, gazing at us deeply. An evil smile spreads reluctantly across his face as if he has barely figured out the punchline to a lame joke. Immediately, as if out of nowhere, Darius is suddenly in front of Donovan. It happened so fast, like a blink of an eye – one moment he stood in the middle of the vast room and the very next moment he is within inches of Donovan's face. His eyes narrow as they transform instantly in front of me from bleach-white to black-as-coal, gazing balefully upon Donovan.

Donovan slowly slides me behind him, pushing me gingerly out of view of Darius. Still holding onto me with one arm, he places his body protectively between Darius and me. Darius's eyes tighten with livid anger. Suddenly Darius thrusts his hand violently around Donovan's neck, gripping tightly. Donovan's muscles stiffen as Darius firmly holds onto him. Reacting to the intense strain being put forcefully around his neck, Donovan lifts up slightly, trying to loosen Darius's grip.

My heart rate speeds up violently in extreme anger at what I am witnessing. Adrenaline pulsates through me as my usual fear is immediately replaced with a fight or flight situation. There is absolutely no way I'm going to run, leaving Donovan behind to be tortured by this monster. Since I'm not going to run from this ominous situation, my only other option is to fight. As I prepare my mind to fight, the situation goes from bad to worse.

Still grasping hold of Donovan's neck, a vicious growl bellows violently from Darius's chest. "Donovan, your inability to embrace what you are is pathetic. Holding on to this ridiculous notion that you have any good left in you has done nothing but make you weak," he roars, sending violent shockwaves of anger through me.

Reacting to the frantic adrenaline rush vigorously pulsating through my veins, I shout out angrily from behind Donovan's protective body. "There is nothing weak about fighting the encroaching evil within. That is what makes him stronger than you – a sinister monster." My heart is pounding as the fire within me begins to race forcefully up toward my heart. Reacting to my obvious outburst, I feel Donovan's arm tighten up around me.

Darius turns his attention violently towards me, causing his black-as-night eyes to burn deep into my soul. Donovan aggressively spins instinctively in front of me, blocking Darius's view. A sharp, squeaking sound escapes ferociously from Darius's hand as it turns tightly around Donovan's neck. Darius tries looking around Donovan again, but Donovan keeps spinning vigorously around, blocking his every move. The more Darius tries to turn toward me, the more Donovan spins his body around, protecting me from Darius's piercing gaze.

Still holding fiercely onto Donovan's neck Darius stops and stares pensively at us. "Interesting," Darius hums in surprise. "Do you honestly think you can protect her?" he questions, gazing deep into Donovan's eyes. Suddenly a vindictive smile spreads maliciously across his face. "Or better yet, do you honestly think you can keep the truth from her?" he mutters proudly.

He shoves Donovan's head slightly to the side so that he is able to completely view my face. I can hear Donovan struggling to stop Darius, but he simply ignores him, placing all his attention on me. "Lauren, did Donovan tell you about the first time he saw you?" The words roll off his sinister tongue like silk through sand. His face erupts with a gleaming expression as he revels in his discovery.

"Darius, stop…now," Donovan warns.

"What do you mean?" I snap in confusion.

"I bet you thought he met you just recently – right?"

"Darius, sto…" Darius's hand constricts even tighter around Donovan's neck, instantly cutting off any sound from Donovan. Darius's hand begins to squeeze tighter and tighter around his neck. Why isn't Donovan fighting back? I can see him struggling to breathe. Somehow I need to stop this.

"Stop it," I yell feverishly. Donovan's arm is still tightly wrapped around me, pressing me firmly against his back. Holding me there vigorously, he tries to prevent me from helping him. Violently I writhe around trying to escape Donovan's firm grasp so

I can at least try to pry Darius's long, lethal fingers from his neck. "Let go of him, Darius."

Lilith slithers hastily over to Darius's side, preparing to intervene whenever necessary. A low, growling laughter rolls fiercely from Darius and echoes sadistically throughout the vast empty space.

Loosening his tight grip on Donovan, he utters spitefully, "Ha, she is a feisty one, Donovan. She seems so brave –" pausing slightly he adds, glaring at me, "– unlike her father." He chuckles maliciously.

My heart stops instantly. "What do you mean, unlike my father? How in the hell did you know my father?" I grunt fiercely.

The internal fire smoldering inside of me ignites violently as though it has set my entire internal organs on fire. Slowly an arrogant smile spreads venomously across his face as if I have responded precisely the way he wanted me to.

"Lauren, what a funny use of the word 'hell.' Donovan didn't tell you?" His voice is low and eerie as he speaks, over-enunciating every sound, "That is exactly how we met. Your father is not dead – so to speak."

"What do you mean? My father died over a year ago." The fiery rage intensifies with every word this monster is speaking.

"Darius, I am warning you…stop." Trying to turn his head towards me, Donovan pleads intensely, "Lauren, please don't give in to the rage. Stay in control – please."

Darius did the same distinct snapping sound with his tongue that Lilith had done earlier. "Shame on you, Donovan, how could you lie to this sweet, innocent young girl?" he mocks. Then turning his attention back to me he utters slyly, "Don't be too angry with him. Maybe he is merely embarrassed that he screwed up, thus forcing me to finish the job for him."

"What do you mean? You had to finish what?" I hiss.

His smile widens in complete triumph. He has thrown me the enticing bait which is luring me in perfectly. "Lauren, a little over a year ago your father's request was granted – by Donovan. So technically he is ours, body and soul."

"WHAT!" I scream. "That's not possible. You're a liar." The rage within me explodes, boiling uncontrollably, making it harder to restrain my immense anger. Instinctively I turn, gazing vaguely over at Donovan for some sort of glimmer that what is being uttered is untrue. The broken expression on his face speaks louder than any words, sending waves of tremendous anguish and anger to crash against me. Heat radiates from my abdomen like a raging forest fire and takes over me as I feel the self-control viciously slip away.

"Lauren, I am not a liar. Unlike Donovan, I want to tell you the truth." His voice is thick with duplicity.

"Donovan, is that what happened to my father? Did you have anything to do with it?" I cry out fervently.

"Lauren – I am sorry," he utters weakly.

"When were you planning on telling me this sickening story?" I snap as the rage begins to take over me.

"Lauren, I was planning on telling you the truth." His voice is muffled by Darius's grip still placed firmly around his neck.

"When?" I shout.

A sharp, sadistic laugh vibrates vigorously from Lilith, causing a high-pitched shrill to echo in the room. She is obviously overjoyed by the game being played, with my soul being the grand prize.

Turning sharply towards Lilith I shoot her a mordant glare. This is not a vicious game being played. This is my life they are messing with. Instantly I feel the rage consuming my entire body like a rushing river, filling me with hate. I begin to violently shake from the pent-up anger – desperately searching for an escape. Every sensory nerve in me is acutely aware of my surroundings, causing my skin to feel like it's on high alert. My breathing intensifies with every breath that I am inhaling. As I look around, all the different vivid colors in the room slowly morph into a bright, vibrant shade of red. The vicious writhing gradually dissipates as I slowly succumb to the raging fire within.

"That's it Lauren, feel the anger, give in to the undying need. Fully embrace the rage within you," Darius beckons with a hypnotic voice.

"Darius, leave her alone," Donovan growls sharply.

Instantly Donovan hurls me backwards with extreme force, causing me to slide aggressively across the tile floor. It feels like I am going to never stop sliding, until suddenly my back slams intensely against one of the massive columns, stopping me instantly. I hit the column with such extreme force that it causes my head to whip back, making my vision spin as though it is swirling out of control. Pain instantly rushes through me, knocking some sort of reality back into my conscious mind.

Though my vision is still affected by the rage within me, I'm now acutely aware of the imminent situation. Shaking my head vigorously I try to clear my vision of this encroaching evil within. Gazing disquietly around the room I suddenly catch sight of Donovan. I can hear a low, sadistic growling sound echoing from him as he forcefully grabs Darius's arm, yanking it violently off of his neck. Thrusting his hand around Darius's neck, Donovan lifts him into the air with just one hand. Out of the corner of my eye I notice a smear of colors rushing towards Donovan.

I try warning Donovan of the approaching danger, but nothing will come out of my mouth. There is no air left in me to support my voice. When I slammed up against the column it knocked the wind right out of me.

The anger begins to flare up within me again as I witness Donovan's precarious circumstance. A sharp, penetrating pain in my stomach doubles me over in anguish. I can feel the intense internal fire engulfing my core, causing severe pain. All the muscles within me coil into a tight ball, forcing my eyes to close. Wrapping my arms firmly around my stomach, I lay here in a fetal position as I scream in excruciating pain. The rage billows violently within me, causing me to convulse rapidly.

Though the pain is completely consuming me, I can still hear the fierce thundering of a violent battle reverberating all around. The terrifying noise rips through the room like a horrendous storm trapped inside. Vigorously I struggle to relax the muscles around my eyes. But with every bellowing growl I hear, it causes the pain in my stomach to intensify, forcing my muscles to stiffen up again.

Fighting against my uncooperative muscles, I pry my eyes open. My vision is no longer corrupted by the sinister color. Instead of the harsh red, all the vivid colors have returned. I look frantically around the now disheveled room for Donovan. The substantial vacant space looks as if a giant tornado has centered its destruction in the middle of this room. The large cement columns have been nearly shattered by something or someone who has obviously slammed against it. As I take in all the destruction I suddenly catch sight of something lying lifeless on the ground. My heart drops instantly as I focus intently on the motionless figure. A wave of relief washes over me as I notice the multiple tattoos streaming across the motionless form. Hovering over the pirated girl's unconscious body is Lilith's dark, malevolent shadow.

Suppressing my excruciating pain, I anxiously begin looking for Donovan when suddenly I see Darius with his hands wrapped vigorously around Donovan's neck, hoisting him up violently in the air. Darius's face is dark with revolting shadows sprawling across his face, making him look like the terrifying monster he is.

"Donovan," I'm able to cry out feebly. The pain I am feeling echoes loudly in my voice.

Darius turns viciously, gazing at me. This is exactly the distraction Donovan has been waiting for. The very second Darius turns his attention toward me, Donovan thrusts his foot aggressively against Darius's chest. The force of Donovan's kick rips Darius's hands free from around Donovan's neck, sending Darius flying aggressively across the room. Donovan drops violently to the ground, quickly jumping to his feet and preparing for another attack. Turning ruefully towards me, Donovan discovers my obvious predicament as I lay here vigorously fighting the evil burning within me.

As I peer at Donovan the internal rage bursts vehemently inside of me again. A cocktail of anger floods my thoughts with ferocious waves of poisonous guile in my veins, doubling me over in pain again. I don't know how much longer I'm going to be able to hang on. I'm losing the battle within. The overwhelming desire to give in to the rage is winning. My strength is spent and I have nothing to fight for any more.

"Lauren, fight it. Hold on a little bit longer – please," he implores. Donovan's hands suddenly slap securely together, forming a tight grip against each other. The muscles in his hands visibly vibrate under the extreme pressure he is placing on them. As his hands slowly pull apart I notice a bright translucent fluttering mass forming between his powerful palms. Slowly he pries his hands further apart, making the mass increase in size as if he is causing the elements within his hands to move at an extraordinary speed. The intense velocity they are spinning with looks like a large glowing ball of translucent whirling matter. As Donovan's clear white eyes focus intently on the implausible process, his hands look as though they are clasping onto an over-inflated bubble.

Darius staggers to his feet as a flash of horror races vigorously across his monstrous face. His dark, sunken eyes gaze maliciously upon Donovan, warning him this is a traitorous act. Reacting to the apparent impending danger, Darius coils up into a tight crouching position. A deep snarl rushes vigorously through Darius's mouth as he springs ferociously towards Donovan. At that very moment Donovan aggressively throws the swirling matter, hitting Darius with such extreme force it hurls him violently against the thick cement wall. Darius hits the wall with such power it crumbles the cement behind his impacting form. Darius slowly staggers against the demolished rubble scattered all around him.

"Donovan, you may think you are winning the battle, but you have lost the war. It is too late for her. The all-encompassing rage is already eating away at her soul," he utters portentously. Darius suddenly shuts his hands with a sharp slapping motion, instantly causing the same swirling matter to appear within his hands.

As I fiercely look towards Donovan, a piercing pain rushes violently through my head, slowly eating away at my core. Donovan is immediately at my side, hastily scooping me up in his arms like a hurt child. Trying to fight Donovan's hold on me, I begin to writhe about in uncontrolled anger. A frightful, bellowing laugh echoes in the distance.

"It's too late, Donovan," Darius chides.

A rushing sound of spinning matter echoes in the distance as Darius prepares to throw it at us. Donovan's arms wrap tightly around me in a near vise, controlling my violent outbursts. Leaning down he faintly whispers into my ear, "Hold on, Lauren. It will soon be over – I promise."

CHAPTER 22

Remembrance

Holding me close to him, he tucks my head firmly against his chest as I instantly feel the rate of the wind increase. The rushing air hits my back with such severity it forces me vigorously against Donovan's chest. My hair whips fiercely out of control like we are traveling at the speed of light. Other than the intense wind, it feels like we are standing still. Though we have done this before, this time the power of the wind has intensity behind it.

The wind slowly subsides as I feel the cool, damp night air softly hitting my back now. Donovan tenderly releases the firm grip on my head, allowing me to lift it slightly. I notice dark shadows of what appear to be tall trees blocking the glittery night sky. The nearly full moon casts silvery light all over the tops of the leaves. Their dancing motion makes them appear like shimmering silver dollars hanging delicately from the massive branches.

The cool moisture radiating from the night air strokes my skin, soothing my overheated body. There is a calm peacefulness looming all around me which is such a sharp contrast to the hell I have been involved in. The anxiety that has been building up within me subsides slightly, but the intense anger still radiates fiercely from my emotions.

Glaring viciously up at Donovan, I push aggressively against his chest. "Let go of me," I snarl, shoving my hands fiercely against him. No matter how hard I push against him, he still holds me firmly in his arms. My strength is nothing compared to his. Like a wafting feather in a tornado, I am completely in his power.

As I thrust my hands insistently against his chest, he suddenly opens his arms, causing me to drop vigorously to the ground. Though I land firmly, to my surprise the drop doesn't hurt as much as I was expecting it to. I'm on a soft, spongy bed of grass. The lawn is extremely thick, and judging by the immense moisture covering the area it has recently been watered. A thin layer of fog blankets the entire area. Silhouettes of the enormous trees are sporadically located between large cement statues dotting the entire space. To my horror it appears Donovan has brought me to a familiar cemetery. Though it looks somewhat recognizable, the blinding night sky – coupled with the ground fog – is making it difficult for me to know exactly where we are.

Rage and disgust billow violently within me at why Donovan would be so insensitive to bring me to a cemetery at night. As I roll briskly over onto my side, I catch sight of a heartbreaking image. There, standing above me, is a large rectangular-shaped marble headstone with tormenting words etched deep into the stone – and my mind. *Maxwell "Max" Cowley, a Loving Husband and Father*. The intense anger suddenly is replaced by an overpowering amount of sorrow and disappointment.

"Lauren, you need to release your anger before it destroys you," he whispers apologetically.

I peer relentlessly at the headstone as the wrath boiling over within me is now overtaken by a severe feeling of grief. Lifting my hand I slowly start to trace my father's name etched deep into the headstone. I have been here so many times before, but this time it feels different. Instead of the feeling of loss being center stage, disappointment and abandonment is now painfully present. Grief fills my mind as the tears well up in my eyes. A rush of streaming tears freely spill out of my eyes, pouring down my cheeks with their salty sting, etching my anguish permanently in my skin. Feeling the rough engraving of my father's name on my fingertips causes a vast array of emotions to rise to the surface. Curling my hands up into a tight fist, I forcefully start hitting his deceptive headstone in complete disgust, crying out, "Why dad – why?!" I yell viciously as my hands continue thrashing his headstone.

The pain rushing intensely through my hands with every hit can in no way be compared to the pain flowing rapidly over my quivering body. Extreme emotion flows from me, causing me to collapse under the pressure. I lay here over my father's grave as I begin sobbing uncontrollably. "Why did you leave me? Your stupid, asinine choice destroyed my life."

The sharp, penetrating pain consuming me slowly dissipates with every outburst I am exhibiting. For the first time tonight I feel like I am able to release the energy building rapidly within me. A year of regret and sorrow flow feverishly through my thrashing fists. My ragged breathing intensifies with every uncontrollable tear as my quivering breath pulls in the cool air – extinguishing the fire within me.

"Lauren, I am so sorry." Donovan's soft voice ripples in the wind as it tenderly lands against my back.

"Aren't you tired of apologizing?" I whimper sharply.

A soft, dejected exhale escapes from him as he continues regretfully, "Yes, I am, and I'm afraid the apologies aren't over yet."

I gaze up at Donovan, not wanting to hear anymore. "What do you mean, Donovan? I thought I heard it all tonight. I am not sure if I can hear any more."

"Lauren, you need to hear the full story – from me, not Darius."

When he utters Darius's name fear shoots through me, sending shivers to dance vigorously on my spine. "Donovan, my heart is completely ripped out and my world – though worthless – has been completely ruined. I don't know how much more I can handle," I whisper weakly as I gaze over at the headstone of the man I thought I admired. But now the only feeling left is hate.

"Lauren, your life is not worthless. Maybe knowing the truth will give you the missing pieces of your puzzling life so you can see how amazing you are. You are a lot stronger than you give yourself credit." He slowly sits down next to me, gently lifting my hands to his face. Delicately he examines my injured hands, wiping the blood off of them with his clean shirt. Tearing off the bottom of his shirt he wraps my bleeding knuckles with the rags formed by the soft, soothing material. "Do they hurt much?"

"Not as much as my heart," I state almost inaudibly, staring vacantly down at my wrapped fists.

"They will all heal. Time has a way of fixing things," he mutters, gently wiping away my tears.

"Not everything. Some things simply can't be forgotten."

"Lauren, that is not true. Remember what happened to my father when I took his place?"

"Yes," I state reluctantly, not quite sure where he is going with this.

"That is what happened to you. You see, Darius was right when he told you we have met before – just over a year ago, to be exact."

"What? I don't understand," I mumble. "You are saying my memory has been taken away – by you?"

"Not exactly. You see, your father did come to me with a deep desire for something."

"What was it?" I ask, wondering what could have been so important as to lose his soul over. "What did he want so badly that he would have gone against everything he ever taught me?"

"Lauren, it wasn't anything terribly bad, in fact it can happen to the best of people. He was going bankrupt and was going to lose everything. He couldn't do that to your mother – or you, for that fact. I was able to grant him what he needed in return for…"

"I don't want to hear it, please," I interrupt, not quite sure if my broken heart can actually hear the words he is going to utter.

He smiles ruefully in response to my request. Then instantly he clenches his teeth down firmly as if he is dreading the rest of what needs to be said. Hesitating slightly Donovan regretfully continues his dubious explanation of the events, "Lauren, when I came to collect him you walked in. You were supposed to be at work, but you came back early. When you barged through the door I instantly caught sight of your face. Something pulled me to you like a magnet calling me home. In that instant I saw the fear in your eyes and I knew what I was becoming. I could see in your eyes the same pain I felt when I walked in on my father. I knew I was becoming the same sinister monster who came to collect my father's soul. I was turning into the very demon I hated – Lucius," he spits the words viciously from his mouth. "I knew I couldn't follow through with it. Lauren, I was planning on letting your father go, but Darius was not about to let that happen. He caught wind of my desire and instantly showed up to finish what I couldn't."

My tears vigorously flow down my face as my memory of that tragic day floods back into my consciousness. It's as if the closed curtains over my memory have instantly been flung open, revealing all the hidden truths. Instantly I recall the agony on my father's face when I walked into the room. His face went completely white, robbing him of all the vitality that usually existed within him. Tremendous pain rushed across my father's face as his guilt seemed to crush his soul. He began pleading for me to leave, but I wouldn't leave him alone with a questionable stranger. Though this dark stranger had ulterior motives, something unexplainable pulled me toward him. Then, to my horror and devastation, I discovered what this stranger really was. During the moment of discovery fear and rage overwhelmed me, but I wasn't about to let my father go without a fight.

With every tragic event vividly being replayed in my mind, extreme pressure envelops my heart as if someone is squeezing it violently between their hands. Everything I thought I knew has been viciously ripped from me. Throwing my hands up dejectedly over my eyes, I begin sobbing uncontrollably. "I remember now. You choked me. You nearly killed me," I cry out in anger and despair.

"No. I had to take you to the brink of death in order to remove your memories. If I hadn't then Darius would have killed you."

"That is why I couldn't remember the situation surrounding my father's death then. You removed my memory of that tragic day so I wouldn't have to live my life in fear and sorrow." Instant panic violently shoots through my veins as I remember there was someone else there that day. Forcing the lump in my throat down, I utter softly, "William was there."

"Yes, he was there also. He discovered what your father had done only a few days before I arrived. William tried to talk him out of it, but he knew it was too late. He had already made the deal."

Suddenly I recall the disheveled picture hanging on the wall at William's house. It appeared as if someone had taken their rage out on the picture. William must have been disgusted with what my father was giving up, thus destroying the photo representing what my father had willingly destroyed. Mentally visualizing the image, I can see my father's face clearly in the wrinkled picture. A terrified expression is etched into creases around his fearful eyes.

"William tried to go in my father's place, didn't he?" I ask reassuringly.

"Yes, he did. Your father wouldn't let him though. He told William it was his mistake and he needed to be the one to accept the punishment."

My mind recalls all the sordid details of that day. "He asked William to take care of me and my mother – didn't he?" I utter. My voice is thick with lament as the tears stream freely down my face. Turning sharply towards my father's grave I rest my head against it, crying, "You chose to leave me, dad. Why?"

"No, he didn't choose to leave you," he reassures softly. "I was going to let him go, remember, but Darius came in. Completely infuriated by my obvious remorse he quickly snatched your father away, leaving both you and William wallowing in pain. I did the only thing I could do for the both of you, I removed all memory of the insidious situation." Pausing briefly, he adds, "Lauren, this may sound ridiculous, but seeing you caused something to collide deep within me. I knew I would never be the same anymore and I haven't until I..." He hesitates, not wanting to finish what he is saying.

"Until you were sent for me – right?" I finish his statement. "Who sent you for me, Darius or my father?" I ask, choking out my father's name, horrified that he could possibly be put in the same category as Darius.

"Lauren, I honestly don't know where your father is," he hums, avoiding answering the question. "Lauren, there is one more thing I need to tell you," he adds regretfully. "William does know what is going on with you, but you already figured that out. The thing you don't know is we have discussed him taking your place, so your soul can be set free. He was already planning on going in your fa–"

"–NO!" I shout as I quickly stand up, visually overpowering him. "You can't take both of them away from me. I will not allow it."

"Lauren, he feels it is the right thing to do. He believes if your father would have let him go in his stead, you would have had a happy, normal life."

"So is this what you talked about yesterday?" I snap. "I thought you took his memory away also." Impatiently I begin pacing across the thick grass surrounding my father's headstone as I try to fight back the excruciating anguish pounding aggressively within my heart.

"I did, but his memory slowly came into fruition when he started answering all of your questions. Lauren, it may be possible to hide your memory, but it is always there. Certain triggers can shove those memories to the forefront of your mind," he explains softly as he bends his knees, wrapping his arms tightly around them. Resting his chin delicately on his knees, his eyes move back and forth, following my every move. Though his low, velvety voice tries to soothe me, nothing at this point is going to help me. The intense sorrow I am feeling right now is overwhelming.

"Well, I hate to break it to the both of you, but my happiness depends on me – not on William's sacrifices or you trying to fix everything. How do you expect me to be happy if everything I love is taken away from me? I won't allow it." The pain circles within me like vultures ready to feed on my broken heart. My free-flowing tears stream down my face too fast to even control.

My trembling legs vibrate aggressively beneath me as I realize I'm about to lose everything important to me. Instantly the sensation that I'm going to collapse at any moment rushes over me, forcing me to sit back down. As I slowly collapse next to my father's headstone I notice the bouquet of now dried red roses lying next to his headstone. These are the same flowers I noticed several weeks ago. Picking up the disheveled remains of the once vibrant flowers, a small card falls out of them. Holding the card ruefully in my hand I slowly open it. Written across the card in beautiful handwriting reads four simple words, *I am Sorry Lauren.*

The words instantly prick my memory. These are the same words Donovan utters all too often. Holding the card tightly in my hand I quickly look up at him. His stunning, melancholy face lies gently against his knees as his eyes gaze remorsefully down at the ground. His once strong masculine physique appears disheveled and broken as the anguish pours out of him. He continues to focus blindly on the ground, refusing to look up at me.

Holding up the card and withered roses, I ask sharply, "Did you leave these here?" Trying to get his attention I shake them aggressively in my hand, causing several dead petals to fall onto the damp ground around him.

After shooting me a quick glance he looks back at the ground, uttering, "Yes, I did, and you are right – I am tired of saying I am sorry. I don't want you to hurt any more. I can make it so you won't remember this any more – or me. Your life can go on like normal."

His voice is weak as he sits here defenselessly. Looking up at me he gazes depressingly into my eyes. His eyes burn with a vivid reality that if he removes my memory I will never see him again. Though I am extremely livid with him right now, I can't imagine not having him in my life. I have been unequivocally altered by Donovan. I'm not sure I can ever go back to a normal life any more. My life before him was bland and pointless. I walked through life with a blindfold on, not letting myself see or feel the beauty around me. Since Donovan appeared it feels like I can see for the first time – see who I really am, a strong, vibrant woman who has more power than I believed. I can't go back – I won't allow it. My strength starts now.

"You think you can simply make me forget everything that is important in my life? I won't allow you to do that. I have already lost my father in the most horrific way. I will be damned before I lose everything I love. No matter how hard you try to make me forget…I swear I will remember," I warn as I fervently gaze upon his face.

I turn and stare firmly at my father's grave I realize how much I am about to lose. The overwhelming overload of devastating information floods my mind, causing the butterfly effect as I burst from my chrysalis, becoming a stronger girl, one willing to fight for everything I love. There is so much I need to resolve and I can't do it with Donovan distracting me.

Suddenly I feel Donovan's fingertips slowly caress my injured hands. Disappointment intermingles with a sudden internal strength consuming me as my mind tries to make some sense out of all this shit I have been dealt. I can't be around him right now. I need Donovan to leave me alone with only my thoughts right now. Pulling my hand away I utter fervently, "Donovan, I need to be left alone for a while please."

His brows stitch together firmly as he stares at me with an appalling expression streaming across his face, "I am not about to leave you alone in a graveyard, Lauren."

"I will be fine – trust me." Holding firm to my request, I speak with sincere determination.

"No. I will not leave you unprotected after what we have gone through tonight."

"Donovan, I'm not joking. I need you to leave. There is a lot that – yes – you have put me through, but I have a lot of things I need to think about. I have found out that everything I believed and have been living through this past year is a complete lie."

"Lauren, please don't ask me to do this," he pleads softly. His glorious, broken-down face looks as if I have asked him to do something entirely against his nature.

"Donovan – please. I need this time to mourn the loss of what I thought my father was, eradicating myself of the anger I feel for the both of you." His eyes snap up in regret. "I'm not only angry with my father, but Donovan, I am also disappointed in you for hiding the truth from me. I deserved to hear it in a better way…not from Darius." I stare firmly at the broken-down expression on his face asking softly, "Please, Donovan."

His usual emotionless eyes have revealed all his pain to me tonight. If he was capable of shedding a tear I'm sure he would have allowed me to witness his full emotions, but I know he can't. Reluctantly he stands up, staring at me with apologetic eyes as he slowly walks dejectedly away from me.

I watch him until suddenly he vanishes into thin air. Wrapping my arms tightly around my bent knees, I throw my head down as I cry hysterically. My tattered soul feels like it is being slammed up against a rocky shoreline as strong waves crash violently against the shore, slowly eroding away at the firm foundation I thought I had. Laying my head mournfully against my father's headstone, my soul cries out to the father I believed he was. "Why, dad? Why did you do it?"

Leaning back against his headstone I gaze sorrowfully at his name engraved in the marble. My mind tries to fathom all the tragic information forced upon me tonight. How could my father, who was always my hero, freely choose such a dark and sinister path? Despondently I rest my back against the headstone as I gaze out into the ominous darkness.

All alone on this hallowed ground the dark blinding night seems to wrap around me like black wings, embracing me within their delicate embrace. The night mist slowly invades the multitude of headstones. I watch the low fog rise and fall with every gentle breeze blowing through the area. The hypnotic, bubbling motion of the fog puts me in an exhausted trance. Slowly I sink deeper into the soft grass as I gaze pensively at the hypnotic fog. Every muscle in me seeps into a state of hazardous relaxation, making it very difficult to keep my eyes open. The skin of my eyelids feels like they weigh a hundred pounds.

Reality washes over me as to the precarious situation I would be in if I was to fall asleep in the middle of a deserted graveyard. Using the top of my father's headstone, I pry my aching body up off of the damp ground, brushing the wet grass off of me. Hesitantly I walk out of the graveyard, when to my horror I realize my car is still on the seedy side of the city. Like an idiot I sent Donovan away, completely unaware that I have no way of getting home. Panic washes over me as I realize I'm not only miles away from my home, but my car is in an area of the city I hope I never have to return to. My heart pounds viciously against my chest while I frantically contemplate how I am going to get out of this situation. Being stranded in a cemetery is not helping me feel any less nervous, either.

Hastily I gaze all around for some sort of help as my internal fear rushes to the surface. Suddenly my eyes behold a welcoming sight. There, parked directly in front of the entrance, is my saving grace – my car. It has been perfectly positioned just outside the main entrance so I can simply hop in and leave. Somehow Donovan must have retrieved my car from the city so I won't have to walk home. I have no idea how he did it – I haven't been here for very long – but at this point I don't care.

Rushing over to my car I grab hold of the unlocked door, flinging it open and jumping into the driver's seat. Instinctively I reach over to start my car when I notice my keys glistening in the moonlight, dangling delicately from the ignition. A wave of relief rushes out of me when suddenly I notice a delicate piece of paper lying across the dashboard of my car. It's folded in half with my name elegantly written across the top. My hand moves slowly across the soft linen paper as I gently unfold the note.

> Lauren,
>
> Forgive me, but I cannot completely leave you unprotected.
> I understand you need to be alone, but if you need me I will be within yelling distance.
> Again, I am sorry. Please remember that I love you.
> Donovan

A warm sensation fills me as I read the tender words. No matter what has transpired, I still – and will always – love him. He is not this sinister monster like Darius. He doesn't want to be this creature he sacrificed himself to become. I can never forget him, nor will I allow him or William to be punished for me. I have to think fast before William or Donovan go and do something stupid. I have been dancing on the edge of a knife for too long now. Tomorrow I have to jump off of the edge so I can put an end to this madness.

CHAPTER 23

Redemption

Anxiously my foot vibrates against the gas pedal as I impatiently wait in the morning traffic. With every slow, creeping pace I inch closer to work, I can feel the anxiety boiling within me. I know I have to get there soon, but this traffic is not cooperating with me. My extreme exhaustion from the lack of sleep is not helping to decrease my highly irritable mood. I spent the entire night curled up on my bed, holding onto a photo of my father, building up the strength I am going to need for today. Sometime during the middle of the night I had an epiphany: I need to accept my punishment of servitude. By doing this it will give me, and hopefully Donovan, the opportunity of trying to locate my father. Once I find him we can come up with a way to release ourselves from the unyielding torment. I know I have to find my father and there is no other way for me to do this than to embrace the darkness. I hope I can get to William before he decides to do something stupid, like his asinine idea of surrendering his soul for mine.

Pulsating shocks of energy rush over me, causing me to twitch with nervous vigor. Raising my hand insistently I attempt to slam it down onto the horn, when suddenly the traffic begins breaking up. Overwhelming joy replaces the anxiety eating away at me. I slam my fidgeting foot against the gas, weaving relentlessly in-and-out of the slower cars. Noticing my exit up ahead I swerve hastily through three lanes of traffic, gliding off the freeway at an extreme speed. This type of driving is not typical for me, but my adrenaline is allowing me to drive as if I am a race car driver.

Hastily I park my car and rush through the large glass doors of the office building. William typically is the first one to arrive in the office, giving me the opportunity to talk to him uninterrupted. But the traffic this morning put a damper on my plan, placing me here a lot later than I had intended. Increasing my pace, I burst through the door, feverishly passing the maze of cubicles, when suddenly my focus is interrupted by a soft, gentle voice.

"Lauren, are you all right?"

Turning abruptly toward the kind, yet obtrusive voice I notice Larry leaning up against the wall. His arms are folded ruefully against his torso as if he is waiting for something – or someone. His eyes scan my disheveled appearance as if he is scrutinizing my every move.

"Larry, what are you doing here so early?" I utter breathlessly, slightly startled by him. It didn't help that I was still jumpy from yesterday's horrific experience.

Gently using his shoulders to push himself away from the wall, he walks carefully over to me. "I'm making sure you showed up for work," he hums delicately.

"What do you mean?" I ask accusatorily.

"Lauren, are you all right?" he reluctantly asks, gazing pensively upon my red, irritated eyes. "Don't take this the wrong way, but you look like hell."

If my anxiety level isn't already through the roof, I would have laughed at his choice of words. He has no idea how accurate his comment is. Not only do I look like hell, but I feel like it too. If he had any idea what I have endured he would completely understand why my appearance is so disheveled. Not wanting to deal with this confrontation, I turn abruptly away from him and begin to walk away.

"Lauren, I didn't mean to offend you. I only want to make sure you are all right," he adds apologetically.

Something he just said piques my curiosity. This is the second time he has asked if I am all right. "Larry, why are you checking on me? Why would you think I'm not all right?" I stop and turn towards him with a sharp glare.

"Lauren, I simply didn't trust the guy you left with last week – that's all. There is something about him that's not right. I can't put my finger on it, but I don't trust the guy." The resentment in his voice begins to increase as the words spill out of his mouth with an acidic edge. "I know the guy is good-looking and all, but don't you think you could have found someone less questionable? He is the reason you are upset…isn't he?"

"Stop, Larry," I snap. "I appreciate your concern, but it's none of your business who I date or what I am going through right now. Besides, it's way more complicated than you could ever imagine." My words may have been harsh, but I'm astonished at how perceptive Larry is. I truly appreciate his concern, but I need to keep him out of this as much as possible. The less he knows, the safer he will be.

"He didn't hurt you, did he?" he growls. His hands begin wringing aggressively around each other as his blue eyes burn fiercely.

"No." A line creases my brow as I gaze at him defensively. "Donovan would never intentionally hurt me." Instinctively I place my hand on my back, rubbing it gently. It is still extremely sore from where my back slammed into the massive column after Donovan pushed me aggressively out of the way. If he would have known the force with which I hit the column he would have never forgiven himself, but I knew he pushed me out of the way to keep me safe.

Just then I hear the large office door swing open, followed by the echoes of over-exaggerated laughter. Closing my eyes despondently I realize everyone I tried to avoid this morning is beginning to pile in. Shaking my head in dismay I sigh sharply as I turn to walk away.

"Hi, Larry, how was your weekend?" Stacie's pretentious voice echoes.

"It was fine. How about yours?" he asks politely, grabbing hold of the back of my shirt and gently stopping me from leaving. "Hold on, don't leave just yet," he whispers to me.

Larry's strong grip holds tightly onto my shirt. Violently I turn, breaking free from his grasp. I look up at Stacie, attempting to give her a gracious smile only to discover she is glaring at me vindictively. If looks could kill, she would be charged with my murder.

"Hi, Stacie," I utter courteously.

"Hi," she snaps in response, giving me a smug look. Instantly Stacie walks away from me. Turning vigorously to Maria she huffs, "What do guys see in her? She looks like crap. Not only does she have Larry pining all over her, but the most gorgeous guy I have ever seen was waiting for her," she complains jealously.

Deep down I have to agree with Stacie. I have no idea why Larry – or for that fact, Donovan – are even interested in me. Donovan hasn't been able to completely convince me that he is totally attracted to me. I know he said he loved me, but why, I don't understand. He is so good-looking and could have enticed any girl. Why he chose me is beyond my understanding. Stacie simply solidified my deepest thoughts at how ordinary I am in comparison to Donovan's completely extraordinary looks.

Larry utters meekly, "Lauren, don't listen to her, she is only jealous. You are extremely beautiful outside, but even better, you are stunning inside."

"Thank you, Larry, but I think you need to go see an optometrist." I laugh sharply, trying to make light of the situation. Though I am grateful to Larry for his compliment, I can't lose sight of why I'm here so early in the morning. "Larry, I don't mean to be rude, but I need to go talk to William privately."

He glances down at me with bewildered eyes. "Lauren, William is not in yet."

"What do you mean? He is always here early." My voice cracks slightly as I begin to panic.

"I know, I thought it was strange when I didn't see him here this morning." Turning hastily I rush towards William's office. "Lauren…" Larry's voice resonates in the distance.

As I rush vehemently down the makeshift hall I can feel the terror flash through me at the possibility that I'm too late. What if William already went and did something stupid? But if that were true I think I would feel different right now. Suddenly I realize something is different. This is the first time in weeks I haven't completely lost my temper or wanted to kill Stacie after her snide remark.

Stopping hesitantly in front of his office door, I suddenly became conscious of the fire which has constantly burned within me slowly diminishing. "Please be in there, please be in there," I chant silently. Overwhelming grief begins to flow rapidly over my tortured heart. Panic floods my emotions as I fling the door violently open.

There is an air of stillness looming in his office I have never felt before. An eerie silence hovers delicately overhead. Holding my breath, I gaze hastily around his office, looking for any sign that he has been here. Instantly my eyes catch sight of something unusual propped up on the center of his desk. My overanxious heart thunders as I notice this object appears to be a picture frame propped up precisely against some books. The trembling fear consuming me is starting to take over my despondent thoughts. Deep down something reaffirms a sense of familiarity to this picture frame.

Slowly I walk closer to this looming object. Swallowing deeply, I hesitantly peer over at the picture. To my horror there, resting purposefully in the center of his desk, is the disheveled picture of my father and me taken just days before his mysterious death. Leaning up against the tattered picture frame is a note addressed to me. Reaching over to the note my fingers gently trace the edges of the letter. I can't open it. If I do, then it means he is really gone. As long as I feel some sort of rage within me then there is still hope. Tears stream down my face as I instantly realize what this means. I know I am running out of time because the fire within me is slowly beginning to diminish.

Grabbing the picture and letter I race out of his silent office. Fear guides my every action as I hastily maneuver the makeshift hallway. Rushing past Larry I can hear him shouting nervously, "Lauren, what is wrong? Stop." His voice seems to resonate in the distance as I make my way out the door.

I try as hard as I can to hold on to the rage for as long as possible. Perhaps this will slow the trade down and buy me some time so I can stop this sacrifice from occurring. Quickly I head to the only place I can think, William's house. Donovan said my father was at his home when he came for him. So maybe William is going to be doing the same thing.

The low, vibrating growl of my car rolls around me as evidence to the sheer extremes I am putting it through. Though there is no traffic I'm not sure if I am going to make it on time. Glancing helplessly around, I catch sight of Donovan's letter he left on the dashboard of my car last night. Instantly I recall his words – he will only be a yelling distance away. If I am going to make it in time I need Donovan to take me to him – quickly. Instead of taking me thirty minutes, he can get me to William in a matter of seconds.

Gripping onto my steering wheel I shout firmly into the air, "Donovan. Please, I need your help." Terror consumes every part of my mind as I sit here in silence for what feels like an eternity.

This time I yell even louder, "Donovan! Please help me." I wait again in silence.

A heavy weight presses down on me as I realize the severity of the situation. Fully aware that I have very little time left, I slam my foot viciously down on the gas pedal.

I arrive at William's house in what seems like a brief moment. As I race down William's street my heart rate speeds to practically an unhealthy pace. The frightening realization of what I might be walking in on overwhelms my already anxious body. An adrenaline rush takes over, endowing me with the strength I need in order to continue.

As I race down his road, the driveway appears to lengthen right in front of my eyes. The sides of the road begin to narrow as if they are pushing in on me, lengthening the distance between my car and William's house. The faster I drive, the further away William's house gets. This illusion is under a sinister control, causing me to realize that I am in the right place. Obviously someone is trying to stop me from entering his house. Pure determination takes over as I realize my family is in there and nothing is going to stop me. Grabbing firmly onto my steering wheel I glare at the distancing house. Gunning the gas pedal as hard as I can, my wheels spin out of control, causing the gravel beneath my car to explode out at a violent speed.

Peering vehemently at the possessed prison ahead, my mind calls out to the home in front of me. Instantly the drive between me and William's house shortens tremendously, causing me to immediately slam on my brakes, stopping my car just in time to keep from slamming into his house.

Catching my breath, I gaze fervently upon the front entrance to William's house. A sinister aura radiates from the house in a virtual mocking manner. Something is messing with me, trying to scare me away, but it isn't going to work. Instead of fear taking control of me, a deep, resonating strength consumes my thoughts. Glaring fervently at William's porch, I see a dark, billowing shadow slither across the porch and rest triumphantly on the swing. Immediately I recognize this sinister soul. Lilith is having fun. I can almost sense her victorious jubilee.

Sliding aggressively out of my car I glare in the direction of the dark shadow. "Lilith, you don't frighten me anymore, because you have no power over me. I am not living in a way that gives you permission to take me over. I'm entering this premise with or without your permission," I growl.

The dark shadow swirls violently in rage, rushing toward me fiercely. I stand here firmly holding my ground. My body may have been eminently holding its ground, but my spirit is shaking in terror as I watch the furious shadow swirl attackingly toward me. The fierce wind caused by Lilith twists rapidly all around me, but the darkness never consumes me. In complete agitation she viciously spins around, slamming her all-encompassing darkness through the front entrance. Holding my breath once again, I vigorously push open the front door.

There standing in front of me is Darius with his dark, intimidating shadows encircling his black-as-coal eyes. He stares at me portentously as his sinister smile widens in complete amusement at the game Lilith played on me. Lilith meanwhile is encircling herself victoriously around a tall, frightful and deviant-looking being standing directly in front of Darius. Simply gazing at him sends shivers throughout my soul. His shiny black hair is slicked back tightly. What little light there is reflects off of his black hair, causing an illusion of a black halo encircling his head. His eyes are jet black with deep, dark pigmented circles enveloping them as if his eyes are sunken into the hollow spaces behind his eyes. Shadows wrap vehemently around his dark gray lips, making them look as if they are oxygen-deprived. His terrifying mouth is taut as his disapproving eyes glare at me frightfully.

Though he has a dark, practically ancient appearance to him, he looks as if he is only in his mid-thirties. His well-built figure is accentuated by a dark slimming suit. Thrown authoritatively over his shoulders is a thick, black enveloping cape. His eyes bore deeply into mine as he grips the edges of the cape firmly between his long, tapered fingers. Fear viciously rolls through me as his gaze frightfully begins tearing open my soul, peering deep inside. Grabbing my chest I double over in excruciating pain. As I turn my head, trying to look away from his all-embracing eyes, I catch sight of someone.

There, standing behind Darius and this frightful being, is Donovan. His tortured gaze floods over me as the pain he is experiencing quivers off of him. He appears to be under duress from Darius and this frightening being. The crease between his eyes deepens as he gazes at me apologetically. They stand here in front of him, relentlessly preventing Donovan from helping me. This has to be the reason why he didn't come to me when I called for him.

"Donovan," I shout as I stand up and rush towards his broken-down form.

The dark, sinister being raises his finger slowly, shaking it back and forth as he snaps his tongue sharply against the roof of his mouth in a clicking, disapproving tone. His taut lips part slightly, revealing his bright, shimmering teeth amidst his dark, engulfing mouth.

"Lauren, I don't think so. You will stay right where you are," he commands in a low, growling tone.

Every word he utters rolls smoothly off his tongue and then explodes resolutely out of his mouth. The low, booming force erupting from him sends violent waves of fear through my veins, stopping me dead in my tracks. When he speaks, his voice seems to resonate powerfully within the room as if we are standing on the edge of a large canyon instead of in William's living room.

Donovan's tranquil blue eyes shatter in piercing pain. "Lucius, please don't hurt her," he pleads in an inaudible whisper of reverence. This being standing in front of me is the ominous monster that Donovan fearfully spoke of. Instinctively I begin to violently convulse in fear.

Lucius turns abruptly toward Donovan. "You will be silent. I will deal with your treachery later," he bellows firmly. His piercing voice resonates, echoing every sinister word.

Turning slowly back towards me with his dark, malicious eyes, he looks at me reassuringly. "Donovan is only overreacting, dear child. I am not going to hurt you." His dark voice seems to mock me as if I am an infant.

"You're not going to hurt Donovan, are you?" I whisper fearfully. My voice is trembling from the convulsions I'm exhibiting. It takes all the energy I have to be able to muster up the strength I need to be able to speak.

A forceful laugh breaks through his terrifying mouth. "Lauren, for such a tiny, insignificant girl, you sure have caused a lot of problems." He eyes flash over at Donovan so quickly at first I'm not sure if it really happened, but as I look up at Donovan I can see his face darken in fear.

"Lauren," he slowly, letter by letter, speaks my name as it rolls maliciously from his dark tongue. "You shouldn't worry about Donovan. Once we leave, you will have no recollection of him. It will be as if he never existed."

"What do you mean?" I hesitantly ask.

"Lauren, your penance has been paid," he states emotionlessly. A large knot wedges its way into my throat, forcing me to swallow deeply. My stomach quivers in pain as the reality of his statement clenches down on my heart.

He gazes contemptuously upon me. "Which is actually too bad, considering you were the one Donovan was summoned to get. I really didn't want to accept his offer, but William made a very persuasive argument," he hums mockingly.

"No. I didn't want him to go in my place. Please, you can't take William. If you want me, take me." My voice quivers as I fight back the tears building up.

"Oh Lauren, that is too bad, if I only would have known." His pretentious voice is laden with sarcasm. As he speaks, his face falls to a glum, angry appearance. I know he is messing with me; he is completely aware of why I was rushing here. This is exactly what he wanted to happen.

Anger fills my brain, giving me a tremendous rush of adrenaline. Extreme rage towards this monster explodes within me, devouring all my fears. I am not about to let this happen. He is not going to take everything I love away from me. "You knew exactly what you were doing," I snap. "I want them back," I demand adamantly. The adrenaline is pumping vigorously through my veins now, giving me the strength I need to stand up to this monster.

Darkness overtakes his face as his eyes narrow in a rebuking tactic towards me. His hands that were once gripping the edges of his cape are now balled up into tight fists. The shadows around his eyes intensify, making it appear as though his coal-black irises are leaking violently onto his skin. These bleeding dark shadows pouring down his face emerge like black tears staining his pale skin. His now morbid appearance takes on a nearly grotesque look.

"Lucius, no. Leave her be," Donovan yells vigorously as he rushes towards me, trying to protect me from the obvious retribution I am about to receive. Lucius turns rapidly towards Donovan, bellowing out a low, ferocious growl which fills the entire room. Instantly Darius is on top of Donovan, wrestling him violently to the ground. Lucius nods approvingly toward Lilith, sending her dark shadow swirling aggressively in the air. Spinning violently toward Donovan she instantly flings her dark, sinister spirit into him.

An eerie stillness spreads slowly across Donovan's once struggling form as if something sinister has taken over him. Darius gingerly releases his firm grip on Donovan, allowing his now calm body to be set free.

"There, I think you will be a good boy now," Lucius growls.

Donovan slowly stands up, stretching and twisting intently. His eyes are closed tightly as he finishes writhing. Slowly his eyes open, causing me to take a step back in horror. His tortured crystal blue eyes have been replaced by piercing coal-black ones. Donovan glances over at Lucius, giving him an approving smile. Slowly Donovan slithers his now deviant-looking body between Darius and Lucius. Donovan's dark, ominous eyes glare at me with a terrifying expression in them.

"Donovan, are you all right?" I plead, fully aware that something is definitely wrong with him. Donovan's countenance has changed drastically in front of me.

"Lauren, he is just fine. He's never felt better," Darius replies sarcastically.

"I didn't ask you, I asked Donovan," I snap. Instantly I look over at Donovan, hoping to get an answer from him when I notice something different about his posture. Instead of his typical masculine stance, he stands here with an effeminate posture. His shoulders are rolled back, forcing his chest to extend forward while his hips slightly favor the right side of his figure. This transformed being in front of me is not the Donovan I am completely familiar with. It's as if something – or someone – has invaded his total being. Suddenly, I remember Lilith has the power to possess her victim's bodies only if they are living in a deviant way. Even though Donovan is trying not to embrace his demonic side, that part of his soul allows Lilith to capture him.

Gazing ruefully at Donovan's controlled frame I utter harshly, "Or shall I say, Lilith?"

Lilith smiles sharply through Donovan's occupied and now controlled body. "Well, aren't you smart?" Her sinister, high-pitched shrilling voice reverberates vulgarly from Donovan's lips. The thought of Lilith inside of Donovan right now sends shivers racing up my spine.

"Let him go, Lilith," I snap.

Instantly Lucius is within inches of my face. His dark, seeping eyes pierce right through me like two sharp needles pushing relentlessly into me, attacking my very soul. Raising his hand up to my face, he slowly and gently traces the outline of my jaw with his long, tapered fingers. Extreme heat radiates off of his fingers, sizzling the top layers of my skin. I inhale quickly then hold my breath in complete fear while he continues to trace my face with his burning touch. My petrified body stands erect as the terror of what he is going to do to me floods my mind. His hand slides abrasively down my neck as he traces the creases on it.

His eyes remain affixed on my face, holding me captive in his dark, ominous gaze. As I swallow hard I can feel his burning touch pressing firmly against my throat, nearly stopping me from swallowing. Wrapping his long, sinuous hand around my neck he gently squeezes, sending shivers of panic racing over me.

"Lauren, you have no right to make any demands here. All I have to do is slightly squeeze and you will be dead," he warns fiercely. His low, rumbling voice booms deep into my mind, as it vibrates aggressively throughout my thoughts.

A single tear streams down my face. "Just do it then. You already took everything away from me. You might as well take my life too." I have to strain the words out through the restricted air flow in my neck, causing my voice to squeak.

A twisted smile spreads vulgarly across Lucius's face. "Don't be dramatic, Lauren. Your father was fully aware of his choice and William, well, I think you already know that one." His voice suddenly gets darker. "You have no right to make any demands when you are the source of the problem. Besides, by the time I am done here, you will have no recollection of what occurred," he bellows unrelentingly.

"You can't make me forget William or Donovan."

"Lauren, should I remind you? You forgot what happened to your own father. If it wasn't for Donovan, you would have never remembered. Besides, I didn't say you would forget William. Donovan you will forget, but William, you will always remember him, like you have always remembered your father. The only thing is that –" shaking his head dramatically, he snaps his tongue against the roof of his mouth, uttering harshly, "You'll simply have to endure another loved one's funeral." He loosens his firm grip from around my neck.

Still feeling the intense burning sensation around my neck, I hastily pull myself away from his torturing hand. Reaching my hand up I wrap it around my neck, gently messaging at the searing pain. Keeping my hand protectively enveloped around my neck, I gaze up at Lucius's frightfully dark face.

"Why are you doing this to me?" I question hesitantly, staring into his bleak, black eyes that sear through my soul.

"Lauren, do you honestly think you are something special to me? Because you are not. You are merely another nameless soul for me," he growls fiercely.

"But Donovan said you sent him to capture me," I state weakly, trying to clarify the confusion swimming around in my head. If I truly am a nameless soul to him, why did he send for me?

"I wouldn't believe everything Donovan told you. Remember he is a demon, bred to deceive and lead astray." He adds cynically, "I am sure he even told you he loved you." His dark voice makes a grotesque sound as he utters the word love, causing him to shiver in revulsion. Gazing at me morosely, his eyes relish in the obvious displeasure he is causing me. My heart stops for a moment realizing perhaps he is right, maybe Donovan was deceiving me the whole time.

Turning my head toward Donovan, I gaze up at his ravenous face, seeing for the first time this obvious demon standing before me. Though it is Lilith's soul controlling Donovan right now, I can still see the monster pent-up deep within him. His face seems to have a disdainful smirk to it as if Lilith is using Donovan's face to solidify what Lucius is saying. I look ruefully upon his dark face for some sort of sign, when suddenly a flash of piercing blue rips through his coal-black eyes. At this moment I know he is fighting Lilith's spirit internally.

Gazing at Lucius I utter firmly, "Aren't you a demon too, who is also bred to deceive? Why should I believe what you say? You are trying to drive a sliver of doubt within me. Once you have done that, you win – right? Thus leading me away from Donovan, because you know love is a powerful thing and that frightens you."

Lucius's ominous countenance darkens even more, causing violent waves of ravenous anger to encompass him. Shaking viciously, he crouches into a tight coil. His eyes burn sadistically into me, causing shivers of fear to radiate violently from me.

Instantly I hear my name bellow in the distance. Looking up I catch sight of a dark shadow being flung ferociously across the room. Within seconds Donovan is on top of Lucius, hurling him vehemently to the ground. A great tumult erupts as Darius leaps into the middle of the uproar. Donovan instantly grabs hold of Darius's arm, throwing him forcefully across the room. Darius slams violently through the kitchen wall, sending debris flying everywhere.

Lucius whirls around instantly, causing his black cloak to spin violently and knocking Donovan to the ground. Jumping vigorously up to his feet, a loud, sadistic roar explodes powerfully from Lucius's mouth. Fiercely peering down at Donovan, Lucius's eyes gleam with violent hatred. I know I need to help Donovan before he is destroyed.

Intensely I look around for something, when suddenly out of the corner of my eye I catch sight of a large, sharp fragment of wood that had splintered off the wall when Darius slammed through it. Securely grabbing hold of the stake I rush over to Lucius and firmly impale the large piece of wood through his back. A low, painful growl violently explodes out of Lucius as he staggers backwards, reaching for the penetrating source of his pain.

"Lauren, no," Donovan shouts fearfully.

Immediately I realize what I have done as my fear takes over me. Slowly I back away from Lucius's reeling body as he struggles to grasp hold of the piercing object. Suddenly his hand wraps firmly around the part of the wood still protruding from his back. Gradually he pulls the piece of wood from his back as it glides slickly out. A loud exhale breaks through as he holds the source of his pain up in the air. The large piece of wood is covered with a thick black tar-like substance. Grabbing hold of the once-penetrating object, he slides his free hand slowly up the piece of wood, wiping off the thick substance then shaking it violently to the ground with a loud splash.

Turning towards me he lets out a loud, vicious laugh. "Do you honestly think you can kill me? Have you forgotten who you are dealing with? You stupid little girl, we don't have the same laws as you – I can't die," he laughs vehemently.

Fearfully I back up, fully aware of the retribution going to soon come upon me. My pleading eyes fervently watch Lucius as I stammer to speak. Immediately he is standing directly in front of my face again as his hand firmly wraps vigorously around my neck. As he lifts me aggressively in the air, I begin struggling to breathe.

Donovan leaps up, rushing to my side, when Lucius's hand suddenly causes a translucent ball of spiraling elements to appear directly above his hand. He flings the swirling substance urgently at Donovan, hitting him with such force it hurls him viciously across the room. He forcefully slams against the wall, causing his now malformed frame to lay there motionless on the floor.

Tears flow freely down my face as I look upon Donovan's broken figure. "Please, I beg of you, don't hurt Donovan. He was only trying to help me," I plead wistfully, straining my voice through his tight grip on my neck.

His hand lowers me slightly, causing my face to be placed directly across from his. His monstrous face glares fiercely upon my pleading eyes. "Lauren, I have had just about enough of you. Your begging and pleading have landed upon deaf ears. This is the end of our conversation. I have grown tired of your childish antics."

"Lucius," I hastily interrupt him. "If demons are real then so are angels and I promise I will pray every day for their guidance to stop you and save the ones I love."

He gives me an ominous glare like he is truly frightened of the impending battle between good and evil. Widening his eyes vigorously a blooming light of reality spreads across his face. "Lauren, you don't frighten me, you won't be able to remember anything." He smiles arrogantly as he utters resolutely, "Goodbye, Lauren."

Suddenly his grip tightens, causing the darkness to slowly engulf my vision. Everything in the room slowly fades into the blackest night as I start floating, weightless in the air. Straining against the blackness I scream out sharply, "Donovan!" Then instantly the seeping blackness fully consumes me, leaving me floating in the thickness of the all-encompassing gloom.

My weightless body lies on what feels like a tremendous sifter as the darkness incrementally filters through the tiny imaginary holes beneath me. With every seeping shadow that falls, it takes with it my most recent intimate thoughts and desires, leaving me feeling empty and void of any emotion. I lay here on the sieve, fully giving in to the emptiness that now engulfs me as my most cherished memories are ripped from me, leaving a hollow abyss behind.

CHAPTER 24

∞

Sadness

Intently I watch as they slowly lower the coffin into the ground. With every descending inch the casket takes, the deeper my sorrow plummets. The realization that William is actually dead overpowers my ravenous thoughts. It feels as though I am sinking deeper into the depression that has consumed me since I was informed of William's sudden and tragic death. My memories of the past several weeks can only be described as Swiss cheese, multiple holes dotting my mind.

I sit in a seemingly catatonic state on a cold, hard metal chair as a procession of dark-clothed mourners line up to give the few distant family members, me and my mother, their condolences. My eyes never leave the descending casket as I habitually shake every hand reaching out for mine. They all robotically utter some type of apologies or words of comfort for what we have lost. I feel like I'm merely going through the motions, nodding vaguely as I mutter some incoherent response to their attempt at words of encouragement. Though my mom and I were technically just friends, we were the closest thing to a family William had left.

My mother, who had to rush back from her European vacation the moment she was informed of William's tragic and horrific car accident, wraps her arm affectionately around my waist. "Are you ready to proceed back to William's house for the luncheon?" she whispers into my ear.

For some strange reason, since my mother's hasty return she has been attempting to be supportive of me. She made a comment to me the other day in passing saying how my outburst a few weeks ago had an effect on her, but I can't remember an outburst with her. The past several weeks of my life are a blur with very few details. The more I try to remember the details, the more my head begins to pound.

My mind is riddled with holes and missing pieces that seem to coincide around William's death. I even tried going to a counselor the day after William's horrific car crash, but it didn't help. The more I attempted to dig into my lost memories, the darker my mind became. The counselor informed me that it is very common for someone who has experienced several tragic losses in such a short time to shut down certain parts of their memory. In time it will fully return. Something deep inside, though, feels like I'm not displacing my memory, but that it has been purposefully stolen. A huge portion of me is void as if a gaping chasm is looming where memories once existed. Though a part of me whispers to give up and just go on living, something within the dark void screams out to search deeper for answers.

My eyes gaze morosely upon the now lowered casket, when suddenly I hear a voice echo into my subconscious, "Lauren, are you ready to go?"

Turning vaguely toward my mother I ask softly, "Sorry, did you say something?"

"Yes. I am wondering if you are ready to go to William's house for the luncheon," she repeats for the third time, this time with zeal in her voice.

My mother decided to have the luncheon at William's house, considering the space that will accommodate all the guests. Though for some strange reason every time we drive out there a violent shudder of fear ripples throughout my mind. Perhaps it's because I know he is no longer there, but since his death I can't enter his house without feeling a creepy sense of danger.

Ruefully I ask my mother softly, "Mom, can I have a few minutes here alone before I head over?"

My lower lip quivers violently as I attempt to fight back the overwhelming emotion ready to burst out at any moment. I can't leave him yet. An overwhelming desire to rescue him suddenly rushes over me – not allowing me to leave. I know it is ridiculous – he is already dead. How can I rescue someone who is already gone? A disconsolate moan billows from my mouth, sending pounding surges of sorrow to flood over me.

Grabbing hold of my trembling hand she whispers softly, "Sure, take your time." Then leaning over she gently kisses the top of my head. "I will see you there."

Gradually the supportive congregation begins to disburse, leaving me to sit out here all alone with only my miserable thoughts. Constant streams of tears instantly wash my face with stinging floods of sorrow. Hesitantly I stand up, walking weakly over to the gaping hole enveloping William's casket. My heart cries out with the loss like a wild banshee. Wrapping my hands relentlessly around my stomach, I hold tightly onto a single rose, trying to control the violent shuddering I am exhibiting.

Slowly I watch as two brawny men begin backfilling the dirt over the casket. Slowly I drop the crisp red rose. It delicately lands on the fresh dirt – gently burying it. With every heavy thud the dirt makes against the casket, it reverberates into my heart, with aching stings pushing down on me. At that moment I want to jump into the pit and be buried along with him. There is nothing left for me here. My father and William are both gone, leaving me here to suffer alone.

The cool, moist air exudes from the damp grass below me, casting a heavy morning mist across the plush carpet below. Suddenly a vague hush softly washes over me as a warm sensation radiates out from my disheveled body. The cool breeze instantly increases, blowing vigorously around my dilapidated form, sending chills racing up and down my spine. Trying to warm myself from this sudden change in the air, I tighten up the grip I have woven around myself. The cool air suddenly changes, gently hitting me with penetrating hot wisps against my cheek. The warm air caresses my cheek with what feels like gentle kisses. An unexplained joy replaces my morose feeling of loneliness. Closing my eyes I completely succumb to the intoxicating sensation the wind is providing me with. My mind slowly sinks into the deepest, darkest parts of my memory as a soothing touch of warmth sears down my arm. Heat radiates vigorously from my skin, sending me into a hypnotic trance.

There is a familiarity to this sensation, something I can't put my finger on but it pricks my mind with peace. The wind feels like extremely hot, yet smooth fingertips gliding down my arm. Tranquility rolls up my spine and flows over me, filling the void within my mind with hope. A warm gust of wind instantly rushes through me as it seems to moan my name audibly in the distance. The utterance of my name in the wind causes me to snap out of my mesmerizing trance. Immediately I realize no one is standing next to me. Instinctively I gaze down at my entangled arms, when I notice bright red marks streaming down my arm where it felt like the wind was caressing me.

My heart flutters in fear as I notice the shocking similarities between the red marks on my arm and the mysterious singe marks that were around my neck the day of William's death. Standing here nearly frozen, I slowly examine the mysterious marks when all of a sudden my name resonates loudly in the near distance, snapping me back into reality.

"Lauren," the low, tender voice utters just behind me.

Turning abruptly towards the low voice, I realize to my happy surprise it is only Larry. "Larry, you startled me," I huff breathlessly. My overactive imagination is on full display. It must have been Larry's voice I heard seemingly uttering my name in the wind.

"Sorry, I didn't mean to scare you. I guess I should have said your name further back instead of sneaking up on you like this."

A sharp line forms between the furrows of my eyes, in complete bewilderment. "You didn't sneak up on me. Didn't you utter my name twice?"

"No, I just now called you," he utters, slightly confused by my question. "Why?"

"Nothing really, I only thought I heard my name a few moments ago – that's all. It must have been my imagination." I try to hide the disquiet searing in my voice. Trying to change the subject, I ask, "Did you need something?"

"Well, I hope you don't mind, but I was about to leave when I saw you standing here all alone. Something whispered in my mind, pushing me toward you to make sure you are all right."

He pauses remorsefully, then adds, "Lauren, I am so sorry. I know he was like a father to you. If there is anything I can do please don't hesitate to ask. I will be within shouting distance."

"What did you say?" I quiver inexplicably.

"I said, I am sorry –"

"No," I interrupt. "The last part."

He stares at me questionably while the expression on his face changes from concern to confusion. "I said I will be within shouting distance."

"That's what I thought you said," I reiterate. "Have you ever told me that before?" I question enigmatically, needing verification as to why that statement sounds so familiar and meaningful to me.

"No, I don't think so…why?"

"I don't know, it sounds familiar like I have heard someone tell me that before – that's all."

I know I have heard those exact words before, but I can't put my finger on it. There are so many holes in my life right now. I feel like I'm constantly trying to put together a giant jigsaw puzzle missing half of the pieces.

"Lauren, I truly mean it. You can call me anytime." Larry wraps his arm gently around my waist as he pensively gazes down into William's resting spot. "I can't believe he is gone. I didn't know him on a personal level like you did, but he was a great boss to work for." He lowers his voice to a near inaudible whisper, gently squeezing my waist as he utters sympathetically, "Lauren, I know you only work there because of William, but I hope you won't quit. I know it has been hard to show up to work when no one, especially Stacie, has ever been very nice to you. Stacie's contemptuous and overbearing personality has been completely inexcusable, and for that I am sorry. I hope you know you still have an advocate and friend at work. Though William may be gone, I will always be there for you."

"Thank you, Larry," I utter weakly.

Glancing apprehensively down at my lower waist, I catch sight of Larry's fingertips tenderly curving around my waist. Am I missing something? I know there are several holes in my memory, but I seriously don't recall Larry and I being an item. I only recall a few recent events involving Larry. One recent event is the night a few of us from the office went dancing, but to my recollection he was with Stacie, not me. Though there are even huge voids in that specific memory also.

Out of all the times I need a friend, this is one of them, but I am not sure if Larry thinks we are more than just friends. Emotionally right now I am not sure I can handle it, but physically this is what I need, to not be completely alone. Momentarily I forget the sadness I am entirely immersed in as I inconspicuously begin to slide my hand towards his. The overwhelming need for sympathy is my only governing action at this point. As my fingers gingerly inch their way closer to his, a queasy nervous energy pulsates through my frame. It starts in my stomach then radiates out from there. The queasy churning within my stomach is laced with a horrific feeling of betrayal. The closer my fingers get to his, the more intense the feeling is. Without warning a sharp, excruciating pain shoots violently down my arm, exactly where the wind left the red burning streaks on me. Grabbing hold of my arm I inhale deeply in pain.

Lunging back slightly, Larry grabs hold of my arm as he begins to examine the four red marks. "What happened to your arm, Lauren?" he questions sharply.

"I don't know, it just happened right before you got here," I reply, my voice still audibly quivering from the intense pain pulsating through my arm.

"Lauren, this isn't nothing." He raises my arm up for me to see it better. "You look like your arm lost a battle with a hot branding iron. Do you need me to take you to the hospital?"

I snap instantly, "Don't be ridiculous. I will be fine." My mind races for some credible excuse for the marks. "My skin reacts strangely to the intense sun – that's all. Instead of your typical sunburn, I break out in splotchy burn marks all over," I utter weakly, hoping he will believe my preposterous explanation.

Hesitating slightly, he then responds suspiciously, "If this happens a lot, next time you are in the sun I think you should wear long sleeves." He looks deep into my eyes trying to search for the real answer. He wouldn't believe me if I told him the truth. Hell,

I'm having a hard enough time believing it myself. How is it possible for the wind to be able to do something like this?

"Lauren, maybe we should get you out of the sun then."

"Yeah, I guess I should leave," I state hesitantly. A sense of abandonment rushes over me. I don't want to leave William yet, but I know I have to. I can't spend the entire night in a graveyard.

Quickly I gather my things when Larry gently removes the items from my hand. "Lauren, let me carry those for you," he smiles wistfully.

"Thank you," I express appreciatively. "You are a really good guy."

"Thank you, I guess. I suppose I'll take that as a compliment," he states blandly.

"You should, I meant it as one," I smile reassuringly. Contemplatively I gaze up at Larry's tender face, wondering if perhaps he might be able to clear up some mysterious recent missing memories. I see him almost every day. Maybe he noticed something strange going on with me, causing me to inadvertently put it out of my memory. "Larry, can I ask you a question?"

"Anything."

A heavy sigh escapes as I utter timidly, glancing down at my twirling thumbs. "Have my actions in the past month or so been strange, or have you noticed anything different with me?"

He looks at me questionably. "In what way?"

"Well, I am having a hard time remembering certain events lately and I'm merely hoping you might be able to fill in some of the missing pieces."

"Funny you should say that, I have been having a hard time recalling certain events as well. It seems my memory has gotten worse with my age," he humorously adds.

For some strange reason I don't find it funny. In fact, it is completely bizarre that we both are having memory problem lately. "Don't you think it's strange we are both having a hard time remembering things?" I question feverishly.

"Not really, I have always had a problem remembering things. It always drove my mother crazy. So if you are asking me to help you recall certain events, I am the wrong person to ask," he adds frankly so as not to offend me. "Have you ever thought of seeing a professional about it? That is, if it is really bugging you?"

Rolling my eyes in embarrassment I moan dejectedly, "I already have and she didn't help much. She only told me it was normal for someone to experience a mild memory loss after a tragic event, in time it will return."

"Well, there you go – you're normal," he jokingly hums. Taking on a more serious posture, he suddenly stops walking, turns towards me respectfully and adds, "Lauren, give it time, things will get better, I promise."

I want to believe him, but an overwhelming feeling of doubt quivers deep within me. Unwarranted fear begins to radiate over me as we silently walk to my car.

Quietly I open the passenger side door so he can put my things on the front seat, when Larry reaches down, removing something from the front seat of my car. "Planning a vacation?"

"What?" Looking pensively over at what he meant by that ridiculous question, I notice a stack of travel brochures in his hand. I must have left them in my car, but I don't remember them ever being on my front seat. "No, I'm not planning on going anywhere. I just got them for fun – I guess. Again I can't remember why."

"You have some great places here. You know, I've been to Italy –" he begins flipping through the small stack of brochures, "– it's absolutely beautiful." Pulling one of the brochures out, he utters flatly, "This one though, you must have grabbed on accident. It doesn't fit in with the other destinations. You've got Paris, Canada, Italy, and then this one on New Orleans."

Holding up the brochure of New Orleans, my heart instantly stops. A familiar rush pulsates through me as I stare at the picture on the front of it. My breathing increases while every hair on my arm stands straight up like I have walked into a static-laden room. Ragged, short breaths pulsate through my pursed lips as an overwhelming rush comes over me.

"Larry, I hate to do this, but something has come up and I need to leave right now," I utter frantically. I inhale deeply as I try to slow down my panting breath pouring rapidly out of my anxious mouth. "Can you please tell my mother I can't make it to the reception? Something has come up. I will call her tonight."

"Is everything all right?" he asks, slightly confused by my sudden change of attitude.

"I hope so." I gaze ruefully up at his questionable expression. "Can I call you later this week? And perhaps I can take you up on your offer of coming over and helping me." Giving him a coy smile, I lean in and kiss him respectfully on the cheek. Slyly I remove the brochures from his imprisoning hand. "Thank you Larry, you really are a great guy."

Driving hastily down the deserted Main Street my heartbeat intensifies as I get closer to the narrow yellow Victorian building. Parking in front of the travel agency I gaze anxiously upon the thin, plastic 'open' sign. The mere thought of what I'm about to do causes my stomach to churn violently.

Springing viciously from my car I proceed up to the white porch of Martha's Travel Experts, fully aware of what I'm about to embark on. I have no concrete validation for my madness, but something familiar burns vehemently within me, causing me to react fully on my instinct. Closing my eyes tightly I grip the handle of the door firmly. While taking a deep breath in I gently open the door.

"Hello, welcome to Martha's Travel Experts, I'm Martha. Can I help you with anything?" Martha replies in a gentle, sophisticated voice.

Getting up from her chair, she proceeds to walk closer to me, suddenly remembering me from my last awkward experience here. As she lifts her delicate hand to respectfully shake mine, she utters enthusiastically, "Oh, welcome back – Lori, right?"

I have completely forgotten how rude I was the last time I was here. I can't believe I lied to her, telling her my name was Lori for fear my mother would find out. How childish I was to do such an impolite thing.

Raising my hand to hers I proceed to shake her hand apologetically. "Martha, I need to apologize to you for my rude and deceitful behavior I exhibited toward you the last time I was in here."

"What do you mean? You were perfectly delightful."

"No, I wasn't. You see, my name isn't Lori." An air of confusion streaks vigorously across her face. "My name is actually Lauren – Lauren Cowley."

Her refined eyes widen. "You're Naomi's daughter?"

"Yes, I am sorry. I shouldn't have lied to you. I know it is inexcusable what I did, but I was afraid my mother would find out I went to a travel agency. I know that is no excuse and for that I am sorry," I utter in regret.

"Don't worry about it. I am not the kind of lady who holds grudges. No harm, no foul, right?" A sudden change washes over her, replacing her exuberant expression with one of sorrow and grief. "Lauren, I'm so sorry for your loss. William was a good man."

"Thank you. I appreciate it," I whisper as a cold shudder races through me, instantly causing me to remember the tragic event I have been immersed in today. My mind has been so engrossed in what I am doing I momentarily forgot the intense grief that had engulfed me. Biting my bottom lip extremely hard, I try to fight back the tears, believing if I cause myself enough physical pain it will overshadow the internal pain rising to the surface.

"Lauren, why are you not at the reception for William?" Resting her hand on my shoulder she adds softly as if she is trying to explain her actions to me, "I wanted to be there, but I had two clients who were finalizing their vacations today, so I couldn't leave. You, on the other hand, should really be there."

"I will once I'm done here," I state over-vigorously.

"Then what can I do for you? Did you make a decision on where you want to go?" She walks gracefully over to her desk, sitting down in her oversized swivel chair in front of the computer.

Following her eagerly to her desk I utter anxiously, "Yes, I have."

"Great, is it going to be Paris, or perhaps Italy then? It is absolutely beautiful in Italy, you will love it there." She continues to type in general information on a vacation package to Italy.

"No, that is not where I intend to go. I want to go here." Gently I slap the brochure I removed from Larry's hand onto the desk in front of her. There on the top, in large bold letters, reads New Orleans.

"You decided on New Orleans," she states flatly. Her once-excited voice deflates like I have killed her overwhelming excitement for me.

"Yes, and I want to stay here if I can." I point to the picture on the front cover of the brochure. There, sprawled across the front page is a picture of a large plantation home with eight massive two story high columns rising vigorously through the two enormous decks. A narrow gravel road leads to this tremendous residence, flanked by incredibly large cypress trees laden with an overgrowth of Spanish moss. The invading moss hangs victoriously from the overgrown, substantial trees, giving the residence a haunting appearance.

There under the picture of the incredible plantation home, in tiny typed words, reads: *The Adam's House Bed and Breakfast.* A flowing warm sensation rushes over my anxious body like a raging river, consuming every part of me. This house for some strange reason holds the answers to my loss of memory. A rush of excitement races through me as I realize I'm going to find out why this massive plantation sparks some kind of déjà vu. My heart thunders rapidly with excitement as I peer into Martha's eyes, uttering firmly, "Book this as soon as possible please."

END OF BOOK ONE

Acknowledgments

I want to thank Greg, my loving husband, for showing me what a true love story is like for nearly twenty years – it is hard work, but worth it.

To my two wonderful children, Evan and Ashlyn, for encouraging me to never give up, especially on the tough days, and being okay with having fast-food for dinner on numerous occasions.

To the best parents anyone could ask for, thank you for not only believing in me, but showing me that the ability to share stories has run in our family for generations.

Season Burch and Pattie Godfrey-Sadler, thank you for being my support and inspiration. Your talents amaze me.

To my Tribe, you know who you are, thank you.

To Shawndra Johnson, my editor and friend, thank you for all your hard work; To Season Atwater, who designs my covers, Thank you.

To my true friends – you know who you are – thank you for your undying support and love.

And to the ones who doubted me…thank you for giving me the motivation to fly.

CHRYSALIS

Book Two in COLLIDE series

Coming 2017

* 9 7 8 1 9 4 5 3 8 4 0 1 1 *